# THE SCARLET AFFAIR

## Elise Noble

Published by Undercover Publishing Limited

Copyright © 2018 Elise Noble

ISBN: 978-1-910954-77-5

Edited by Nikki Mentges at NAM Editorial

Cover design by Abigail Sins

www.undercover-publishing.com

www.elise-noble.com

Blood is that fragile scarlet tree we carry within us.
- *Osbert Sitwell*

# CHAPTER 1

THE FIRST OF July. Thirty days since I left my old life, and twenty-nine days since Taylor Hancock came into the world.

But nobody lives forever, right?

Glowing white letters spelled out the date on the plasma screen behind the reception desk as I ran a duster over the surface, then the display switched to eight clocks showing various times around the world and finally to the shield-and-halo logo of Blackwood Security, the company I worked for.

Two weeks into my new job, and my days had changed beyond all recognition. Back home in California, I kept our beachfront home spick and span, but with only two of us living there, it didn't take much effort. And now? Now I had two floors to clean in an office that was home to hundreds of people. Somebody else did the basement and the other restricted areas.

Behind me, reflected on the screen, the glass doors of the atrium slid to the side as an employee stared into the retina scanner that provided security after office hours. Another man hovered at his shoulder, awaiting his turn. The external security system was a little over the top, but it didn't bother me. Why? Because I'd already gotten past it. No, my problem came from the scanners to get up to the third floor, because those were causing me difficulties.

The men walked past, talking softly as they headed for the stairs. Nobody took the elevator here. Rumour said that one of the bosses made anyone caught using it do twenty push-ups so they realised the error of their ways, although that was possibly why all the employees were so fit. Coming to work was like walking into a fantasy world where Magic Mike met the Navy SEALs, but while most women might see that as a perk of the job, I only had eyes for my husband.

Other than a brief glance in my direction and the merest flash of a smile from the blond guy on the left, the newcomers didn't acknowledge the woman doing her best to fade into the background, and that was the way I liked it. I wore Taylor's anonymity as a cloak, a cloak that kept me safe and cocooned me from the evils in the world, like the ones lurking on the top floor. The ones trying to ruin my husband's biggest client.

The door slid open once more and a flame-haired lady walked through, her heels clicking on the floor I'd just polished. Mackenzie Cain. I recognised her from her picture in the staff directory. With the added height those stilettos gave her, she had to be close to six feet tall.

"Hey." She raised a hand as she opened the door to the stairwell.

"Hi," I mumbled, but she'd already gone.

At any other company, the amount of foot traffic at ten o'clock in the evening might have been considered unusual, but Blackwood Security worked twenty-four seven, and even at this late hour, the place gave off a quiet buzz that made me nervous. When I agreed to help Dean out with this project, I'd expected it to take a week, two at most, and I hadn't planned on there being so many people around. He'd made it sound so simple, but every time I walked through the front door, I wanted to throw up.

"You just need to find their mainframe and upload a file onto it, that's all," he'd said.

"But what if there's a password?"

"Doesn't matter. As long as you can get the USB key into the port, the code I've written will do the rest."

The idea of plotting something so underhanded didn't sit well with me, but neither did the prospect of Blackwood destroying Dean's career, which was what they were trying to do.

"Can't you go?" I'd asked.

"Not and keep working. Looking after the Draupnir contract is a full-time job, and getting into Blackwood's system will take time."

I hadn't managed it yet. The comms room was in the basement, secured by not only biometric security but a key as well, and constantly monitored by security cameras. And I wasn't a spy, I was a freaking housewife.

When I'd explained the situation to Dean, he'd fallen silent for a few minutes, thinking. Then he came up with a new plan.

"I bet there's another way into the system. Their top IT people will have a back door because they won't want to run down to the comms room every five minutes if there's a problem. Mackenzie Cain, that's who you need to find. We'll try the USB key in her computer."

Except she sat on the third floor, protected by yet another retina scanner, and even if I could have gotten through the door, there were always other staff around. I longed to run back to California, to our pale-blue villa with its high walls and its peaceful garden filled with bougainvillea and lilac and honeysuckle, but more than anything, I desperately wanted to get away from all these *people*.

"Evening."

A voice behind made me jump, and I turned to find a blonde woman standing three feet away. Her. Emerson Black. The one who hated elevators with a passion. Where had she come from?

"Hi."

"Taylor, right? You're new."

Emerson knew my name? Or rather, the name Dean had created for me?

"That's right. Is something wrong?"

"No, nothing's wrong. I just like to know the people who work here. I'm Emmy."

She held out a hand. Long, slim fingers and nails painted a vivid red. No chips in her manicure, so apart from a penchant for making hot men do callisthenics in the hallway, I figured she spent most of her time behind a desk.

"Yes, Taylor. I've been here two weeks."

"And how long have you been in Richmond? You're from California, right?"

During the flight across the United States, I'd agonised over Taylor's cover story—where she came from, why she moved, and her family, or rather the lack of it. Dean told me to keep interactions to a minimum, and I was only too happy to comply, but I couldn't avoid them completely. Nor could I do much about my accent. When I first arrived, I'd practised something more southern in my tiny apartment, but I'd ended up sounding like a poor imitation of Scarlett O'Hara, probably because I'd watched *Gone with the Wind* more times than was healthy. No, it was far better to stick close to my real background, because at least that way I wouldn't make so many mistakes.

"I've been here for a month. I just moved across from the West Coast."

"Not for the weather, obviously."

Ah, a typical Brit, talking about the weather. When Dean and I visited London three years ago for a vacation, almost every conversation had opened with a comment bemoaning the lack of sun or the gale blowing outside. And Emmy was using the trait to fish for information.

"I don't think it's stopped raining since I arrived."

Emmy stayed silent, watching, and the intensity of her gaze made me fill in the silence.

"I just needed a fresh start, and when I looked on the internet, Virginia seemed like a nice place to live."

"A fresh start." Emmy nodded, seemingly satisfied with that answer, then glanced at her watch. "I guess I can understand that. Well, I'd better not keep you."

Her footsteps echoed through the hallway as she headed into the depths of the building, and I sprayed lemon-scented polish onto the desk, rubbing the cloth in circles until the wood shone. At least I could do that part of my job. When I'd called Dean to suggest I just come home, he'd insisted I stay, never mind that carrying out his wishes seemed a near-impossible feat. And worse than that, he'd sounded nervous.

"You've got to get that software installed. Draupnir got hit by another cyberattack this week, and even though the hacker masked their IP address this time, it's got the same signature. I don't need to remind you that if my client goes under, we go under with it."

No, he didn't need to remind me. Dean had bought the house before the property market plummeted, and it was mortgaged up to the hilt. Then soon after we got married, he'd fallen out with his former business partner, and our income had taken a dive too. Months passed before he found another job that paid anywhere near the same amount, and we'd been on the brink of bankruptcy when he finally landed the contract with the Draupnir Foundation, based near Richmond, Virginia.

"I still don't understand why Blackwood is doing this."

"Draupnir's one of their competitors."

Another security company? Okay, that made sense. Dean rarely discussed his work, and every time I showed any interest, he glossed over my enquiries with comments about it being top secret. And he'd once mentioned signing a confidentiality agreement. At least he showed his ethical side by not speaking about classified information—I had to admire that.

"But surely Blackwood resorting to sabotage is illegal?"

"Only if they get caught, and someone in that organisation is good at what they do. Apart from that one mistake, every move has been flawless. They're bad people."

Bad people, but everyone had been nice to me so far. "What if you're wrong?"

Dean's harrumph of annoyance told me he didn't like being questioned, but his voice quickly lightened and once more, he became the man I loved.

"The other possibility is that Blackwood has a rogue employee. Someone working against them from the inside. If that's the case, we can help them to find their mole."

That didn't sound so bad. Besides, I'd never seen Dean so stressed as in the month before I left California, which meant when he'd asked me to do this thing, this one little thing for him, of course I said yes. No matter how much it scared me.

Because I owed him. After the way he saved me six years ago, I owed him, and now it was time to repay his kindness.

# CHAPTER 2

CADE DUCHAMP TOOK the long way home from Oakley. A trip out into the countryside, looping around —he got halfway to Virginia Beach before he felt sure he hadn't been followed and turned back again. Ten miles outside Richmond, he stopped at a safe house, a nondescript property on a quiet street where the lots were small and the lawns neatly trimmed. A couple of heads turned as his Harley rumbled past—a mom loading her daughter into an ageing minivan and an old man watering his lawn while committing the gravest of crimes against fashion: pairing socks with sandals. Damn hog. It was ugly as hell and drew too much attention. Cade avoided revving the engine as he pulled into the garage at the side of the beige duplex and parked next to a scarlet Ducati with all the extras. Now, that was his kind of bike.

The house stood empty, unused since the last snitch to stay there gave his testimony and returned to wherever he came from. Cade stared into the retina scanner by the back door and waved to the hidden camera as the bolts shot back.

"Honey, I'm home," he muttered into the silence.

A thin layer of dust covered the furniture, but Cade ignored it as he jogged upstairs to the back bedroom. Fuck, he needed a wash. His biker brothers weren't too hot on cleanliness, so he'd had to let his hygiene slip along with his monthly haircuts and his daily shave. He caught a glimpse of his face in the mirror on the far wall. Bad skin, lank brown hair. Damn. Yeah, he'd cross the street to avoid himself.

At least he could grab a shower and a day or two of respite in civvies while he pretended to visit his grandma in the Hickory Falls assisted living complex just outside Hanover. And Blackwood Security, his employer, didn't do anything by halves. There really was an eighty-one-year-old lady living in room forty-seven, and despite her failing eyesight, she was as sharp as a tack. If anyone called, Beryl would assure them that her grandson had just popped out to the store to feed her candied fruit habit.

Meanwhile, Cade could head to the office for an update, then sleep in his own bed for a night. He wrinkled his nose as he peeled off his dirty jeans and slung his leather jacket onto the bare mattress. As a prospect for The Darkness Motorcycle Club, Cade didn't yet wear the sleeveless cut of a full patch-holder —a biker who'd earned the right to wear the three patches on his back, proudly proclaiming himself to be a member of The Darkness MC out of Richmond, Virginia. No, Cade still had to prove himself worthy, which meant doing all the dirty work around the clubhouse while trying not to blow his cover. Wearing a digital recorder in his underwear was getting really old.

He began folding the jeans out of habit, then shook his head. What was the point? He tossed them into the bottom of the closet and pulled out his own clothes— clean black jeans, a white T-shirt, and a pair of sneakers instead of the heavy boots that made his feet sweat. Fifteen minutes in the shower scrubbing the grime away, and he felt almost human again. *Almost.* After some of the shit he'd seen over the past couple of weeks, he'd begun to think he was one of the animals he hung out with.

Before he left the house, he shrugged into his favourite leather jacket. Red and white, it matched his bike and would have looked more at home on the racetrack than in The Darkness's dingy clubhouse. A quick check of the security system showed nothing untoward, and he was soon speeding back towards Richmond on his beloved Ducati.

"Nice beard." Emmy, Cade's temporary boss and the woman who ran Blackwood Security's Special Projects team, greeted him with her usual snark. "You could make pigtails out of it."

"Maybe a braid," Dan piped up from behind.

"Pack it in, would you?"

The beard was just one more thing that made this job hell. It itched, food got stuck in it, and if he didn't trim the moustache every couple of days, it dipped in his beer. Facial hair might suit some guys, but it made Cade look more ape than Adonis.

Emmy reached for the carafe of coffee in the middle of the conference room table and raised an eyebrow. Cade nodded. Yes, he desperately needed caffeine.

"Any problems getting here?" she asked.

"Nope. If somebody followed me, they were damn near invisible."

Cade felt slightly more human after a night in his

own house and a morning catching up with regular chores. The place still felt foreign to him, seeing as he'd signed the lease only a month before he went to play biker, but despite its sterility, his home was infinitely more comfortable than the grubby room he rented near the bar The Darkness had claimed as its own. He'd be back in the pit tonight, but the occasional breaks helped to preserve his sanity.

"Ready to start?" Emmy asked.

"Yeah. Did you get all the audio?"

"Mack spent most of yesterday sifting through it. Those assholes don't half talk a lot of shit."

"Tell me about it."

More people filed in, and as well as Emmy and Dan, who was number two in the investigations team, he recognised Mack, the red-haired computer geek, and Logan, who often helped out on projects like this one. The only unfamiliar face was the blonde chick sitting next to Mack. Those thick-rimmed glasses she wore with pigtails should have been a turn-off, but the whole effect was kind of cute.

At least, it would have been if Cade hadn't sworn off women.

After all, it had been a woman who got him into this situation. His... Well, she wasn't even an ex, because it had never got that far. Five months ago, Cade had made a play for Tia, a friend of Emmy's, and got knocked back in favour of a washed-up pop star. That had hurt. Fuck, it had hurt. Right after the incident, Cade had considered quitting, then running back home to Minnesota to lick his wounds and let his heart recover. But dammit, he'd worked hard for this job. Four years in the army and one more slogging away in

Blackwood's New York office, to be precise. So instead, he'd thrown himself into work and finally been rewarded with the coveted transfer to the Richmond office he'd wanted since he started at the company. A job in the investigations department he'd hoped would lead to a spot in Emmy's Special Projects team if he played his cards right.

Except he'd barely got his feet under the table in his new role when he visited Emmy's estate, Riverley, for a party and accidentally walked in on Tia having a moment with her new beau. He might have sworn before he slammed the door. Three days later, he found himself assigned to a long-term undercover job that Emmy dressed up as an opportunity, a secondment to the Special Projects team, but Cade wasn't stupid. He'd been sidelined so he didn't cause another scene.

"It's a joint project with the ATF," Emmy had told him. "Somebody's distributing unlicensed hand grenades, and there've been rumours a biker gang's involved. The ATF doesn't have enough resources to look at all of them, so they've asked us to help out."

"Hand grenades?"

"Yup. And in the last two months, the cops have recorded three instances of them being used in robberies in Virginia alone. In the last one, a man died, and the Bureau's taking flak for it."

"So what do you want me to do?"

"Research The Darkness MC and hang out where they hang out. Infiltrate the gang. They're getting money from somewhere, and we want to know whether any of their income streams contribute to innocent people getting blown up."

"What's the timescale?"

"As long as it takes." Emmy must have noticed Cade's total lack of enthusiasm. "Three children have to grow up without a father now. I wouldn't ask you to do this unless it was important."

She'd done that on purpose. Emmy knew Cade had also grown up without a father, and now she used that knowledge as a weapon against him. But in all honesty, he'd have expected nothing less from her. Not only could she shoot someone between the eyes without hesitation, she'd always been a manipulative bitch, and even though she was smiling now, there was a hardness to her eyes no expression could hide.

And he really did want to get a permanent spot on her Special Projects team. Professionally, there was no bigger challenge, no bigger rush than being part of that elite group.

"Sure, I'll do it."

He'd hang out with The Darkness, even if it meant wearing grimy leather for a few months and watching his colleagues have fun without him.

Today at Blackwood, he'd been called into a meeting, one that seemed more serious than the regular updates he'd been attending, purely due to the number of people sitting around the table. He'd hoped that today Emmy would recall him back to Blackwood to work the big case he knew was going on, but that didn't seem too likely right now.

Emmy blew steam off her coffee and took a sip before speaking. "Shall we start?"

Murmurs of assent came and Mack fired up her laptop, displaying a mugshot of Wolf, the club's president, on the screen. By the looks of it, the photo dated back to his stint in jail for drug possession a decade ago.

Emmy looked at Miss Pigtails. "Let's have a quick recap for Agatha's benefit, shall we?"

Agatha? That was her name? She didn't look like an Agatha, more of a Sammi or a Lexi. Something cute but a little nerdy.

"Cade, we stole Agatha from the FBI to give Mack a hand."

Agatha gave him a tentative smile, and he grinned back. Her front teeth weren't quite straight, but rather than detracting from her appearance, the flaw added to the intrigue.

"Nice to meet you." Agatha's accent said she had southern roots, much like Mack herself.

"Likewise."

Damn this beard. She didn't look particularly impressed by it.

Cade counted up the number of months since he'd been with a woman, grateful that the beard at least hid his grimace. Ten months. Ten fucking months, or rather, ten not-fucking months. Any longer and he'd develop carpal tunnel syndrome.

Mack cleared her throat, interrupting his thoughts. "Dave Hauser, also known as Wolf. Fifty-seven years old. As well as running the most secretive outlaw motorcycle club in the state, he's done two stints in prison plus one in hospital after he got on the wrong side of a Hells Angel."

Agatha tapped away on her tablet with slim fingers, making notes as Mack carried on talking. Pink nail varnish, the colour of bubblegum. Cade looked down at his own nails, and despite his shower, there was still dirt trapped underneath the edges. He slipped his hands out of sight below the table.

Finally, Mack got to the end of her spiel. "Cade, do you have any insights to add?"

"So far, I haven't seen or heard anything about grenades or any similar destructive device being sold through the club. Other dodgy shit, sure, but nothing that requires a licence from the ATF."

"What kind of dodgy shit?" Emmy asked.

"Drugs, handguns, knives. And a fuck of a lot of stuff tends to fall off trucks when they're around. Yoga accessories last week."

Dan spluttered out a laugh. "Yoga accessories?"

"There's big money in sportswear. They've been selling it all online. I've lost count of the number of trips I've made to the post office on that fuckin' bike."

Cade got stuck with the jobs nobody else wanted to do, and if he hoped to become a full member of the club, he had to suck it up and get on with everything from cleaning to cooking. If the fridge ever ran out of beer, he'd be packing his bags. In addition to taking on the menial tasks, he'd also had to pledge his Harley to the club, and if he didn't make it to patch-holder, they'd keep the bike as a forfeit. As far as Cade was concerned, they were welcome to the damn thing. Emmy had dredged it up from someone who owed her a favour, and Cade spent more time fixing it than riding it.

Agatha giggled, and Emmy rolled her eyes.

"What next? Herbalife? Pampered Chef? Will they start holding Amway parties?"

"More like AK-47 parties if what came through the warehouse last week is any indication. Now that I'm hanging out in the clubhouse, I can get a better handle on the inner workings, and as far as I can ascertain, the bulk of their money comes from dealing crystal meth. But if an opportunity to make a few bucks comes up, like the online auction shit, they'll take it. And I reckon the auto repair place they own doubles up as a chop shop."

"Interesting... As long as The Darkness isn't selling weapons to known terrorists, the ATF won't move on them at the moment."

Cade sensed a "but" coming, and he was right.

"But now we've got another issue. As most of us already know, three years ago, a wealthy businessman named Keith Welbey was eating dinner with his wife and kids when an armed gang broke in. At least three men, maybe more. Mrs. Welbey was a little hazy on the details, which is understandable seeing as one of the intruders cut her husband's throat and another held her down as he bled to death."

Agatha's colour dropped a shade. "And the kids?"

"Locked in a wardrobe—it seems the gang weren't completely heartless. But that was only the start. Thirty-four months, seven home invasions, and seven men dead. They never touch the kids, and they always make the wives go into a different room. Even so, the last widow suffered a breakdown and she's still in the hospital."

Mack flashed details up on the screen. Jacqueline Price. Thirty-six years old, and in a picture taken a week before her husband's murder, she'd looked twenty-five. In a more recent photo beside it, she'd aged two decades. Finding a man's brain leaking all over the sofa would do that to a woman. While Cade and the others watched, sipping coffee in the comfort of their sterile conference room, Mack scrolled through each case. Descriptions, pictures, videos. At the end, she ran from the room, looking green.

"How did Blackwood get involved?" Agatha asked.

"Widow number five hired us to find the men who killed her husband, Randall Granger," Dan said. "He and Tracey had been married for eleven years, and now their six-year-old twin boys will grow up fatherless." Her knuckles went white as she gripped the edge of her tablet. "Which is why we need to stop these people."

Dan's eyes cut sideways to Cade, and he knew she'd read his file too. Okay, he'd bite.

"What's that got to do with me?"

# CHAPTER 3

"WE'LL GET TO the details of your involvement in a minute," Emmy told Cade. "Dan, can you carry on?"

With Mack presumably puking, Dan took over. "Whoever's committing these crimes, they're phantoms. They come in, *bam*, and they get away clean. So far, they've stolen money, jewellery, electronic goods, and a painting, but that's where they got sloppy. They chose to take a cheap watercolour by a local artist when there was a genuine Modigliani hanging on the wall in the next room."

"Maybe they couldn't sell the Modigliani?" Agatha suggested.

"Maybe. But in home two, they took all the costume jewellery off the wife's dressing table and left a box full of gold in the closet. Plus Tracey Granger was wearing two-carat diamond earrings and they didn't touch them."

"Probably thought they were fake," Emmy said.

"So, we've got a gang who can hit a house with precision, murder without blinking, and make a near-perfect getaway, yet they don't do enough homework to know what's worth stealing? This whole case is strange."

"What's the value of the goods they've taken so far?" Agatha asked.

"Half a million dollars, give or take. They got thirty thousand in cash from the Prices alone."

Agatha let out a low whistle, and Cade's privates stirred. Too long. It had been too damn long.

"Crime pays, then. How did we get from the home invasions to Wade being embedded with a motorcycle gang?"

"Cade." He couldn't help correcting her.

Her cheeks turned a pale pink. "Cade. Yes, of course."

"After Mrs. Granger hired us, we canvassed the area as well as going through all the old case files. In three of them, neighbours mentioned hearing bikes nearby in the week leading up to the invasion, and two days before incident number four, a security camera half a mile away caught one of the riders on camera. Mack enhanced the video and we traced the bike to Tank."

Mack came back, wiping her mouth, but nobody said anything about her sudden departure. Did that happen often? She put a photo up on screen—a man astride his Harley holding his middle finger up to the camera. It didn't take a genius to work out where Tank's nickname had come from. He dwarfed the bike.

"That's the only evidence?" Agatha asked. "It's tenuous."

"Not quite. After Granger's death, the clerk in a gas station on the way out of town recognised Rev." Mack gestured to the screen, where Tank had faded away, replaced by a man in his late twenties looking into the distance as he stood by his bike. The picture had been taken covertly, but the lens was powerful enough to capture the thin scar bisecting his left eyebrow. "Pure, dumb luck. All the way over in Blacksburg, and she went to the same school as him here in Richmond."

"And she had a crush on him," Dan said. "Throughout the interview, she kept saying how misunderstood he was, and when I showed her a photo, she licked her damn lips."

"Did he recognise her?" Agatha asked.

"Not likely. I pulled her old yearbook photo before I visited, and between high school and now, she ate *all* the Twinkies. She must have put on two hundred pounds."

"It's still not much."

"No, it's not, and that's exactly what the cops said. But in the absence of other leads and with a pretty much unlimited budget from Mrs. Granger, we thought it was worth briefing Cade." Dan grinned at him. "Are you having fun undercover? Ladies love bikers, right?"

"Not the right kind of ladies." Yes, he got scantily clad groupies throwing themselves at him in the bar every night, but the thought of tapping those made his balls shrivel. He'd rather not catch herpes, thanks. "And I'm not there to get my dick wet."

"Have you heard any talk about home invasions by The Darkness?" Emmy asked. "Or any rumours of rival gangs being involved?"

"I haven't heard a thing. Do we have any other leads?"

Dan shook her head, not looking particularly happy. "Nope. But based on the pattern of the previous home invasions, we expect another strike within a few weeks."

A few weeks. With Cade growing ever closer to The Darkness, the next step would be his initiation. If the rumours were true, that could involve anything from being pissed on by his drunken clubmates to eating raw bull testicles or even committing a crime, all to prove his loyalty to the men he now supposedly considered to be his family.

Family. Yeah, right. Cade might not have had much of one himself, but a gang of bikers made a poor substitute. While he wasn't bound to Blackwood by blood, that was where his allegiances lay.

Much as he'd have liked to return to his life, the crime scene photos from the seven home invasions were something he'd never erase from his mind. If he could help to bring the killers to justice, he would, even if that meant dealing with a little discomfort in the meantime.

"I'm staying in?"

Emmy nodded, her decision made. "For now, yes. We've done too much work to throw it all away if The Darkness is involved in the home invasions. And even if they aren't, we'll be gathering intel to trade for favours, and better still, we'll be doing it on somebody else's dollar."

"Then I'd better head back to Oakley. The assholes are expecting me at the bar tonight." Cade pushed his chair back and stood up, checking his watch. Leaving now would give him enough time for a leisurely trip to the safe house to swap bikes.

"Beryl says hi. Oh, before you head off, Nate's got a new voice recorder for you. Better battery life, apparently, and it..." She tried to keep a straight face. Failed. "It shouldn't chafe your balls so much."

Cade rolled his eyes, then glanced at Agatha. Was it him, or did her gaze drop to his crotch when Emmy said that? He should have worn tighter jeans. After all, he had nothing to be ashamed of in that department. If only he didn't have to go back to the clubhouse, he might be tempted to break his self-imposed vow of celibacy and ask her out for dinner. Something fancy—maybe Claude's or even Rhodium if he didn't order the expensive wine. He'd just have to remember to protect his heart better this time.

A knock at the door interrupted his thoughts, and Emmy's office assistant, Sloane, poked her head into the conference room.

"Eugene on the gate called. There's a visitor here for you, Cade. I wasn't sure whether you'd left yet."

"For me?"

"That's what she said."

"She? Who?"

The only women who knew he worked here were his mother, who never left their hometown, and the Blackwood girls, who wouldn't have to buzz and wait.

Sloane shrugged. "She said it was a surprise. Do you want to go? Or shall I say you're not here?"

"No, I'll go." Cade had to admit he was kind of curious.

Emmy's grin came back. "I'll wander down with you."

"Do you ever stop being nosy?"

"Nope."

"Fine. But we'll have to hurry because I need to help with dinner back at the clubhouse."

"Biker's bitch," Dan muttered under her breath.

"I heard that."

# CHAPTER 4

CADE FIGURED THAT since his visitor had turned up unannounced, she wouldn't mind waiting for a few minutes until he'd collected the new voice recorder from Nate. That way, he could make a quick getaway afterwards rather than having to come back inside.

"It's sweat-proof and shock-proof, and the battery'll last seventy-two hours before it needs a recharge."

"Do I download the audio like before?"

"Exactly the same way. It's got a micro USB port on the side, and you can use the clip to attach it to your waistband or jacket...or elsewhere."

Emmy stifled a giggle. At a previous catch-up meeting, Cade had explained about the older Darkness members' habit of stumbling in for breakfast in their boxers, and as the newbie, he could hardly break with tradition. He'd had to clip the damn recorder onto his short-and-curlies. It was either that or duct tape.

"Thanks."

Even Nate smirked. "No problem."

Agatha was nowhere to be seen as they headed outside, and Cade tried to block her from his mind as they walked up the driveway. There was no point in even contemplating a date until this job was over.

"Any idea who the girl is?" Emmy asked.

"No, I don't." Cade spoke through clenched teeth.

"No girlfriend?"

"You already know the answer to that."

"Look, I'm sorry about what happened with Tia. I don't suppose it's much consolation, but she was cut up over that whole episode too."

"I'm just glad she got through it."

Eugene, the daytime security guard, stepped out of the guardhouse as they got closer. Why did he look worried? Eugene never looked worried. His expression varied between bored and downright unwelcoming, which fitted quite well with his role as a human guard dog.

"What's up?" Emmy asked.

"Uh, I'm not sure. The lady stepped away to make a phone call, then she got in her car and took off."

"Oh, so she's gone?"

Emmy had already turned halfway around when Eugene shook his head.

"*She's* gone, but she left the kid behind."

Emmy paused mid-stride as Cade asked, "Kid? What kid?"

Eugene pointed to the open guardhouse door. "In there."

"What kid?" Emmy mouthed at Cade, and he shrugged as they both hurried to look inside.

A little girl sat on Eugene's chair, feet dangling a couple of inches from the ground as she clutched her pink backpack tightly against her chest. She reminded him of... No, he didn't want to think about that. Not after he'd spent so many years blocking out the pain.

Emmy raised an eyebrow, and Cade gave his head a barely perceptible shake. No, he'd never seen this child before in his life. How old was she? Five? Six?

"What's your name, sweetie?" Emmy asked.

"Scarlet."

Emmy crouched down, putting her just below Scarlet's eye level. "Can you tell me your last name too?"

"Bonner."

"Do you know where your mommy went?"

A shrug.

"Do you know her phone number?"

Nothing.

"Your address? Do you know where you live?"

"Huntswood."

Cade's heart stuttered. Huntswood? That was his hometown. *Should* he know this girl? How long since he'd last been back? Six, no, seven months. A flying visit to wish his mother a happy birthday and put flowers on his sister's grave. Apart from waving to the neighbours, he'd barely seen another soul.

From Emmy's sideways glance, she'd made the connection too.

"I don't know her," Cade said.

"Eugene, did the woman say anything else? I mean, who abandons a child with a bunch of strangers?"

"She just asked for Cade, and when I said he wasn't available she burst into tears, so I figured I'd call Sloane to see if he could spare a few minutes."

"Tears? Oldest trick in the book. You shouldn't have fallen for that one."

The big man stared at his feet.

"I didn't know she was gonna do a runner. She said she needed to make a call and she couldn't get a good signal. Next thing I know, her car's speeding down the road."

"Did you get the licence number?"

"Sorry."

"Never mind. I'll get Mack to check the cameras. Or Agatha. She should learn how to do these things."

"What do we do with the little girl in the meantime?" Eugene asked.

Emmy looked down at her, brows knitted together. "Uh, do you know anything about kids?"

"Never had any."

"Okay. Someone around here must have one. I'll..."

She trailed off as the little girl sniffed then rummaged in her bag with shaky hands. "Mommy said I have to give this to Cade."

He and Emmy stared at each other, then Emmy took the envelope and handed it to him.

"Go on, open it. This is gonna be good. I can tell."

Cade didn't know whether to be worried or angry as he peeled open the flap. What he did know was that he needed to read the damn letter quickly so he could ride back across Richmond to The Darkness's clubhouse and check the fridge was fully stocked with Bud.

Eugene backed off a few steps as Emmy leaned over Cade's shoulder to read.

*Cade,*

*Sorry to drop this on you, but I don't know what else to do. I'm not sure if you remember that night in the back seat of your car after prom, but I sure do, because six weeks later I found out I was pregnant. Maybe I should have told you, but I kind of had a thing going with Reed Bonner at the same time, so I figured it was more likely to be his as I only went with you that once.*

*Anyhow, me and Reed split, and he wanted a paternity test, and it seems I got it wrong. Scarlet must be yours.*

*But I've got no money and Reed kicked us out, so I'm moving someplace else. My new man don't like kids much, and your mom told me where to find you, so I figured you could take a turn for a while. Till I get settled, sort of thing. She's not much trouble, honest. Mostly she watches TV. She don't like pizza.*

*I'll call when I get a chance.*

*Cindy*

No. *No, no, no.* This could *not* be happening. Cindy... Cindy... Cade remembered the night of the prom all right—a hasty, drunken fumble in the dark where he'd embarrassed himself by coming after about six thrusts —but he couldn't even recall Cindy's surname at first. Barker? Baker? Something like that. And she'd ended up pregnant? This had to be some kind of joke, right?

He looked at Emmy. She wasn't laughing. In fact, she looked a little nervous.

"Uh..." What did a man even say in this situation?

"Shit." Emmy summed up the position perfectly.

Eugene wagged a finger at her. "I might not know much about children, but I don't think you should use words like that in front of them."

"Boll— Oops." She scrunched her mouth to one side. "Okay. We need a plan. Cade, you've got a job to do, and kid or no kid, we can't afford to screw it up with the time ticking down to the next home invasion. You're sure this Cindy never mentioned being pregnant?"

"Reckon I'd fu— flipping remember."

"You didn't see her around?"

"I left town and joined the army two weeks after I graduated. Only things I've been back for are birthdays and Christmas."

"Fine. Fine, okay, we need to track her down. She can't have got that much of a head start. I'll put a team on it while you go back to Oakley. We can sort this out. Don't worry."

Cade wandered towards the door, dazed. How could he have a kid? Allowing for nine months of pregnancy, the little girl must be almost six now, and she clearly knew as little about him as he did about her. What if Cindy was lying? She'd been doing the dirty with two men, so why not a third? What was the margin of error in a DNA test?

He and Emmy got halfway out the door before Eugene coughed behind them. "The little girl?"

Emmy stopped mid-stride. "Fu-dge." She closed her eyes for a brief second. "Right, we can deal with this. I'll call Ana. Or Carmen, or Georgia. They've got kids. One of them'll know what to do." She crouched down to the kid's eye level again. "How about you come with us? I'll find you juice and crayons or something."

Scarlet stood silently, a tear trickling down her cheek. "When's Mommy coming back?"

"Soon. We'll find her for you."

"Where did she go?"

"She needed to visit a friend."

"What about my daddy?"

Fuck. She must have meant Reed Bonner. After all, that was whose surname she'd been given. The man had dumped a five-year-old child as well as ditching her mother, and that made an old, familiar anger resurface like an inmate done serving its time.

It pulsed hot in Cade's veins as he dropped to his knees next to Scarlet, studying her features as he did so. Her eyes were the same colour as his—a shiny brown his mother always said reminded her of buckeyes in the fall. And the same eye colour that Christie had once had.

"Can you walk to the other building with us?" Cade asked.

"My feet hurt." More tears fell, and Scarlet wiped her face with her sleeve.

"Do you want me to carry you?"

She paused for a few seconds and then nodded, although she kept sniffling. Cade passed her little pink bag to Emmy, who looked at it suspiciously then held it at arm's length. Emmy might have been a brilliant soldier, but she sucked at being a mom.

Cade lifted Scarlet onto one hip, and she clung to his neck as they set off up the drive, leaving a relieved-looking Eugene behind. The child weighed almost nothing. Was she getting enough to eat? Had Christie been heavier when she was the same age? Cade thought so, but it could just have been that he wasn't so strong back then. After all, he'd only been seven years older than her.

The receptionist gave them a curious look as they strode past into the stairwell and up to Emmy's office on the third floor. Eyes followed them the whole way. How was Cade supposed to explain this situation to his colleagues when he could barely comprehend it himself?

He had to peel Scarlet's fingers away from his jacket to sit her in Emmy's leather chair, which dwarfed her tiny frame and left her looking more vulnerable than ever. Whether or not she was really his daughter, his heart ached for a young girl who'd been abandoned by everyone she knew.

"You okay?" Emmy asked.

No, he was far from okay, but admitting that to a boss whose nickname was Diamond because she was so fucking hard wasn't something he wanted to do.

"Yeah."

"What about Oakley?"

"I have to go, don't I? It's not as if someone else can take my place."

"We'll be in *scheisse* if you don't. Hard evidence or not, my gut says those bikers are mixed up in the home invasions."

So did Cade's, although it didn't have the same track record as Emmy's for being right. "What about Scarlet?"

"I'll look after her." Emmy crinkled her nose. "Well, I'll make sure she gets looked after. I promise. And I'll get a paternity test done. We've got your DNA on file."

If Emmy promised Scarlet would be safe, she'd be safe, Cade was certain of that much. And hopefully they'd find her mother soon. Although when Cindy did turn up, Cade would be having words, that was for sure. How dare the bitch keep her pregnancy hidden from him if she had so much as a hint that the kid might have been his?

Tempting though it was to stay in Richmond and get to the bottom of the mess, Cade couldn't live with the idea that another child might end up fatherless if he didn't go back undercover. Another man dead, another family broken. Who would be next?

With no other clues, he needed to get back on his bike and leave.

# CHAPTER 5

SHITTING HELL.

EMMY looked at the kid, and the kid looked at her. Then Scarlet started to cry. As one quarter of the team who owned Blackwood Security, Emmy could look down the barrel of a machine gun without flinching, but tears? Nothing in her sixteen years of training had prepared her for this.

"Okay, uh, what's up?"

Dammit, stupid question. Emmy already knew what was up. Some bitch called Cindy had abandoned her five-year-old daughter while she went swanning off to fuck-knows-where with her boyfriend. The anger Emmy felt at her own mother simmered dangerously close to the surface, and she fought to maintain an expression that didn't suggest she wanted to kill someone.

Tissues. Tears needed tissues. Emmy grabbed a handful from the box on the credenza by the window, blue ones covered in tiny silver stars that could only have been left there by Bradley, her assistant.

"Here you go."

Scarlet wiped her eyes while Emmy patted her awkwardly on the back. A few of Emmy's friends had children now, but so far she'd managed to avoid any involvement that went beyond the superficial—buying gifts, attending the occasional birthday party, pretending to gush over photos.

Except now there was a small child needing assistance, and no responsible adult around to supervise.

Okay. Deep breaths. Emmy could do this. All she had to do was find somebody who *did* understand children and call them for pointers, or better still, convince them to come and help.

But who? Emmy ran through a mental list.

Carmen was in Mexico with her son, visiting her family, so she couldn't offer practical help. How about Georgia? Her daughter may only have been seven months old, but the fact that she had a child must count for something, right? Emmy was scrolling through the G's on her phone when she recalled her husband's comment yesterday morning—Georgia had gone down with gastroenteritis and was confined to barracks. Ana? Ana wasn't in the country either, but surely she'd have some ideas...

"*Da*?" Ana answered almost immediately, letting her Russian accent come to the fore.

"I need help. What do I do with a child?"

Emmy left Scarlet sitting in the big leather chair behind her desk and stepped out into the main office, which was almost deserted since there was a raid going on in town as well as a brainstorming meeting in the big conference room. Only Logan sat in the Special Projects department, his head bobbing in time to the music playing from his headphones as he concentrated on the laptop in front of him. Emmy began pacing. Yes, the pacing was a bad habit, born out of stress, but if any situation called for her to wear a hole in the carpet, it was this one.

"You're pregnant?"

"No! Hell, no. She belongs to Cade."

"Cade? Since when?"

"Since some woman dumped her off at the office with a note."

A bark of laughter escaped. "*Eto pizdets.*"

Yes, thanks, Emmy had already realised the whole affair was fucked up. "And Cade's gone back to work on that undercover thing."

Ana only laughed harder. "So you got left with the kid? Was there literally nobody else in the entire building?"

"It's not bloody funny."

"Yes, it is. When Tabby wanted a piggyback the other day, you went four shades paler."

Tabby was Ana's daughter. Three years old, and she'd already perfected a stare that could intimidate most grown men, just like her mother.

"I was worried about dropping her."

Ana's voice softened uncharacteristically. "For six months after she was born, I worried about everything, but it got easier. How old is the girl?"

"Scarlet. Her name's Scarlet. Five, as best we can work out."

"That's not so bad. At least you can talk to her."

"But I've got no idea what to say."

"Start with the simple things—tell her that she's staying with you while the grown-ups get their shit together."

Ana's boyfriend piped up in the background. "Try not to use the word 'shit.'"

"No shit. Got it."

"Has she eaten?"

"I've got no idea."

"Okay, start by getting her dinner. Are you still in the office?"

"Yeah. And I'm supposed to be meeting with an informant in three hours then doing a little breaking and entering. When I catch up with Scarlet's mother, it ain't gonna be pretty."

Emmy was already organising the search in her head. She may not have known how to care for a child, but she could plan a manhunt in her sleep. First, check the CCTV to find out the details of the woman's vehicle. Next, run an in-depth background check and pass the details on to her ever-growing network as the information came in. Nobody could disappear completely—they always left clues. Always. And— Oh, shit.

Emmy glanced over into her glass-fronted office and saw the empty chair.

"Uh, I think I lost the kid."

"Remind me never to ask you to babysit."

"I don't think there's any danger of that. Besides, all of my time's gonna be taken up looking for Cade's ex so I can remove her ovaries and ensure she never has another child."

"Emmy?"

"Yeah?"

"Stop talking and find Scarlet."

"Okay, right." Of course. "Talk later."

Where the hell had the girl gone? Emmy checked under her desk, and then her husband's opposite, but all she found was a packet of Reese's Peanut Butter Cups she'd tossed there when her nutritionist turned up unexpectedly, extolling the benefits of organic tea that looked like shit and tasted worse.

The private bathroom at the back of the office yielded nothing either, so Emmy ventured out into the open-plan office.

"Logan?"

No answer. Logan was engrossed in whatever was on his screen, which knowing him, could have been a detailed plan for his next job or a video of Kate Upton. Emmy picked up a squeezy stress ball from the nearest desk and scored a bullseye. Logan plucked out his headphones, scooped up the ball, and hurled it back, but Emmy ducked behind a decorative palm Bradley had insisted on bringing in for therapeutic purposes.

"What was that for?" Logan asked.

"Have you seen a little girl walk past?"

"The one who came in with you earlier?"

"That's her."

"Nope, sorry. Why? She's gone?"

"I turned my back for two seconds. Two fucking seconds, and she's disappeared."

"Well, she can't have got far. If she's not in here, she might have pushed the button to go out into the hallway, but she can't get in anywhere else without a retina scan."

"Can you check the stairwells while I head to the surveillance room?"

Logan was already on his feet. "What's her name?"

"Scarlet."

He walked off, chuckling. "Can't believe you lost a kid."

# CHAPTER 6

SIX O'CLOCK IN the evening on the second of July. While the rest of the country geared up for the Independence Day celebrations in two days' time, I was cleaning as slowly as possible in the hope that divine inspiration would strike and I'd figure out a way to get the freaking USB key into Mackenzie Cain's computer. Thanks to Dean's arrangement with the agency who supplied Blackwood's cleaning staff, I'd gotten the job at the company's head office with just a cursory interview, but only working in the non-secure areas. A security clearance would have meant deeper background checks I couldn't pass, even with Dean's meticulously crafted cover story. Still, I had time on my side if nothing else. As long as I didn't put in for any overtime payments, nobody seemed to mind me staying at the office for an extra hour, and even if I didn't succeed with my goal, I could hang out in the kitchen. The drinks machine made perfectly frothy hot chocolate. Even in summer, I couldn't resist it.

But first, I had to finish cleaning. Toil then reward, that's how it worked. I'd just started wiping the electronic booking screens outside each of the conference rooms when a figure scuttled around the corner and startled me into dropping the duster.

"Hey, are you okay?"

The little girl looked nervous, eyes darting from side to side as she fidgeted.

"Where's your mommy?"

"I don't know."

Oh dear. The tears came thick and fast, but luckily I had a package of tissues in my pocket. When I handed one over, the girl scrubbed at her face but kept crying just as hard. Surely she must have a parent nearby? I'd never seen a child in the office before, let alone on her own.

"How about your daddy?"

No answer, just a quiet shaking of her shoulders.

"Is your daddy here?"

"I-I-I don't know."

I held out a hand, and the child just stared at it.

"Why don't we go and look for your mommy or your daddy?"

"My feet hurt."

"Do you have something in your shoe?"

She stayed silent, so I lifted her onto the nearest chair, and when I knelt beside her to check, it was soon clear what the problem was. What kind of parent sent a child out in shoes three sizes too small? Her toes were squashed right up against the end. I loosened the laces and took them off, rewarded with a tentative smile when she freed her feet. The rest of the girl's clothes weren't much better—the waistband of her jeans cut into her skin, all too obvious because under her coat, her grubby pink T-shirt was short enough that I could see her belly.

The sight made me groan, and not just out of pity for the little girl. Rather because when I did eventually track a parent down, I'd have to say something for the child's sake, and I hated confrontation. Confrontation brought consequences.

But in the meantime, the child could stay in her socks. The floors were clean enough—after hours of washing and polishing, I'd made sure of that.

"What's your name?"

"Scarlet."

"Hi, Scarlet. I'm E— Taylor."

Darn it, I'd almost used my real name. I needed to be more careful, especially around here where Nate Wood, another of the directors, was rumoured to bug rooms for a hobby.

"Come on, let's go find your mom and dad."

I held out my hand again, and Scarlet slipped hers into it, her tiny fingernails decorated with chipped pink polish.

"Which way did you come?"

She pointed along the hallway towards the stairwell.

"Did you climb up or down the stairs?"

"Down."

That meant she'd come from the second or third floor, either Investigations or the Special Projects department. Seeing as my whole problem was that I didn't have clearance for Special Projects on the top floor, I figured we'd start with Investigations. Did one of her parents work in there?

Curious faces looked around as we walked through the door, but nobody leapt up to claim Scarlet. Were we in the right place?

Scarlet didn't show a flicker of recognition either.

"Is your daddy here?"

A shake of her head, and Scarlet stared at her feet.

Wonderful. That meant I had to speak to one of the men, and they were so...intimidating. One, two, three... eight men, all big, all dangerously good-looking, and all oozing the kind of confidence that made me want to lock myself in a bathroom stall. Alone.

Trying not to show my nervousness, I headed for the nearest occupied desk. While the employees here had been nothing but polite to me, the idea of getting within striking distance of any man other than Dean set my heart racing.

"Uh, hi."

The guy looked up, focusing blue eyes on me from under a shaggy fringe. "Can I help?"

"This little girl was meandering in the hallway. I'm not sure where her parents are."

"Sorry. Never seen her before." He turned to the guy a few desks away. "Slater, you know who this girl is?"

The blond-haired surfer type shook his head. "Nope. But she must have come in with somebody."

A voice from behind made us turn our heads. "Hey! Is that the kid Emmy lost?"

"Emmy lost a kid?" Slater asked.

Emmy... She with the penchant for making people do push-ups in front of elevators had a daughter? Well, she really should look after her better. Yes, I understood it must be difficult to balance motherhood with a career, but children got into all sorts of trouble if you took your eyes off them, even for a second.

"Yeah, she walked off while Emmy was on the phone." The new guy held a hand out to Scarlet. "Here, I'll take you upstairs."

Scarlet squashed herself behind me and pressed her

face into my back, although with all the attention, I wasn't sure which of us was more scared.

"Maybe it's best if you bring her," the man suggested.

"I really need to finish my work."

"You're a cleaner?"

I nodded, hoping he didn't notice as I took half a pace back.

"Place looks sparkling to me. Come on, nobody'll care if you take ten minutes off."

Scarlet sniffling behind me made up my mind. For the little girl's sake, I could cope with the man's company while we returned her to Emmy. We followed him out of the investigations department and over to the elevator, where he pushed the button for the third floor.

A rebel. *Please, don't let us get caught.* I didn't know how to do push-ups.

He must have read my mind, because he turned with a finger over his lips. "Shh. I won't tell her if you don't."

Upstairs, Scarlet curled her fingers into my sweater in a death grip as the man held the door open, and I gave her a smile I hoped was reassuring.

"Is she Emmy's daughter?"

The man burst out laughing. "You're kidding, right?"

"I just assumed..."

"Emmy doesn't have any kids." He dropped his voice so Scarlet couldn't hear. "I don't know why the girl's here either, but I'm sure as hell curious to find out."

The man showed us into a side office, the biggest in

sight, and waved me onto a sofa in the corner with
Scarlet. I heard him muttering into his phone outside,
telling somebody, presumably Emmy, to "get your ass
back up here."

That gave me a minute to take in my surroundings.
Of the two desks, the one nearest the window was the
largest, a heavy, dark wood affair bigger than the
hallway in my apartment, but apart from a giant
computer monitor, a blank jotter, a fancy pen, and an
ornate statue of a rearing black horse in one corner, it
was empty. A more modest glass desk faced it, equally
stark, its only decoration a purple orchid in one corner.
His 'n' hers? A framed copy of Rudyard Kipling's "If"
graced the wall to my left, silver script on a black
background, and I'd gotten halfway through the second
verse when Emmy strode towards me in a flurry of
blonde hair. The bearded man who'd accompanied us
upstairs was a pace behind.

"Thank goodness." Emmy sagged onto the edge of
the glass desk. "Uh, Scarlet? You can't just wander off
like that."

Scarlet burst into tears. "I-I-I want my mommy."

"Believe me, I want to find your mom too, but I
can't look for her if I have to hunt for you instead."

Scarlet sobbed harder, and Emmy looked at the
man, who shrugged. I put an arm around the little girl
and dried her face with the bottom of the polo shirt
they gave all the cleaning staff as a uniform.

"Do you have any idea where her mom is?"

Emmy drew a note out of her pocket and passed it
over. "Your guess is as good as mine at the moment."

I unfolded the paper and read, growing more
incredulous with every sentence. A woman had

abandoned her daughter with a father she'd never even met? The bearded man had been reading over my shoulder and I turned to him, unsure whether to feel sympathy or anger for a man who didn't know what a condom was.

"You're Cade?"

"Hell, no. I'm Logan."

Oh. Oops. It seemed I'd misjudged him.

"Cade's one of my men," Emmy said. "He's working undercover, and if he gets distracted by this situation, that's three months of work down the toilet."

"How can work be more important than his daughter?"

"He's working two cases right now. Across them both, eight men have died so far. Eight families torn apart, eight wives widowed, and fourteen kids traumatised. Time's ticking, and we're due another murder anytime soon. I'd say solving that problem is kind of important, wouldn't you? Besides, we don't even know if Cade's really Scarlet's father. All we've got is the word of a woman who's already lied to one man about the girl's parentage."

Well, when she put it like that.

"Sorry." I cast my eyes downwards. "I'm just worried about Scarlet. Somebody needs to look after her."

"Have you got kids?"

"No."

I wanted children, but Dean didn't, and I couldn't imagine ever being with another man. Over the years, I'd come to accept that I'd never be a mother.

"You're good with her. I thought you might have a child of your own."

"I used to babysit a lot when I was a teenager."

I'd been brought up by my Grandma Frances, and money had been tight throughout my childhood. Babysitting most nights brought in some much-needed cash as well as allowing me to study while the children were sleeping. Then as a nurse, I'd spent six months working in the paediatrics ward before we moved house. I'd planned to do the same in our new town, but Dean wanted me at home instead.

"Fantastic. How would you like to do some overtime?"

"Cleaning?"

Emmy shook her head and pointed at Scarlet.

"I'm not sure..."

"Look, Scarlet likes you, you've got experience with children, and we already background-checked you as part of your employment application. It's perfect."

Ah, yes, the background check. I'd been nervous as heck until the results came through, even though Dean assured me he'd made the necessary arrangements for me to pass a basic inspection—a few database alterations here and there and a false job reference from an old acquaintance of his. While I might have got away with that, I didn't want to tempt fate by hanging around near people who sniffed out lies for a living.

"I'm quite happy doing the cleaning."

"I'll pay you double."

I broke away from Emmy's gaze, and out of the corner of my eye, I spotted another glass-fronted office opposite, except this one had three—no, four—computer monitors set up on the desk. Did they belong to Mackenzie? If so, this could be my only chance to load Dean's program or virus or whatever was on that memory stick onto the network and get back home.

No, I couldn't afford to turn the opportunity down. "Okay, I'll do it. How long do you want me to stay?"

"Well, all night. I need to work."

I eyed up the couch. "But I don't have any spare clothes with me. Do you even have blankets?"

Emmy burst out laughing. "Not here, for fu— goodness' sake. Logan can take you both to my place. There's plenty of spare rooms, and my assistant'll be back in the morning to find you both something to wear."

Oh, no. No, no, no. How did I go from vacuuming to staying at my boss's house overnight? Talk about uncomfortable.

"I'll be fine staying here."

"No way. Scarlet's already escaped once, and my house has perimeter security. I can't risk losing her again because Cade'll flip out. Besides, you both need to eat."

"It's a nice place," Logan said. "It's been remodelled after it got blown up a while back."

"Blown up? I don't think—"

Emmy put an arm around my shoulders, and I went rigid.

"Honestly, it's fine. The people who set it on fire are all dead now."

Oh, that was comforting.

"Please, I—"

"Why isn't Scarlet wearing shoes?"

"Because they're too small and they were hurting her feet."

"I'll get my assistant to take you both shopping tomorrow. You can buy whatever she needs."

Logan fished a set of car keys out of his pocket. "Let's go. No point in hanging around here all evening."

Part of me wanted to carry on protesting, but what was the point? I was no match for a strong personality like Emmy. Besides, life went so much more smoothly when I didn't argue. If I disagreed with Dean, he gave me *that* look. The one that said how disappointed he was, and on particularly bad occasions, he'd rewarded me with the cold shoulder for days.

I mustered up a smile I absolutely didn't feel. "Okay, let's go."

If I got lucky, I might get another shot at Mackenzie's office when I brought Scarlet back tomorrow.

# CHAPTER 7

"WOULD YOU RATHER follow in your car?" Logan asked as we headed to the front door.

"I don't have a car. I catch the bus to work."

That wasn't entirely true. Back in California, I had a compact BMW, nearly new, but Dean did most of the driving.

"Don't worry, Emmy'll sort out a chauffeur so you and Scarlet can travel around."

"What do you mean? I'm only sitting with her for one evening."

"Fifty bucks says you'll still be there tomorrow night."

I'd feel guilty taking money from Logan when I already knew what the outcome would be. "No, I won't."

He chuckled as he bleeped open the doors on a black Ford Explorer parked near the entrance, and I helped Scarlet into the back seat.

"She needs a booster seat, really."

"Just tell Emmy's assistant. He'll sort it out."

He? I'd assumed Emmy's assistant would be another woman, and the thought of having to spend tomorrow morning with a man made me regret my decision to help all over again. No doubt there were wonderful men out there, but between Mr. Wilson, the fifth-grade teacher who accused me of copying my first homework assignment and then made the rest of that year a living hell, my old boss, who took pleasure in humiliating me after I spurned his advances, and finally Harlan Lake, the drug addict who'd attacked me in the hospital on the worst night of my life, I had no desire to find out for sure.

Apart from Dean, I'd decided that when it came to the opposite sex, avoidance was the best policy.

In fact, I'd almost chickened out of working at Blackwood entirely during my interview when the HR lady had shown me the gym and informed me I'd need to wipe down the sweaty machines each evening while a bunch of muscle-bound jocks jostled for space. But Dean was counting on me, so I'd swallowed my misgivings. At least Logan seemed kind. He held the door open for me before jogging around to the driver's side and hopping behind the wheel.

The sky darkened as we drove, the light fading in a spectacular show of yellows, oranges, and finally pinks. I'd never ventured in this direction before, and my discomfort at having to spend the night at Emmy's house was tinged with worry for the girl sitting beside me. How long before her mother came back for her?

The streets grew quieter, the houses got bigger, and we passed through the suburb of Rybridge and out into the country. I'd imagined Emmy would live in a swanky apartment in Richmond, but it seemed I'd been wrong. The closer we got, the more my nerves jangled, eclipsing my curiosity. The words *Please, just take me home* weighed heavy on my tongue, begging for release, but I held them in for Scarlet's sake. One night. I could deal with company for one night.

Then we were outside a pair of tall metal gates, solid yet ornate, modern in style. A man in a polo shirt that matched mine stepped out of a guardhouse and motioned to Logan to wind down the window. *Little Riverley*. That's what the sign on one brick pillar said, although from the size of the gates, the "Little" part was a misnomer.

"Evening, Logan." The guard stooped to peer in at Scarlet and me. "These the girls Emmy called about?"

"Taylor and Scarlet?"

"Yeah. Mrs. Fairfax is making dinner for everyone, and Bradley's on his way back from Milan."

The gates swung open and Logan trundled the car along a winding driveway. Heck, this place was huge. Security work must make Emmy even more money than I thought. And when I saw the house... Whoa. Could anybody even live there? It was all fancy glass and metal put together at strange angles, more of a modern art installation than a home. Quirky. That was the best word to describe it.

"That's Emmy's house?" I asked, just to check.

"Yeah. We reckon the architect was on drugs."

Something hallucinogenic, no doubt. LSD would do it. "The place does look a little unusual. Who's Mrs. Fairfax?"

"The housekeeper."

"Does she have a first name?"

"Nobody ever uses it."

"And Bradley?"

"He's the assistant I mentioned earlier. He...hmm... Between you and me, let's just say he and the house suit each other perfectly."

Bradley took drugs? And Emmy thought it

appropriate for a five-year-old child to spend time with him? My opinion of her dropped a notch, and I vowed to shield Scarlet from the man until I could tell her exactly what I thought of that idea. Drugs held the power to turn even the most mild-mannered person into a monster. Whether she was my boss or not, she needed to know.

Logan parked in front of the house, and I lifted Scarlet out of the back seat. She still didn't have shoes on.

"After you," Logan said, holding the door open.

If the outside of Little Riverley was spectacular, the inside took my breath away. A life-sized silver horse reared majestically in the foyer, spotlights twinkling off its hooves. The rest of the decor in there was white—white floor, white couch, white side table. The only splash of colour came from a painting on the far wall, where an ornately decorated skull stared down from its empty eye sockets.

A grey-haired lady bustled out of a doorway on the far side of the room and smiled when she saw us. I couldn't help but return it. She reminded me of my grandma, from her tight curls to the way she dusted her hands on her apron.

"This must be Scarlet?"

I nodded, and she reached down to cup Scarlet's cheek.

"Aren't you a pretty little thing? How old are you, missy?"

"Five."

"A fine age. I'm just making us all something to eat. What's your favourite food?"

"Chocolate ice cream."

"Well, I'm sure we can rustle some up for dessert as long as you eat your vegetables."

Her eyes widened.

"Scarlet, what's your favourite vegetable?" I asked her.

"I don't know."

"How about carrots? When I was your age, I loved carrots."

A shrug.

"What does your mommy normally give you to eat?"

"Chips. Fish fingers. Fries. Cookies."

So basically junk food. What a way to bring up a child. I'd seen it all too often in the hospital waiting room, kids placated with candy rather than a kind word, and it filled me with sadness.

And it filled Mrs. Fairfax with horror, judging by her expression.

"We'll be changing that right away," she muttered. "Logan, I've made up the bedroom that overlooks the tennis court. Could you show the girls up?" Then to me, "I thought it would be better if you shared, seeing as Scarlet's in a new house tonight."

I wasn't sure sharing with a stranger would be much better, but I nodded anyway. The last thing we needed was for her to disappear again.

"I don't suppose there are any shoes she can wear? Hers are far too small."

"Sorry, dearie. The only children who come here are younger, apart from Nate's boy, and he's much bigger. We can sort out some more clothes for her tomorrow. Do you have an overnight bag?"

"I don't have anything. We came straight from the

office, and I didn't expect to be staying away."

"Not to worry. We've got plenty of clothes for grown-ups. Just have a rummage around in the closet and help yourself."

Borrow other people's clothes? No way, not without asking them first. I'd made that mistake once when I borrowed one of Dean's T-shirts, and he'd grumbled for days. Besides, I'd be back in my apartment tomorrow. Still, I nodded and smiled, because that was easier than disagreeing.

Although when Logan opened the door to our temporary lodgings, I almost changed my mind about going home. The furnishings could have come straight from one of those luxury living magazines. Puffy pink and cream cushions covered half of the twin beds, perfectly matched to the lavish drapes. Scarlet didn't need to worry about going barefoot in the deep carpet, and through a door on the far side, I glimpsed a spacious bathroom.

Back in California, Dean felt compelled to keep up with the neighbours, even when it cost more money than we could really afford. The top-of-the-range cars, the expensive house, the fancy dinners that I really didn't enjoy—we had them all. Once, he'd even bought a boat because the couple opposite did, only to sell it two months later when he kept getting seasick. But Little Riverley put his aspirations to shame.

"Which bed do you want?" I asked Scarlet.

She pointed at the one next to the window. "Where's Eric?"

"Eric who?"

"Eric the elephant. He always sleeps in bed with me."

"I don't know, sweetie. Did you bring him?"

Her bottom lip quivered. "He was in my bag."

What bag? I hadn't seen a bag. "I'll try to find him, I promise."

*Please, don't cry.*

For a second, it was touch and go, but then she managed a tiny smile. "Can we have dinner now?"

"Of course. Wash your hands, and we'll go back downstairs."

As long as I could find the way. Logan had abandoned us, and the house was plenty big enough to get lost in. Oh, how did I end up in these situations?

After two wrong turns where I found a fully equipped beauty salon and what looked like a flight simulator, we made it back downstairs. The aroma of something Italian, lasagne maybe, drifted through the house, and I followed my nose until we got to the kitchen. Logan was sitting at the counter fiddling with his phone while Mrs. Fairfax sliced up a ciabatta.

"Everything okay?" Logan asked as I lifted Scarlet up onto one of the stools.

"Did Scarlet have a bag with her? Her favourite toy's inside."

"Not that I saw. Let me check."

He dialled somebody, and I heard Emmy's, "Shit," from across the table, too late to cover Scarlet's ears. But from the gist of the conversation, yes, Scarlet had brought a bag. Some good news at least.

Logan hung up and raised an eyebrow as he lifted a bottle of wine. I shook my head. The last thing I wanted to do was let my guard down among strangers. He poured himself a glass, a large one. Guess he was staying overnight too.

"Emmy left Scarlet's bag in her office. Someone's on their way with it now."

"Thank you."

I'd guessed right with the food, and Mrs. Fairfax slid a plate of vegetable lasagne and mixed salad in front of each of us before taking a seat next to Logan. My mouth watered, but Scarlet eyed up the meal suspiciously.

"I don't like it."

"But you haven't tried it."

"It's green."

That would be the spinach. "But it tastes nice, and it's good for you." I took a forkful of my own food, pleased to find out I wasn't lying. Mrs. Fairfax was a superb cook. "See?"

"Can I have fries?"

"Not today, sweetie."

"Mommy would let me have fries."

Dammit, what should I say to that? I could hardly point out that her mother wasn't there and might not be for the foreseeable future.

"Mommy's set you a challenge. If you try twenty new foods before she comes back, she'll give you a special gift."

Scarlet brightened a little. "Really?"

"For sure." I'd buy her the gift myself.

"Can I go to Wonder World? I saw it on TV."

Nothing like aiming high, eh?

"She might not be able to take you there, but I'm sure she'll buy you some Wonder toys. How about that?"

Scarlet picked up her fork and gingerly tasted a small piece. Well, she didn't spit it out, so that was a good sign.

"Okay," she said.

"Okay, you'll eat it?"

"It's not as yucky as I thought."

Thank goodness for that. Between encouragement and some bribery with ice cream when she faltered, we got most of the plateful down her. Just as well, because when I carried her earlier, I'd felt the outline of every rib hard against my arm. Her mother may have fed her trash every day, but she'd clearly skimped on the quantities.

By the time Scarlet had finished a scoop of ice cream with fruit on the side, her eyes were beginning to close, and just watching her made me yawn.

"Her bag's here," Logan announced when his phone lit up with a message.

Phew. At least she'd have Eric back for bedtime. When I was her age, I'd had a giraffe called Lenny, and just thinking of him now brought a tear to my eye. Because six days after my seventh birthday, I'd buried Lenny with my parents so they'd sleep well too. My grandma brought me a zebra instead, but it wasn't the same. I knew how Scarlet felt to be alone, but at least her mom would come back, hopefully sooner rather than later.

"I'll walk you up," Logan said once a man had handed me Scarlet's tiny pink backpack.

I opened it and found Eric, one ear tattered and stuffing coming out of his bottom. If Mrs. Fairfax could find me a needle and thread, I could fix that tomorrow.

The only other essentials Scarlet's mom had thought to include were a crinkled T-shirt and a package of cookies. People like her didn't deserve to have children.

"Thank you. This place is a maze."

"I'll give you a proper tour tomorrow."

I had to admit that as men went, Logan seemed like one of the better ones. A rare gem. I managed a smile as I bid him goodnight, and he returned it twofold.

"If you need anything, I'm at the other end of the hallway. Just knock."

"I'll see you in the morning."

He gave me a salute as he turned away. "Sleep tight."

I always called Dean last thing at night, but with Scarlet in the room, that was out of the question. Instead, I tapped out a quick text.

*Dean, I got asked to babysit at Emerson Black's house. I'm there now, so I can't talk. But I think I know where Mackenzie Cain sits. Xx*

Even if I didn't have a clue how to get near her desk undetected, I wanted to give Dean some good news. I'd heard the disappointment in his voice last night when I'd told him I hadn't made any progress, and the night before. And his message a few minutes later made me smile inwardly.

*Good girl. I knew you could do it. Don't forget—I'm counting on you.*

# CHAPTER 8

CADE NEARLY TURNED his Ducati around a hundred times on the way back to the safe house. He had a daughter? Technically, Emmy still had to run a DNA test to confirm it, but he'd have had to be blind to miss the similarities between himself and Scarlet. How had Reed Bonner thought she was his for so long? Granted, when they were at school Reed was famed for his muscles rather than his IQ, but even so... The hair colour should have given it away, surely? Both Cindy and Reed were blond, and Scarlet's hair was a soft brown, the same as Cade's.

Only the memory of the video interview he'd seen of another little girl kept his wheels pointing forwards. Five-year-old Alice Finch, the daughter of home invasion victim number four. She'd been inconsolable as she asked over and over why her daddy had left to live with the angels. Didn't he love her anymore? And Alice's mom, sobbing as a police liaison officer tried to comfort her. Alice had always been a daddy's girl. How would she cope without him?

And so the miles passed as Cade thought through the prospect of being a father himself. The upheaval in his life. Although he'd left the army now, working for Blackwood was hardly compatible with being a single father. Because that's what he'd be until they found

Cindy. And even when they did find her, the idea of sharing Scarlet with a woman who'd tossed her to the side in favour of her latest piece of ass filled Cade's veins with a cold fury he hadn't felt since another little girl left his life. Christie had been seven years old but not much bigger than Scarlet, and they shared a lot of the same features. Looking into Scarlet's eyes earlier had been like seeing his sister again.

Okay, so maybe Alice wasn't the only thing that kept Cade riding away from Blackwood's headquarters. There was also an undercurrent of fear. Fear he wouldn't be good enough. Fear he'd let Scarlet down the way he'd failed Christie. Fear that the little girl would be better off without him. No matter how much of a bitch Emmy could be, Cade had seen how strong her instinct was to protect others she cared for, and he knew that would extend to Scarlet. His daughter would be safe until he returned, perhaps safer than she'd be if he stayed.

"All right, Pool Boy? How's your grandma?" Doc asked.

Ah, his biker nickname, another thing Cade wouldn't miss when he finally left this nightmare. Although he looked good in a pair of trunks, that wasn't where it came from. No, he'd got it one night soon after he started hanging out at the club bar in the small town of Oakley, the night he got promoted to prospect with Doc as his sponsor.

It had all started when two assholes walked in like they owned the place, when everyone in town knew The Darkness ruled the roost. The newcomers weren't bikers, that much was clear from their clothes—baggy jeans, no belts, open shirts over pale-blue T-shirts. Cade had surreptitiously snapped a photo, and using her custom facial-recognition software, Mack had tapped away from the comfort of her desk at Blackwood and identified them as members of Chaos, an up-and-coming gang who were trying to gain a foothold in Richmond. Wannabes, and worse, they had something to prove.

The bulges under their shirts hinted at the weapons they carried, and Cade watched from the pool table as the pair got drunker and rowdier. Or more lairy, as Emmy would say. Then they made their big mistake. Dickwad number one, full of bluster, reached out to pinch the barmaid's ass, only she wasn't the regular barmaid. Doc's old lady, Taz, was standing in, and she upended a bottle of beer in the guy's lap in return. Two seconds later, World War Three broke out.

Cade had served his country in Afghanistan as well as a few other places he hated to talk about, but he'd never come so close to a bullet as the one that passed a hair's breadth from his neck before embedding itself in the wall behind him that night. While ordinarily he'd have stood back and let the rest of The Darkness take care of the situation, he picked up a handful of pool balls from the table next to him and hurled them in the gunman's direction. His second ball scored a direct hit and laid the guy out on the floor. Hawk, the MC president's son, had tackled his buddy and made it two for two.

That was when Doc had patted him on the back and said, "Nice throw, Pool Boy," and the moniker stuck.

And now Cade nodded to Doc and answered his

question.

"Grandma's not so bad. She has her good days and her bad days, and today was one of the better ones. All I can do is make the most of the time she's got left."

"Family's important."

"It is."

Cade's chest seized at the thought of his possible daughter, left behind with strangers. How long before he could get back to her?

"But your brothers are more important. 'Bout time you earned your patch."

Thoughts of Scarlet fled from Cade's mind. "Tonight?"

"Got a little job to do. You up for it?"

At times like this, you didn't ask for the details, and Cade fought back the urge to whoop with joy. Another home invasion? Could this be the break they were looking for?

"Sure am. Like you said, the brothers come first."

"You got a problem with breaking and entering?"

The question served two purposes. One, did Cade have a personal problem with committing a crime, and two, was he undercover? It wasn't unusual for new recruits to have to participate in illegal activities to earn full membership, and that was one way they weeded out the cops, who couldn't break the law as well as enforce it. There were ways around it—indeed, one ATF agent had staged an elaborate murder as part of his initiation—but this was the point at which most agencies were caught out.

Luckily, as a private contractor, Cade had more leeway. Emmy's instructions? *Do the necessary, and we'll fix it afterwards. Just try not to kill anyone, yeah?*

She was one cold bitch.

"No, I don't have a problem with it, as long as we don't get caught." Cade forced a laugh, and Doc joined in.

"Don't plan on that, son. That's where you come in. We need a lookout."

And Cade needed to get a message to Emmy.

An hour later, Cade and three of his so-called buddies assembled in front of the clubhouse. Boone, the club's treasurer, was one of the old school. The president's right-hand man, he wore his hair long and his jeans tatty. Cade needed to impress him tonight if he wanted his Darkness patch. Next to him was Tank, the club's muscle, who was as solid as his name implied. Rev sat astride his Lowrider, smoking a cigarette while they waited for the final member of their group. Deke was Boone's son, Cade's age and a grade-A asshole.

Cade wasn't on his bike tonight. He'd been assigned truck duty behind the wheel of the battered pickup the club used to carry spares on their road trips. Would it serve as transport for stolen property tonight?

Earlier, Cade had been hopeful, and he'd prepared accordingly. After messaging Emmy and her team to be on standby, he'd headed back to the shared bathroom in the clubhouse and turned on more electronic equipment than flew on the first Apollo mission., A miniature camera hidden in a stud on his jacket, a voice transmitter with a range of fifteen miles, a tiny in-ear microphone, and a kinetic energy-powered locator on his watch, which also held his panic button. He checked himself in the mirror. The Darkness didn't go in for vanity, and brown age spots on the glass marred his reflection as he arranged his shaggy hair over his ears. No, the mic was invisible.

As always, battery life was a problem, but he'd recharged everything and he'd have enough juice to last out the night. Usually, he stuck with a simple miniaturised recorder that sucked minimal power and, and then uploaded the data via his laptop each time he went home, but tonight, he needed the safety net that real-time transmissions afforded. The team behind the home invasions didn't hold back.

But now that the men were preparing to depart, Cade wasn't so sure he'd been right about Boone's intentions. They seemed remarkably relaxed for a crew about to commit murder.

"Ready to go?" Boone asked as Deke stumbled out of the clubhouse, doing up his fly.

Deke had been with Ginger, no doubt—his girlfriend, and the only woman hanging around the club who might have been a class act if she weren't so downtrodden. Cade struggled to understand what she saw in the man, but her air of sadness suggested a difficult past, so he could only assume she was driven by desperation.

In answer to Boone's question, three bike engines started up, and Cade turned the key in the truck's ignition.

"We're ready to go too."

Emmy's voice came through crystal clear in Cade's ear. Where was she? Somewhere close, he trusted that much. Emmy's one-word reply to his earlier message—

*okay*—let him know she'd canned her plans for tonight and followed the protocol they'd set out in their earlier briefings. Yes, she'd arrived, but he wouldn't see her until he needed to.

Boone led the way out of the compound, heading north towards Glen Allen. Cade followed at the back, tamping down his fear. He'd never gotten nervous like this in the army, but Boone had been worryingly light on the details of their job tonight. Cade didn't know what would be worse—participating in a home invasion with the potential to end in carnage, or the anticlimax if that turned out not to be the case.

Twenty miles outside Richmond, they pulled over into the deserted forecourt of a long-dead diner. The wind blew the remains of an old wooden sign against the metal siding with a slow *thwap-thwap-thwap* that echoed into the gloom once the engines were turned off. Boone beckoned everybody closer, and Cade couldn't help taking a covert glance around for any sign of Blackwood.

Nothing.

Boone rubbed his hands together, his face twisting into a smile in the headlights from the truck. Boy, that guy needed a visit to the dentist. Then he got a gleam in his eyes that Cade didn't like.

"Thought we'd make a little change to the plan. Deke, you stay here in the truck. Pool Boy, you can come with us and get a piece of the action."

Oh, shit.

Cade didn't want a piece of whatever action they had planned. He wanted to stay in the truck and keep an eye out for Emmy and her band of merry men as they rolled in to back him up. Deke didn't look too happy with the situation either.

And he was the first to protest. "But, Pop, you said I could join in with this one."

"Son, you went too far last time and the cops sniffed around our asses for weeks."

"I don't wanna stay in the truck."

Great, a twenty-five-year-old teenager. Cade didn't know whether to back the prick up or go along with whatever Boone was cooking.

"Tough shit. Cade, you're with us. You can ride behind me."

Looked as if he didn't get a choice in the matter. "What's the plan, boss?"

"Bobby Lee Gibson backed into Tiny's bike the other day." Tiny was the designated cook and gave Tank competition in the size stakes. "That old drunk needs to be taught a lesson."

Not a home invasion?

Cade stifled a groan. Dammit. Not only had he jumped the gun by getting Emmy's team out, now it looked as if he'd have to help beat up a defenceless man or blow his cover. Why had this particular role ever seemed attractive?

"Just go, Cade," Emmy said. "We'll be right behind you."

With little alternative, he swung his leg over the back of Boone's bike, dread pooling in his stomach. This whole night was fucked up.

Emmy updated him as they rode, getting her information from Mack, no doubt, or maybe Agatha. A small smile tugged at Cade's lips at the thought of Miss Pigtails, but it soon faded again as they got closer to their target.

"Bobby Lee Gibson," Emmy said. "Forty-eight years old, married, no kids. Lives half a mile from your current location. Doesn't look like he pays taxes, and his credit history's fucked."

None of which meant he deserved three angry bikers and one reluctant recruit turning up at his door late at night, intent on causing him harm.

What should Cade do? Back out? Protest? Suggest a different way of doing things? Stand by and do nothing, or worse, join in?

He'd never been in this situation before, forced to go along with something against his moral code in the line of duty. What would Emmy do? He'd have given anything to press pause and talk things through with her.

But Boone was turning off the road and into an overgrown driveway.

Cade's time had run out.

## CHAPTER 9

NOBODY STIRRED IN the house as four leather-clad shadows slipped past the old pickup abandoned at the far end of the driveway. Light from the full moon glinted off a fresh dent in the back. From Tiny's bike?

Boone didn't bother to knock when they reached the front door, just stood to the side as Tank shouldered his way through. One hit, that was all it took. He didn't even pause. Then they were inside and the stench... The stench was unreal. Stale beer mixed with damp mixed with rotten food. Cade stepped over a pile of dog shit and swore under his breath as an ageing mutt staggered out of a room to the left, barking in a hoarse whisper. Tank kicked it into the bathroom and slammed the door.

This whole—Cade didn't want to dignify it by calling it an operation—was wrong. Ill-thought-out, morally abhorrent; these men were nothing but a bunch of thugs. And what was more, he couldn't see any of them acting with the precision needed for one of the seven home invasions pulled off so far.

Snoring from up ahead alerted them to the house's occupants, and there they were. Bobby Lee Gibson and his wife, sprawled across a filthy king-size, still dressed. The woman barely stirred as Tank grabbed her scrawny husband by the arm and hauled him out into the tiny lounge. Boone stumbled around in the dark, cursing as his boot squelched in something Cade hated to contemplate, and then the light came on.

Bobby Lee wasn't a shining example of manhood, that was for sure. He couldn't stand up on his own, and although his eyes were open, he struggled to focus on the group of men gathered in front of him.

"Bobby Lee, you know why we're here?" Boone asked.

Nothing.

Boone belted Bobby Lee across the stomach, and he threw up on Boone's boots.

"Ah, fuck!"

Boone hopped around, spewing profanities, while Rev stepped forwards to kick Bobby Lee in the shin. The man barely moved. Either his pain receptors were wired up wrong, or he was too drunk to notice. Cade was going with the latter.

"Gibson's got a record," Emmy said in Cade's ear. "Seems he spends most of his time on the sauce."

No shit, Sherlock.

"DUI, DUI, DUI, all with no licence because that got revoked years ago. Seems he's a regular visitor to the drunk tank. One spell in jail a decade ago. He ran over a mom and kid in his truck and killed them both, and guess what? He was four times over the limit while he did it. The arresting officer's report said the only miracle was that he was still conscious."

Suddenly, Cade didn't feel quite so sorry for the man anymore. His spell in prison hadn't changed his behaviour one bit.

Rev let fly with another vicious kick, then stepped back and beckoned to Cade. "Your turn, Pool."

Now what? Whether Bobby Lee deserved retribution or not, Cade didn't want the man's murder on his hands, and if he went in soft, he wouldn't get his damn patch.

*Think, dammit. Think!*

"I could use him as a punching bag, but the asshole's out of it. He doesn't even know what lesson we're trying to teach him."

"He'll work it out from the bruises in the morning."

"But he won't know it was The Darkness." Cade waved a hand in front of Bobby Lee's eyes, and he didn't even blink. "See?"

Boone folded his arms and raised an eyebrow. "You got a better idea?"

"Yeah, I do. Take out his truck so he can't drive into people's vehicles anymore. Way he lives, he won't be able to afford a new one."

Boone stared, eyes narrowed, chewing on the end of an unlit cigarette while Cade did his best to look confident in his suggestion.

Rev surprised him by chipping in. "It's not a bad idea."

Finally, one corner of Boone's mouth quirked up. "Fine. The truck. Show us what you got here, boy."

"Nice one," Emmy said. "We'll back off a bit."

Now, improvising IEDs was something Cade had gotten plenty of practice with during his army days. A rummage around in the kitchen produced a thermos and a handful of batteries, and by using his trusty multitool, he quickly extracted the lithium and packed it into the bottom of the flask. Next, he dropped in the can of deodorant he'd spotted on the overflowing dresser. Full, by the feel of it. Figured. It wasn't as if

Bobby Lee ever used it.

"I hope you know what you're doing, boy," Boone said, looking over Cade's shoulder.

"The fruits of a misspent youth."

Next, Cade filled the pair of condoms that had been gathering dust in his wallet with water and carefully blotted them dry. If a drop got on the lithium too soon, he'd blow up the house as well as himself and everyone else in it rather than just the truck. A piece of wadded-up tissue held the condoms in place at the top of the flask, and he screwed the lid on.

"Okay, we're ready. Is Gibson still in the lounge?"

He was. His left hand rested in the pool of vomit, and it didn't look as though he'd moved an inch. Cade breathed a sigh of relief as he pulled the sagging front door closed behind the rest of the gang and headed for the bikes at the top of the driveway. He and Gibson would both live to face another day. The battered Ford would be the only casualty.

The Darkness fired up their bikes, and Cade shook the flask to break the condoms, rolled it under the truck, then ran.

Emmy's voice crackled in his ear as he hopped up behind Boone. "Hate to tell you this, but you've got company. There's a cop car at the end of the road."

Cade barely had time to process those words before the explosions came. First his rudimentary grenade, then the fuel tank on the truck, which, by Murphy's Law, must have been full judging by the way the damn vehicle lifted clear off the ground. A siren pierced the air before they'd even got out of the driveway.

"Shit, boy," Boone muttered as they swung into the road, red lights flashing in front of them.

The bikes blew past the cruiser, kicking up dirt as they went. Cade twisted around and saw the cops already turning. A police chase. The perfect end to a perfect night.

As Boone manhandled the Harley down the road, Cade glanced at the deserted gas station and saw Deke slumped in the front of the pickup. Asleep or dead? Didn't matter, really. If they got out of this alive, the lazy asshole wouldn't be breathing by the time Cade finished with him.

Cade soon realised where Rev's nickname came from as a gap opened up between him and the others. Whatever engine he had on his bike, it sure wasn't the manufacturer's standard. The Electra Glide would have given Cade's Ducati a run for its money. Boone wasn't a bad rider either, but being helpless on the back of another man's bike filled Cade with a fear he'd never experienced.

Of course, Emmy was cool as the damn Arctic.

"Don't worry; we've got a plan as long as you stay on the main road."

Like Cade had a say in that.

"Did I mention Carmen came for the ride tonight?"

Oh, shit. Because if Carmen had come along, she'd have brought a gun. Probably several guns. And that meant there would be shooting. Cade had a Colt .45 tucked into his waistband, and everyone else was carrying too. A vision of bleeding out in a hail of gunfire flashed through Cade's mind, and he thought of Scarlet.

His daughter. The one he'd barely met.

If he avoided arrest tonight, when this job finished, he'd spend the rest of his life being the best father he could for her.

*Emmy, whatever you're planning, get it over with.*

The *pop* of an exploding tyre came from behind, and the cop car spun out of control. Boone slowed enough for Cade to watch the lights twist sideways as the vehicle came to rest in a ditch.

"Bullseye. Carmen strikes again."

Cade owed Carmen a damn fine box of chocolates for that one.

Back at the clubhouse, Cade didn't get the chance to swing at Deke, who admitted to waking up as the siren wailed past him. Because Boone did it himself. Deke stormed from the building sporting a bloody lip and glared at Cade as if the incident were all his fault.

A little animosity? Cade would have to tread lightly around him.

Boone bore no such ill will as he passed the beer around, recounting the tale of the explosion and subsequent chase.

"We got lucky when the cops got that blowout, eh, Pool?"

Cade mustered up a smile. "Something like that."

Wolf Hauser lifted his bottle as a shadow floated behind him. His son, Hawk. Cade hadn't seen much of Hauser junior, and the man gave off vibes that said "stay away." But tonight, after a brief conference with his father, he gave a rare smile and raised his arm in a toast as well. Cade caught sight of a dark bruise on his biceps, the size of a man's boot print. Hell, that had to sting.

Wolf broke into Cade's thoughts when he held up a

patch with The Darkness's insignia on it and beckoned Cade forwards.

"Welcome to the club, Pool Boy. You're one of our brothers now."

While the other men cheered and laughed, Cade's feelings were mixed. Being inducted into a band of assholes who beat men for sport was hardly something to be proud of, but in a way, it was his greatest achievement. He'd proven to his team, his real brothers and sisters at Blackwood, that he could do the job they asked of him.

A job which had only just begun.

# CHAPTER 10

WHEN I WOKE the next morning, I forgot where I was for a second, confused by the pale-pink wall next to me rather than the usual grubby cream one. Then I turned over and saw Scarlet sleeping a few feet away, and beyond her, the sun rising over a forest in the distance.

What a view. I climbed out of bed, drawn to the window. If I lived here, I'd never close the drapes. As Mrs. Fairfax had said, there was a tennis court below, glistening with early morning dew, and on the far side, a pair of horses grazed peacefully in a paddock. Gently rolling pastures sloped down to the trees, lit up in a blaze of yellow as the sun inched higher. And what struck me was the silence. No noise at all apart from the clock ticking on the wall next to the closet. In Richmond, my apartment was on a busy road and the traffic never stopped, and even in our quiet community in California, there were occasional cars and worse, lawnmowers.

With Scarlet still dead to the world, I tiptoed into the bathroom and pulled the door shut. After dinner yesterday, I'd been so tired I hadn't even cleaned my teeth, and my tongue was all fuzzy. Please say there was a spare toothbrush.

There was. A whole bunch of them, in fact, tucked into the cupboard under the sink alongside little bottles of shampoo and conditioner and lotion. Was this a house or a hotel? Whichever, I decided to take a shower before Scarlet stirred, because then I'd have to get her cleaned up too.

As I stepped into the double-width stall, I dug my nails into my palms to stop myself from bolting right out again. Taking a shower was such a normal thing for most people, but I rarely did it anymore, not since that night at the hospital when my boring life got tipped on its head.

The Saturday evening shift was always the worst in the ER. Prior to that, I'd been working in paediatrics where there was more of a routine, but six weeks earlier, budget cuts meant I had the choice of rotating to the emergency room or losing my job. Already two months behind on the rent, I didn't have a lot of choice in the matter.

As Saturday nights went, it hadn't been any worse than usual. A kid who'd glued Legos to his face, one bad car smash, and the usual parade of drunks. I'd been looking forward to going home via the twenty-four-hour diner down the block when Dr. Finnegan ordered me to bring him a cup of coffee, skim milk, no sugar. Ever since he'd hit on me at the staff Christmas party and I'd thrown a glass of white over him, he'd been giving me all the crappy jobs. Asshole. Back then, I'd been a little braver, and I'd so nearly told him to get the damn coffee himself. That was my biggest regret in life, I think, that I'd obeyed his command.

Because if I hadn't, I wouldn't have found Harlan Lake in that quiet hallway, preparing to shoot up. And I wouldn't have shouted at him that I was calling security, and he wouldn't have bundled me into the empty shower room opposite and raped me. As he held me down and thrust inside, he'd reached up to the faucet and turned on the water, soaking us both as he got his perverted kicks. Every time I felt a gush of water on me now, it took me right back there. I could still hear his animalistic grunts as he stole what I didn't want to give, still feel his hands around my throat, choking the life out of me. He'd have succeeded, too, if Dean hadn't heard my strangled cry as he walked past outside.

Dean had saved me that night, the first night we met, earning himself a broken nose for the pleasure. And he kept on saving me. When I couldn't work for months afterwards, he'd settled my rent arrears and offered his spare room. Then he'd taught me to forgive Harlan Lake and ensured my attacker got the help he needed to recover from his addiction. And slowly, slowly, I learned to trust a man again. Just one. My friend, my lover, and now my husband. He'd never hurt me.

I was still shaking when I walked into the kitchen for breakfast. After enduring a five-minute shower, I'd helped Scarlet to wash her hair, and halfway through, I'd had to excuse myself to retch over the sink. Luckily, she'd accepted my explanation of a sore tummy with a childlike innocence I'd long since lost.

Mrs. Fairfax was in front of the stove when we got downstairs, and my mouth watered at the sight of pancakes. The sweet smell of syrup drifted on the air too, and I spotted Logan already halfway through a plateful.

"Sit yourselves down, dears," she said. "I'll bring breakfast over."

Usually, I made all of Dean's meals, so being waited on was a novelty. Even back when I'd lived with Grandma, I'd been the one to cook in the later years.

"Thank you."

"Can I have chocolate sauce?" Scarlet asked.

Mrs. Fairfax smiled. "Do you promise to eat your vegetables at lunch?"

Scarlet nodded solemnly. "I will."

"In that case, Taylor, could you get the bottle out of that cupboard next to the refrigerator?"

I was happy to oblige, and when Mrs. Fairfax set two pancakes down in front of the little girl, she duly squirted so much sauce on them it was more like chocolate soup.

Logan smothered a laugh. "I can't say anything. I did exactly the same at her age, and look how I turned out."

A sarcastic comment about him being saucy almost escaped, but I stopped it just in time. Dean hated it when I talked that way, and the chances were that Logan would feel the same. Best I stayed quiet.

I went with maple syrup for my pancakes, and for a moment, I wished I could come to Little Riverley for breakfast every morning. Grandma used to make me pancakes when I was a small girl, and my mom before her, but Dean had insisted on eating the same brand of muesli every day for the past six years. He said it was the healthiest option, but secretly, I thought sometimes it was nice to do something a tiny bit bad for you. Which was why when Mrs. Fairfax asked who'd like seconds, I held my plate out.

"Your food's delicious."

"Thank you, dearie. After breakfast, I thought young Scarlet here could help us make lunch."

"Emmy said her assistant was taking us shopping so Scarlet could get some new shoes?"

"Change of plan, I'm afraid," Logan told me. "Bradley got held up in Milan with a small legal issue. He'll be with us as soon as the police let him leave, but that doesn't look as if it'll be today." He gave his head a little shake. "It was only a matter of time before his habit got him into trouble like this."

The drugs. Logan was talking about the drugs, wasn't he? And if so, it was best that Bradley stayed away from Scarlet for good. There were too many Harlan Lakes in this world, driven by their demons and desperate for their next fix, and the police precinct was the best place for them until they could get the help they needed. Either that or rehab, but not everyone was lucky enough to find a space at a good facility.

"That's fine. I'm sure I can find shoes for Scarlet on the internet and have them delivered."

"No need. Tia's coming over after lunch to take you both into Richmond. That girl shops like a pro."

And I was a pro at buying things online. I did it all the time. No bustling streets, no people bumping into me, no sideways glances. Dean was only too happy for me to do things that way. He'd even bought me a shiny new computer. A tiny part of me missed the old days when I'd gone for coffee with girlfriends and jogged in the park, but I'd joined a couple of internet chat forums so I didn't get lonely, although according to Dean, those could be full of weirdos as well. But it wasn't as if I was totally agoraphobic—I still went out as long as Dean came along to keep me safe.

"I can get the shoes delivered the same day by courier."

"Shopping won't take long, and I've already lined up Tia. If I try to cancel, she'll lynch me."

Well, didn't she sound like a charmer? All I wanted to do was return to my apartment, but if I freaked out about a tiny shopping trip, that would only draw unwanted attention. No, best to go along with it, then get back to my original objective, vague though that was. Plant Dean's computer program thingy so he could find out what Blackwood was doing to Draupnir, then get the heck out of Richmond.

I might have enjoyed cooking with Scarlet and Mrs. Fairfax if the clock hadn't been counting down to Tia's arrival at two o'clock. Scarlet had obviously never helped out in the kitchen before, but we soon had her kneeling on a stool, up to her elbows in the mixing bowl as she helped to make shortcrust pastry. Now she was sitting in front of the oven, watching our quiches bake.

"Scarlet, can you help to set the table?"

Her little brow furrowed in confusion. "Set the table?"

"That's what we call it when we put out the place mats and plates and cutlery."

"Why do I have to eat at the table again? At home, I always sit on the floor in front of the TV."

"Eating at the table's what grown-ups do. Don't you want to learn something new?"

She looked doubtful but clambered down from the stool anyway. "What do I do?"

First, I needed to find out where the dishes were kept, so I walked over to the utility room to ask Mrs. Fairfax. That lady never stopped. The second the quiches went into the oven to bake, she'd headed off with a pile of laundry.

Only now she was on the phone. I was about to back away because Dean always hated when I hovered, but I heard Bradley's name and got curious.

"Bradley will be the death of us all. He's still with the police?"

The answer was clearly yes.

"That addiction of his is out of control. It's costing a fortune. I don't know why Emmy doesn't stop him, I really don't."

I didn't understand it either. With the amount of money Emmy had, surely she could send her assistant to a good rehabilitation centre?

"So he won't be back until tomorrow night? That's cutting it awfully fine for the party."

A party? A drug addict shouldn't be at a party. It was the worst possible place for him.

"Okay, keep me updated."

I backed away before she finished her conversation because I didn't want to be caught eavesdropping, and when Mrs. Fairfax came back through the door, I'd made it to the kitchen island and assumed what I hoped was a casual stance.

"I'm not sure where the place settings are for the table?"

"I'll show you where everything lives, dearie. Then you'll know for next time."

Next time? Why did everybody keep saying that?

# CHAPTER 11

A PRETTY BRUNETTE glided in at five minutes to two, hugged Mrs. Fairfax, then stared at Scarlet and me. Was this Tia? She was younger than I'd imagined, barely out of her teens by the looks of things.

"Are you ready to shop? I've lined up a driver, so we don't need to worry about parking." Her British accent matched Emmy's.

"Is that really necessary?"

The part of me who'd once counted every cent would never die, even though Dean had provided me with a comfortable life for years.

"Emmy said Scarlet didn't have any shoes. This way, we can stop right outside the shop to buy her a pair."

I hated to admit it, but Tia did have a point, even if poor Scarlet hadn't complained once about her lack of footwear.

"And if I have to carry loads of bags, my arms'll fall off. It's far easier to just keep putting them in the car."

Okay, maybe Tia didn't live in the same world as the rest of us after all.

Rather than the limousine I'd half expected, Tia led the way out to a black SUV driven by a man who looked as though he'd be more at home as a getaway driver. Thankfully, he didn't handle the car that way, and we made it to downtown Richmond in one piece. Tia had already planned our itinerary, and I carried Scarlet into a children's shoe shop at our first stop.

"We need shoes," she told the assistant, stating the obvious. "Ballet pumps, flip-flops, slippers, boots, tennis shoes. And we need them in different colours. What do you have?"

The assistant's eyes lit up, and she beckoned to a colleague. "I'm sure we can help. Do you know what size?"

Tia pointed to Scarlet. "She'll need measuring."

While the two ladies got to work, taking Scarlet to the other end of the store to check her feet, Tia sank back into a chair by the window, clearly accustomed to being waited on. I perched next to her, not feeling quite so comfortable.

"You do a lot of shopping?" I asked to break the silence.

"I love it, plus it helps Emmy's assistant out."

"Bradley?"

"You know him?"

"I've heard about him. Isn't he stuck in Milan?"

She shook her head. "The poor guy. I mean, he just couldn't help himself, and now the police won't let him fly back."

"Doesn't Emmy get upset about his addiction?"

"Sometimes, but as long as she looks good when she needs to, she lets it slide. Bradley's amazing at hair and make-up."

What a shallow attitude. That way of thinking was why America had so many problems, and now an innocent child had been dropped into the middle of it all. Abandoned by her mother, and with her father nowhere to be seen. While Tia was talking, I decided to try and find out more about him.

"Do you know Cade?"

"Why?" Her tone turned from friendly to a little hostile.

"I was just wondering what he was like, seeing as he's supposed to be Scarlet's father, but it doesn't matter."

"Oh. Cade's a nice guy. A really nice guy. He just wasn't the right one for me."

Ah, so they had a history. "I'm sorry things didn't work out between you."

"Don't be. It was for the best, and we're still friends. Well, sort of. It's awkward."

"I just hope he'll be a good father to Scarlet."

Tia scrunched her face up. "Honestly? I don't know what sort of father he'll make, if she's even his. Emmy wants us to take her to Blackwood's office on the way back so the doctor can collect a DNA sample and give her a check-up."

That poor girl, getting passed around from person to person. Did anyone want her? I looked across in time to see Scarlet's face light up as she tried on a pair of sneakers that fitted, and soon she was running around the store, laughing.

"Taylor, look! They're pink!"

"They're really pretty, sweetie."

"I love pink. It's my favourite colour."

"She'll get on well with Bradley, then," Tia muttered. "Especially if her favourite animal is a unicorn. Hey, Scarlet? Do you like unicorns?"

"I love unicorns!"

"There you go."

Fantastic. Wasn't there *anybody* who thought it was a bad idea to leave a small child with a substance abuser?

Once Scarlet had picked out a dozen pairs of shoes, we carried them all out to the car and headed for the nearest department store. Tia knew most of the assistants by name, and we sat in a private room while they brought clothes to us, so the experience wasn't as painful as I'd feared.

"Here, this one's for you." Scarlet solemnly placed a necklace made of fat pink beads over my head. I winced as I caught sight of the price tag—sixty dollars.

"Scarlet likes you," Tia whispered. "I didn't get a necklace."

"We can't buy it. Have you seen how much it costs?"

She flipped the tag over. "Is that all?"

"It's made from plastic."

"Designer plastic, and I've got Emmy's credit card. Don't worry about it."

And so it carried on. By the time we'd finished, we could barely fit in the car, and Scarlet had more clothes than I did back home in California. Hers were more fashionable too.

"Where are we going?" she asked.

"Blackwood. Back to the office you were at yesterday."

Scarlet's smile faded. "I don't wanna go back there."

"It's not for long. I'm sure someone will take you back to Little Riverley later."

"I want you to take me."

"I need to go home, sweetie."

We hadn't had any tears yet today, but now they

came. Tia fished around in her purse for a tissue while I gathered Scarlet onto my lap.

"There are plenty of nice people to look after you."

And Bradley.

"That blonde lady scared me. And the man with all the hair on his face, he scared me too."

A beard? What man? Logan? He only had a goatee, and I thought Scarlet had liked him. I raised an eyebrow at Tia, and she mouthed, "Cade."

"I didn't know they'd met," I whispered.

"Briefly, before he went back to his job."

Oh dear. It looked as though when he did get back, Cade would have a lot of bridges to build, assuming Scarlet was his daughter. And in the meantime, she had nobody she trusted. Except me.

And heaven help me, but I didn't want to abandon her. How could I even begin to explain that to Dean?

At Blackwood, Tia waved me into the elevator and pressed the button for the third floor. Obviously, Emmy's rule about callisthenics didn't apply to fashionistas. Tia also had the necessary clearance to get into the Special Projects department, and she led us inside and over to Emmy's office. Nothing had changed since yesterday apart from the addition of three empty coffee cups on the edge of the glass desk.

"Emmy's here somewhere," Tia said. "I'll go and find her."

When she left, I peered out of the glass at the office I'd spotted yesterday. Today, the vivid red of Mackenzie's hair was visible behind the bank of monitors, shining under the lights above her. I was getting closer to achieving Dean's objective, but how could I take that final step?

"What are you looking at?" Scarlet asked.

"Nothing. Just looking."

Scarlet pressed her face against the glass, only she was interested in something much closer.

"Is that chocolate?"

"Uh, I'm not sure."

It was. A bar of Hershey's on the nearest desk.

"Can I have some candy?"

"Maybe later, if you eat all your dinner."

She flounced off in annoyance. "Mommy always lets me have candy."

Scarlet flopped onto the sofa with her arms folded just as Emmy walked in, and the big boss looked far from happy.

"The doctor's on her way up. How did shopping go?"

"Good, I think. We got more stuff than she really needs."

"Tia's got a habit of doing that."

"I'm sure she and Scarlet'll have fun playing dress-up this evening."

"What? No, they won't. Tia's just left for a rock concert with her boyfriend."

"So who's looking after Scarlet tonight?"

Emmy yawned. "I was kind of hoping you would."

"I'm not sure..."

"Look, in the last thirty-six hours, I've had five meetings, two horrific sessions with my personal trainer, one police chase, a nasty development in an ongoing investigation, and no sleep. Even if I could stay awake to take care of a child, I wouldn't have a clue what to do. I'll pay you whatever you want, but please, would you just help me out here?"

Scarlet's eyes pleaded too, adding to the guilt trip.

"Okay, one more night."

"How about two? We're having a party tomorrow since you Americans insist on celebrating Independence Day, and you're welcome to come if you don't mind keeping an eye on Scarlet."

My face must have given away what I thought of that idea.

"Oh, don't look so horrified. There'll be other kids there, fireworks and all that sh...shizzle. Bradley's organising it, and he'd better be back in time."

Bradley was going to be there?

"Fine, I'll do it."

Somebody had to keep Scarlet safe from that man.

# CHAPTER 12

CADE BARELY SLEPT on the night of his initiation. Probably he should have been grateful he'd avoided some of the more extreme rituals his acquaintances at the ATF had described—being forced to drink vomit from an old boot, for example—but once the initial high of escaping the cops had worn off, his body felt like a deflated balloon while his mind went into overdrive.

What if they'd gotten caught? Would Emmy have pulled strings to get him out of jail and risked blowing his cover, or left him there? So far, this whole operation had been...not quite a waste of time, because Cade had gathered plenty of information on the petty crimes The Darkness were committing, and in Blackwood's world, information was currency, but it had been damn frustrating.

He forced away those thoughts, only for Scarlet to replace them. How was she? Who was looking after her? If Cade had to guess, his money would have been on Bradley, at least temporarily. No doubt Scarlet would adore the man. Kids always did.

The morning brought more bad news, at least from Cade's point of view. Boone held up a bottle of beer in a salute as Cade stirred on the dirty couch in the clubhouse just before midday.

"We've found a room here at the clubhouse for you.

Kinda small, but it'll save you rent."

That meant Cade could get closer to the action. The problem was, he wasn't convinced there was any action worth getting interested in.

But a new member didn't turn down an offer like that.

"Appreciate it."

"We'll get the new prospect to clear the junk out." Boone waved at a skinny guy leaning on the bar in the far corner. Cade's replacement. Didn't take long.

Cade raised a hand, and the guy nodded back. "Better pick up my shit from the apartment."

"Take the truck. Deke don't need it anymore."

At least picking up his belongings gave Cade the chance to call Emmy. He needed to apologise for last night's debacle, update her on his new living arrangements, and see what she wanted him to do next.

From the outside, his phone looked like a normal handset, but Nate, Blackwood's resident gadget man, had modified the software to hide his communications with Blackwood. Unless anyone being nosy typed Cade's PIN into the calculator, they'd think he spent most of his time calling Grandma Beryl and the local pizza place.

As soon as he got into his apartment, he dialled Emmy's hotline number, the one she called her red phone, knowing her PA would pick up if she didn't.

"You got back okay?" Emmy asked.

"Yeah, and then they welcomed me into the club. Not sure whether that's a good thing or a bad thing."

"Jury's still out on that one. There was another home invasion while you were messing around with Bobby Lee Gibson."

Cade sagged back against the rickety kitchen counter. "Where? How bad?"

"Rybridge. One man dead, his wife and kid left alive."

"Well, we know it wasn't the assholes I was with."

"No, but we did catch a break, because who lives in Rybridge?"

"Nick?"

One of the owners of Blackwood, director of the company's executive protection division, and a former Navy SEAL to boot.

"You got it. And when we checked the footage from the camera on his gatepost, we caught a pickup driving past two hours before the house got broken into. Guess who it was registered to?"

"Just tell me already."

"Brendan Hauser."

Shit. "Hauser? As in Wolf Hauser?"

"His son."

"They call him Hawk."

"Whatever they call him, I don't believe in coincidences like that."

Cade thought back to the mark he'd spotted on Hawk's arm when he got back last night. "Was there a struggle?"

"Yeah, there was. According to the kid, the wife belted a dude wearing a JFK mask with a marble statue, but then he knocked her out and she doesn't remember anything. Why do you ask?"

"Hawk had a bruise last night when I got back.

Upper arm. Looked fresh."

"All these little bits of circumstantial evidence are piling up. I'll let Dan know and she can dig into his background. Any chance you can get some up-to-date photos?"

"I'll try. I haven't seen him around much. He stops in to visit from time to time, but he's not officially a member of the club." Cade's throat went dry at the thought of getting closer to Hawk. The man might dress like a bum, but he kept fit and moved with a stealthy grace that reminded Cade of a leopard stalking its prey. And Hawk's eyes... His eyes looked flat at first appearance, but if you held his gaze, they bored into you with the benevolence of a red-hot poker. Cade didn't want to admit it in present company, but Hawk scared him.

"Does he own a bike?" Emmy asked.

"A Harley. I doubt his father would let him ride anything else. But I've seen him in a truck too—a black Ford, right?"

"Dark-coloured Ford. That's what was on the camera. We need to focus on him now, and anyone he hangs around with."

"I've seen him with a couple of guys, but I don't know their names."

"Find out. The clock's already ticking down to the next attack. We've got less than six weeks if they stick to their current schedule."

"And we still haven't found any definite connection between the victims?"

"Apart from three of them being members of the same golf club? No. They move in the same social circles, so there could have been some casual interaction, but the wives can't recall anything concrete and we can't find a link through their businesses. A lawyer, a real estate mogul, an importer, one owned a chain of opticians, three inherited their money, and the latest victim was a low-level politician. But people are scared. Revenue at Blackwood's home-security division has rocketed."

"Did the latest property have security?"

"It was in one of those gated developments with a guard patrol every hour. They didn't notice anything until it was too late. The alarm was turned off because the family were home, and the gang took out the security lights. A catapult maybe."

"Did they steal much this time?" Cade moved across to the sink and poured himself a glass of water.

"Cash, jewellery, two laptops, a coin collection. Oh, and cameras. The husband was a keen photographer and some of those lenses cost the same as a small car, apparently."

"I wonder if Hawk's using Wolf's contacts to get rid of it?"

"Whoever the fence is, they're good. Nothing's surfaced so far." Emmy smothered a laugh. "I guess after your experience with the sports gear, we should check eBay."

"Hawk would have to be dumber than a rock to go that route."

"Yeah. And so far, he's been anything but. He's also a ghost. Apart from the basics like his truck and his address, we haven't found anything on him yet. No job, no record, not even a parking ticket."

"Nobody's invisible."

"I know. Mack's on it, but things are crazy here and

she's exhausted. She fell asleep at her desk yesterday. Normally, Luke would lend a hand, but he's busy opening a new branch of his own company this month."

"What about the new girl? Agatha?" Miss Pigtails.

"Yeah... She's good, but we need to keep an eye on her."

"Why?"

"Agatha's keen, but between you and me, she can make mistakes. A couple of weeks back, she was working on some extracurricular activities in the office, and she forgot to mask her IP address or something. Mack caught it, and we don't think it caused a problem, but she needs to prove she's being more careful before we let her loose on the sensitive stuff."

"Understood. I'll get what I can from my end."

"Just be damn careful. If Hawk is behind these home invasions, he's not fazed by violence."

*Thanks for the reminder.*

With the investigative focus shifted to Hawk, Cade allowed himself a few moments to think of his daughter. "How's Scarlet? Is Bradley looking after her?"

"Bradley's stuck in Milan, but I found someone else to help."

"Who?"

"Her name's Taylor. She's one of the cleaners at Blackwood."

Cade almost spat out the mouthful of water he'd just taken. "You've got a cleaner looking after my daughter?"

"Jumping the gun a bit, aren't you? We haven't done the DNA test yet."

There was no need. Cade knew in his gut who

Scarlet's father was, and he didn't need a piece of paper to tell him.

"Stop splitting hairs. Why have you entrusted a child to the cleaner?"

"Scarlet got talking to Taylor the other night, and she really seemed to like her. And Taylor's got babysitting experience, plus we background-checked her when she joined the company. It seemed like the perfect solution."

Really? Or just the most convenient one?

"I want to talk to Taylor. What's her number?"

"I'll get Sloane to email it to you."

"Fine. But if I pick up any hint of a problem when I speak to this girl, you'd better be ready to find a replacement or I'm out of here."

# CHAPTER 13

CADE PACKED AS slowly as he could, waiting for Sloane to send Taylor's number, but that plan backfired when the club's new prospect knocked on his door.

"Boone sent me. He thought you might need a hand."

Help was the last thing Cade wanted, and he thanked his lucky stars that he'd stowed away anything sensitive before the kid arrived.

"I'm almost done packing."

"I can help carry everything down to the truck. I'm Bugs, by the way."

Named for his teeth, that much was obvious. Cade longed to send him away, but that would look odd.

"Thanks. Just start with what's in the hallway."

Bugs followed on Cade's heels for the rest of the evening, so close Cade nicknamed him Tailgater instead. And when he finally got some solitude in his room, not only was it midnight, the walls were thinner than a supermodel on Jenny Craig and he had to listen to Deke fucking Ginger all damn night. He didn't get to sleep until past three, and when he cracked his door open in the morning, Tails was already waiting with coffee.

Who the hell said undercover work was glamorous? James Bond had a lot to answer for.

It wasn't until evening that Cade managed to sneak out under the pretence of paying his final month's rent to his now ex-landlord. Tails offered to drop the cheque off for him, but Boone spoke up to remind him the beer fridge needed restocking, and Cade made a grateful escape.

A fine drizzle hung in the air as the Harley roared down the main road. It ran better now Cade had tuned it up, and he was grateful to his late grandpa for imparting his mechanical knowledge when Cade was a teenager. He still missed the old man who'd stepped in as a father figure when Cade's dad ran out on his mom before Cade was even born. Another reason he was determined to be there for Scarlet.

Would he get to speak to her tonight? He wanted to, but he didn't know where to begin.

He was more nervous than he cared to admit when he steered the bike off the road and parked it behind a stand of trees. At least the overhanging branches would shelter him while he called Taylor. He didn't know what to say to her either. Usually, his conversations with women started when they gave him their phone number, so going in cold was a foreign concept.

The phone rang once, twice, then he heard a nervous, "Dean?"

"No, Cade."

Who the hell was Dean? Her boyfriend? He didn't want some stranger around his daughter.

"Oh, I mean, sorry. Nobody ever calls me, and I just thought..."

"Who's Dean?"

"Nobody. Just an old friend from back home. He said he'd call sometime this week."

"Where's home?"

"California. But I moved to Virginia a few weeks back."

Cade relaxed a little. An old friend on the other side of the country wasn't a threat to Scarlet.

"Sorry if I came across terse. It's been a rough couple of days."

Taylor's voice softened, and Cade strained to hear her over the music in the background.

"I can understand that from the little Emmy's told me."

"I don't suppose it's easy for you either. You signed up for cleaning and ended up babysitting. I guess I should thank you for stepping in."

"Emmy didn't..."

Cade missed the last part of her sentence as a car sped past. "What was that? I can't hear you very well. Any chance you could turn the music down?"

She raised her voice instead. "Not really. There's a DJ and everyone else is enjoying it."

"A DJ? Is Scarlet with you?"

"Emmy's having a party. I didn't want to come, but like I tried to say, she doesn't give people a lot of choice."

Scarlet was at one of Emmy's parties? Hell, no. Those events ended in carnage with alarming regularity. After the last one Cade had attended, he'd woken up on a sun lounger wearing a damn dress.

"Where *is* Emmy?"

"I'm not sure. She's on roller skates, so it's easy to lose track."

Cade's teeth clenched so hard his jaw cracked. "Do me a favour and find her, would you? I need to have a word."

"Uh, okay."

The music faded in and out, and Cade heard Taylor talking softly to somebody. Scarlet? He couldn't make out the words.

Then Emmy's dulcet tones came through the phone. "You managed to get away from your new besties, then?"

"What the hell is my daughter doing at one of your parties?"

"Oh, did someone give you the DNA results already? It was a clear match. Congratulations, Daddy."

"No, nobody did, but I knew anyway. And you didn't answer my damn question."

"At this moment, she's eating a sausage roll."

"That wasn't what I meant, and you know it."

"Look, she's having fun. Bradley sorted out a bunch of acrobats to perform. Tabby's here too, and she's younger than Scarlet."

"Tabby's not a normal child. She's three years old, and she already knows how to reload a revolver."

"These things are important. She's not a bad shot with it either."

Cade's temples began to throb. How did he get into these situations? His peers in the army had raved about Blackwood as the crème de la crème of companies to work for after being discharged, but they forgot to mention that half the people at the top were batshit crazy.

"I don't want Scarlet near guns, or alcohol, or acrobats, or loud music. I want her in my house, sleeping in my spare room like a five-year-old child should be doing."

Emmy sighed, loud enough to be heard over the music. "Well, you'll have to ask Taylor if she'd mind putting her to bed there, because we've just hired her as Scarlet's nanny until you get back. I'll pass you over. Have fun biking."

*Deep breaths. Don't punch the tree. Deep breaths.*

"Cade? That didn't sound like it went too well?"

*In and out. Relax.* Luckily, Blackwood had a good dental plan, because Cade feared he'd cracked a tooth.

"You could say that."

"Sorry. Emmy's quite wilful, isn't she?"

Cade laughed. He couldn't help it. Talk about understatement. "Emmy does what Emmy needs to do to stay on top. She said you'd agreed to work as Scarlet's nanny. Is that right?"

"She's such a sweet girl, I just couldn't say no. Especially with Emmy's assistant back from Milan."

"Why? What's he done?"

"Maybe I shouldn't say anything. I never like to gossip."

"Just tell me, would you?"

Taylor's voice dropped to a whisper. "I mean with his drug problem."

Drugs? Bradley had been taking drugs? But Bradley wouldn't even take an aspirin unless a limb was about to drop off. He swore by all that weird herbal shit Emmy's nutritionist came up with.

"What kind of drugs?"

"I'm not sure exactly, but I heard he got arrested in Milan, and I also overheard someone mention his addiction."

"Find Emmy again."

This time, Cade was more confused than angry as

he waited for his boss to speak. Had he totally misjudged Emmy's assistant?

"Now what?"

"What are these rumours about Bradley having a drug problem?"

"Beats me. I haven't heard any."

Cade imagined Taylor withering under Emmy's gaze, because it didn't take Einstein to work out where the rumours had come from. The music faded more, then there was a *click* as Emmy closed the door to whatever room she'd ushered Taylor and presumably Scarlet into.

"Okay, you're on speaker. Who's going to tell me about these rumours?"

Taylor coughed nervously. "I heard he got held in the police station in Milan due to his addiction."

Emmy roared with laughter. "Oh, fu...duck me. He did end up in the *stazione*, but not for drugs. Bradley's addicted to shopping. He bought thirty pairs of shoes in one boutique, and as he was dragging them out to the car, some punk tried to snatch his manbag. So Bradley got him full in the face with a can of hairspray, which blinded him, and the asshole stumbled into the road and got hit by a truck. Of course, Bradley freaked out, mostly because he got blood on his Gucci loafers, and the whole mess took days to unravel."

Cade couldn't help laughing too, although Taylor sounded close to tears when she spoke.

"I'm so sorry. I thought... I got it all wrong."

"Don't worry about it. Next time, just talk to me, yeah?"

Emmy may have been a bitch, but she was an understanding bitch.

"I will. I promise."

"Now, did you get the logistics for tonight sorted out? Cade wants you to take Scarlet to stay at his place. Apparently, my parties are too much fun."

"But...uh..."

"Please, Taylor," he said. "I promise it's not a dump. I only lived in it for a month before I came on this job."

Emmy joined in, and for once Cade was glad of her forceful personality.

"It's a perfectly nice house, and it'll be good for Scarlet to get settled, especially as we haven't had any luck finding her mother yet. I'll arrange a car to take you both, and Bradley can sort out any groceries and cr...things you need in the morning."

"You won't tell him I thought he took drugs, will you?"

"It'll be our little secret."

## CHAPTER 14

OH, HOW DID I end up in this situation? I cursed Dean under my breath as Scarlet and I followed Emmy out of the house to the waiting SUV. First, I'd been worried enough about leaving Scarlet with Bradley to agree to be her nanny full time, then when I realised how wrong I'd been about Emmy's assistant, I'd panicked and offered to move into a stranger's house. The only saving grace was that I'd have privacy when I broke the news to Dean.

"Do you need to pick anything up from your apartment, ma'am?" the driver asked.

Yes. My brain and my sanity. Because I'd clearly forgotten to bring them with me this evening.

"Just a few clothes."

"I'll wait in the car with the little girl while you run in."

Shoving everything I owned into my suitcase only took five minutes, mainly because I'd never unpacked properly. I'd kept hoping that every day in Richmond would be my last and I could hop on a plane back to California. Emmy said she'd take care of the rent on my apartment while I stayed in Cade's house, but I'd be happy if I never saw the place again.

Outside, the driver hefted my case into the trunk, and then we set off again. I didn't even know where

Cade lived. *Please, don't let it be in a rough part of town.* The houses got bigger, the lots neater, and I began to relax. At least until we passed one mansion with what seemed like half a police force parked outside. Floodlights bathed the lawn in a harsh glare as white-suited forensic technicians milled around.

"What happened in there?" I asked the driver.

"Another one of those home invasions the night before last. They've been all over the news."

"I don't watch the news."

It only depressed me. The rare happy event was overshadowed by war, riots, and politicians arguing.

"Well, a bunch of rich folks' homes have been broken into over the last few months, and whoever's doing it murders one of the family as well as just stealing their valuables."

And I found this out just as I was going to stay at a house nearby on my own? At least in my cramped apartment building, I had neighbours on all sides to hear me scream.

"Will Cade's home be safe?"

"He wouldn't send you there otherwise. The gang only targets places full of money, so you don't need to worry."

I bit my lip, fighting back tears. I worried about everything at the moment. Dean and his job, our mortgage arrears, my impossible task at Blackwood, being entrusted with a stranger's child, the Harlan Lakes out there waiting to hurt me. I'd been away from home for weeks, and every day grew more difficult.

A few minutes later, the driver pulled up outside a modern detached house on a quiet street. Small, but tidy. The driveway lay empty, but a light gleamed from an upstairs window.

"Is somebody home? I thought the house would be empty."

"The lights are on timers. I'll come in and show you how to work the alarm."

Scarlet didn't say a word as I carried her up the path, the driver following behind with my case and a small bag containing Scarlet's essentials. Her eyes kept trying to close, and despite what Cade thought about the party, she'd enjoyed herself earlier watching the acrobats. Although I did agree with his assessment of Tabitha that I'd overheard. Seeing eyes so calculating on a child gave me the creeps.

The driver opened the front door, and after he'd disarmed the security system, he handed me a key attached to a plastic tag.

"The utilities should all be on. Any problems, you've got Emmy's number?"

"Yes, she gave it to me."

"Bradley'll call in the morning before he comes around, and he'll arrange for the rest of Scarlet's things to be brought over."

Bradley's arrival—something else to look forward to. After a quick lesson in how to arm the perimeter sensors to monitor the doors and windows while we slept, the driver departed, leaving me alone to begin my next nightmare.

Which started with calling Dean. As soon as I'd got Scarlet into her pyjamas and off to sleep in the bedroom at the back of the house, I picked up the phone.

"Hi. It's me."

"Where have you been? I tried calling earlier, but

you didn't answer."

"At a party."

"A party? But you don't go to parties."

No, I didn't. Not by choice. "It's a long story. Uh, I kind of got shifted off cleaning duties."

"You what?"

I told him the story about Scarlet, and how I'd been drafted in to take care of her, leaving out the part where I'd mistaken Bradley for a drug addict. That was just plain embarrassing. I'd expected Dean to be unhappy, and in the past, him being grumpy with me meant he ignored me for anything from hours to days, depending on the severity of my transgression. But I wasn't prepared for his explosion.

"What the fuck are you playing at? One simple job, and you've wasted weeks. The management at Draupnir's blaming me for their lost income, and worse, whoever's breaching security is causing difficulties for the senior staff personally."

"I-I-I'm sorry."

"We'll both be sorry if I lose this client."

"Dean, you're scaring me."

He drew in a breath at the other end of the line. "Look, I'm stressed, okay? The CEO is on my back ten times a day to seal up the holes in their network, but every time I plug one, another appears."

"Can't you get somebody else to help?"

"It's not that simple. The data I'm dealing with is very sensitive. Anyone new would have to be carefully vetted, and that would take months."

I tried to come up with something positive to placate my husband. I'd never seen that angry side of him before, and I didn't like it.

"Looking after Scarlet might even help. In my cleaning job, I never had clearance for the third floor where Mackenzie Cain's office is, but I've been up there twice with Scarlet to see Emerson Black."

Dean sounded a little calmer when he replied. "I'm sorry I yelled." He drew in a long breath. "Yes, if you can use Scarlet to get closer to Cain, that'll help both of us. But watch out for Emerson Black. My research indicates she's a real wildcard, and she can't be trusted."

He was definitely right about the wildcard part. "I'll be careful around her."

"Call me when you've got more news."

He hung up, leaving me with dead air.

"I love you too."

My hands shook as I tossed the phone onto the leather sofa in Cade's lounge. He said he'd only spent a month in the place, and that much was obvious from the boxes still stacked along one wall. The lounge held only two sofas, a widescreen TV with a DVD player underneath it, and a stereo on a sideboard. I flipped through the tracks on the MP3 player in the speaker dock to distract myself. An interesting selection— country, pop, ballads, even classical. Who exactly *was* Cade? Lana Del Rey was loaded up on the playlist, and I turned the music on softly to ward off the loneliness of the near-empty house.

As Lana sang about gods and monsters, I explored the rest of what was admittedly a reasonable property. A lot smaller than the one I shared with Dean, newer and not in such a nice location, but still okay. The kitchen was perfectly serviceable but devoid of food— only a few condiments sat in one cupboard next to a half-empty jar of coffee, and a whole collection of takeout menus was stuck to the fridge with colourful magnets. Mickey, Pluto, Daffy Duck. Looked as if Scarlet and her father at least had one thing in common —a love of cartoon animals.

Upstairs, I ran into my first major problem. While the house had three bedrooms, only two contained beds. The smallest one had been turned into a study with a desk, a chair, and bookshelves. Scarlet needed her own room—because how would she ever settle otherwise?—which meant the only spare bed was the king-size in the master, and from the wrinkled sheets, Cade had been using it. Sleeping in another man's bed felt awkward—no, just plain wrong—even if he wasn't in it. But unless I wanted to put my back out on the sofa or share with Scarlet, I didn't have much choice. Thankfully, I found a fresh set of linen, and by the time I'd changed the sheets, I was so tired that my eyes closed the moment my head hit the pillow.

And as usual, Harlan Lake visited me in my dreams.

Scarlet woke me up in the morning, crawling onto the bed to give me a hug. Her sweetness brought tears to my eyes, no doubt because of the fragile emotional state I'd been in lately.

"Can I have breakfast?" she asked. "Please."

"I'll have to buy food first. There isn't anything in the kitchen."

"But I'm hungry."

Her exaggerated sad face got me out of bed, and I

glanced at my watch as I headed for the stairs. Eight thirty, and I needed coffee. What time would Bradley arrive? Soon? Or should I try to find a store nearby? I looked down at myself, tastefully attired in pink ice-cream-print pyjamas. Before I did anything, I needed to get both of us dressed.

As soon as the kettle boiled, I made myself a mug of coffee, black because there was no milk, added a splash of cold water, and took a grateful sip.

"Scarlet, do you know how to take a shower by yourself? Or a bath?"

"Of course I do. Mommy hasn't helped me since I was four. I can clean my teeth too."

Why didn't that surprise me?

I followed her to the bathroom anyway, because when I'd babysat for kids Scarlet's age, they might have attempted those things, but they rarely remembered to brush the teeth at the back of their mouth and when they got out of the shower, their hair was invariably full of shampoo suds.

Scarlet did a surprisingly good job, and I found some cartoons on TV for her to watch while I took my turn in the bathroom. When I got out, I found a message from Bradley saying he was on his way.

I'd avoided him at the party last night, but that wasn't possible when he pulled into Cade's driveway in a yellow Ford Explorer, bounded up the path, and let himself in without bothering to knock.

"Never fear, Bradley's here." He stopped short and looked around. "Where's the rest of the furnishings?"

"This is it."

Some rooms felt quite cosy compared to our minimalist home in California. Dean didn't like clutter.

"But... But the walls are bare. The couch doesn't have cushions." I trailed Bradley through to the kitchen. "There's no fruit bowl. Everyone needs a fruit bowl."

"I guess Cade doesn't."

He sucked in a breath. "Well, we'll have to fix that." Abandoning his critique of the decor, he crouched in front of Scarlet. "Hi, I'm Bradley."

"I'm Scarlet."

He shook her hand, his silver nail polish flashing in the sunlight flooding in through the window, and she giggled.

"Scarlet, I brought you a little gift." He reached into the bag slung over one shoulder and produced a cuddly lion. "I heard you like toys."

She beamed at him. "I love toys."

"Then we'll have to go to the toy store together one day soon. But first, we need to buy you some food, missy. Are you ready to go shopping?"

Scarlet nodded enthusiastically as Bradley looked up at me, questioning.

"Me as well?"

"Of course."

Bradley already had a booster seat installed in his car, and my opinion of him crept up, more so when he pulled out of the driveway at a sensible speed and hung well back from the car in front. Rather than heading straight for the grocery store, he pulled into an IHOP just as my stomach grumbled.

"I thought we'd get breakfast to start with."

Scarlet clapped her hands together in the back seat, and while I hated to admit it, Bradley had gained two more fans.

At five o'clock, the time when I'd normally be pulling on my Blackwood polo shirt ready to start my cleaning shift, I flopped back onto the sofa next to Scarlet, shoving a couple of cushions out of the way as I did so. The lounge already looked more comfortable thanks to whirlwind Bradley, although I wasn't sure what Cade would make of the six-foot-high Warhol-esque print of a cow hanging opposite the television. Or the pink-and-yellow stripy rug, but Scarlet had picked that out, so her father couldn't complain too much.

A man was coming to measure up for drapes tomorrow morning, and a florist would be popping around with a few "essentials." Most importantly, we had a full refrigerator, a Mr. Coffee drip machine, and well-stocked cupboards.

But I couldn't stay on the sofa for the whole evening, because we needed to eat. I knew if I asked Scarlet what she wanted for dinner, she'd say pancakes, seeing as she'd eaten them for breakfast and lunch and still kept asking for more all afternoon. So I didn't ask her. I was determined to get her to embrace healthy eating before her mom came back, and my home-made fish fingers went down surprisingly well.

By the time I'd loaded the dirty plates into the dishwasher and got Scarlet to bed, my eyes were fighting to stay open. I'd always wanted to be a mom, but I'd imagined days of yoga lessons, lunch with other moms, and afternoon play dates. The reality was somewhat different.

My phone rang, and I sighed as I reached into my

pocket. Dean? I'd avoided calling him because I had no news, and I didn't want him to shout at me again.

No, not Dean. Cade. I didn't really know what to say to him either, but I picked up anyway.

"How are you?" he asked. "How's Scarlet?"

"Your daughter's exhausting. I'm half-dead. No, on second thoughts, I'd need more energy to die."

Cade chuckled softly. "Sounds like you've had a difficult day."

"Between Scarlet and Bradley, I haven't stopped. I don't know how moms do it. I mean, I used to babysit, but that was only in the evenings."

"I wish I could be there to help." He meant it. There was no mistaking the sincerity in his voice.

"How much longer have you got left on your job?"

"Who knows? Some days I wonder if it'll ever end."

"That bad, huh? What are you doing? Or can't you say?"

"Sorry, I can't. But the living conditions aren't great, the company's worse, and my stress levels are off the charts. I was hoping you could tell me a little about Scarlet to take my mind off things."

"Sure. Well, firstly, I've learned that it's not a good idea for her and Bradley to go shopping together..."

I spent five minutes describing our trip, and Cade listened quietly. When I finished, he let out a long sigh.

"I hate that I'm missing all this."

"Even the shopping? I'm worried that she'll want to buy as much stuff the next time we go."

"Even the shopping. It's not so bad. Just agree with her what she can buy before you leave, and if she wants anything else, it goes on a list."

"You sound as though you're speaking from

experience."

"My mom used to do that with my sister."

"You have a sister? Is she younger than you?"

"She was seven years younger."

Was? His tone didn't invite further questions, and although I wanted to offer sympathy for the sibling he'd lost, I kept quiet. After all, as an only child, I couldn't truly understand what he'd gone through.

Cade spoke again before I did. "I won't be able to call every night, but when I can, will you tell me what Scarlet's been up to?"

"Of course. Can you receive photos? Or isn't that safe?"

"My phone's got encryption software."

"Then I'll send pictures of her so you don't miss out."

"Thank you. I mean that. I don't know what I'd have done if you hadn't stepped in. I'd probably get back to find Bradley and Emmy had turned her into a diva who'd only wear designer combat gear."

I couldn't help laughing, because he spoke the truth. "Well, I promise to keep Scarlet's feet firmly on the ground."

"Then I'll speak to you soon."

Scarlet had gotten lucky with Cade, even if he wasn't there. Because he cared, certainly more than her mother appeared to, despite parenthood having been sprung on him in the unkindest of ways. And when he returned, I was confident he'd prove himself worthy of being her father.

Which was just as well, because soon I'd be leaving her too.

# CHAPTER 15

"WHERE'S MY MOMMY and daddy?" Scarlet asked over breakfast. I'd made her toast, which was sitting untouched on the plate as she sulked for Lucky Charms.

"They're away at the moment."

"When are they coming back?"

"Not for a while, sweetie."

She still didn't know that Cade was her real father, and I didn't want to be the one who had to tell her. How hard would it be to shatter a little girl's world?

"Mommy lets me have Charms."

"You remember what we said about trying new foods? That you'd get a new toy?"

"I've got lots of new toys now. I don't need another one."

Damn Bradley and his penchant for shopping. After we'd bought groceries yesterday, he couldn't resist taking Scarlet to The Toy Box, the biggest toy store in the area, and he'd let her run wild. Now I'd lost my main bargaining chip.

"How about I do your hair all fancy if you eat your toast?"

She brightened a tad. "In a French braid?"

"Yes, I can do a French braid."

I was wrapping a hairband around the ends when

the screech of tyres outside made us both jump. We ran through to the master bedroom in time to see Emmy slam the door of a Corvette and stride up the driveway. At least she knocked first rather than wandering in like Bradley.

"Have you got coffee? I need caffeine."

I followed her through to the kitchen. "Good morning to you too."

"I thought I'd better stop by with an update." She glanced up at Scarlet standing in the doorway. "Did Bradley get you new toys to play with?"

Scarlet nodded.

"Then why don't you go play with them?"

Scarlet looked up to me, and I forced a smile. "It's okay."

As Scarlet ran off to the lounge, Emmy sat at the counter while I checked the coffee machine. Luckily, there was enough for two cups in the jug. She might have caught up on some sleep, but she still looked rough.

"Is something wrong?"

"Depends on how you look at it. We tracked down Reed Bonner."

That name rang a bell, but from where? Ah, yes, the note that came with Scarlet. I dropped my voice to a whisper.

"Scarlet's...stepfather?"

"Ex-stepfather. He wants nothing more to do with her. Says he only stuck with Cindy because she was pregnant, they argued through their whole relationship, and as Scarlet got older, he realised she looked nothing like him and demanded a DNA test. In Reed's own words, 'Scarlet ain't my problem now.'"

How cruel could a man be? "Does he know where Cindy went?"

"No, and he doesn't care. Says he hopes she's gone for good."

I fetched two mugs from the cupboard beside the sink. "Do you take sugar? Cream?"

"Nope."

Once I'd added a splash of cream to my own drink, I took a seat beside Emmy.

"Has Blackwood had any luck finding Cindy?"

"Not a lot. According to Bonner, she skipped town with a door-to-door salesman. Guess when he got to her place, he bought rather than sold."

Wow. Just wow. How could a woman do that? Run off with a man she barely knew?

"But you'll find her, right? She can't have disappeared completely."

"We'd find her if we hadn't stopped looking."

"What?"

"I spoke to Cade earlier. He doesn't want Scarlet going back to Cindy, not if she won't take care of her properly. He reckons she'll be better off here with you."

Talk about piling on the pressure. "But long term... I'm not sure I can commit to that."

"We'll cross that bridge when we come to it. For now, our goal is to keep Cade's head in the game on a case that's going to hell, and make sure Scarlet's happy while we do it."

"She keeps asking for her mommy and daddy. I don't know what to tell her."

"Me neither. In case you hadn't noticed, I'm not exactly an expert on childcare. Besides, I think the decision about what to tell her should be made by her father."

"You're probably right." And it meant I wouldn't have to be the one to break the news. "He does seem to care for her."

"Yeah, he does. I was worried at first, because he's not exactly a guy I pictured settling down in the near future, but...he's got some history that means him wanting to look after Scarlet isn't a complete surprise."

"You mean his sister?"

Emmy's eyebrows shot up. "He told you about that?"

"Not any details. Just that he used to have a younger sister. What happened to her?"

"That isn't my tale to tell, I'm afraid." She sipped her coffee, staring out the window at a utilitarian yard. Plain patio, plain lawn, no plants. "I'll just say that if you ever get the urge to bring a man over while Cade's daughter is in the house, make sure that urge passes."

"I don't have a boyfriend."

At least I didn't have to lie about that, and it wasn't as if Dean would be popping over to visit from California.

"Good. For the moment, I'd suggest it stays that way."

Now she had me more curious than ever about what happened, but I didn't dare to press for more information. Would Cade ever tell me the whole story?

"Do you know how much longer Cade'll be away?"

"We haven't got a handle on that at the moment. This case is tricky."

"He said he'd try to call me in the evenings so I could update him on Scarlet. Is that safe if he's undercover?"

"He'll be careful. He might visit at some point too."

"Is that normal? I mean, whenever I watch cop dramas, those undercover guys are dug in deep."

"Some agencies prefer to work that way, but we don't. Being cut off like that brings its own problems. Agents can get a little too sympathetic to their new cause and switch sides, or the stress gets too much and they burn out early. If we can come up with a way for our guys to get some respite from what is, let's face it, a shitty job, then we'll take it. Cade's got a cover story that allows him to spend time away from his operation."

"As long as he's safe. Scarlet's already lost two parents."

"Nothing's ever one hundred percent safe, but we strive for ninety-nine."

My nerves didn't settle completely, but it wasn't as if there was anything I could do. "So I just stay here, then?"

"Nah. That would get boring, don't you think? You can use one of Blackwood's drivers to go wherever you want, and feel free to visit us at Riverley. Or the office, since it's closer."

The office—hallelujah!

"I might just do that."

"I'll get your clearance changed so you can come straight up to the third floor. Best to call first in case we're all out."

"Of course."

"And Nick Goldman doesn't live too far from here." Nick Goldman... I knew from Dean's research that he was one of the other directors. "He's got a place in Rybridge. His girlfriend said she'd stop by to keep you company this afternoon. Lara's a real sweetheart, and we don't want you to get lonely."

The thought of a lady from the wealthy part of town coming to visit brought me out in a cold sweat. I didn't speak fancy.

"I'll be fine with Scarlet. She's very entertaining."

"Nonsense. It's always good to have friends." Emmy swallowed the last of her coffee then pushed her stool back and stood, fishing her car keys out of her pocket. "I'd better get going. Got one hell of a day coming up. Have fun with Lara."

Despite my nerves, I knew within five minutes of meeting Lara that I liked her. Not because of the chocolate cake she brought, although that certainly charmed Scarlet, or because she was so damn pretty, but because of her smile and her positive outlook on everything. She was just so *nice.*

"And if you ever want a break for a few hours, I'm happy to look after Scarlet."

"Do you have children of your own?"

"Not yet, but hopefully one day, so I suppose I'd better get some practice in."

"Maybe you could join us for dinner sometime?"

Hang on. What was I doing? I didn't invite people over for dinner voluntarily, and certainly not girls whose boyfriend's company I was supposed to be spying on.

But Lara was already nodding enthusiastically. "That would be lovely. And we'll have to return the favour. Do you swim? We've got a pool, and I'm trying to use it every day. That and yoga—I want to get fitter."

"I don't have a swimsuit."

"We can go shopping and get you one. It'll be fun."

She looked so happy at the prospect, I didn't dare to say no. "I'd like that."

"And when Scarlet starts kindergarten and you've got more time, maybe we could go to the spa or something?"

"Kindergarten?"

Some nanny I was. I hadn't even considered that.

"She's five, right? So she'll be starting soon?"

"I guess. I suppose I should discuss it with Cade. Or Emmy."

When did the next term start? Mid-August? That gave me a little over a month to get organised, and I barely knew my way around Richmond.

"I can help, if you like. Does she know how to read? Or count?"

"I'm not sure."

But if her mother's efforts with everything else were indicative, the answer was no. It seemed being Scarlet's nanny would be even more difficult than I thought. How did a person teach a child those basics? I thought back to my own childhood, to the alphabet friezes my mom had pinned on the wall, to the flash cards and the books about a dog named Spot. She'd taught me to count using Cheerios. My grandma had done a wonderful job of bringing me up, but I still missed my parents like crazy.

"What's wrong? Why are you crying?"

I wiped away the tear that rolled down my cheek. "Nothing. Just thinking of my parents, that's all."

"Are they not around anymore?"

"They died when I was six."

"I miss my momma too. I lost her to cancer when I was twenty-five."

"My parents died in a car crash."

"I'm so sorry." Lara reached over and squeezed my hand, but that only made my eyes water harder.

"Me too. About your mom, I mean." I swiped at my face with my sleeve again. "Look at me. I shouldn't get upset like this, not after all this time."

Dean said if I kept mourning my parents, I'd never move on, and I always tried to put on a brave face for him.

Lara pulled me into a hug. "It's okay to cry. Grief never truly goes away, no matter how much time passes. But it's important to remember the good times too."

"I'll try."

"I'm helping to organise a fundraiser at the moment, and the proceeds are going to the American Cancer Society. That way I'm remembering Momma and doing something good at the same time. I can get you a ticket if you'd like to come?"

"I'm not sure I'm the sort of girl who goes to fundraisers."

"I always thought that too. My first one was a disaster—I ended up in the ladies' room in tears—but now I quite enjoy them. And I bet we can find you a hot date. That's one good thing about Blackwood. There are always single men happy to oblige."

A date? Hell, no. "I'm not sure..."

"Think about it." Lara glanced at her watch. "I need to pick something up from the office for Nick, if you guys want a trip out?"

"From Blackwood's office?"

She giggled. "Unless he's got another job he hasn't told me about."

Oh, I was going to hell when this adventure was over.

"A visit to the office sounds wonderful. It's always nice to get a change of scene."

Lara's Porsche 911 put Dean's Boxster to shame, and Scarlet oohed and ahhed over the candyfloss-pink leather seats as she clambered into the back. Thankfully, Lara didn't drive much faster than Bradley, and we made it to the office in one piece.

And I was no longer just the cleaner. The receptionist called me over when we got inside to let me know I now had access to the third floor. All I had to do was look in the retina scanner. One more piece of the impossible jigsaw Dean had challenged me to complete fell into place.

With Lara in the lead, we took the stairs at a jog—part of her fitness efforts, no doubt—and she let me do the honours when we got to the secure part of the third floor. *Click.* The lock opened, and we were inside.

Only there were people everywhere.

"What's going on?" I whispered to Lara.

"There's a big case in progress. I think it's something to do with those home invasions that've been on the news."

I really needed to start watching CNN, didn't I?

"I didn't realise Blackwood was working on those."

"Nick didn't come home until midnight yesterday."

I spotted Emmy pacing her office on the phone, and she gave me a wave before turning her attention back to whoever she was speaking to. Mackenzie was there too, ensconced behind her bank of computers. Darn it. I wouldn't be getting near them today.

"I'll take Scarlet into the break room," I told Lara.

The last thing I wanted to do was get in the way, and besides, it gave me the chance to be nosy. Each break room housed a computer terminal with access to Blackwood's intranet, and the intranet contained the global staff directory. What did Cade look like?

There were two Cades working for Blackwood, but only one in the United States. Cade Duchamp. And... Hot damn. Since Scarlet was such a cute kid, I should have realised she'd got a lot of those genes from her father. Intense brown eyes, straight nose, a strong jaw, and Cade had a hint of stubble. With Dean waiting for me back home, my heart shouldn't have started beating faster, but it did.

"He doesn't look like that right now."

I almost fell off my stool when I heard Emmy's voice behind me. "I wasn't— I mean, I didn't..."

"Hey, I'd be nosy too. Cade's a little rough around the edges at the moment. Part of the whole undercover thing."

"It doesn't matter. I'm only here for Scarlet."

She gave a funny little smile as she headed for the coffee machine. "Of course you are."

# CHAPTER 16

AFTER LARA DROPPED Scarlet and me back at Cade's house, I spent half of the evening worrying about work while I avoided calling Dean. Yes, I'd managed to gain access to the third floor now, but I didn't think he'd be happy if I told him getting near Mackenzie's computer still seemed like an impossible task.

Frustrated, I decided to concentrate on Scarlet instead, determined to do my best to help her in what little time I had. She needed a routine, basic schooling, and trips out so she could see what went on in the world. That last part would be the hardest for both of us. Now I was away from California, I could see I'd turned into a bit of a hermit there, only leaving the house if it was absolutely necessary. I'd been scared to go out after the rape, and Dean had always encouraged me to stay at home if I felt more comfortable there.

Twice a week. I'd start by taking Scarlet out twice a week, even if it was only to Lara's house to go swimming. No child should be stuck inside just because her appointed guardian had an unnatural fear of public spaces.

And I'd ask Bradley to bring us half a dozen suitable books so I could teach her to read. An hour's search on the internet gave me some pointers about methods, and I couldn't bear the thought of sending her off to kindergarten so far behind her peers.

For as long as I was in Richmond, I'd do the best I could.

A week later, I reflected on my plan with a mixture of pride, guilt, and worry. The pride came from Scarlet's progress and a few small wins of my own too.

From nothing, Scarlet could now count to ten, sound out the letters of the alphabet in lowercase, and spell her name. Bradley had brought enough books to stock a small library, and I'd begun reading to her instead of parking her in front of the television like her mom apparently used to do. Next week, I had three appointments lined up at various kindergartens, and Lara had agreed to come with me to give a second opinion.

And what about my own achievements? Well, when we went out—first to a playground on Tuesday and then to a children's art workshop on Thursday, one of Bradley's ideas—I hadn't succumbed to a single panic attack. With Blackwood's driver waiting for us outside each venue, I didn't feel the fear that usually came with being out in the open. And as an added bonus, we'd visited Lara's house—or rather, Lara's mansion—to swim. Scarlet had been swimming twice before, but only in a friend's blow-up pool back at her old home, and seeing her splashing around so happily made me smile. Not only that, Lara treated me as a real friend.

That was a strange concept. I'd lost contact with all my former girlfriends after I moved in with Dean. When I hadn't wanted to go out, their visits had gradually tailed off. Looking back, I had to admit that Dean had never made them particularly welcome in the house, so I suppose their absence wasn't surprising. Lara, on the other hand, rolled out the welcome mat when we arrived and even had a Wilbur the Wonder Hound mug for Scarlet in the kitchen.

So, those were the things I was proud of. The worry came because I'd done little to achieve Dean's objective, the whole reason I'd come to Richmond in the first place. Dean hadn't been too happy about my lack of progress either when I'd spoken to him on Wednesday.

"I thought you said you'd got clearance for Mackenzie Cain's office now? What's stopping you from plugging in the damn memory stick?"

"I can hardly walk into her office while she's in it, can I?"

"She must take a coffee break or something."

"But her office has a glass front. If I go in there and start fiddling around, twenty people will notice right away."

"Well, find a way. Draupnir refused to pay half of my invoice last month because of the security breaches, and now we're even further behind on the mortgage."

That was where the guilt came in. Because I didn't care as much as I should have. While Dean worked to keep our home, I'd been enjoying myself with Scarlet, making a mess with poster paints, exploding popcorn in the kitchen, and learning ever-more-complicated hair-braiding techniques from YouTube.

And speaking to Cade.

He'd called on Thursday while I was trying to dig three different colours of paint out from underneath my fingernails. Okay, so the art workshop was technically for Scarlet, but I hadn't been able to resist joining in. A few more sessions and I'd be able to do better than the weird abstract mess Bradley had hung in the downstairs hallway.

"Hey," Cade said.

"Hold on a minute." I dried my hands and settled back onto the sofa, more at ease in the house now but still not so comfortable talking to its owner. "Hi."

"I don't have long—I've only made a trip out to pick up beer. How's Scarlet?"

"She's good. We've been cooking together, and she went to an art class today."

Cade released a breath. Relief? "Thank fuck. I've been worrying all week."

I couldn't help wincing at the F-bomb. "Honestly, she's fine. I'm teaching her to read and count, and Lara's helping too."

"Nick's Lara?"

"You know her?" Lara hadn't mentioned meeting Cade.

"No, but I know Nick, and from the way he talks about her, she's a good woman."

"Definitely. She's coming with me next week to check out kindergartens. We figured Scarlet should probably enrol in one until her mom comes back."

"If she comes back."

"You think she won't? Emmy said Blackwood had stopped looking for her."

"Cindy Bekker was a bitch back in high school, and I don't suppose she's changed much. That night I spent with her... I was drunk as fuck and there's no way my dick would have gone near her otherwise. If I'd known about Scarlet before I did, sure as shit I wouldn't have left Cindy to bring her up."

Okay, that was a little blunt. And crude. Dean never swore like that, but with Cade being my boss, I could hardly object.

"I suppose I can understand that. Scarlet's so clever, but she's not very advanced for her age in terms of skills because nobody's ever taught her."

"*Cindy* never taught her."

"Right. But at the moment, she still thinks Reed Bonner is her father, and she keeps asking when her mommy and daddy are coming back."

"What do you tell her?"

"Mostly I'm changing the subject, but I found her crying in bed last night because she thinks Cindy abandoned her."

"Shit. I'll have to talk to her, but I don't know what to say either."

"I don't think having that conversation over the phone is a good idea."

"No, it isn't. I'll visit. As soon as I can get away, I'll visit."

"You'll come here? To the house?"

"Technically, I do live there. Fuck, I've got to go. I'll get there when I can."

Cade hung up, leaving my pounding pulse as the loudest noise in the room. He was coming to visit. A virtual stranger, and with me alone in the house apart from Scarlet. That thought might not have worried any normal woman, but it terrified me.

A week passed, and while I hadn't heard anything more

from Cade, I'd suffered through two strained phone calls with Dean. By the second, I'd gotten so worried over the impossible task of getting into Mackenzie Cain's office as well as Cade's impending visit, I'd suggested coming home.

"I haven't managed to get into the office again, and I miss you," I told my husband.

"Do you know how many hours I worked yesterday? Twenty. Twenty! Because someone hit Draupnir's servers again, and they're blaming me."

"What if it wasn't Blackwood? What if I'm just wasting my time trying to get at their computers?"

"I traced the origin to Richmond again. It doesn't take a genius to work out someone at that company has a vendetta against my client."

"But if you saw the setup they've got there... It's an open-plan office."

"Use your imagination, would you? Cause a distraction. Set off the fire alarm. Or use that brat you're looking after—make her run into Cain's office or something."

Involve Scarlet in something...well, maybe not criminal, but perhaps not entirely ethical?

"She's just a child, Dean. I'm not doing that."

"Well, you'd better do something, or when you do finish messing around over there and get home, we'll be living in a fucking shack."

He hung up, and I stared at the phone, scarcely able to believe he'd spoken to me that way. What had happened to the Dean I knew? If working for Draupnir made him that stressed, maybe we'd be better off living in a shack. Anything was better than this awful situation we'd found ourselves in.

That night, it was me rather than Scarlet who cried myself to sleep.

And the state of affairs only got worse the next day.

I'd just returned from a walk with Scarlet—half a mile and back—and I was feeling quite pleased because I hadn't gotten that far from home on foot for years, not since before Harlan Lake came into my life, when my phone rang.

"It's Cade."

"Hi."

"I'm on my way. I'll be there in a couple of hours."

He didn't say anything else, and the moment he hung up, I fought down the bile rising in my throat.

"What's wrong?" Scarlet asked.

"Nothing, sweetie."

"Then why are you shaking?"

With it being eighty degrees out, I could hardly tell her I felt chilly.

"Somebody's coming to visit tonight, and I haven't met him before."

"Is it my daddy?"

Little did she know. "His name's Cade."

"Cade." She tried the word out. "Cade with the beard who carried me after Mommy left?"

"Yes."

He'd carried her?

"I don't like his beard. It's scratchy. And Cade's a girl name like Katie. I've got a friend called Katie back home. She lives next door, and she's six. Is it September yet?"

"Not yet. Why?"

"Because Katie's gonna be seven in September, and she said I can go to her party. Can I have a new dress?"

"I'm sure we can sort something out."

Scarlet squealed and bounced up and down. "Will you do my hair like Jasmine out of *Aladdin*?"

Right now, I doubted I'd be around in September, and I had no idea whether she'd ever see Katie again.

"Why don't we talk about it nearer the time?"

She skipped off ahead, singing "A Whole New World," while I rued the day I'd ever come to Richmond. Cade's visit notwithstanding, every day I spent here made it more difficult to leave.

# CHAPTER 17

I'D BEEN WAITING for a car to arrive, or maybe a pickup, but the bright-red motorcycle that roared into the driveway caught me by surprise. Was that Cade?

It had to be, the way he parked up in front of the garage and swung his leg over the back, and I found myself holding my breath as I waited for him to remove his helmet. But first, he bent down to check something by the rear wheel, giving me a prime view of his ass. Holy moly.

I stepped back from the window as he turned towards the front door, but not before I caught a glimpse of his face. When Emmy said he looked rough, she hadn't been kidding. Scruffy hair curling past his collar, a bushy beard—not a man I'd want to bump into alone at night.

To my surprise, he knocked rather than letting himself in, and I wondered if I'd been mistaken over his identity. Thank goodness there was a security chain, and I slotted it into place before I opened the door.

"I didn't want to just walk in because of Scarlet," he said quietly, his gaze going past me into the hallway.

I quickly pushed the door closed to take off the chain, then let him in. "She's in the lounge watching TV."

I'd given in to her badgering and put on a cartoon

DVD because my stress levels were through the roof, and I couldn't concentrate enough to read her a story.

"Did you tell her I was coming?"

"I said we'd be having a visitor, and she knows your name, but not that you're her father."

We stood awkwardly for a few moments, neither of us sure what to do or say next. Finally, Cade broke the silence.

"I should go and say hello."

"Why don't you take off the leather jacket first? It makes you look a bit, er..." Scary. "Tough."

"Good idea." He shrugged out of it, revealing a white T-shirt stretched across a well-muscled chest, but I wasn't sure the tattoos on his right arm were much of an improvement.

"On second thoughts..."

He followed my eyes. "No better?"

"Do you have a sweater?"

"Upstairs. I'll run and get one."

He took the stairs two at a time, and when he opened the door to the master bedroom, I sagged against the wall and groaned. What would he say when he saw I'd made myself at home in his bed? I suppose at least I hadn't evicted his belongings from the closet.

Cade came back a minute later, jogging down the stairs. With a thin black knit sweater on, he looked less like a thug, and I wondered whether to mention Scarlet's dislike of his beard. No, best not.

"I'll be sleeping on the couch tonight, then?" he said.

"Sorry, I didn't know where else to sleep. I mean, I considered the couch, but long term, I..."

"It's fine." He cut me off with a wave of his hand.

"What's with all the pillows everywhere?"

"Bradley. Uh, he kind of decorated the lounge too."

"Do I want to see that?"

"It's a little bright."

"Does Scarlet like it?"

"She seems to."

"Then it's all good." He took a deep breath and closed his eyes for a second. "Guess I should go talk to her."

"I suppose so."

Better to get it over with. Scarlet was sitting on the floor, cross-legged, and she didn't look away from the TV screen until I tapped her on the shoulder.

"Sweetie, our visitor is here."

Rather than greet Cade, she shuffled closer to me and wrapped an arm around my legs.

"Aren't you going to say hello?"

She shook her head.

I crouched next to her. "Please? For me."

"I don't want to."

"But Cade's come a long way to see us."

Nothing.

Cade tried, holding out a plastic bag with the logo of a nearby gas station on it. "I brought you a gift."

Scarlet reached for the bag and pulled out a cuddly dog. "It's not Wilbur the Wonder Hound."

Oh dear. "Scarlet, say thank you to Cade. It was kind of him to bring you anything."

"Thanks," she mumbled. Then silence again. What happened to the chatty girl I was used to?

"I made spaghetti with cheese for dinner."

Ah, that got me a smile. "And carrots?"

"And carrots." Out of all the vegetables she'd tried,

those had fast become her favourite. "But we can't eat until you get up and help Cade to set the table."

"O-kaaaaaaay."

She levered herself to her feet and ran into the kitchen. The house wasn't big enough for a separate dining room, but it did have a four-seat table by the back door.

I nudged Cade. "Go on. Help her."

He flashed me a smile as he followed, and damned if that didn't make my belly flutter. Was that nerves or...? No. It was definitely nerves.

Dinner was an awkward, stilted affair. Cade sat next to me with Scarlet opposite, and while the spaghetti may have gone down well with one of my dining companions, the other, not so much.

Cade cursed under his breath when Scarlet got up to get another juice box out of the refrigerator.

"I hate this fuckin' beard. Shit keeps getting stuck in it."

I tried to be diplomatic. "It doesn't look that bad."

"Yeah, it does. Some dudes are meant to wear beards, but I'm not one of them."

"Can't you cut it off?"

"Not right now. Every other asshole on this undercover job's got one, and I need to blend in."

"Maybe you could trim it?"

"Maybe."

Scarlet sat back down, and after three tries at getting her straw into the juice, she gave a quiet sniffle.

"Cade, could you help Scarlet?"

He reached out and fixed it for her, and that was the first time she smiled at him. Not a grin, more of a flicker, but I'd take that.

"Why don't you tell Cade about your day?"

"I watched *Frozen*."

"That's the one with the ice princess, right? Elsa?"

Scarlet looked as surprised as I felt. "You saw it?"

"Yeah, a while back. That prince is one nasty man."

"And the duke. But I love Elsa and Anna. And Olaf the snowman. When I grow up, I want to live in a palace made from ice."

"Won't you get cold?"

"No, because I'll dance and sing and wear pretty dresses."

And that started a whole discussion of the plot, which ended with Scarlet singing the songs from the movie in between spooning chocolate ice cream into her mouth. By the time she'd finished, I was exhausted just from watching her.

"Time for bed, sweetie," I told her once she'd loaded her bowl into the dishwasher. When we first got to the house, she'd tended to abandon her utensils once she finished eating, but now she was getting the hang of basic chores. "Do you want Cade to carry you upstairs?"

"I can walk. I'm five."

He smiled at her. "Fair enough. When will you be six?"

A look of panic came over her face. "I don't know. I have to ask Mommy. When are her and Daddy coming back?"

Dammit, we'd got through nearly a whole evening without her mentioning them. I glanced at Cade, and his face mirrored his daughter's.

"Sweetie, we're not sure yet. But I promise we'll do lots of fun things while you're here with me. Why don't we go swimming again tomorrow?" Surely Lara would oblige.

"Yay! I love swimming. Will you read me a story now?"

"I need to clear up in the kitchen, but how about if Cade reads you a story?"

"All right."

Scarlet ran for the stairs while Cade lagged behind.

"Thanks for that. I had no idea what to say."

He may have looked like a thug, but he didn't act like one. "I'll do my best for her. She's got a pile of books on her nightstand, and she likes the ones about the wizard."

Cade gave me a salute as he walked backwards out of the door, and another one of those dangerous smiles.

Okay, so being alone in the house with Cade wasn't as bad as I'd feared.

The kitchen was spick and span by the time I heard quiet footsteps on the stairs, and a moment later, a shadow appeared in the doorway.

"She's asleep."

"So am I, just about."

Cade headed towards a lockbox on the wall, one I'd never had the combination for, and took out a key.

"Better put the bike in the garage before I turn in. Looks like we're in for a storm tonight."

"It's felt sticky for days. I've been hoping for this hot spell to break."

"Back in a minute."

He let himself through the internal door into the garage, and I heard the big door at the front roll up, closely followed by the burble of his motorcycle engine. While he busied himself with that, I went upstairs to find him a blanket and pillow for the couch, feeling decidedly awkward about the sleeping arrangements.

"Are you sure you don't want me to sleep down here?" I asked when I heard him come back.

"You're kidding, right? What sort of man would I be if I let a woman take the couch?"

"Uh, I don't know."

When I'd first moved in with Dean, right after the Harlan Lake incident, I'd slept on the sectional in the lounge for two weeks until he bought another bed. At the time, I'd just been grateful to have a sympathetic ear and some moral support.

"No, Taylor, you're not sleeping on the couch. It's more comfortable than my usual accommodation, anyway." He held up a bottle of wine. "Do you want a glass of red before you turn in?"

I hadn't drunk alcohol since I arrived in Richmond, but after the last few weeks, I figured I deserved a glass.

"Yes, please. The glasses are in... Oh, you probably know already."

I trailed him through to the kitchen, careful not to spend too much time looking at his ass. I was a married woman, for goodness' sake. Only when he reached up to the top shelf for the wine glasses, his shirt rode up and I got a glimpse of washboard abs instead. Freaking heck.

Back in the days before Dean's sense of humour deserted him completely, he'd used to joke that he had washboard abs too, only they were hidden under steak and beer. Not that he was seriously overweight. He just spent most of his time at his desk working, providing for us both. I had to be grateful for that.

But Cade... I made an effort to focus on his face. "I took you for more of a beer drinker."

"The assholes I'm living with spend every evening drinking beer, and I'm sick of the fuckin' stuff. Lucky I had a case of wine stashed in the garage. Help yourself if you want any when I'm gone."

"I don't normally drink much."

Cade found the corkscrew and poured us a generous glass each. Back in the living room, I curled my feet under me on one sofa while he stretched out on the other.

"Gimme a second, would you? I need to check in with Beryl."

"Who's Beryl?"

"My cover story."

He reached for his jacket, slung over the back of the sofa, and pulled out his phone. A moment later, he smiled as Beryl, presumably, answered.

"How's the knitting? You finish that sweater yet?"

Knitting?

"They did, huh? Figured it was time someone checked up on me... You're a star, lady... Yeah, Oreos, I got it. I'll send them."

He chatted softly about needlepoint for another minute or two, then hung up and stared at the wall behind me, deep in thought.

"Everything okay?"

"Think so. The people I'm monitoring reckon Beryl's my grandma and I'm with her tonight. Someone called her saying they needed me to pick up a package on my way back tomorrow. She told them I was in the john, and she'd pass the message on. Guess I've got an errand to run."

"Is this package important?"

"Doubt it. Ten to one, it was just an acquaintance making sure Beryl existed. I figured they'd have called her before now."

"Is this job you're on dangerous?"

"Yeah."

"Doesn't that worry you?"

"A few weeks ago? No. If shit happened, a couple of people would have turned up at my funeral and the world would have kept turning as normal. But now?" His gaze flicked to the ceiling. "Now I've got a reason to live, and that scares me more than the job ever did."

"I'm sure you'll finish the job okay."

I wasn't—I didn't know anything about it—but I could hardly be all doom and gloom, could I?

"It's not just the job. I don't know the first thing about looking after a kid." He took a long swallow of wine then topped up his glass. "I want to do everything right for Scarlet, but I don't know where to start. I've spent every spare moment thinking about this for the last few weeks, and I'm so fuckin' angry."

He punched the cushion next to him, and I shrank back, wine slopping over the edge of my glass onto my cream top.

Cade leapt up. "Shit! I didn't mean to scare you. Here." He passed me a tissue from the box on the side table. "I'll buy you a new top. Or pay for dry cleaning. Whatever."

"It doesn't matter."

Not really. The top was one of my favourites—well, Dean's favourites—but it was only a piece of fabric. What upset me more was the violence.

"It does. I'm not angry at you or Scarlet. I'm pissed Cindy didn't tell me about her, and I've missed out on five years of her life."

"But you can make up for that now."

"Can I?" He leaned forwards, elbows on his knees as he focused on the floor.

"You even knew about *Frozen*."

"Pure luck. Bradley's obsessed with cartoons and he insisted on watching it one day while I was at Riverley. If she'd picked any other movie... I don't know if I can do this. I don't know if I can be a father. I want to be, but I let everyone down."

"I'm sure that's not true."

"I let my sister down."

Oh, heck. The sister who wasn't with us anymore. I might have been curious, but from the pain in his voice, that wound ran deep, and I was afraid it might open up again. Thankfully, Cade seemed to feel the same way. He slugged back the rest of his wine and stood.

"Better use the bathroom before I get some shut-eye."

Good plan. And I made sure I was safely tucked away in the sanctuary of the master bedroom before he got back.

# CHAPTER 18

THE NEXT MORNING, I made a big mistake.

Half-asleep and desperate to pee, I stumbled out of my—no, Cade's—bedroom and into the bathroom, just as he dropped his towel to step into the shower.

"Uh, I..."

I didn't know where to look. Not down. No, definitely not down. Okay, maybe a glance. Freaking heck! I screwed my eyes shut and stumbled over my own feet as I backed out of the bathroom.

Cade turned, and I clutched at the edge of the door as I fell. Bigger mistake. Huge. I trapped my fingers against the frame as I pulled it shut. The string of curse words that left my mouth would have made a biker blush, but I hastily swallowed them as Scarlet trotted out of her room and stared down at me.

"What's wrong, Taylor?"

"Nothing. I tripped."

"Why did you scream?"

Between my nosedive and the red-hot throbbing in my fingers, I'd missed that part.

"I just caught my hand in the door."

The door that opened to reveal Cade, thankfully now with a towel around his hips.

"You okay?"

Did I look okay, lying on the floor and clutching my

hand?

"Honestly? I've been better."

"I felt the crunch. Hold on, and I'll get some ice for your fingers."

Scarlet stared at him, at the tattoos that covered not only his arm but part of his chest as well.

"Why did somebody draw on you?"

I closed my eyes again, but Cade's artwork still scrolled across the insides of my eyelids. A skull. A gun. A mermaid.

"Ooh, is that Ariel? Where are her shells?"

*Dammit, Cade. You can't have a bare-breasted siren on your arm if you've got a five-year-old daughter.*

"She lost them. But don't worry, I'm gonna get her new ones."

"I've got an Ariel doll at home. I miss her."

"We'll get you a new Ariel."

"Today?"

"I've got to go to work today."

"But... But I want Ariel."

Scarlet's voice cracked. No, please—it was too early in the morning for tears, and my mind was fuzzy with pain.

I risked opening my eyes. "I'll take you to the toy store, how about that?"

"Before we go swimming?"

"Okay, yes."

"Yay! I have to tell Eric."

She ran back into her bedroom, leaving me looking up at Cade.

"Who the hell is Eric?"

"Don't worry, he's only a toy elephant."

"Sorry. I didn't mean to snap. It's just... I hate the idea of other men in the house with Scarlet."

Emmy had said the same thing. "Believe me, I'm the last person who would bring a man home."

Apart from Dean, obviously, but I could hardly tell Cade about him.

"You prefer women? Not that there's anything wrong with that," he added quickly.

"No! I mean, I know there's nothing wrong with that, but I'm not a lesbian."

He stared at me expectantly, and under the steady gaze of his blue eyes, I panicked. "I got hurt once. By a man. It kind of made me lose my trust in them."

"Shit." His expression softened into sympathy. "I'm sorry."

"It's in the past. I learned to forgive and move on."

"You forgave the guy?"

"It was for the best."

That was what Dean said. The bitterness in my heart was a poison I hoped would hurt somebody else, but ultimately, the only person who would keep suffering was me. I won't lie and say forgiving Harlan Lake was easy, but by refusing to press charges on the condition he went to rehab, I'd given him the best chance of understanding his wrongs and righting them.

"I couldn't have done that." Cade's tone told me he spoke from experience.

"You were attacked too?"

"Not me. My sister." His jaw ticced, stiff with tension as he held out a hand to help me up. "Come and sit down. I'll get you that ice."

His grip was cool, firm, but he let go the instant I was on my feet. And once he'd settled me on the sofa with an ice pack, he headed back upstairs. Two minutes later, I heard the shower running.

What a morning, and I hadn't even had my first cup of coffee yet. So far, I'd managed to blurt out one of my biggest secrets, pry information out of my boss that he didn't particularly want to share, and ogle him naked.

Surely the rest of the day could only get better.

"You did what?"

Lara spluttered into a smoothie as I recounted the story of Cade's naked bottom and Ariel's naked chest. I hadn't wanted to tell her, but I couldn't hide the fact that my fingers had swollen to twice their normal size, and I didn't want to break my promise to Scarlet that she could go swimming. Lara had driven us to the mall too, and we'd bought Scarlet a new Ariel doll, plus an Wilbur the Wonder Hound playset complete with a fully equipped dog house. They were all lying abandoned on a sun lounger as Scarlet splashed around in the shallow end.

"It never even occurred to me that he might be in the bathroom. I'm so used to just walking in there, and the door doesn't have a lock."

At home, Dean and I had separate bathrooms. I didn't go in his except to clean it, and he never came into mine. Cade only had the one shower room with a half bath downstairs for visitors.

Lara kept laughing, so hard that some of her drink slopped out of the glass and landed on the tile. "Was the pain worth it? Cade works out, right? All the Blackwood guys do."

"It's not funny."

"You didn't drool, did you? When I used to work as Nick's housekeeper, he answered the door to me once in nothing but a towel, and I nearly died. I dreamed of him standing there for weeks afterwards, and he didn't even drop it."

"No, I didn't drool. My vision went double when I shut my hand in the door."

"Oh, I'm so sorry. Wait a moment, and I'll get you more ice."

The whole afternoon felt surreal. If someone had asked me a decade ago what I'd like to be doing in ten years' time, spending the afternoon reclining in luxury beside a private pool with a girlfriend while the sweetest child played in front of us would have been close to my dream. But every time I tried to relax, a little voice at the back of my head reminded me that this life was just an illusion. I was a low-paid employee, Scarlet wasn't my child, and I'd betray Lara and all my other new friends before I disappeared back to the West Coast.

The first niggles of a headache started up, caused by the two conflicting sides of my psyche using my skull as the battlefield. And in the middle of the mental war zone, Scarlet stood, smiling, then whispered, "What if you don't go back to California?"

# CHAPTER 19

WHILE TAYLOR TOOK Scarlet shopping with Lara, Cade headed for something less enjoyable—an update meeting at Blackwood. He received daily summaries by secure message, but there were so many ears at the clubhouse that talking was difficult, and besides, there was nothing like sitting with the team to brainstorm ideas.

Because face it, he had precious few of those at the moment.

On the way into the building, he passed Emmy's husband coming the other way. Never a cheerful man, he looked downright pissed today. Had the golden couple had an argument?

And if so, was the newcomer seated at the conference room table anything to do with it?

Cade studied him without being obvious, something he'd gotten a lot of practice at lately. Tall, well-built, the stranger held himself like a military man. A new Blackwood employee?

Mack filed in with Agatha and Dan, then Emmy arrived with a steaming mug of coffee and a donut. Her nutritionist clearly had the day off.

"Okay, we're ready. Cade, before we get started, this is Alaric. He's stopped by to help us out with some information."

Alaric? No, the name didn't ring any bells. Emmy didn't elaborate further, and Alaric merely nodded at him.

"Shall we start with an update on The Darkness? Cade, we've received the photos you sent over and put together bios of Hawk's buddies, but I'd like to get your take on things first."

"Now that I'm living at the clubhouse, I've seen more of them. Hawk drops by to see his old man every couple of days, and the others come into the auto shop to work on their bikes. I've been helping out in there as much as I can."

In between doing a couple of protection runs and trying to shake off the new prospect, whose company was about as welcome as a verruca.

"We've run your pictures and made some IDs. Mack?"

Five mugshots popped up on the screen, with Hawk at the top. Brendan Hauser didn't look much like his father, but there was a similarity in the shape of his face.

"Brendan and his guys don't hang out with the others, and I've never seen them messing with any of the drugs either," Cade said.

Hawk might have made him nervous, but he didn't have the same effect on Miss Pigtails, it seemed. Cade didn't miss the way her eyes widened when Mack brought up his picture, nor the small sigh that escaped her lips. Hell, if he were a chick, he'd probably react the same way. Cade was straight as a damn ruler, but the guy looked like a model despite his grungy clothes. The leather the old guard of The Darkness wore made ordinary folk cross the street in avoidance, but Hawk's beat-up jacket acted like a magnet. Women wanted to fuck him and men wanted to be him.

"What's your take on Hawk?" Emmy asked.

"He's as sharp as the switchblade he carries."

She nodded. "I'll go with that from what we've found. Okay, let's move on to the rest of his crew. We've got Sailor, Snake, Smith, and Mouse?"

"Sailor, Snake, and Smith are mean sons of bitches, but Mouse spends most of his time playing computer games on his laptop."

*"Grand Theft Auto?"*

"Some shit with dragons. Out of the five, he's the only one who seems friendly."

Cade had shared a few beers with him, talking about bikes, mainly. Mouse insisted on drinking his Miller Lite from a blue plastic cup, which should have been funny, but nobody else had laughed. And the man couldn't keep his hands still. He fidgeted constantly, usually with his phone, but occasionally with random pieces of computer hardware. He'd told Cade he wanted to build a more powerful machine for gaming. When Hawk motioned at Mouse to leave, the guy had packed up and followed, very much under the tougher man's influence. It seemed like an odd friendship, one that Cade hadn't quite gotten to the bottom of yet.

"From our research, Hawk and the three S's don't appear to be the epitome of compassion either."

"What have you found?"

Agatha cleared her throat, reaching out for her laptop. She had those braids again, but Cade's dick didn't twitch at the sight of them today. Mainly because he couldn't get the picture of a hot brunette out of his mind. Thank fuck Taylor hadn't walked into the bathroom five minutes earlier when he'd had his cock in his hand, stroking slowly as he thought through all the things he wanted to do to her. Not that he'd ever act on those fantasies. Taylor was amazing with Scarlet, and he needed her in his life to provide stability for his daughter, not for a quick fuck that would complicate everything.

*Mental note: fit a lock on the bathroom door.*

Cade had felt like a complete asshole when Taylor got hurt, and even worse when he'd had to leave so soon afterwards. Right now, he'd much rather have been escorting her to the store so Scarlet could buy Wonder shit. But he...

"Cade? Are you with us?" Emmy raised an eyebrow.

"Yes, boss."

Agatha started with Sailor, projecting a larger picture of him up onto the screen.

"Sailor was named, we think, because he spent five years in the navy. He made it to Petty Officer Second Class before he got a dishonourable discharge for striking a commanding officer."

"Why did he do it?" Emmy asked.

"According to the file, he accused the officer of assaulting a female enlisted while she was drunk. The master chief denied everything, and the girl couldn't remember what happened. Then another officer came forwards to say Sailor attacked unprovoked."

"And do you think he did?"

Dan spoke up. "I did a bit of digging, and I don't think so. Sailor and the master chief suffered several run-ins. By all accounts, they weren't fond of each other, and the new witness was a drinking buddy of the master chief's. Plus a year later, the pair of them were among a group of three accused of rape by a new recruit."

"So Sailor lost his job and may harbour a dose of bitterness towards the establishment."

"I'd say that's possible. He hasn't held down a steady position since he left the navy. A month as a barman here, a few weeks working in a warehouse there."

"A handful of break-ins may have seemed like an easy way to make cash. How'd he hook up with Hawk?"

"We don't know that yet."

"Okay, next. Agatha?"

"Smith. Only his name isn't Smith, so we don't know why he's called that."

"It's because he carries a Smith & Wesson," Cade put in. He'd heard that much from the chatter at the club.

"But can he hit anything with it?" Emmy asked.

"By all accounts, yes," Agatha said. "He's a champion marksman. He was well-known on the Virginia club circuit as a teenager, but he dropped out of sight after he came back from college."

"College? Where? What did he study?"

"Harvard. Would you believe he studied philosophy?"

"Interesting choice. Does he have a job?"

"He doesn't need one, not when he has a trust fund."

"Then why the hell would he need to get involved with home invasions?"

Agatha shrugged.

"Perhaps for the thrill of it?" Dan suggested.

"If he wants kicks, why not take up skydiving? Or

white-water rafting? Or parkour? Why break into someone's home and start killing people?"

Dan didn't have an answer for that.

"Shall we move on to Snake?" Agatha asked.

Emmy took a mouthful of coffee. "Why not?"

"Out of the four of them, he's the only one with a full-time job. He runs a tattoo parlour in Oakley with his wife, Maggie."

Which explained the green-and-black snake inked onto his arm, curling around the muscles until its fangs bit into Snake's neck. A boomslang, if Cade wasn't mistaken. Native to sub-Saharan Africa, they delivered their highly potent venom through two large fangs. Victims died from internal and external bleeding. Information on deadly snakes had been part of the briefing before his army unit was deployed to Angola a few years back, an operation that had opened Cade's eyes to the evils lurking in the world.

"Any trouble with the law?"

"Only in the last couple of years. His daughter died, and he got picked up for a handful of minor infractions after that—drunk and disorderly, a fight in a bar."

"Understandable. Grief affects people in different ways. How did she die?"

"Snatched from a playground while her mom was buying ice cream. They found her body two weeks later in nearby woodland. Maybe that tipped him over the edge?"

Stories like that made Cade want to ride straight home and never let Scarlet out of his sight again. At least Taylor didn't seem overly keen on going out. He needed to remember to drop her a message: no playgrounds.

"What about financial problems?"

"He got behind on his mortgage payments after the murder, and his truck got repossessed," Agatha said.

"Caught up now?"

"Seems so, and he's got a few thousand in the bank."

"So he had a motive. He needed the cash, and he most likely had anger burning inside him. How about Mouse?"

"Mouse attended Harvard too, which is probably where he met Smith. But I can't see him being involved in the home invasions—he got excused from gym class in high school because of a heart murmur, and he still lives with his mom."

"Doesn't seem like the type to hang around with The Darkness."

"He's heavily into Harleys," Cade said. "He's been in the auto shop three days this week."

"What does he ride?" Emmy asked.

"An Electra Glide, and he's rebuilding a vintage Nova. Hawk was helping him to weld the exhaust yesterday."

"What does The Darkness get out of that arrangement? Could Mouse be helping to fence the stolen goods?" Emmy mused. "Can we check out that angle?"

"We already are," Dan said. "But we haven't found any evidence of that yet."

"So that leaves Hawk."

Agatha pulled up his photo with that faraway look in her eyes again. "Brendan Hauser. Twenty-seven years old. Joined the army at eighteen, did one tour of Iraq when he turned nineteen, then disappeared. We can't find any information on where he went or what he did until he reappeared in Oakley aged twenty-five. The man's a ghost."

"A phantom, actually." Alaric spoke, his voice soft, his accent unplaceable. "Hawk was recruited by the CIA after they saw his performance in Iraq. He made up one-quarter of the Phantoms, an elite unit tasked with infiltrating terrorist units abroad and destroying them from the inside out."

"Shit." Cade's expletive was echoed by others in the room. Only Emmy didn't look surprised, probably because she'd already spoken to Alaric earlier.

"They brought down cells in Georgia and Serbia as well as several in mainland Europe. But three years ago they made a mistake in Ukraine, and their targets ambushed them. Hawk was the only one who got out alive. The CIA tried sending him out on another job, a softer target, but he got busted after a couple of months. Seems he lost his edge."

"So he quit?" Dan asked. "Reckon he's hurting for cash?"

"Turned his back on the whole agency, but a hundred bucks says he's got a healthy nest egg stashed away offshore, just like the rest of us."

Was Alaric CIA? Or ex-CIA? He had to be from some sort of government agency at the very least.

"And he's got the skills to carry out the home invasions?"

"Undoubtedly."

"But what would his motive be?"

"Maybe he thinks he's got something left to prove?"

After the revelations about Hawk, they batted ideas back and forth, but the overriding premise was that

Cade needed to "dig deeper, and do it fucking carefully." Agatha and Mack would continue to root through electronic evidence while Dan and her team acted as boots on the ground to chase down any other leads in the investigation.

When he rose to leave, Cade wished more than ever that he'd never agreed to work on this operation, and he vowed to never again let a woman get to him so much that he abandoned all rational thought. Emmy and Alaric walked ahead of him to the door, Alaric's hand resting on her lower back. Strange. Few people touched Emmy without risk of losing a finger. Did she have more than a professional relationship with the man? Was that why her husband had looked so unhappy earlier?

"Take care of yourself," she told Cade as they left the conference room.

"Take care of Scarlet."

"We'll keep track of her, don't worry."

But Cade did worry. With his daughter a reminder of the sister he'd failed to protect, how could he not?

# Chapter 20

AS CADE PULLED his bike into an empty spot outside the clubhouse, Rev's mangy dog barked at the end of his chain.

"Easy, boy."

Cade often brought the mutt a treat or two, but today his pockets were empty. Unlike the parking lot. Sixteen bikes belonging to the club members were lined up near the front door, plus Hawk's Sportster and Sailor's Softail at the end. It was a full house tonight.

With the package he'd picked up on the way home tucked safely under one arm, Cade climbed the steps into the clubhouse. Many years ago, the place had been a cookie factory, but two generations of The Darkness had stripped it bare and rebuilt it as their home. Now the inside looked tired, and the wet bar at the back of the main lounge sagged under the weight of a thousand secrets shared over its scarred surface.

Cade spotted Wolf on the opposite side of the room, deep in conversation with Hawk. Neither man looked happy. When Wolf glanced over in Cade's direction, he held the package up with a grin and placed it on a table near the door. Wolf nodded, distracted, before turning back to his son.

From the amount of beer flowing, nobody planned on riding again tonight, so rather than stand out, Cade grabbed a bottle of Miller Lite and joined Rev in front of the TV. He and Tiny, the cook who shared Tank's collar size, were watching *Sons of Anarchy* from the battered leather couch.

Cade barely saw the show. He kept one eye on Hawk and his mind on the task at hand—find out more about the man. But how? Hawk's demeanour didn't lend itself to the casual approach. Sailor acted more relaxed, which was to say, his gaze wasn't designed to slay anyone who looked in his direction. But he'd settled in on a stool at the bar with Boone and Doc, his group tight-knit, not the sort of huddle a new member wandered over to join.

Cade sighed quietly. Despite their name, The Darkness were less hostile than other biker gangs Cade had come across over the years, but infiltration still took time, care, and a little luck. Cade could manage the second, but time he didn't have, and he hadn't been so lucky lately. With the gang members getting more raucous and the tales of past glories increasingly outrageous, Cade could do nothing more than sit back and enjoy the show.

How much beer had Cade drunk? He woke up on the sofa, squashed between Tiny and the arm. What had stirred him? Tiny's flatulence? The infomercial starring a perky blonde trying to sell the latest miracle skin cream? Cade didn't feel a burning need to spread extract of sea urchin on his face, thanks.

Nor did he have a desire to spend more time inhaling the by-products of Tiny's poor digestion.

The strip light above the bar flickered as Cade stepped over the prone form of the new prospect, who clearly needed to make improvements where holding his liquor was concerned. Lightweight. Cade fished a packet of aspirin out of his pocket and tossed it down next to Bugs's outstretched hand. He'd need it in the morning.

As Cade got closer to his room, the faint sounds of whimpering reached his ears. Where was it coming from? A television? He paused at each door in turn, listening. Nothing from Doc except snoring. Only silence from Tank. But when he got to Deke's room, the whimpering got louder.

Shit.

Ginger.

Cade knew busting into Deke's room was a dumb idea, especially as Deke habitually carried a gun, but if Ginger was in there hurting, he couldn't just walk by. A quick check ensured his own pistol was easily accessible in the back of his waistband, his knife clipped to the front.

A gasp came from the far corner of the room as Cade shouldered the door open, just in time to stop Deke from taking another swing at his old lady. Ginger was crouched down, arms wrapped around her knees.

"Get away from her."

"Not your business, brother." Deke spat the final word as an insult.

"When you're hurting a woman, it's everyone's business."

"Get the fuck out of my room."

"I'll leave, but I'm taking Ginger with me."

She looked up, cheeks streaked with tears and

mascara. A trickle of blood ran from the middle of her bottom lip.

"Don't," she whispered.

"I'm not letting him hurt you."

Deke advanced, anger rolling off him in waves. Even from six feet away, Cade could smell whisky on the man's breath.

"You been here five minutes, boy, and you think you own the damn place?" Deke's knuckles cracked as he balled his hands into fists. "Someone needs to teach you a lesson."

"But it's not gonna be you."

The voice came from behind Cade, sending a chill through him. He hadn't even heard Hawk approach.

Deke stopped in his tracks, and although he stayed rigid, his fists uncurled slightly.

"Ginger's fine. Women are always gettin' emotional. You know how it is."

"They always splittin' their own lips too?"

"Gotta keep the bitch in line."

"You don't keep a lady in line. You keep her happy." Hawk held out a hand, reaching past Cade, and Ginger scrambled to her feet. "If you can't keep your fists to yourself, it won't matter who your daddy is."

"That a threat?" A little of Deke's swagger returned.

"No, it's a fact."

As soon as Ginger got close enough, Hawk pulled her into his side and stepped back. Cade followed. The slam of Deke's door echoed behind them as they retreated along the hallway, heading for Wolf's apartment at the back of the building.

"What can I do?" Cade asked.

"I need a drink," Ginger groaned.

Hawk paused to unlock the door, Ginger tucked under one arm. "You don't need a drink." Then to Cade, "She needs ice, Advil, and an antiseptic wipe. First aid kit's under the bar."

"I know where it is."

Cade jogged down the hallway to get the supplies, thankful to have avoided the need for medical help himself. Deke might have been drunk, but he was a big man and angry too. Cade had no doubt he'd have come out on top, but Deke would have done his best to get in a few swings first.

Painkillers, antiseptic, ice... Cade rounded up what he needed and hurried back to Ginger. Hawk had her propped up on the couch as he crouched in front.

"Is she okay?"

Hawk fixed Cade with ice-blue eyes. "She won't be okay as long as she stays with that prick. Gimme the antiseptic."

Cade handed it over, then wrapped the bag of ice in a bar towel. "How about tonight? Did he hurt her bad?"

"Not as bad as he has in the past. I oughta nail his ass to the wall, but...politics. Boone promised to get him help." Hawk sighed. "He's been dry for five months, and I thought he might've finally got himself sorted out, but I shoulda known."

"Has he hurt her often?"

"Once is too many times." Hawk dabbed at Ginger's lip with a tenderness Cade hadn't expected, then sighed. "Five incidents that I know of. Now six. I laid him out last time, but it seems he still didn't learn."

No, he didn't, and now Ginger had paid the price. Again.

"I'll get her some water to go with the Advil."

"Glasses are in the cupboard to the right of the sink."

Hawk pointed at an open door on the far side of the room, and Cade walked through to the kitchen. Wolf's apartment was normally off limits, and after seeing the state of the rest of the clubhouse, Cade was surprised at how neat the place was. No dirty dishes in the sink, mail stacked neatly on the table, a couple of saucepans scrubbed clean on the hob.

He ran the water until it was chilled then took the glass back through to Ginger. She was sitting a little straighter, leaning into Hawk as he spoke to her softly.

"Thanks." Hawk took the glass and passed it to her. "You sleep in my bed tonight, and I'll take the couch."

"I can't, Hawk. Not again."

"You're not going back to Deke. Not tonight."

"But he'll be mad at me."

"No, he'll be mad at me and Pool Boy here."

"I'm sorry," she whispered.

"Don't be. I can take care of myself, and from what I've heard, Pool's smart too." Hawk looked up at Cade. "You worried?"

Cade shook his head. "I can deal with Deke."

"Do me a favour, would you?"

Now wasn't the time to enquire what that favour would entail. This was the longest conversation Cade had had with Hawk since he'd arrived in Oakley.

"Sure."

"Keep an eye on Ginger, and if Deke gives either of you any shit, call me."

Hawk reached into his jacket pocket and pulled out a card with a number printed on it, nothing else.

Cade knelt in front of the woman. "You don't have

to go back to him. I'll... We'll..." Cade glanced at Hawk, who nodded. "We'll help you out. Find you a place to stay."

"He loves me. He always says so."

"If he loved you, he wouldn't have hurt you tonight."

"He d-d-doesn't mean it. Mostly I deserve it."

"Did he tell you that?"

She nodded, and Hawk rolled his eyes. "Been through this a hundred times, Pool. Just look out for her, yeah?"

This whole situation was fucked up, but Cade couldn't push things.

"Yeah, I will."

"Get some sleep. I'll sort Ginger out."

# CHAPTER 21

TWO MORE WEEKS passed before Cade was able to get some time alone, aided in no small part by Beryl, who called while he was helping Snake to change the back tyre on his Harley. Hands covered in tyre grease, he flicked the phone onto speaker with one pinky and quickly told her that everyone could hear her.

"Are you with those nice young motorcycle men?"

"Yes, Grandma."

"Ooh, if I was fifty years younger..."

Snake didn't bother to hide his grin. "I like your grandma," he muttered. "Hey, lady, you ever ridden a Harley?"

Cade gave a mock sigh. "Please, don't put ideas into her head."

"Constance in the next room's got one of those leather jackets," Beryl said. "She used to date a rock star, did I tell you that?"

"At least fifty times. You know I always want to talk to you, but can I call you back later? I'm in the middle of fitting a tyre."

"No need, I just wanted to know when you're next coming to see me. I've run out of candied fruit and I'm hoping you can bring me one of those roll-up jigsaw mats. Betsey Kessler's got one and she won't stop crowing about it."

"I'm sure I can sort something out. Uh, I'll try to come sometime this week. It depends what's going on here."

"Don't leave it too long. I'm old, you know. I might die before you get around to visiting again."

"I won't, Grandma."

Snake was still smiling when Cade hung up. "Your grandma sounds like mine."

"In that case, where the fuck do I get a roll-up jigsaw mat?"

"Can't help you there. My nana wanted a magnifying light so she could read her dirty romance novels at night without my mom finding out. Try asking Mouse—he's good at finding weird shit online."

Good—an excuse to talk to him. "I might just do that."

The Darkness was surprisingly big on family, and Wolf had no problem when Cade said he needed to take off for a couple of days. Mouse helped too, organising next-day delivery of an extra-large jigsaw mat for Beryl. Cade bought a bunch of puzzles too—she deserved that much for her well-timed phone call.

In the past couple of weeks, between his biker brothers looking over his shoulder, tiredness, and work in the auto shop, he'd only managed a handful of brief messages to Taylor. And when he'd been searching online for a replacement seat for his bike because the old one was made of fucking granite, Mouse had borrowed his phone and installed a custom search application, leaving Cade paranoid that the computer nerd could track his communications. Until he got Mack to check the phone out thoroughly, he couldn't risk using it to contact Blackwood or Taylor or even to check his messages.

Up until then, Taylor had been sending daily photos of Scarlet, and he missed them both like crazy. No, he missed Scarlet. Not Taylor. He shouldn't have been missing Taylor, although she did have that sexy-yet-innocent thing going on, a combination that made his pants tighten whenever he spent time around her. Dammit.

He wanted nothing more than to go home, but before he could do that, he needed to head into the office for an update.

Agatha was already seated at the conference room table when Cade walked in, having made a quick stop off at the coffee machine for a cappuccino first. He was sick to death of the bitter instant that was a staple in The Darkness's clubhouse.

"Is Mack coming?" he asked her.

"Afraid not. She had to go to the Boston office."

Shit. He slid his phone across the table towards Agatha. "Mouse put an app on my phone. It's supposed to be a search app, but I'm worried there's something more."

"We figured there was a problem, so we got Beryl to call. Here, I can check it out for you."

Agatha's previous mistake niggled at Cade, but he slid the phone across the table. He had to trust that she could do her job properly.

"Thanks. It's the app with the question mark on the first screen. But make sure you don't turn it on anywhere it can get a signal because they can track me through that as well. I always keep it off when I'm supposed to be with Beryl. Nursing home rules and all that."

"Don't worry, we've got a shielded room in the basement. I'll get onto it right after the meeting."

"Where are the others?"

"Dan had a small problem with her car, and Emmy went to pick her up. They shouldn't be long."

Cade had heard about Dan's legendary prowess behind the wheel. "What kind of problem?"

"A mugger and a wall were mentioned."

"Is she okay?"

"Fine, but I understand the mugger's got to have his jaw reset. There may have been paperwork."

"Ah. In that case, I'll be at my desk."

Cade had only spent a couple of weeks in Blackwood's Richmond office before he went undercover, and his desk was devoid of any personal effects. No photos, no planner, no sorry-looking potted plant. But it did have a phone, and he used it to call Taylor.

"Hey, it's Cade."

"Thank goodness. You didn't reply to my messages, and Emmy didn't know anything. I was worried."

"Just a little phone trouble. I've escaped for the night, but I've got a meeting at Blackwood before I can come home."

"Will it take long?"

"Maybe. Emmy and Dan are running late, and they haven't even arrived yet."

"Oh. We visited the playground today. It's Scarlet's favourite thing right now, and I finally managed to tire her out. She's exhausted."

The playground? Fuck, he'd forgotten to warn Taylor off that. But how could he if it was Scarlet's favourite?

"Just be careful taking her there. Some real freaks hang out at the playground."

"I never take my eyes off her; I promise."

"What's she doing now?"

"Watching TV, but her eyes keep closing. She might not be awake when you get back."

The disappointment Cade felt was on a par with his eighth birthday, when he'd asked for a new bike and received a hand-knitted sweater with one sleeve longer than the other.

"I guess I'll have to see her in the morning, then."

"Do you want me to make you dinner?"

"If it's not too much trouble."

"No trouble."

Half an hour passed before Emmy and Dan walked in, the latter wearing a skirt suit and blouse rather than her usual attire of skintight jeans and a leather jacket.

"What happened to your wardrobe?" Cade asked.

"Parent-teacher conference happened. Last time, Caleb's tutor kept getting distracted by my tits, and he repeated everything twice. I don't have that sort of time to waste."

Emmy took her seat at the head of the table just as Sloane came in with a tray of drinks and snacks. Cade's stomach grumbled—his departure from Oakley had been delayed by a drop-in customer at the auto shop, and with Sailor hanging around, he'd had to oblige and change the man's oil. That meant he'd skipped lunch.

"What is this shit?" Emmy asked.

"Uh, cranberry-and-rose-hip tea, rice crackers with

houmous, and crunchy edamame beans."

"Shit. Has Toby been around again?" Toby was her nutritionist.

"Apparently, he saw you eating a cheeseburger late last night, and you're supposed to be on a detox."

"I was bloody starving. He fed me pumpkin soup with grilled chicken for lunch and confiscated all my chocolate."

"Well, these are the consequences."

"Sometimes I hate Toby and his obsession with my well-being."

Sloane laughed as she pulled the door closed behind her.

"Okay, Cade." Emmy grimaced as she bit into a cracker. "Tell us what happened. Why'd you stop talking to us?"

Cade explained about Mouse tampering with his phone. "I couldn't exactly tell him not to install it, not when any other new recruit would have acted grateful for his help."

"Agreed. If we find anything dodgy in that app, you'll need to take a second phone in. Now, let us know what else has been happening."

"Well, it all started when Deke got drunk..." Cade told the team about Ginger and how Hawk had stepped in to back his play. "Hawk left the next morning, but he's called me a few times since to check up on her, and a couple of days later, he stopped by to see her again. Brought her a box of fancy chocolates and made her smile. I talked to him afterwards, and he said she still refuses to move out of Deke's room."

"She needs to leave him in her head first, and that can only come from within," Emmy said. "Has Deke caused any more problems?"

"He's perfected his death glare, but as I've been spending more time with Sailor lately, he's kept off my back."

"What do you think of Sailor?"

Cade had spent many nights asking himself that same question. "If we didn't suspect him of being involved in the cold-blooded murder of eight men, I'd probably invite him over for a beer."

"Interesting. I had the pleasure of meeting Smith this week."

"Under what circumstances?"

"He works part-time for his daddy's real estate company. I went along to an investor's event he was speaking at."

Emmy, of course, would have fitted right in there. Rumour had it that the Blacks' investment portfolio rivalled that of some Wall Street banks.

"What were your thoughts?"

"Not sure I'd invite him over for a beer. He struck me as more of a red-wine man. Or perhaps a good scotch. But apart from that? He didn't turn on the sleazy charm that so many of those wealth-management guys ooze. We talked about sustainable developments, and he seemed genuinely interested in the technology rather than just spouting off facts and figures to get a sale."

"So another contradiction?"

"Maybe. He did ruin the impression somewhat when he hit on the waitress afterwards. Asshole waited until he thought she was alone in the corridor, but he didn't notice me in the shadows."

"It didn't go well?"

"He backed off when she slapped him. For the record, bragging about the ride you can give a girl is not the best way to get a date."

"Seems to work okay in the club bar."

Emmy rolled her eyes. "I don't want to know. Just don't catch any diseases, yeah?"

Cade didn't want to admit he was still only getting action from his hand.

"Have we worked out how these guys know each other yet? They seem like an odd group."

It was Dan's turn to speak. "Hawk and Snake went to school together, and played Little League, at least until Hawk got kicked off the team for hitting another kid. Alaric did some digging on Sailor and found he and Hawk spent time on the same boat in the Gulf of Aden. A couple of months together, in close quarters—that's enough time to form a strong friendship."

"When did Sailor move to Oakley?"

"Couple of years ago, the same time as Hawk came home."

"And how did they hook up with Mouse and Smith?"

"We haven't worked that out yet, but Mouse and Smith hung out at Harvard. According to Mouse's medical records, which we absolutely haven't seen, he's autistic, but after the initial diagnosis, his mom refused the full spectrum of tests."

"Autistic? That could explain why he's sometimes difficult to talk to."

"Yes, but he's also smart. He's got an IQ of a hundred and forty-nine. According to one of his professors at Harvard, Mouse is a genius when it comes to computers, and he speaks better with machines than he does with people. The same professor said a group of jocks was bullying Mouse, and Smith stepped in to stop it one day. After that, they hung out."

"We haven't managed to access his computer network yet," Agatha said. "Mack and I have both been trying."

"And we've been running loose surveillance on all five men. Nothing. Nada. Mouse rarely leaves his mom's house, which, incidentally, she rents from Smith. Snake goes to work, and then he comes home. Smith does the same, interspersed with the odd round of golf, dinner dates, and time in the gym. Hawk and Sailor hang out at the clubhouse, or in their apartments, and so far, the whole group's only gotten together twice. We've had to be careful, though. Hawk's been taking evasive manoeuvres, and we've lost him three times."

"You reckon he's onto us?"

Dan chewed the corner of her lip. "I don't think so. It seems more like countermeasures are ingrained in him."

"My husband's the same. It makes going out for the evening interesting," Emmy said. "How about women? Any involvement apart from Hawk's concern for Ginger?"

"Only Snake's married. Sailor seems to have a casual thing with the barmaid at the club bar, Smith dates anything in a skirt, and we've never seen Mouse with a girl. Or a man, for that matter. And none of the stolen goods have turned up. Not one single item."

"So however they're being sold on, someone's being bloody careful about it," Emmy said. "Either that or they're hoarding them for a rainy day."

"This is one of the weirdest cases I've ever worked on," Dan said. "At first, everything was clear-cut, but the more we dig into it, the less it makes sense."

"And all we can do is keep digging. Just don't let the sides of the hole cave in."

# CHAPTER 22

WHEN CADE ARRIVED home, it was just after ten p.m. and dark. I'd left a light on in the lounge to welcome him and spent the past hour yo-yoing between the kitchen and the front window in case I'd somehow missed the roar of his bike. Finally, it came. I scooted through the internal door to the garage and rolled the front door up for him to ride straight in.

"I figured you'd be tired, so I thought I'd help out."

"Fuck knows how I'm still awake. Has Scarlet gone to bed?"

I nodded. "Two hours ago. But I told her you'd be here in the morning."

"How'd she take that piece of news?"

A giggle escaped my lips. "She's been into arts and crafts this week, so she made your Ariel a clamshell bra before she went to sleep. But you have to act surprised, okay? I wasn't supposed to tell you."

"I can manage surprised."

"Do you want dinner right away? I'm making Kung Pao chicken, and I just need ten more minutes."

"Really? That's my favourite."

I sort of knew that because when Cade called earlier, first I'd panicked because I hadn't cleaned for three days, which led to a frenzy of vacuuming and dusting, and then I'd phoned Mrs. Fairfax for advice on what to cook. She remembered Cade raving over her Kung Pao chicken when he visited Riverley for dinner a while ago, and emailed me the instructions with a promise to send over a whole collection of recipes for every occasion, "just in case."

But I couldn't admit that to Cade.

"Uh, that was lucky." I hurried off to the fridge. "And I've got white wine and a ribbon salad."

Cade poured the wine and took a seat at the table while I fried the chicken then added garlic and ginger. By the time I'd finished making the sauce, my mouth was watering. I hadn't eaten Chinese food in...how long? Since before I met Dean. He didn't go in for foreign cuisine, apart from the expensive French type we occasionally ate in restaurants. No Chinese, no Indian, no Italian. Even when we went on vacation to England, he'd insisted on eating in burger restaurants half the time. Apart from his weird fetish for healthy breakfasts, most of our food came from the barbecue.

Back when I was a teenager, I'd loved to experiment in the kitchen, and although Scarlet could be a little fussy, I'd enjoyed creating different dishes over the past few weeks. Mostly for myself, but Lara had come over for lunch a few times. And I was supposed to be joining her and Nick for dinner the day after tomorrow, something that left me with butterflies. What if me being on my own with a couple got awkward? I'd always dreaded those types of events, even when I had Dean by my side.

Speaking of Dean, I'd done a terrible thing. I'd lied to my husband. When he called for the third time this week, pushing me to do "one damn thing, just one damn thing," I'd panicked and told him I'd been into

Mackenzie Cain's office, but I couldn't find the slot to put the memory stick in.

Part of me had hoped he'd call the whole ridiculous plan off and fly me home to California, while the other part wanted to stay in Richmond for good. On my own. Okay, so that was possibly over the top, but this past month had taught me that Dean wasn't entirely the man I thought he was.

And I wasn't the girl I thought I was either.

For so long, I'd hidden away in Dean's house, and I say Dean's because it was never mine. He'd bought it, he decided how we'd decorate it, and he set my cleaning schedule and dictated the furnishings. Yes, he looked after me, and he'd helped me to no end after Harlan Lake did that awful thing, but rather than pushing me to regain the confidence I once had, Dean had sheltered me from my fears instead of helping me to face them.

And I'd let him. I'd collapsed in on myself like a dying star.

Being away from California, I'd learned to fend for myself, and for Scarlet. Okay, I'd had help, but six months ago I'd been terrified to go to the grocery store alone. When I returned home, I couldn't carry on being the girl Dean knew. The girl he'd created.

I wasn't sure he'd appreciate that.

But I didn't need to go home, at least, not yet. When I'd told Dean of my struggle to find the right port for the memory stick, rather than sending me a plane ticket, he'd sucked in a deep breath.

"For heaven's sake. We've been together six years, and you can't find the USB port on a computer?"

"It's more complicated than mine. Than yours,

even."

"But USB ports all look the same."

"It was kind of dark, and there were wires everywhere."

More huffing. "Leave it with me. I'll sort it out." Then, so quietly I thought I might have imagined it. "Just like I have to sort everything else out."

That was four days ago, and I hadn't heard anything from him since. Right now, I was trying to decide whether that was a good thing or a bad thing.

"Smells great," Cade said, breaking me out of my thoughts.

"I hope it tastes great too."

It did, if I said so myself. Whether Dean liked it or not, I'd be cooking this when I got back to California. The wine wasn't bad either—crisp, fruity, and from a vineyard in Portugal, according to Bradley, a vineyard that Emmy and her husband owned but never visited. If I owned a vineyard, I'd probably live there and become an alcoholic.

"I'm afraid I don't have much for dessert. The store was closing, so I just grabbed a lemon meringue pie."

"You didn't have to buy anything." Cade sat back, rubbing his temples. "Shit. I haven't even asked where you're getting the money to buy Scarlet's stuff. I should be giving you cash."

"Bradley gave me a company credit card. I guess you'll need to settle up with Emmy at some point."

Although I'd bought tonight's food with my own money because I felt guilty about Blackwood paying for everything. Taylor's salary got paid into the account Dean had set up for me as a cover, and with Emmy also reimbursing me for my rent, I had few other expenses.

"Yeah. I'll add that to the list of a thousand other things I need to do when I get my life back. You mind if I head through to the couch?"

Cade sounded thoroughly tired of his undercover life.

"Not at all. I'll bring dessert."

Except by the time I'd put a slice of pie into a bowl, added cream, and carried it through to the lounge, Cade was sprawled out on one sofa, asleep. I curled up on the other with the TV on low to catch up with the day's news. In Richmond, I found myself wanting to know what was going on in the world, although with Scarlet around, I mainly put cartoons on during the day.

President Harrison was on a tour of France, and I couldn't help pausing to admire the man. They didn't call him the pin-up president for nothing, and the first lady was so damn beautiful too. I concentrated on my pie through a story on the war in the Middle East then tuned in again for a local piece on those home invasions. They still hadn't caught the people responsible. I'd travelled past the latest crime scene in Rybridge several times on the way to Lara's, and there was still a police car parked outside, only hinting at the horrors that went on behind the gates. At least Cade was here tonight. I made sure to double-check the doors and windows every evening, but even so, having him downstairs made me sleep a little easier. Although for me, that was relative.

The talking heads switched over to a feel-good story about a puppy rescued from a storm drain, and I got up to tuck the blanket I'd brought down earlier around Cade. He looked so tired, I couldn't bear to wake him.

The extra bowl of pie on the coffee table taunted me, the cream pooled around the bottom. Cade wasn't going to eat it, right? And it would be rude to waste it. I took a mouthful, feeling slightly guilty, although I'd burned off so many calories running around after Scarlet that my jeans were starting to feel loose. The news finished, and a sappy romcom movie came on. Romance was a bit of a foreign concept to me. Dean had made some effort before we got married, bringing me flowers and chocolates and so forth, but that petered out after we tied the knot. Yes, his lack of attention had saddened me, but I'd forced myself to think positive. I had a beautiful home, Dean was kind, and until recently, we'd been financially secure. Only now did I realise what was missing—friendship. Dean had become more of a business partner, and at the moment, I was the incompetent employee.

"Taylor?"

"Go away." I pushed at the chest in front of me, but it didn't move. "Get off me!"

"I'm not touching you. What's wrong?"

The note of panic in Cade's voice cut through the darkness, and Harlan Lake faded away. But he'd be back. He came most nights.

"Sorry. It's nothing. Just a nightmare."

Cade reached out to wipe my cheeks with his thumbs, and I forced my eyes open.

"It's not nothing when you're crying in your sleep."

"Really, it's fine. I have nightmares most nights. I'm used to it." Dean had bought himself a pair of custom-made earplugs, so at least he didn't complain about the noise anymore. And in Richmond, I always slept with the bedroom door closed so I didn't wake Scarlet, except when I fell asleep on the sofa, of course.

And now Cade crouched in front of me. "Shit, Taylor, that doesn't make it okay."

I shrugged.

"Have you spoken to someone about this?"

"You mean like a professional? A shrink?"

"It might help."

"No, it won't. My h—" Dammit, I nearly said husband. "My, uh, ex said that if I kept talking about it, I'd never be able to forget."

"Forget what?"

Ah, dammit. "It doesn't matter."

"It does." He spoke more softly. "Is it something that could affect Scarlet?"

"No! I swear it's not. I only saw him that one day."

"Saw who?"

I closed my eyes again, wishing the whole world would go away. "The man who raped me," I whispered.

Silence. When I found the courage to open my eyes again, the world was still there, including Cade, who'd gone a few shades paler.

"A man what?" His hoarse voice echoed my own.

"Don't make me say it again."

He reached a hand out, stopped an inch from my knee, withdrew it, stood up. Took a couple of paces back, then forwards, then crouched down again.

"That was what you meant before when you said you'd been hurt by a man?"

I could only nod.

"Aw, fuck. I thought... Tell me the bastard's still in

prison."

"H-h-he didn't go to prison. I never pressed charges, on the condition he went to rehab instead."

"What? Why?"

"B-b-because if I stayed bitter, the only person I'd end up hurting was myself."

Another quote from Dean.

"Nobody says you have to stay bitter, but this is obviously still eating away at you. Those nightmares—are they always the same?"

I nodded, throat thick with tears threatening to escape. "He's coming for me again. Every damn night. Which is stupid because I haven't laid eyes on him in six years."

"It's not stupid. It's natural. You never got closure, and he's most likely walking around a free man. Want me to find out where he is?"

"No. I just want to get on with my life, but the silliest things scare me. Going out by myself. Strangers getting too close. Having to take a shower instead of a bath."

"A shower? That's where it happened?"

"In a shower room at the hospital where I worked. I used to be a nurse." I tried to fake a smile, but it didn't work. "I couldn't go back there after it happened. I had to transfer."

A lock of hair flopped over my face, and Cade leaned forwards to tuck it behind my ear. That tender gesture undid me like no other, and I burst into great wracking sobs that shook my whole body.

"Aw, fuck it."

The sofa dipped as Cade sat beside me, and then I was in his arms, sobbing all over his shirt.

"I'm s-s-so sorry."

"Don't be sorry, Taylor. You've got nothing to be sorry for."

At that moment, I wanted to tell him everything. My real name, my past, the fact that I was married to a man I liked less with every passing day. But I didn't, because admitting why I'd come to work at Blackwood would be a sure-fire way to get my ass kicked all the way back to the West Coast, and I wasn't sure I ever wanted to see Santa Barbara again.

It barely registered as Cade picked me up and carried me upstairs, tucked me into his bed, and wiped away the last of my tears. His lips brushed across my cheek.

"Sleep, Taylor. Call me if you get another nightmare, and I'll come and sit with you for as long as you need."

Forever? How about forever? Because I was permanently broken.

Again, I tried to smile, and it flickered for a second. "I'll be fine."

Cade backed away, but the look on his face said he didn't believe me.

I didn't believe me either. I only managed to hold it together until his footsteps sounded on the stairs, then I buried my face in the pillow and cried again.

# Chapter 23

BREAKFAST THE NEXT morning was an awkward affair. Cade and I both tried to be cheerful for Scarlet's sake, but with the enormity of what I'd told him last night hanging over us like a thick fog, our conversation was stilted.

Not that Scarlet noticed. She presented Cade with Ariel's bra before he'd finished his coffee, and we taped it on. Many men might have balked at something so silly, but not Cade. He took it with good humour and listened intently as Scarlet chattered away, demonstrating how she'd learned to count using Cheerios.

"And I've got a new game. Will you play it with me?"

"What kind of game?"

"Hide-and-seek. I go hide, and you have to find me."

"Lara taught her," I explained.

At least in Cade's home, we stood a chance of finding her. At Adler House, the mansion Lara shared with Nick, we'd spent hours searching, but Scarlet was enjoying herself so much it was difficult to say no to her.

"Sure. How about we play after breakfast?"

Scarlet snarfed down two slices of toast and a glass

of orange juice, informed us we had to count to a hundred before we moved, and ran off. Her footsteps faded, leaving us with a gaping silence.

"Scarlet seems happy," Cade said finally.

Thank goodness. He hadn't brought up my little confession.

"She's settled over the last couple of weeks. Uh, we got her a kindergarten place. I hope that's okay. We tried to get ahold of you, but when you didn't answer, Emmy told me to pretend I was her mother and just sign the paperwork."

"I'm sure you've picked out somewhere good."

"It's the best in the area, on the other side of Rybridge. Emmy's arranged a driver to take us each day."

"Is Scarlet still asking for Cindy and Reed?"

"Not so much. I've been trying to keep her days full of fun stuff so she doesn't think about them. Do you think Cindy will come back?"

"Honestly? I've got no idea. I barely know her."

"Reckon we've got to a hundred yet?"

"I'd say so. I'll take upstairs, you look down here."

We spent an hour playing hide-and-seek with Scarlet, the tension gradually dissipating. Even in such a small house, she found some creative hiding places.

"My kid's a contortionist," Cade muttered when we found her in one of the kitchen cupboards after ten minutes of looking. She'd even managed to pull the door shut behind her.

Then Cade received a phone call, and between his expression and the muttered curses, I knew it wasn't good news.

"Everything okay?"

"Not entirely. Someone's bugged my regular phone. I suspected they'd done it, but I can't swap phones without arousing suspicions."

"So we won't be able to contact you anymore?"

"I'll take this extra one with me, but I won't be able to carry it all the time without people asking questions. Here, I'll write down the number for you." He picked up the notepad and pen from next to the house phone.

"Should I stop sending you updates on Scarlet?"

"That's probably best for now." He sounded so damn sad when he said that, I wanted to give him a hug.

"I'll save them up. Trips out, craft projects, her first day at kindergarten."

"I wish I could be here for that."

"I'm sure your job's important, and by doing it, you're providing for Scarlet."

"That doesn't make missing out on most of her life any easier to take."

"I know. Promise you'll stay safe, and we'll see you soon."

Cade gave us a salute as he headed through to the garage to get his bike out. "Won't be soon enough."

After Cade left, I settled Scarlet at the kitchen table with glue and glitter and scraps of material so she could make a collage.

"Be careful with the scissors, sweetie."

"I'm always careful."

I poured myself a cup of coffee, then stared out the window at the garden as I sipped. Maybe we could plant some flowers? Or vegetables to teach Scarlet where food came from? I dismissed that idea almost as fast as I had it, because I'd be gone soon, and the plants would wither and die.

"Taylor, can you help me to cut this out?"

"Sure I can."

Our peace was shattered an hour later when the front door opened. My heart lurched, but the sound of a cheerful, "It's only me," made me roll my eyes instead.

By the time I got to the lounge, Bradley had dumped half a dozen bags on the floor and collapsed onto a sofa arm.

"I've brought clothes for you, toys and a few outfits for Scarlet, cakes from Mrs. Fairfax plus her entire database of recipes..." He dropped a memory stick into my hand. "She arranges them by breakfast, lunch, and dinner followed by name. Oh, and I need to measure your bathroom."

"What? Why?"

Bradley was already back on his feet, and I followed him upstairs.

"Why do you need to measure the bathroom?"

"Cade said he needs a new one. He wants to rip out that fancy-ass shower stall and put in a tub instead. I'm seeing a corner unit with whirlpool jets. What do you think?"

Aw, hell. This was because of me, wasn't it? I told him I got nervous taking showers, so Cade planned to install a whole new bathroom. A bathroom I wouldn't even be here to use. A tear rolled down my cheek because that was the sweetest thing anyone had ever done for me.

"What's wrong?" Bradley asked. "You don't want a

whirlpool tub? We can put a plain one in if you like. Something modern to match the house. I really don't think a claw-foot would work in here."

"We don't need a new bathroom."

He stared, aghast. "This one came with the house. It was somebody else's vision."

"But there's nothing wrong with it." No, the problems were all in my head. "Can't we call Cade back and discuss this?"

"No can do, doll. He's incommunicado, and I've got my orders. You're getting a new bathroom."

"What about the landlord? What will he say?"

"The landlord's Emmy. She said Cade can change it however he wants."

With that knowledge, I even tried voicing my concerns to Emmy that afternoon when I bumped into her at Lara's. She was in the gym with Nick, attacking a punching bag as if civilisation's future depended on it.

"Uh, have you got a minute? When you're finished, obviously."

"I can take a break. Gives Nick a chance to recover."

He was lying on a mat in the corner, and he raised one hand to give me a little wave. Despite his size, Nick was one of the sweetest men I'd met, and when Scarlet and I had come over for dinner, it hadn't been the uncomfortable affair I'd feared. Far from it. After putting Scarlet to bed in a spare room, I'd chatted with him and Lara for half the night until eventually it got so late that I'd ended up sleeping there too.

"Okay, what's up?" Emmy asked, gulping water from a bottle.

Without going into the details, I let her know that something I'd inadvertently said may have led Cade to order a whole new bathroom, and while it was very generous of her to allow him to make modifications to the house, none of it was actually needed.

"So?" she said. "It's not as if you forced him into it."

"It doesn't seem to you like he overreacted?"

"Maybe. But as long as Bradley's replacing Cade's bathroom, he's not messing with mine, so it's all good."

"But what if Cade wasn't thinking straight? I mean, he's been stressed with this case he's working on and also Scarlet arriving."

"Has he seemed stressed to you? You've spent more time than any of us with him lately."

Cade seemed less stressed than Dean at the moment, and my conscience carried on eating away at me. Guilt that I was adding to Dean's burden, and more so, regret that I was misleading Emmy.

"Cade hasn't said anything about work, but I know he misses Scarlet terribly. He was upset he wouldn't be there for her first day of kindergarten, and I can't even send him pictures."

"How's he taken to being a father?"

"He adores Scarlet."

"Interesting. And what does she think of him?"

"She's gradually coming around to the idea of him being there, but she still doesn't know their true relationship, and it's difficult to build up a bond when he's only spending a night here and there. He got home so late yesterday, she'd already gone to bed."

"We can't take him off this case, not yet, not when we're finally getting somewhere. But I'll see if I can get him some extra time with her. That'll have to do for now."

"And what about the bathroom?"

"I'd try to talk Bradley out of Italian marble if I were you. It takes ages to arrive."

With that, Emmy jogged back to the punching bag and pulled on a pair of boxing gloves, leaving me to curse myself for ever agreeing to come to Richmond. When this house of cards collapsed, the fallout would affect not only me, but the people I'd come to care for too.

## CHAPTER 24

KNOCKING ON THE front door woke me early on Saturday morning, and I rolled over in bed, groaning. Harlan Lake had made his presence felt again last night, and that meant I'd only gotten a couple of hours' sleep.

The bedroom door clicked and Scarlet appeared.

"Who's come to visit?" she asked. "Is it Cade?"

"I don't know. I don't think so." But as I tugged on a robe, my heart lodged in my throat. What if something had happened to him?

I ran down the stairs and only just remembered to check the peephole before I flung the door open. Why was Emmy here?

"What's the—"

"No problem. Cade's on his way and I've arranged a surprise trip for you guys. Do me a favour and pack some shit for all of you, would ya?"

"Cade as well?"

"Yeah. He won't have brought much with him."

"Where are we going?"

"Like I said, it's a surprise. It'll be warm, though."

Oh, heck. What would Dean say if he found out that while he was waiting for me to get back into the third-floor office at Blackwood, I'd gone on a freaking vacation? I'd spoken to him the day before yesterday, and he'd sounded relaxed for the first time in months.

"The attacks on Draupnir are still coming, but I've managed to block three so far this week."

"Is it Blackwood again?"

"The hallmarks are the same."

I should have been angry that my employer was still threatening Dean's livelihood, but instead, with my head clearer than it had been in years, I began to ask myself *why?* Why was Blackwood so determined to harm Draupnir?

"Do you know what they're after?" I asked Dean.

"Oh, the usual. Payment details, customer lists, proprietary information."

"What for?"

"Why do hackers ever attack innocent businesses? I expect they want Draupnir's customers to lose confidence and go elsewhere."

"What does Draupnir actually do?"

He'd hinted at security work, but never elaborated on the details.

"Does it matter?"

"I just thought that if you could work out a definite motive, it might help us to stop them."

"Money, that's the motive. Everything's about money. Anyhow, I've come up with a plan for you. There's a package on its way. It'll be with you tomorrow, and it contains a miniaturised camera and a headset. Next time you get into Mackenzie Cain's office, I can guide you to the right place to put the memory stick."

Oh, hurrah. Another impossible task. I managed a hollow, "Great."

Dean's voice mellowed. "And then you can come

home. I've missed our dinners together, and our Saturday night movies."

At first, I smiled at his words, but my happiness faded as I repeated them back to myself. Dean hadn't missed me. Not *me*. He'd missed dinners and movies with my company as an incidental. Come to think about it, he'd never once expressed that sentiment. I'd said the words to him plenty of times, when he went on business trips or out for meetings, but he'd never once reciprocated. A slip of the tongue? Or did his choice of words have a deeper meaning?

Emmy waved a hand in front of my face. "Earth to Taylor? You won't need to bring much, but you'll need comfortable shoes."

"Oh, uh, yes, of course."

It didn't take long to pack a small bag for Scarlet and me, but what would Cade want to wear? I'd only ever seen him in jeans, but they weren't suitable for the heat. After some deliberation, I opted for board shorts and T-shirts, plus a pair of sneakers so battered he must be fond of them.

"Where are we going?" Scarlet asked.

"It's a surprise, sweetie."

I wasn't prepared for her to burst into tears.

"What's wrong?" I crouched beside her and pulled her hands away from her eyes. "Look at me. What's wrong?"

"That's what Mommy said and then she left. I don't want you to leave too."

I gathered her up in my arms, close to tears myself. "We're just going somewhere nice for a few days, and Cade's coming too. Then we'll all come right back here. Don't forget, you've got kindergarten to go to."

"Do you promise?"

"I promise."

But I couldn't bring myself to tell her I wouldn't be around forever.

"Are you ready?" Emmy yelled up the stairs.

"Just coming."

I'd never ridden in a car with Emmy, and the experience wasn't one I'd care to repeat. Buildings, cars, and trees flashed by along with my life as she inched the speedometer higher and higher.

"There's a child in the back," I muttered. "Can't you go slowly?"

"I am going slowly."

But she sighed and eased back a touch, much to my relief. I'd assumed we'd be heading for Little Riverley, so when we pulled up at a small airfield next to a private jet, my jaw dropped. Dean liked to fly business class, but this was in a whole other league.

"Are we riding in that?"

"Cade's only got two days. Better to take the Lear than waste hours at the airport."

"Whose is it?"

"My husband's."

Wow. I'd known they were wealthy, but a freaking jet?

Cade seemed confused rather than awed when he arrived fifteen minutes later, not on the Ducati this time, but sitting astride a Harley Davidson, complete with faded jeans and a battered black leather jacket. He looked...scary, if I was honest, and Scarlet thought the same judging by the way she hid behind me. Was Cade undercover as a biker?

He parked next to Emmy and hopped off.

"What the hell is going on?"

I covered Scarlet's ears with my hands as Cade continued.

"Some doctor called at six a.m. telling me Beryl's gone into emergency surgery and I need to get there pronto, but when I arrive at the hospital, she's sitting up in bed eating a box of chocolates from Fortnum & Mason, and Bradley confiscates my phone and tells me to get my ass over here."

"Surprise. You're going on a little holiday with Taylor and Scarlet."

"Are you insane? We're in the middle of an investigation. They're watching me. Someone had been through my room when I got back last time."

"Do you think your cover's blown?"

"I can't see them taking the 'softly, softly' approach if they thought I was a mole. No, it's more like they're checking me out."

"Vetting you? Then that's good, because when you pass, they might let you into their secrets. But that doesn't change the fact that you need a break, and you need time with your daughter. Snake's booked solid with tattoo appointments for the next three days, Smith's flown to Vegas for a real estate convention, and Hawk got on a plane bound for England late last night. We don't know why, but Slater's sitting three rows behind to make sure he doesn't come back unexpectedly, and we've also got teams on Sailor and Mouse. Nothing's gonna happen on the case for a few days, and we're taking advantage of that."

"By putting Beryl in the hospital? Is she even ill?"

"I don't think so, but I'm sure they'll give her a check-up while she's there."

"How the hell did you manage that?"

"My husband practically bought the new children's wing. We get perks." She backed away towards her car. "Have fun, kids."

Cade wheeled his bike over to the hangar before heading back to where I was waiting with Scarlet.

"It's okay, sweetie. It's just Cade."

"But he's all black."

Cade stopped six feet from us, looking devastated as his daughter cowered away from him. The only good point was that he'd trimmed his beard.

"I brought you some clothes to change into. That bag over there."

"Thanks. Give me a minute, yeah?"

He jogged back to the hangar, and two minutes later, he emerged in a pair of shorts and a T-shirt.

"Better?"

"Much. Scarlet, are you ready to ride on the airplane?"

She peeked out from behind me and nodded.

"You want Cade to carry you up the steps?"

"I can do them myself."

She ran on ahead, and Cade picked up our bags.

"From the clothes you packed, I guess we're going somewhere hot?"

"Apparently, but I don't know where. It's a surprise, although Scarlet isn't that keen on surprises." I recounted the tale of Cindy's effort.

"Damn that woman. Wherever we end up, we need to make sure Scarlet has a good time."

"Absolutely."

And Cade too. He'd developed fine lines on his forehead since I'd met him, most likely from frowning too much. He needed to relax, even if it was only for a couple of days.

"Wonder World? We're going to Wonder World?"

I read the sign next to the road as the limo that had picked us up from yet another private airfield sped along the highway.

Scarlet squealed loud enough to wake the dead three states over. "Wonder World?"

"Is that where we're headed?" Cade asked the driver.

"Yes, sir, but you'll be staying at the Black Diamond hotel outside the park."

"Another piece of Emmy's empire," Cade muttered.

"Will we see Wilbur the Wonder Hound?" Scarlet asked. "And Sleepy Kat?"

I brushed her hair out of her eyes. We'd left in such a hurry I hadn't had time to braid it.

"I'm sure we will."

She pressed her face against the glass, watching the scenery pass by. "I can't wait!"

"Have you ever visited Wonder World before?" Cade asked.

"I've only been on vacation twice in my life, once to London and once to Aspen." Not that I saw much of either place, because I preferred to stay out of the way of people. And Aspen had been a total disaster. Several of Dean's business associates had raved about it over dinner one night, so he decided we'd go and learn to ski, only to discover he hated it. He'd spent most of the two weeks on his laptop, complaining about the temperature. "Uh, I'm not really one for crowds."

"I'm not sure Wonder World's my thing either, but I'll keep you both safe. I promise."

Cade's smile was genuine, his intentions noble, and if anyone could help me to get over my nervousness, it would be him. When I was with him, the horrors of the outside world faded just a little.

At the Black Diamond, a concierge met us at the hotel desk the second we walked into reception. She'd obviously been waiting.

"Mr. Duchamp? Miss Hancock? We've reserved you one of our suites. I've got a pack of information for you about Wonder World, and your driver will be waiting to take you there as soon as you're ready. Oh, and Mrs. Black sent a camera for you."

Was there anything she hadn't thought of?

It seemed not, because breakfast was waiting for us when we got to our suite, everything on the menu, it seemed like. And the suite itself... Wow. The lounge, the dining area, the kitchenette, two bedrooms—they looked like something out of a movie.

"Have you ever been anywhere this fancy?" I asked Cade as Scarlet ran around, whooping at all the shiny things.

"Nope. And for the last few months, I've been living in a converted warehouse with a bunch of men who consider personal hygiene to be optional." He gave one armpit a sniff. "Speaking of which, I need a shower."

One of the bedrooms had a king-sized bed, the other two doubles, and each had an en-suite with a bath as well as a shower stall. That made me breathe easier.

"I'll share with Scarlet. You can take the big bed.

And you didn't need to install a new bathroom at home, by the way."

He stepped closer, making me gasp as he cupped my face in both hands.

"Yes, I did."

Then he was gone.

# CHAPTER 25

IT DIDN'T TAKE long for Cade to shower and come back wearing shorts and a long-sleeved T-shirt, and my cheeks still burned from his touch. What did it mean? Something or nothing? Given that my experience with men consisted of a drunken fumble with the only straight male nurse in the short-stay surgical unit—an embarrassing mistake which had led to me moving to the geriatrics ward because it was the only place with an immediate opening—then being attacked by Harlan Lake and finally sleeping with Dean, I was hardly qualified to guess. Certainly Dean had never made me shiver that way. I mean, Dean was always kind and gentle, but he never acted like men from the movies. The only thing I'd ever seen him get passionate over was a new Intel processor.

"Did you check out the brochures?" Cade asked.

"Uh, sort of."

Scarlet had been poring over them, goggling at the pictures and sounding out the few words she knew, while I'd flicked through without truly registering anything.

"So, where do you want to go today?"

There were realms, right? I turned back to the index page, hoping for inspiration.

"Princesses," Scarlet announced. "I want to see the

princesses."

"Where are the princesses?" Cade asked.

A photo of a blonde in a crown jumped out at me. "In the Royal Realm, I think."

Down in the lobby, the concierge organised tickets while Cade checked through the wallet the pilot had handed him on the plane.

"Emmy's gone overboard with the undercover thing again. According to this, we're now Cade and Taylor Walker. Here, have a driver's licence."

Holy crap, it looked just like the real thing. A part of me wondered if I could really use it to rent a car, because then I could start driving and not stop until I was far away from the mess Dean had helped me to create.

"You want a credit card too? For crying out loud, she's even included wedding rings and a condom. She realises we've got a five-year-old child with us, right?"

I nearly choked. "Maybe it's her idea of a joke?"

"Yeah, maybe."

The five-year-old child was currently six feet away by the front desk, telling the receptionist and anyone else who would listen that she was going to meet all the Wonder Princesses today, and that when she grew up, she wanted to be a princess too. I'm sure the other hotel guests were as relieved as us when our ride pulled up outside the front door.

"You have to stay close, sweetie. Okay? You hold my hand or Cade's hand, and you don't run off."

"Okay. Can I have an ice cream like that one?" She pointed at a passing teenager eating two scoops out of a cone.

"Sure, we'll find a place."

"Where to, boss?" Cade asked.

With Scarlet sitting between us in the car, I managed to banish my hormones and read the brochure properly as well as studying the map and checking the notes from the concierge.

"We should get Scarlet an autograph book first, because then she can collect signatures from all the princesses. It'll be nice for her to take something home to remember the trip by."

"Good plan. And I'll take plenty of photos too."

An hour later, I sat with Cade in Queen Ella's beauty parlour, both of us wearing Wilbur ears while Scarlet got a princess makeover. Hair, make-up, gown, wand—she was getting the works. In fact, Cade would probably have bought her the whole damn castle if she'd asked for it, mainly out of guilt that he couldn't be a bigger part of her life at the moment.

"Do I look pretty?" she asked when she emerged from the boutique dressed as Princess Maya.

"The fairest maiden of them all," Cade told her.

"You got that from Snow White!" she squealed. "I love Snow White! Can I get a Snow White dress too?"

I interrupted before Cade could agree. Snow White wasn't even a Wonder World character. "Don't you want to go on some of the rides first?"

"Yes! And I want to go and see Bella out of *The Enchanted Library*."

We visited Bella in the library for story time, then I rode on the carousel with Scarlet while Cade took pictures. As the day wore on, he seemed more relaxed, happier than I'd ever seen him as he escaped the stresses of his job and acted like a big kid. And when I asked Scarlet whether she wanted me to go on the

Twisted Teacup ride with her, she shook her head.

"No, Cade."

I thought his jaw would crack, he smiled so wide.

"Here, give me the camera. I'll play photographer."

The sight of them together made the early morning and all the travelling worth it. Nobody could deny those two were father and daughter.

"That your kid on the ride?" a man next to me asked.

"Oh, no. I'm just her nanny."

"Then it's nice to meet you, pretty lady."

Maybe he meant it as a compliment, but it came out sleazy.

"Is your child on the ride?"

"Nah. My boy's twelve. He's over at the pirate treasure hunt thing."

He'd left a twelve-year-old boy unsupervised in a park full of strangers?

"Well, don't let me keep you. I'm sure you must be keen to join him."

The creep laughed. "Not my kind of thing. I'd rather stay here and talk to you."

He moved six inches closer, but I couldn't shuffle away because a lady was standing to my left.

"I'm not really that interesting."

"A sweet thing like you? I don't believe that." He reached out to stroke my arm, and his touch made my skin crawl.

"Please, don't..."

He didn't move his hand. "Don't what?"

A strong arm around my waist made me jump, and before I knew what was happening, I'd been pulled backwards against Cade. Scarlet grabbed my hand.

"There you are, gorgeous," Cade said softly, but still loud enough for the sleaze to hear. "Scarlet wants to go see the 3D movie."

I didn't bother to bid the man goodbye as Cade propelled me away from him. As soon as we were out of earshot, Cade loosened his grip, although he left one hand resting on my hip.

"You okay? You didn't look too happy with that guy."

"He touched me, and I didn't even know his name." I gave an involuntary shudder.

"Shit. I wish I could've got there sooner, but the ride was still going."

"It's okay. I'm just overly sensitive about these things." I put on a smile, not wanting to ruin the day, especially when Scarlet was so happy. "Are we really going to watch the movie?"

"It's got Dennis the Wonder Duck in it," she said.

"Sure, if that's what you guys want to do."

I felt grateful when Cade didn't let me go, because my encounter with that weird guy had shaken me more than I cared to admit. Any other woman would most likely have laughed his poor attempt at flirting off, but Harlan Lake's legacy and the sheltered life I'd led since had left me poorly equipped to deal with the unwanted attention of strangers.

Inside the theatre, I expected Cade to put Scarlet between us like in the car, but he lifted her into the seat on the far side of him and sat next to me instead. Once we'd all put our 3D glasses on, which made me feel a bit silly even though it was dark and everyone else was wearing them too, Cade's arm settled over the back of my seat, grazing my shoulders.

"Are you okay?"

I nodded.

"You're trembling." Cade's warm breath whispered across my ear.

Yes, but that was partly because of his close proximity, and when he touched me, I didn't feel my usual nervousness, just an odd flutter in my belly. What was wrong with me?

"It must be the air conditioning in here."

Wrong thing to say. Because Cade muttered, "Fuck, I don't have a sweater to give you," and pulled me tight against him. Only the narrow wooden arm of the seat stopped me from being dragged into his lap.

"Better?"

Heat fizzed through my veins as his lips skated over my earlobe, but while my stomach danced, the rest of me was frozen.

"I think so."

Should I freak out or relish the closeness? The last person to comfort me with any affection was my grandma, and she'd died three weeks after my eighteenth birthday. Dean tried to soothe me when I got upset, of course he did, but he was more about words than actions. One of the things he'd always told me was that time heals. Back then, I'd never believed him, and if he'd suggested that I'd one day take a trip to Wonder World with a man I'd known for only a few weeks, I'd have called one of my ex-colleagues from the psychiatric ward to check he hadn't lost his damn mind.

But here I was.

And Cade's arm felt...nice.

The moment I had that thought, the guilt started,

because Cade wasn't the man I was married to. The smart thing to do would have been to shuffle towards the small boy sitting on the other side of me and concentrate on the movie, but sensible me had been left behind in Richmond. Stupid me dropped my head onto Cade's shoulder and let his warmth soak through my body until the usher reminded us to hand in our 3D glasses on the way out.

Only when we got up, Scarlet didn't.

I leaned over, then burst into giggles. "Someone's overdone it a bit."

"Is she asleep?"

"Dead to the world."

Rather than waking her, Cade picked his daughter up, and her head lolled against his shoulder as he carried her out of the theatre.

"Time to go back to the hotel, I think."

I stumbled as we got outside. "She's not the only one feeling tired."

Crowds flowed past as Cade called our driver and asked him to wait by the exit so we didn't have to walk too far. I almost took the opportunity to snap a bunch of photos, even got as far as pulling my phone out of my bag, but then I remembered that this wasn't my life, and nobody outside of Blackwood could ever know I'd spent a weekend at Wonder World, gallivanting with a man who wasn't my husband. A man who hung up the phone and tucked me under his spare arm again as he steered us out of the park.

And I freaking let him! Had I lost my mind? Obviously. But it felt so...so comfortable. Safe.

So I kept my mouth shut, and I kept walking.

In the car, as in the theatre, Cade settled a still-sleeping Scarlet on his left. The hotel had even provided a booster seat, not that she noticed.

"I have to tell her," Cade whispered as the driver pulled away.

"Tell her what?"

"That I'm her father." He leaned back, eyes closed. "I hate that she thinks I'm just some random guy."

Suddenly, I was awake. "What, tonight?"

He nodded. "I think so. It's killing me that she doesn't know."

Without conscious thought, I grabbed his hand. "Are you sure that's a good idea? I mean, now?"

"There's never going to be a good time. But I think the longer I...we leave it, the more difficult it'll be."

"Okay." I watched the traffic flash by for a few seconds, then looked back to find Cade studying me. "What?"

"Nothing."

I kept staring at him.

"You're just not what I expected."

What did that mean? In a good way, or a bad way?

And why did I wish so much that it was the former?

# CHAPTER 26

BACK IN THE hotel, the concierge hurried towards us the moment we set foot in the lobby, her heels clicking on the black-and-white tiles. The skirt she wore didn't help her speed—tight and straight-cut from thigh to knee, it meant she could barely move her legs. I noticed her eyes flick downwards to Cade's fingers intertwined with mine before she focused back on his face.

"Mr. Duchamp, we've reserved a table in Aston's for you. It's our premier restaurant."

"Thanks. Does it have a children's menu?"

"The chef's been briefed, and he'll make anything this little sweetheart would like."

"What time is the reservation?"

"You can come down whenever you want."

A lady on the far side of the lobby dropped her purse, and the baby in her arms began to wail as her partner stared in horror at the bottles of milk rolling across the floor. The concierge patted me on the shoulder.

"If you'll excuse me, I just need to go and help with the..." She gestured at the lady. "Enjoy your dinner, and call me if you need anything."

The baby's cries must have woken Scarlet, because she blinked groggily. "Can we go on the Dumbo ride again?"

"Sweetie, we're back in the hotel. It's almost time for dinner."

Her face fell.

"But we can go back to the park tomorrow. Do you want to visit the Animal Realm?"

"Are there unicorns?"

"No unicorns, but there are elephants and butterflies."

She scrambled out of Cade's grip and raced across the lobby, flapping her hands. "I want to be a butterfly! I love butterflies! Can I have a butterfly?"

"At least she doesn't want an elephant," Cade muttered.

"Come here." I opened my arms, and she jumped into them. "How about we take lots of pictures of you with the butterflies?"

"Yes! Will there be pink ones?"

"Maybe."

"What's for dinner? Can I have french fries?"

"Sure you can," Cade said, and I rolled my eyes. For a tough guy, he sure was a soft touch.

"But you've got to eat some vegetables too, okay?"

"Potatoes are a vegetable," Cade told me as we climbed on the elevator.

"Don't give her ideas."

He flashed an unexpected grin, and at that moment, he looked exactly like his daughter.

"Just sayin'."

It didn't take me long to change into something suitable for the cool atmosphere of the restaurant, although Scarlet held things up a bit when she couldn't find Eric.

"Where did you leave him?"

"On my bed. I know I did."

I got down on my knees to check underneath, then shook the duvet out, but there was no sign of the cuddly elephant. Not until Cade appeared in the doorway.

"Looking for this?"

Scarlet screeched and skipped over to him. "Thank you!"

"Where was he?"

"On the dining table. You ready?"

"Do I look okay?"

"Beautiful as always, Taylor. As are you, little lady. You want a piggyback?"

Cade swung Scarlet up onto his back and headed towards the door, leaving me giddy. He thought I looked beautiful? Not "okay"? Not "fine"? The most I'd ever got out of Dean in six years was a "nice."

"Taylor! Cade says I can have chocolate ice cream!"

Five years old, and she already knew how to wrap a man around her little finger, which was more than I did.

Down in the dining room, the maître d' seated us in a quiet corner screened off from the other tables by a pair of potted palms. Scarlet bounced with excitement as Cade helped her onto one of the padded leather chairs, and a waiter draped a napkin over her lap.

"Where's the counter?" she asked.

"Sorry?" What counter?

"Where we order."

"The waiter takes our order."

"But when Mommy takes me to McDonald's, we

have to order at the counter, and in the café today, we went to the counter too."

Suddenly, it dawned. "When your mommy took you to restaurants, did you always go to McDonald's?"

"Sometimes Burger King. I always get onion rings at Burger King. Can I have onion rings here?"

The waiter looked faintly panicked. I could only imagine the ear-bashing he'd get from the chef if he walked into the kitchen and announced their young guest wanted fries, onion rings, and chocolate ice cream. But because Emmy owned the hotel, I also had no doubt they'd deliver.

"Onions are a vegetable too," Cade said under his breath, and I rolled my eyes once more.

"We have a wood-fired pizza oven," the waiter suggested. "We could do a children's size."

Scarlet made a face.

"Sorry, she's not keen on pizza. Sweetie, how about spaghetti bolognese?"

"Will I like it?"

"You ate it when I made it last week."

"Okay. Can I pick which toy I want?"

"Could you find her a toy?" I whispered to the waiter. "One of the Wonder characters, perhaps?"

He tried hard to hide his grimace. "Of course, ma'am."

Cade opted for steak with fries, while I went for the Thai chicken noodle bowl, eager to expand my cultural horizons while I was away from Dean. The maître d', bless him, turned up with paper and a box of crayons for Scarlet and a bottle of chilled champagne for the grown-ups.

"Compliments of Mrs. Black."

There it was—the return of the guilt.

But Cade didn't seem to notice as he clinked his glass against mine.

"Here's to the best weekend I've had in months. Maybe even years."

I hoped my smile looked convincing. "To the weekend."

As the evening wore on, I got more and more anxious about Cade's big announcement. When would he make it? Would there ever be a good time? Scarlet needed to know, but how would she take the news?

Cade seemed more nervous than usual too, sneaking glances at his daughter while he made small talk about his favourite foods—spaghetti carbonara and paella as well as Kung Pao chicken—and fiddled with his napkin.

"I drew a picture," Scarlet announced.

Oh, thank goodness—an interruption. "What did you draw, sweetie?"

"You and me and Cade."

A lump came into my throat as she passed me the piece of paper. Three figures, holding hands. There was no mistaking Cade's beard on the left, and the smaller person in the middle was undoubtedly Scarlet. That left me as the brunette on the right. She'd drawn a picture of a family. The family I always thought I'd never have.

And Cade cleared his throat. "Uh, Scarlet? I need to tell you something."

She stared at him expectantly.

"I mean, what I'm trying to say is..." The colour drained out of his face, and he looked at me in a panic. "Shit, I... No, I didn't mean that..."

I took Scarlet's hand. "There are some little girls

who are very special, and that means they get extra family. Your daddy Reed's very busy at the moment, and Cade's offered to help him out by being your new daddy."

She tilted her head to one side. "Cade's my new daddy?"

"That's right. What do you think?"

Scarlet broke into a grin. "I like it! Does that mean you're my new mommy?"

Now it was my turn to falter.

"I'm afraid it do—doesn't..." I choked on my words, trying not to cry.

She scrambled onto Cade's lap and pointed at me. "Cade, I want Taylor to be my new mommy. She's better than my old one."

"Scarlet—"

"Please?" She pressed her face against his beard. "Pleeeeeeease?"

His eyes flicked towards me before settling back on his daughter. "We'll see, okay?"

We'll see? What the heck was that supposed to mean?

The waiter saved us from more difficult questions when he presented Scarlet with dessert. Not only had the chef found three kinds of chocolate ice cream, somebody had added rainbow sprinkles and stuck a sparkler in the top. Half the diners turned to stare at the sound of her squeals. No, we weren't torturing her, honestly.

I put a finger to my lips. "Shh, sweetie."

"Can you take a photo? Please?" she asked, gesturing to the camera beside me.

"Okay, quick, before the sparkles stop."

I snapped a few pictures, and her grin was so wide it barely fitted in the frame.

"Thanks," Cade mouthed as she picked up her spoon and began to eat. "For everything."

The lump in my throat got bigger.

Cade had opted for the strawberry roulade while I chose a crème brûlée. A little decadent, but I'd been on my feet all day so I figured I deserved it, even if I did feel stuffed afterwards.

"Time to go back upstairs?" Cade asked when I pushed the bowl away.

"I couldn't eat another thing."

"I'll get the check."

Cade looked around for the waiter, but our view was blocked by a large lady in a floral dress who bent down to pat Scarlet's cheek.

"Aren't you just a cutie pie?"

"I'm not a pie."

"What a darling." The lady turned to me. "You must be so proud of her."

"Oh, I'm not her—"

"We are," Cade interrupted.

Our visitor spied the camera I'd picked up to put in my purse. "Would you like me to take a photo of the three of you? Such a fabulous restaurant, isn't it?"

"Er, I'm not—"

Scarlet clapped her hands together. "Yes! A photo!"

The three of us squashed together while the lady clicked away, Scarlet beaming from ear to ear. Posing like that should have been awkward, but Cade's arm around my waist and that beautiful little girl in front of me stirred up feelings I didn't want to think about. Because I absolutely shouldn't have been having them.

I managed a weak smile when the lady handed the camera back. "Thanks."

"My pleasure, honey. You make a beautiful family."

# CHAPTER 27

BACK IN OUR suite, Scarlet still buzzed with energy. Where did she get it from? How much sugar did the chef put in her dessert? I needed at least three portions.

"Can we go in the bubble tub?" she asked, pointing out at the terrace.

"Not tonight, sweetie. You need to get some sleep so we can go to the Animal Kingdom tomorrow."

"Awww..."

"I'm sure Lara'll let you use her Jacuzzi again when we get home. Now, let's go brush your teeth."

"I can do it by myself."

"I'll come along so you can show me."

Between Scarlet wanting a story, then scrambling out of bed to look through the window, then insisting that she needed another blanket, it took half an hour before I escaped back to the lounge. Cade was sitting at the bar on the phone, but he hung up when I arrived.

"Sorry. Had to check in with the office."

"At this time?"

"Blackwood never sleeps."

"Neither do I with Scarlet around."

"She doesn't give you too much hassle, does she?"

"Her batteries never run out, but I don't mind. A lot of it's actually fun."

"Just let me know if it gets too hard, right?"

"Okay."

"How did the teeth brushing go? Maybe I could help her with that tomorrow?"

"She thinks she can brush them herself, but if you don't keep an eye on her, she skips all the back ones."

"I'll remember that. Fuck, I wish I could be home to learn these things for myself."

"Your undercover job won't go on forever."

"Right now, it feels like it will. Want a nightcap? This bar's got almost everything. You can tell Emmy stocked it."

Normally, I wouldn't dream of it, but what was normal about this weekend? "I'll have whatever's easiest."

I expected a glass of wine or perhaps a gin and tonic, but a few minutes later, Cade slid an orange-and-yellow concoction over to me.

"What's this?"

"A kiss on the lips."

"Excuse me?"

"A cocktail. Mango and peach schnapps, mango juice, grenadine. I worked as a bartender in my last year of high school, before I joined the army. Kind of ironic that I could make the drinks but I couldn't legally drink them, don't you think?"

All these little things I didn't know about him.

Before he took a seat next to me, Cade made himself something slightly less vibrant then fiddled with the stereo until a Suzi Quade song played softly in the background.

"You're a big fan of hers?" I asked. He had every one of her albums at home, and I loved her blend of pop and country too.

"Yeah. I worked personal protection for her US tour last year, and she's one of the few celebrities who didn't leave a bad taste in my mouth."

"I didn't realise you worked as a bodyguard."

"When I first joined Blackwood. I did a year in their New York office before I moved to Richmond."

"Is undercover work harder?"

"A hundred times harder. There's no rest. I can't let my guard down for a second while I'm there. And now, with Scarlet, I hate every day I'm in that damn place. It's the stupid shit that gets to me, like...like nobody knows how to change a damn toilet roll. Or empty a trash can. And the only music they listen to is heavy metal or Dolly Parton."

"Dolly Parton?"

"One of the guys is a fan, but he's also built like a tank, so no one argues with him."

"I bet. What was New York like? I've only ever seen it on TV."

"Busy. Not as friendly as Richmond, but it's got this buzz about it. And there's so much to do. In the time I lived there, I swear I only spent a couple of evenings in my apartment."

"I've never been a social butterfly. Sometimes I wish I could try a new hobby, or hang with friends, or take a trip." One that didn't involve espionage. "At least with Scarlet, I get out of the house now."

"When this job's over, we can go to New York if you want. You, me, and Scarlet."

"Are you serious?"

"I'm racking up a hell of a lot of vacation time."

Dean. I had to think of Dean. Not Cade. And certainly not a getaway to a more-than-likely luxury hotel in the city that never sleeps with a man who made my heart skip and the cutest kid I'd ever known.

Luckily, Cade didn't press me but pointed at my empty glass instead. "Want another?"

"What else can you make?"

"How dirty do you like your drinks?"

"I've never drunk a cocktail before." And it was kind of delicious.

"Never? Miss California, you haven't lived."

Five minutes later, I found myself staring at a strange green affair decorated with two cherries and a slice of orange.

"What's that? Is that safe to drink?" I gave a tentative sniff. Fruity.

"Sex in the jungle. Try it."

Okay, so it didn't taste as bad as it looked. I nibbled on the orange then sucked a cherry off the stick.

"So, we've done New York. Tell me about the West Coast."

Oh, hell. The cherry wedged in my throat and I began choking. Cade leapt up and thumped me on the back, eyebrows pinched in concern.

"You okay?"

"Fine." I coughed again, and the cherry came loose.

"Just went down...the wrong way." I chugged back half of the cocktail to stop the tickle. "All good now."

Was it too late to jump off the roof? Probably, with Cade staring at me expectantly.

"Uh, the West Coast. It was, uh...hot."

"Whereabouts did you live?"

"Near Santa Barbara, on the beach."

Cade gave a low whistle. "Nice. Bet that wasn't cheap. Sure puts the East Coast coat closet I called home to shame."

"The house belonged to my ex-boyfriend."

And... I was going to hell. Not only was I getting pleasantly tipsy with a man who wasn't my husband, but I'd also demoted Dean to insignificant other.

"Hope the break-up wasn't too painful."

"We just sort of grew apart."

Well, that part wasn't entirely untrue. We had grown apart. Two and a half thousand miles apart, because Dean had insisted on sending me to another state to do his dirty work.

"I don't suppose my place compares to what you're used to."

"It's different. More of a home, because it's got Scarlet in it. Our house in California was...sterile. Too perfect. And my h—ex-boyfriend didn't speak to me much, even though he worked from his home office almost every day. Mostly I talked to people on the internet if I got lonely. Yes, I know that's weird, and I know I should have gone out and met people, but I've never really liked doing that and..." Now I was babbling. "Can I have another drink?"

"What do you want this time?"

"Surprise me."

A short tumbler, something pink, slices of banana, more cherries. And a smile from Cade. Awesome.

"What's this?"

"A tropical orgasm."

"Ooh, I've never had one of those."

"Vodka, rum, lemonade, strawberry daiquiri mix."

"No, I meant an orgasm."

Cade's eyes bugged out of his head, but drunk me still didn't take the hint to stop talking.

"At least, I don't think so. People on the internet talk about the earth shattering and fireworks exploding, but nothing like that's ever happened to me. I mean, Dean tried his hardest, but in my opinion, sex is totally overrated." I grabbed the cocktail and poured half of it down my throat. "Then there's kissing, which also isn't that great. It's like sucking on a lychee."

After we'd been living together for three months, Dean had encouraged me to get over my fear of going to bed with a man, and thanks to his gentleness, I'd managed it. But did I enjoy it? Not really.

Cade gently pried the glass from my fingers. "On second thoughts, I think you've had enough. We should get you to bed."

I tried to take the drink back, but he moved it farther away.

"Hey, I want that."

Cade's arm wrapped around my waist as he helped me to my feet, and I twisted around to face him.

"Do we have any lychees?"

"No lychees."

Our faces were an inch apart, and slowly, so slowly, he leaned forwards and brushed his lips against mine. A giggle escaped as his beard tickled me. But then he deepened the kiss, and I soon learned that Cade was more of a fruit cocktail with a side helping of ice cream. His arms tightened as he nibbled my bottom lip, and I took the opportunity to return the favour, using my fingertips to explore those muscles that rippled in his back whenever he wore a tight T-shirt. His tongue ran along the seam of my lips, and I welcomed him in as some otherworldly force took over my body and pressed it against Cade's.

Warmth spread through my limbs, nothing to do with the Florida climate but from a passion I'd never felt before. And someone was making these little gasping noises. It might even have been me.

"Taylor?"

A small voice filtered into my consciousness.

"Taylor?"

Cade pulled back with a groan that echoed my own.

"Taylor, I'm thirsty."

Cade answered for me. "Coming in a second."

What the hell had just happened? My brain refused to process it as Cade kissed me again, chastely this time.

"You need to sleep." Then, a smile. "Do you still want lychees?"

"No, no lychees."

After that, I never wanted another lychee in my life.

## CHAPTER 28

STRAWBERRIES? WHY WAS I dreaming about strawberries? And not just any strawberries—my strawberries were wearing Wilbur ears and being attacked by an army of cocktail-stick-wielding lychees.

"Taylor! Wake up!"

My bed dipped as Scarlet climbed up next to me, and a ripple of pain ran through my head. I tried opening my eyes, but as the first shards of sunlight hit me through the open drapes, I soon rethought that idea.

"Too early, sweetie."

"But we're going to the Animal Realm."

"What time is it?"

Scarlet shrugged, and I closed my eyes again. She got off the bed, and footsteps padded across the room before the door clicked open and closed. Thank goodness. Now I could get some more rest.

Except then I heard her voice, even louder than usual.

"Cade, Taylor won't get up, and we need to go to Wonder World."

Cade... Cade... Oh, hell. I sat bolt upright as the feel of Cade's lips on mine came flooding back. Was that part of the lychee dream? Or did it actually happen? I prayed for the former, but the pulse pounding in my temples told me alcohol had been involved somewhere.

My boss. I'd kissed my boss. Or did he kiss me? That part was a little hazy. I forced my eyelids apart again and stared at my reflection in the mirror opposite, touching a finger to my lips. The roughened skin around them glowed pink, evidence of the damage done by Cade's beard in the early hours. Shit. My toes curled just thinking about it. Then my belly clenched. Oh my, oh my, oh my... Did I really tell him I'd never had an orgasm? I was staring at the terrace, contemplating leaping off it and falling eleven stories to a welcome death, when a knock sounded at the door.

Cade. Scarlet would just barge right in.

"Please go away. I'm dying of embarrassment in here."

"I have Advil."

Dammit. Advil was tempting.

Scarlet made up my mind for me, shoving the door open and jumping on the bed again. "You can't die. We're going to Wonder World. Cade..." She paused, tilting her head to one side. "Daddy says I can have cotton candy."

His grin matched hers when she called him that, and I couldn't help smiling too. The pair of them were so darn sweet together.

No. *No.* Cade wasn't sweet. Cade was dangerous. Cade was sin and heaven and temptation and fire and darkness all rolled into one, and I needed to remember that. Soon enough, I'd be leaving, and... I came to a sudden realisation. I didn't even *like* lychees.

Cade perched on the edge of the bed and held out a glass of water and a packet of pills.

"Take these. They'll help."

"Nothing will help. Did we...? Last night?"

"Did you what?" Scarlet asked.

Cade beckoned her forwards. "Do you want to play hide-and-seek?"

"And then we'll go to Wonder World?"

"Sure."

"Okay then."

"Right, you go hide, and I'll come and look for you in a minute."

"A hundred. You've got to count to a hundred."

Once Cade nodded his agreement, she ran off, leaving the two of us and a sea of awkwardness behind in the bedroom. He reached out to tuck a stray lock of hair behind my ear. Thank goodness I was still fully dressed from yesterday instead of wearing a pair of flimsy pyjamas. As soon as I'd swallowed the pills, I leaned my head back and groaned.

"I'm sorry. I shouldn't have drunk so much."

"You don't drink often, do you?"

"How did you guess?"

"I should be apologising to you. I've seen enough people in bars to recognise the signs, and I should have stopped making you drinks. How bad is your hangover?"

"It's not the hangover I'm worried about."

"The kiss?"

"What else?" I whispered.

He shrugged. "I just wanted to prove that there are better fruits out there than lychees. Like peaches, for example. They're sweet and delicious, like you."

I threw a spare pillow at him. "You can't say that."

"Why not? It's true. What fruit am I?"

An image of a banana popped into my head, and I

felt my cheeks colour up. "I don't know. Maybe an apple?"

"An apple? Why?"

"I don't know. I just like apples." Oh hell, now I'd just admitted that I liked him too. "No, no. Bad analogy. How about an orange because... No, a blueberry... A blueberry... I don't know."

And I was a tomato—bright red.

Tears pricked at the corners of my eyes, and Cade reached out to wipe them away with his thumb.

"Yes, a peach. Sweet, delicious, and easily bruised." He leaned over and pressed a kiss to my forehead. "I don't want to hurt you."

Too late. It would be so damn painful when I left Richmond.

Cade stood and headed for the door. "I'd better find Scarlet. Are you up to going out today, or would you rather stay here?"

And miss out on a day with the two of them? I couldn't.

"I'll be ready in twenty minutes."

When we got to the theme park, Cade took pity on me and didn't make me go on any stomach-churning rides. We took a trip on the Super Safari Train and visited the gorillas, and then I spent ten minutes trying to explain to Scarlet why keeping butterflies as pets wasn't a practical idea.

"They're not always butterflies, sweetie. They start out as caterpillars."

"I don't mind that."

"They prefer to be outside."

"That's okay. I like being outside too."

"But they need plants to eat, and we don't have any." Apart from the weeds sprouting between the slabs on the terrace and a now patchy, overgrown lawn, Cade's backyard was devoid of vegetation.

Scarlet, being the smart little girl she was, brought out the big guns. "Daddy, we can get plants, can't we?"

"What? Huh?" Cade stopped fiddling with the camera as his daughter tugged his sleeve.

"Plants. We need plants for the butterflies to live in."

"Where?"

"In the garden at home. It's all empty."

"Maybe I could buy a few pots?" I suggested. "And we could do with a sprinkler and a lawnmower."

"You shouldn't have to do heavy work in the garden."

"I don't mind."

"I'll ask Bradley to find someone to help."

"I can look for someone myself if you like? I'm sure there're plenty of garden services around with Rybridge just along the road."

"No."

The ferocity of his answer shocked me.

"Sorry, I didn't mean to..."

He put an arm around me and pulled me a little closer. "No, *I'm* sorry. I shouldn't have snapped. It's just... Any man coming near Scarlet needs to be thoroughly vetted, and you don't have the resources to do that. Blackwood does."

I could understand that, but why such a vehement reply?

"Did something happen? In the past?"

He closed his eyes and nodded. "Yes, but now isn't a good time to talk about it."

As if on cue, Scarlet slipped her hand into mine. "Can we go and see Magic Forest now?"

"Sure we can."

A hundred photos later, we left the tree and headed for the Jurassic Realm play area. In truth, I was exhausted, and the idea of watching Scarlet expend energy while I conserved mine certainly appealed. Cade and I sat at the edge watching her run around. He rested an arm on the back of the bench behind me, but apart from that, yesterday's affection had vanished. Because of the kiss? Had that made him feel awkward? My insides sure as heck lurched just from me thinking about it.

His eyes darted from side to side as he watched Scarlet, and I realised he wasn't only checking up on his daughter; he was studying the other adults present in the playground as well. Every so often, his gaze would linger on one of them for a few seconds, sometimes as long as half a minute, before he moved on to the next.

Was this simply his professional training coming to the fore? Or something deeper?

"Is everything okay?" I asked.

"Yeah. I just hate it when she goes out of sight. This is harder than I ever thought it would be."

"You're doing a great job of being a dad. It's obvious she adores you."

"Not that part. When I have to leave her behind and go to work."

"It won't last forever, and I promise I'll look after her."

That earned me a shoulder squeeze. "I know. I trust you."

And that was the moment I knew I'd do everything in my power to avoid going back to California until Cade could look after Scarlet properly. That little girl couldn't be left on her own. Not again.

I just had no idea how I'd manage to dig myself out of the hole I was in, a hole that got deeper with every passing day.

"I found a fossil," Scarlet shouted, running up to us with a grubby bone in her hand. It was fake, right?

"Well done, sweetie."

At least one of us knew what she was doing.

"We finally did it!" I said to Cade as he carried Scarlet up the steps onto Emmy's plane. "We tired her out."

"A memorable occasion." He passed me the camera. "I think this calls for a photo."

"Blackmail material for when she turns eighteen?"

He grinned. "Maybe."

I took a few pictures of her in his arms before he buckled her into one of the cream leather seats. I still had to pinch myself that I was actually on a private jet, not that I'd ever have anyone to tell about it.

"Would you like a drink before takeoff?" the hostess asked.

"Not sure that's wise," Cade put in.

The Advil had worn off, and I wholeheartedly agreed with him.

"Just a bottle of water, please."

"Make that two."

It wasn't long before the plane rose gracefully into the air, and still Scarlet didn't stir. Two days of running around had taken their toll, and I couldn't help hoping she was still tired tomorrow. Mainly because I needed a rest.

"How's Scarlet doing in kindergarten?" Cade asked.

"No problems so far. She seems to be enjoying it, although she managed to get paint in her hair the other day and it took me three lots of shampoo to get it out."

"Is she too much work? Do you want me to get someone else to do a couple of days a week?" He leaned back and sighed. "I hardly thought this through, did I?"

"I'm fine, honestly."

"When this job's over, I'll take some time off so you can have a break."

"You want me to stay on?"

"Of course. You thought I wouldn't?"

"I guess I figured you only needed me temporarily."

"I'll still have to work long hours, even if I spend half my time in the office."

"Oh."

"You don't want to stay?"

What was I supposed to say to that? I really did want to stay, but the circumstances...

"I love looking after Scarlet."

"I'll make things easier, I promise, starting with a gardener. It's about time the backyard got used. We can get Scarlet a swing and all that shit."

Curiosity got the better of me, and I couldn't stop myself from digging. "What were you saying earlier? About having anyone near Scarlet vetted? Is it something to do with your sister?"

Cade said the problem stemmed from his past, and

I knew she'd passed away. What the heck happened?

"Yeah." His eyes took on a haunted look, one I'd seen all too frequently in the ER when a family lost a loved one. "Christie. She was seven when she died. Cute as hell. Scarlet reminds me of her a lot."

I reached over and curled my fingers around his, offering him what little strength I had. The hitch in his voice told me speaking these words was far from easy.

"I'm so sorry."

"Me too. I was fourteen at the time. She actually my half-sister because my mom got married again, but that didn't matter. I loved her just the same. She used to follow me around the house, asking me to play teddy bears picnic with her, and she had all these soft toys lined up on little chairs with cups and saucers..." He shook his head. "So damned cute."

"I bet she was."

"I had soccer practice after school, and then I was supposed to pick her up from the sitter and take her home, but a bunch of my buddies went to the arcade, and I figured it wouldn't hurt to join them. An hour, that's all it took. One hour." Cade swallowed and took a gulp of water. "Need something stronger than this," he muttered.

"Shall I see if I can—?"

He shook his head. "I arrived at the sitter's house and found her passed out drunk in the lounge while her boyfriend was in the bedroom fucking my seven-year-old sister."

My gasp did little to convey my horror. "He what?"

"The asshole turned around and put a finger to his lips like it was our little secret. Can you believe that?"

"What did you do?"

"He'd left his pants in a heap by the door, and there was this old revolver in a holster on the belt. Piece of shit, but it still did the job."

"You shot him?"

"Yes."

"Oh my..." Words failed me.

"Well, that's my big secret. Ready to run in horror?"

I didn't know what I was ready to do, but stuck in a plane that seemed smaller by the second, I couldn't go very far. "He died?"

"Before he hit the floor. Except he'd already choked Christie. I called an ambulance, and they tried to save her, but..." He paused, eyes closed, and his knuckles turned white as he gripped the arms of the seat. "But it was too late."

"I'm so sorry."

Anything I could say was inadequate, but I had little else to offer.

"It's in the past. But now you understand why I'm so protective of Scarlet?"

I nodded. "Did you get into trouble?"

He shrugged. "A year in juvie. Would have been six months if I'd shown some remorse, but I wasn't sorry. I'd do the exact same thing again."

Dean had spent months teaching me the benefits of forgiveness in such circumstances. Yes, raping a child was awful, abhorrent. So horrible I could hardly bring myself to think about it. But was killing the man really the answer? What if, with help, he could have reformed the same way Harlan Lake did? Dean followed up with the police liaison officer, and Lake had successfully completed rehab and become a changed man.

And it wasn't only the man who Cade had killed

who'd been affected. He'd had a family too. Cade lost a sister, but a mother and father lost their son. Did the man have siblings of his own? Shooting him in the heat of the moment was one thing, but Cade's attitude afterwards left me cold. A chill ran through me, and I shuddered involuntarily.

"You hate what I did, don't you?" Cade asked.

"It doesn't sit well with me."

"I can't pretend now just like I couldn't then. I'm that person, and I always will be."

"I can't pretend either."

A few hours ago, I'd wanted to stay in Richmond for good, but now my world had been flipped on its head once again. Could I continue to be involved with a man whose views were so different from my own?

I wasn't sure.

# Chapter 29

THE TENSION CAUSED by Cade's revelation only eased once he'd departed on his motorcycle for a destination unknown, and I scooped a still-tired Scarlet into the car and took her back home.

Bradley must have been there in our absence because the old bathroom had disappeared, the double-width shower replaced by a white tub with a pale-blue stripe running around the edge. A caddy next to the new basin overflowed with luxury toiletries, and when I stepped onto the tiled floor, it was warm beneath my feet.

Who was Cade, really? He'd done this for me, he obviously adored his daughter, and he'd loved his sister, yet the coldness I'd seen in his eyes when he made his confession scared me. Yes, I could understand why he'd shot that awful man on impulse. It was his complete lack of remorse that bothered me. The world needed kindness and compassion, not vengeance. Dean had taught me that.

But Dean was notable by his absence. When I first came to Richmond, he'd called every day, but now contact had dwindled to once a week at best. It was as if he'd abandoned me. His *wife*. When we got back from Wonder World, I'd tried calling him, finally leaving a message after I'd got his voicemail three times. Now, two days later, he still hadn't called me back.

Cade hadn't phoned either, and I was grateful for that because I didn't know what to say to him, but the feeling of loneliness grew into a monster that pressed on my chest and made it difficult to breathe. What should I do? Try to convince Dean to let me go back to California when he eventually called? Or go all out to stay in Richmond?

Or I could take a third option. The wildcard. A new start far away from Blackwood and Cade and Richmond and the giant mess I'd become involved in. The trouble was, I didn't know if I had that in me.

Old me, the girl I'd been before Harlan Lake and before six years with Dean, would have embraced the adventure, but the girl I'd become was scared of the world beyond her front door. And looking back now, I could see that despite Dean's initial kindness, he'd never really helped me to get over the fears that had taken root in my psyche.

Fears that now ate away at me. Should I stay or leave? I had fake documents from Emmy and six thousand dollars in Taylor's bank account that I could use towards a fresh start, but would it be enough?

"Taylor, can I have pancakes for breakfast?"

"You had pancakes yesterday."

"But I want them again today. Pleeeeease? Daddy would let me have pancakes."

Of course he would. And I kind of understood why now. Not knowing how much time I'd have left with this beautiful little girl, I was tempted to indulge her every wish too.

But I also didn't want her to get spoiled.

"Cereal today. And if you eat all your vegetables this

evening, we can have pancakes tomorrow. How about that?"

"Okay. Can we do painting this afternoon?"

"Sure we can."

Once I'd dropped Scarlet off at kindergarten, the loneliness set in again, together with self-doubt and fear over the future. I should have cleaned the house, but I spent most of the morning pacing the lounge instead. What was I going to do?

I'd practically worn a hole in the carpet by the time I needed to pick Scarlet up from kindergarten. Even the driver asked if I was feeling okay. No, I wasn't, but I smiled anyway and answered in the affirmative. I got him to drop us off at the park on the way back just to avoid any more odd looks.

"Can I go on the slide?" Scarlet asked.

"Sure, sweetie."

She took off to play with the other kids, and my mind went haywire again. I needed a drink. No, not a drink, because alcohol only led to more problems. I needed an anaesthetic.

A blonde lady sat down on the bench next to me, calling out to a child a little older than Scarlet not to go too far.

"They never stop, do they?" she said.

"I don't know where they get the energy."

"Ice cream and jelly beans, at least today. Caitlin, don't go out of sight!" She shook her head. "Blink and they're gone, and that's a scary thought right now."

"Why? What happened?"

"You didn't hear about that little girl in Virginia Beach? Her mom bent to get something out of her purse, and she clean disappeared."

"The police can't find her?"

"Don't you watch the news, honey?"

Not for the last two days. "I try to avoid it."

"A security camera a few blocks up filmed a man carrying her, and nobody's seen her since. Sick freak. My husband bought me a gun. If any pervert comes near my baby, he won't know what hit him."

I glanced down into her bag, the top gaping open to reveal the glint of a silver barrel. "Don't you think that's a bit drastic?"

"No, I do not. Anyone meddling with a child needs to realise their actions have consequences. They have that choice."

"But..."

"You wouldn't do anything—*anything*—to defend your child?"

"I don't actually have children of my own. I'm her... Well, it's complicated."

She patted my arm. "Well, maybe when you do, you'll understand." A quick rummage through her bag, and she produced a package of cookies. "Oreo?"

I shook my head, feeling sick. Maybe one day I'd understand? I thought I was starting to. Because if anyone tried to hurt Scarlet, I'd be tempted to pull the trigger myself, and with that realisation came an empathy with Cade and his actions all those years ago.

"What do you think of the idea of forgiveness?" I asked my companion.

She tilted her head to one side. "Forgiveness?"

"If someone did something really awful to you,

could you forgive them?"

"That depends. Some people have lost their way and need a little help to find it again. Those people deserve a second chance. But I also believe evil walks on this earth, and the people it lives inside don't deserve any chances at all."

Well, that was more flexible than Dean's one-size-fits-all policy, and it certainly made me think. What if my first reaction wasn't always the right one?

"Perhaps I will have that cookie."

She fished the package out and put it on the bench between us. "I'm Jessie, by the way."

"Taylor."

"You sound like you've got some deep thoughts, Taylor. Is that something to do with the 'it's complicated' part?"

"Kind of. Yes, it is."

"A man?"

"Men."

"Isn't it always? Took me six tries to find a good one, and now I'm keeping him."

"But how did you know he was the right one?"

"Where do I start? He treats me like a queen, he makes me laugh, and he's hot as hell between the sheets." She dropped her voice. "Caitlin's not his biological daughter, but he loves her like she is. That means everything."

Even though I was just an employee, Cade had always treated me as an equal, and he certainly had a sense of humour. I could only imagine what he was like in bed. If that kiss was anything to go by, he'd set the damn mattress on fire. And the way he looked after Scarlet... Yes, that did mean everything. And Dean? The man whose ring I'd worn for the past four years? It felt as if he'd given up on me. I choked out a sob and quickly clapped a hand over my mouth.

"So, these men... You've got to pick between them?" When I hesitated, Jessie spoke again. "Sometimes speaking to someone who isn't involved in the situation can help. I unloaded on this poor bar girl once, but just putting it into words helped." A bubble of laughter escaped. "She'd probably heard a hundred times worse."

Who else could I talk to? Nobody.

"I don't know if I'll even have the chance to pick between them. The one I'm with hasn't been treating me too well, and the other... I haven't been entirely honest with him, and if he finds out the truth, I'm not sure he'll ever want to speak to me again."

"Is he worth the risk?"

Whatever happened, carrying on with the status quo wasn't a possibility. I either had to confess everything to Cade, to...hell, to Emmy, and hope they didn't kick me off the edge of the continent, or go back to Dean, which promised to be an uncomfortable experience. Whatever love I'd once felt for him had been left scattered from Nevada to Kentucky. The only other option, to strike out my own, left me shaking inside.

And which of those three lives would I prefer? I glanced over at Scarlet, playing with Caitlin on the swings. The thought of never seeing her or her father again made my heart stutter. I touched my lips, something I'd caught myself doing many times over the past three days.

"Yes, he's worth the risk."

"So, tell him what's eating away at you. If he feels the same way about you as you feel about him, he'll understand. And if he doesn't... Well, it wasn't meant to be."

"I'm... I'm scared."

"If you weren't, it would mean you didn't care for him enough to matter."

She was right. Damn, she was right. I needed to talk to Cade, and what I'd tell him would make his confession about shooting the man who killed his sister seem like a casual remark. And the worst part was, I had no idea when he'd be back. The stress was already eating away at my sanity, and I might not see him for weeks.

All I could do was keep balancing on the tightrope and pray I didn't fall off.

"You were right. It did help to talk."

Jessie leaned over and gave my shoulder a squeeze. "It'll work out. Fate brings two people together, but love keeps them there."

"I'd better go before I start crying."

She rummaged in her bag again and passed me a tissue. "Here. Maybe we'll meet again someday?"

"I hope so. Trust in fate, right?"

Jessie just smiled as I called Scarlet over and took her hand. The walk home was short, but if I'd known what fate had in store for me when I got there, I'd have headed in the opposite direction.

My phone rang as I put a dishful of lasagne into the oven, right after Scarlet had run up to her bedroom to fetch Eric to join us for dinner, and the momentary optimism that it could be Cade soon faded when Dean's name flashed up on the screen. Almost two weeks of radio silence, and now he called?

"Hi."

"Have you done it yet?"

No "how are you?" No "I realise how difficult things must be." Not even a greeting.

"I haven't been to the Blackwood offices for a while. It's difficult, seeing as I don't need to clean there anymore. Mostly I'm being a nanny."

*You know, doing my job?*

"Well, you'd better find a way, and quickly. I'm getting a lot of pressure here."

"I'll try soon, okay?"

I wouldn't. I needed to hold out until Cade got back, then throw myself at his mercy.

"Soon isn't good enough. It needs to be tonight. Whoever's behind this took down an entire server yesterday, and my boss is furious. Actually, furious doesn't even begin to describe it. He wants my blood."

"It's just a computer."

Wrong thing to say.

"It's not 'just' a fucking computer. It represents people's livelihoods, including mine. Who do you think pays for all the things you enjoy? Your music? Your clothes? Your books?"

At the moment? Cade. But until I'd spoken to him, I couldn't risk angering Dean.

"I'll try and go to the office."

"Wear the camera and the earpiece, and I'll talk you through what to do. There's a microphone bundled in with the camera if you've got any questions. If this doesn't work, I'll have to catch a flight tomorrow, and we'll figure out a way for you to get me in there so I can do the damn job myself."

Dean wanted to come to Virginia? Oh, hell no.

"I'll do it, okay? I'll find a way."

"Call me when you've got the kit on. The earpiece and camera should connect to your phone automatically. And hurry up. Time's getting critical."

"We're just about to eat dinner."

"Then you'll need to eat it later."

I could barely speak. "All right."

But I couldn't make Scarlet go without food. That wasn't fair to a child who shouldn't have been involved in this situation in the first place. I pulled the pan out of the oven, scooped a portion of the lasagne onto a plate, and microwaved it instead.

"Aren't you eating too, Taylor?"

"I'm not hungry, sweetie."

I fetched the package Dean sent, but my hands were shaking so badly it took me three tries to put the earpiece in and another five minutes in the bathroom arranging my hair this way and that to make sure it didn't show. Next, I put on the flower brooch containing Dean's hidden camera and avoided the temptation to kick something. Mainly because the one thing I really wanted to kick was on the other side of the country.

While Scarlet ate with Eric in front of the television, telling him he had to finish all of his food like a good elephant, I snuck back into the kitchen and called Dean. For once, he answered right away.

"How's it going?"

Awful. I kept thinking I was going to be sick. "Is the

camera working?"

"I've got a picture. Not much of a kitchen, is it?"

Why did he have to be so critical? It may only have been half the size of ours, but it had something no kitchen designer could install: a soul. I bit back a scathing remark and mumbled a bland response. "It's all right."

"You're doing good. I'm sorry I snapped earlier. You have no concept of the stress I'm under at the moment."

Oh, I had a good idea. "It's fine."

"Turn everything off for now—we need to save the batteries. Do you have the memory stick with you?"

"It's in my purse."

"Perfect. Phone when you're about to go into the building."

The building? Through a portal to hell, more like. I was going to hell. I tried to put on a cheerful expression as I called out to Scarlet.

"Guess where we're going?"

"Wonder World?"

"Not quite. We're going to visit Emmy at the office. Isn't that exciting?"

"I'd rather go to Queen Ella's castle."

"So would I, but we need to thank Emmy for lending us her airplane to go on that trip, okay?" On second thoughts, that was a bad idea. Because Dean would be listening to every word, and letting him know I'd swanned off on vacation rather than taking his work seriously would only invite trouble. "Or maybe we'll just stop by for a chat."

"I know! I'll take her one of my pictures. Do you think she'd like a picture?"

Brilliant idea, and it took a five-year-old to come up with it. My brain was so fried I could barely remember how to tie my own shoelaces.

"I'm sure she'd love that. But we need to be quick, because the car's on its way."

# CHAPTER 30

TWO DAYS SINCE he'd got back from Wonder World, and Cade wanted to be anywhere but in The Darkness's clubhouse. Actually, no. While anywhere else would have been preferable, there was one place he desperately needed to be, and that was at home, trying to work out whether he'd blown his chance with Taylor.

The more time he spent with her, the more time he wanted to spend with her. Although she'd been a little standoffish at first, she'd loosened up during their trip to Florida, and he'd barely been able to keep his hands off the girl who shone through. Then his self-control had lost its battle with alcohol and he'd kissed her. Yes, she'd kissed him back, but when sobriety hit the next morning, things between them had been decidedly awkward.

Cade's brief dalliance with Tia had left his heart fragile, so he backed off, and a day in the Animal Kingdom with his two favourite girls had left them all smiling. But then, in a moment of madness, he'd told Taylor about his past.

As soon as the first words left his mouth, he wanted to suck them back in, but once he'd started the story, he couldn't stop. He'd asked if she wanted to run in horror, but he knew the answer from watching her face. She hated what he'd done.

Yet, even if revealing his secret meant he'd lost her, a small part of his brain told him it was for the best. She talked about forgiveness being important, but if she couldn't get over his past, it was better to find that out sooner rather than later. As long as she stuck around for Scarlet, Cade would have to deal with the fact that he and Taylor weren't meant to be together.

But for now, he was stuck in limbo, wearing a grubby T-shirt, a pair of boxers, and a voice recorder clipped to his pubes. The glamorous life of a covert agent.

Doc farted and held out his hand. "Pass the chips, would ya?"

Cade duly handed over the bowl, resisting the urge to sigh. Doc liked horror movies, and if Cade had to sit through one more poorly acted zombie flick, he'd turn into one of the living dead himself.

But the other option was going to bed, and if the last two nights were anything to go by, he'd lie awake into the early hours thinking of all the things he should have done differently with Taylor.

"Want another beer?" he asked Doc.

"Better not. My old lady's put me on a diet."

Cade levered his ass off the sofa to fetch another drink for himself, plus something to eat that wasn't potato-based. A piece of fruit, maybe, if there was any left.

He'd gotten halfway to the kitchen when the roar of bikes outside announced an imminent arrival. But whose? Apart from Boone, who'd headed upstate to negotiate some deal pertaining to the gang's crystal meth enterprise, everyone was home. Which meant either there was a group of unwelcome visitors, or

Hawk and his buddies had stopped by.

"Hawk?" he asked Doc.

The man was already halfway to his feet, revolver in hand. In the chair opposite, Tank had woken up and was fumbling under the seat for the shotgun Cade knew he kept stashed there. Cade reached for his pistol too. The three of them tensed, ready for whoever was at the door.

Hawk. It was Hawk. But the relief that The Darkness wasn't under attack only lasted moments, because Hawk's arrival brought its own problems.

"What the fuck happened?" Tank asked as Hawk walked in half carrying Snake, who was staggering at his side. Cade's eyes tracked downwards to the red stain spreading out over Snake's jeans. Somebody had tied a T-shirt around it, and above that, a belt made a makeshift tourniquet, but the wound still oozed blood.

"Snake got shot. Doc, you need to look at this."

Doc got his nickname because he'd completed two years of medical school before deciding life in a white coat wasn't for him. He'd ditched his degree in favour of his Harley, but according to Boone, his skills still came in useful whenever any of the gang needed stitching up. Now, he dropped his gun and followed Hawk towards the back of the building.

"Pool, we need the first aid kit in Pop's apartment. Tank, watch the door."

Cade ran to get the bag, thankful it had been put back in the right place after the Ginger episode. As he hauled it off the shelf, he tried to work out what the hell had happened. Was this something to do with another home invasion? Or a completely unrelated incident? Either way, Snake needed medical attention and fast.

As Cade grasped the first aid kit, the front door opened again and Sailor strode in with Smith. Each of them carried a duffel bag.

Fuck.

Cade knew what had just happened, and the thought of helping Snake made the vein in his temple pulse in anger. But with a dozen armed bikers plus Hawk and his crew in the building, now wasn't the time to make his protest. Thank goodness he was wearing the digital recorder, because the potential for catching something incriminating just increased a hundredfold.

When he got to Wolf's lair, the older man was pacing up and down behind the couch where Snake was lying with his pants off. Doc knelt beside him, examining the wound with the help of a flashlight held by Sailor.

"What the hell happened tonight, boy?" Wolf asked.

"We fucked up, that's what," Hawk muttered.

"Still got the job done, though," Snake said, then gasped as Doc prodded his leg.

What did that mean? They'd stolen the loot? They'd murdered another innocent civilian?

Doc filled a syringe with clear liquid and injected it into Snake's thigh before snapping on a pair of latex gloves. "I don't think the bullet hit anything vital, but there's a lot of blood."

Hawk peered over the back of the couch. "Can you deal with it? Or do we need help?"

Snake waved a hand, smiling now. "It's fine. Whatever Doc gave me was the real deal. Barely stings at all."

Doc didn't share his confidence. "I'll need to get the bullet out, then stitch him up. Not gonna be an easy job, but this wouldn't be easy to explain in the emergency room."

A flicker of worry passed over Hawk's face, the first time Cade had seen him look anything but controlled. "If we go to the hospital, it'll take the cops three seconds to connect Snake with the other two gunshot victims."

Two? Shit.

"What happened out there?" Wolf asked.

"Our target hired extra security, and we didn't know about it. They were good. Almost too good. Came out of nowhere after we got inside and started shooting at us."

"Who got hurt other than Snake?"

"The target. I put one between his eyes. And a guy on the security team. They were from Blackwood."

Cade gripped the edge of the desk he was leaning against for support. Blackwood? They'd gone up against Blackwood? This day got worse and worse. How badly had one of Cade's colleagues been injured? He pictured Emmy's face when she heard the news. She wouldn't be visibly upset like Wolf. No, she'd put on that blank mask she wore when she plotted her next move, and that move wouldn't be pleasant for any of the men standing in front of him.

"What about the kids?" Wolf asked.

"They're okay. Smith got them out of the way as soon as all hell broke loose."

That was something, at least. Cade was surprised they'd cared.

The door opened again, and Hawk's hand went to the gun in his waistband before relaxing as Mouse walked in.

The smaller man glanced at Snake then screwed his

eyes up and turned away. "There's blood. I hate blood. I hate it. I hate it. I hate it."

Smith left Snake's side to stand in front of Mouse, addressing him head-on while he shielded him from the gore.

"It's okay. He'll be okay."

"Did you get it?"

Smith stuck out his arm and beckoned, and Hawk carried over one of the duffel bags. "It" turned out to be a slim black laptop, complete with a power cord.

"Here you go."

Mouse hugged it to his chest and hurried into the kitchen, and for the tenth time that evening, Cade wondered what the hell was going on. Hawk had killed a man, Snake was injured, and Mouse cared about a laptop? It didn't even look like a fancy one. How much did a computer cost nowadays? A thousand bucks? Two at most.

Silence fell in the room as Doc worked on Snake. The others assisted, with Sailor continuing to hold the flashlight, Smith passing items from the first aid kit, and Hawk speaking quietly to Snake, only stopping every so often to check on Mouse in the kitchen. Wolf leaned against the wall on the far side of the room, watching, and Cade avoided making eye contact with the man. He felt out of place, an interloper, but since nobody had told him to leave, he kept quiet and gathered all the information he could.

Over an hour passed before Doc stood up, knees cracking. "Reckon that's got it, but I can't guarantee there won't be a scar."

"One more won't hurt," Snake mumbled.

"You'll be out of action for a few weeks. Gotta keep

the weight off that leg."

"Can't you just give me some pills or something? I ain't got time to sit around on my ass all day."

"If you move, the wound'll tear, and you'll need someone better with a needle and thread than me to fix it up again."

"What about the shop? I need to work. Got bills to pay."

"I'll take care of them," Smith said. "Already told you that."

"I don't want no charity."

What had happened to the money from the other robberies? The loot from those totalled hundreds of thousands of dollars. Unless the gang was sitting on it for some reason or they hadn't managed to fence it yet... But if they weren't making cash, then what was the point of all this?

Quick footsteps sounded on the linoleum floor, and Mouse popped out of the kitchen doorway. "Got it! I got the name. That was the easiest one yet, or maybe I'm just getting better at this."

"Who is it?" Hawk said.

"Reuben Lodge. Also known as Barney Sunshine."

Hawk's eyes widened slightly. "The TV presenter? Aw, fuck."

"No, not fuck. He's easier to research. Reuben Lodge lives with his boyfriend in Colonial Beach, and I've already got the layout of the house because he posts pictures of it all over Instagram."

Cade knew Barney Sunshine. Scarlet had been watching his show on Cade's last visit home. Each episode, Sunshine and his sidekick, some weird blue puppet-dog, took a bunch of kids on an adventure, everything from helping out on a ranch to sneaking behind the scenes at a Broadway show.

Hawk began pacing again. "We've got to change the pattern. Blackwood's involved now, and they're worse than the cops. We shot one of their men, and Charles Black won't ever let that go. Don't even get me started on his wife."

"So what's the plan, boss?" Sailor asked.

"Snake's out. We start hitting hard and fast, as many as we can before the fire gets too hot, then we lie low until it dies down."

"That could take years."

Hawk shrugged. "The ring won't stop, and neither will we."

The ring? What ring? Cade was digging through his memories for any mention of a ring when Hawk stopped in front of him.

"We need a lookout, Pool Boy. You in?"

"Huh?"

"Tomorrow night. We need another man to replace Snake, and Pop says you've got guts."

"What's the job? Is it these robberies that have been on the news?"

"Yeah. Robberies. Right."

"Look, I don't have a problem with anything The Darkness does, but shooting innocent men isn't something my conscience agrees with."

Dammit. Why did Cade say that? He should have just agreed, then found a way to get out of it. He needed to perfect the art of thinking first and speaking after. Had he learned nothing from his cock-ups with Taylor?

He waited for the recriminations, for Hawk's wrath,

but they didn't come. Instead, the man began to laugh.

"You believe everything the media tells you?"

"No, but..."

"If CNN reported that little green men had landed on the White House lawn, would you question it?"

"Of course I..."

"And if NBC said Violet Miller was secretly a man, you'd believe them?"

The up-and-coming movie star? Cade scoffed. "She's clearly not..."

"So what makes you think these men are innocent?"

# CHAPTER 31

WHAT MADE CADE think those men were innocent? Well... Blackwood had studied the pattern of the crimes —homes in wealthy areas, usually a family, stolen goods, the man of the house always left dead. But they hadn't found anything to connect the victims other than their lifestyle. What had they missed?

Hawk beckoned Cade over to the couch, and Snake shuffled far enough along it that Cade could perch on the end. Hawk pulled over a dining chair and straddled the seat, leaning forwards over the back, waiting.

"I don't know the answer to that," Cade admitted.

"Every man who's died by our hands was a member of The Ring. We've taken out nine so far, but by our reckoning, there are over a hundred of them. And it's like playing whack-a-mole. You take out one, and another pops up in his place."

"What's The Ring?"

"Virginia's most fucked-up network of paedophiles, and the group that murdered Snake's daughter. My god-daughter."

Snake screwed his eyes shut. "They raped her. My kid. Six years old, and they took it in turns. Mouse found the footage."

Cade felt physically sick, and he swallowed hard to force down the bile rising in his throat. Paedophiles? If this was true, it changed everything, at least for him. He couldn't hate Hawk for doing the same as he'd once done, although Hawk's vendetta seemed a hell of a lot more calculated. Why go down that route?

"Couldn't you have turned the tape over to the cops and let them deal with it?"

"You think we didn't try that? We sent it anonymously to the chief of police, and you know what happened? He buried it. Six weeks passed, and nothing happened. Not one thing. In the end, Snake called for an update, said he'd heard rumours of a video, and the chief brushed him off."

"We couldn't figure the guy out," Smith said.

Hawk shrugged. "Man was evasive as fuck, so I took a trip over to his condo and borrowed his computer. We figured we'd get Mouse here to check his emails."

"At that point, we thought he was just slacking," Snake added.

"But the guy got home while I was still in the house, saw his computer was missing, stepped onto the back deck, and ate a bullet." Hawk shook his head. "Didn't even hesitate. That's when we realised we'd stumbled across something far bigger than we ever imagined."

"He was part of the network?"

"Member number 103. The way it works is that each member only communicates with two others on a day-to-day basis—one they receive from, and one they send to, and they're identified by a number rather than a name. The ringleader sends out a message to number one—might be a photo, a video, or details of an event. Photos or videos just get forwarded around the ring. Sometimes the sick freaks add comments, and those aren't something any of us enjoy reading."

"Fuckers need castrating," Sailor muttered.

"If they're interested in an invitation to an event, they add their number to the list before they send it to the next person."

"What kind of events?" Cade asked, even though he wasn't sure he wanted to know.

"Parties. Live shows so they can get their sick kicks."

"Where are they held? Why not go after a whole group in one go?"

"We don't know where. As best we can ascertain, if their application to attend is accepted, they receive the address by snail mail, then they're instructed to burn it. We suspect the location changes. I know I'd move it around if I was organising something so whacked."

"So, what? You're working your way backwards and forwards around the ring?"

"Only backwards now. Barney Sunshine's number ninety-four. We tried both directions and took out member 104, but 105 died in a house fire before we could pay him a visit. Fell asleep while smoking, apparently."

"Ninety-four left? With the greatest respect, are you crazy?"

Hawk chuckled. "Pretty much, yeah. I know it's not ideal, but the cops are useless, and we're not letting the members of The Ring get away scot-free. And there's always the hope that the ringleader will make a mistake and we'll be able to find him before the countdown reaches zero. What do you say? Are you in or out?"

"You could borrow Rev again," Snake suggested.

Hawk shook his head. "Rev isn't careful enough. Pool?"

Only one little word was required, and it could change everything. Telling Hawk he was out would potentially invite repercussions from a man who'd shown he wasn't afraid to kill if it helped him to reach his ultimate goal.

And that goal was one Cade fundamentally agreed with.

Saying he was in would lead him down a dark path, one where two wrongs might not make a right, but where that second wrong had the power to save a lot of children from unnecessary suffering. Kids like Christie and Snake's daughter. And Scarlet. If anything ever happened to her, Cade would make it his life's work to get through all ninety-four on the list.

But siding with Hawk would also pit Cade against Blackwood. Hawk had injured one of their men, perhaps worse, and if Emmy's past exploits were any indicator, she'd be out for blood. Hell, the sharks were probably circling right now.

There was a third option—for Cade to agree to join Hawk's team and somehow explain the situation to Emmy before he got any deeper into this mess. Surely she'd show some understanding if she found out what Hawk was doing? And she and her husband had connections to every law enforcement agency there was, so maybe they could negotiate a more legal operation than simply bursting into paedophiles' homes and shooting them?

With thoughts jumbled in his head, Cade took the sensible option and stalled. "How did you guys meet, anyway? I mean, it's a big thing to join up for a job like this one."

"I've known Snake since we were kids, and I met

Sailor when we were both in the military."

That much, Blackwood had already worked out.

"And I met Snake when I went on a bender and decided to get a tattoo one night," Smith said. "Passed out on the floor before he could tell me to piss off, and he and Maggie took pity on me and let me sleep it off on their sofa. Never did get that ink, but I made a couple of new friends out of the experience. And I knew Mouse from college."

Wolf pushed off the back wall, where he'd been leaning in silence for the past hour.

"I don't like it. Got a bad feeling. I say you should stop this instant."

"We can't, Pop. Not while there's men out there willing to prey on kids."

"Haven't they realised there's a problem?" Cade asked. "With so many members getting taken out in such a short time?"

"The ringleader must know, but as far as we can determine, he hasn't come clean to the others, and because of the convoluted way they use to communicate, none of them've connected the dots. Each time we take a link out, the number before them gets instructed to send to a new person, but that only happens once for each of them."

Cade's mind cycled through the system. "But what about the person who replaced member 104? The person before him must have changed nine times by now."

"That's where it gets interesting. We believe the person in that slot is connected to the upper echelons, and whoever's running that email address knows what he's doing when it comes to security. Mouse hasn't been able to crack it yet. The rest of the fuckers try to cover their tracks, but we've always found a chink in their armour."

"Come on, Pool Boy," Sailor said. "Tomorrow we're gonna peel Barney fucking Sunshine's chink wide open, and you're either with us or against us."

"Sick bastard's working with kids," Smith reminded Cade. "The TV station's serving him up a fresh batch every damn week. You're a brother now. You can't stand by and let this go."

Wolf began speaking, and everyone focused on him. "One more. One more, and then you re-evaluate. The Ring is one fucked-up freak show, but I'm not losing my boy over it. Pool, Smith's right. You're one of us now, and you need to back the club on this one. Got it?"

Wolf flicked his cut back as he said the last sentence, the gun stuck in his waistband clear for all to see. Cade felt vastly underdressed in his boxer shorts, and he'd left his gun behind the bar when he picked up the first aid kit.

"Got it."

He couldn't have given any other answer, not if he wanted to walk out of there.

# CHAPTER 32

CADE'S FIRST PRIORITY when he got out of Wolf's apartment was to get a message to Blackwood. His second phone was in his closet, tucked into the pocket of a faded pair of jeans. With the walls so thin, he couldn't risk a conversation, but the control room worked twenty-four seven, and if he emailed them, they'd find Emmy or Dan straight away.

Where should he start? With confirmation that Hawk was behind the home invasions? That they weren't simply home invasions, but had a higher purpose? Or with The Ring and their vile activities? The last thing Cade wanted was for Blackwood to act against Hawk without taking into account his motive.

His *real* motive.

Since Cade was mentally composing the message as he fiddled with the sticky handle on his bedroom door, it took a few seconds for the faint cry from the next room to register. He paused, listening, and then it came again.

"No! Get off me!"

The sound was muffled, but there was no mistaking Ginger's voice.

Oh, hell. Of all the nights, Deke picked tonight to start his shit again. Asshole. But Cade couldn't just ignore it.

He blocked out the pain in his shoulder as he crashed into the door, and the flimsy wood flew back and bounced off the wall behind. Deke was on the bed, jeans and boxers pulled down around his knees with Ginger naked underneath him. She was struggling, but his weight pinned her to the filthy mattress as he held her wrists above her head with one hand and covered her mouth with the other.

"Leave her alone."

Cade grabbed a leg and pulled Deke onto the floor, but he slipped on a discarded sock and landed next to the asshole. The faded laminate was solid, and almost as bad, sticky. Cade dodged a swinging fist and scrambled to his feet, but Deke ran at him from a crouch, roaring like a wounded lion. The pants around his knees meant he struggled to get any momentum, and Cade sidestepped, but Deke caught him with one arm and they both went down again. Fuck. Deke landed with an elbow in Cade's solar plexus, and Cade's stomach spasmed as he gasped for breath. That gave Deke an opening for a punch to the face. Pain radiated out from Cade's nose, probably broken, as blood dripped down his cheeks, but he still managed to jerk sideways when Deke tried for a second blow. The bigger man let out a howl of pain as his fist connected with the floor.

Cade got a knee up, and a second after it connected with Deke's privates, the prick puked. Vomit splashed on Cade as a shadow appeared over both of them, and then Hawk hauled Deke back and threw him into the corner.

His head must have connected with the corner of the closet, because he didn't get up again, and the loudest sound in the room came from Ginger, sobbing on the bed.

It only took seconds for Hawk to work out what had happened—Ginger's puffy eyes and lack of clothing coupled with Deke's semi-hard dick flopping over his thigh were the giveaways—and he quickly shrugged out of his own jacket and threw it around Ginger's shoulders. Cade stayed on the floor, trying to get his breath back before he sat up.

"Did he...?" Hawk asked Ginger.

She must have nodded, because a string of curses left Hawk's mouth, finishing up with, "I'll kill that motherfucker."

"Probably high again." Sailor's voice came from behind Cade, and he stooped to pick up a baggie of white crystals from beside the bed. "Looks like he's been sampling the product."

"Is he using again?" Hawk asked Ginger.

"He can't help it."

"Shit. Boone's gonna have to do something about him." Hawk turned to the closet and yanked the door open, then rifled through until he found a flimsy dress. He tossed it over to Ginger. "Put that on." Then to Cade, "You okay, Pool?"

"Reckon the asshole broke my nose."

Hawk held out a hand and pulled Cade to his feet. "We'll get you some ice. Sailor, get some ice, would ya?"

Only Sailor never got as far as the door. He stopped three feet away and bent to pick up a small black object. "What's this?"

With all the other assaults on his body, the tug as the digital recorder got pulled out of Cade's pubic hair hadn't even registered. But there it was, pinched between Sailor's thumb and forefinger as he peered down at it.

It was Hawk who realised its purpose first. Cade didn't even see his fist coming, only the stars after it connected with the edge of his jaw and landed him next to Deke. He did catch the blur of Hawk's boot coming towards his side, but he couldn't move fast enough to avoid it slamming him in the ribs.

"You're a cop?"

Cade opened his mouth to deny it, but the only thing that came out was a groan.

"I'll kill you. Don't give a fuck about the badge."

This time, Cade saw Hawk wind his arm back for another punch, but all he could do before his vision faded was click the panic button on the side of his watch and pray.

# CHAPTER 33

"BIT LATE TO be going to the office, isn't it?" the driver asked as we purred through Rybridge in a town car. Emmy's assistant had apologised for not having an SUV with a bodyguard available and sent a uniformed chauffeur instead. Oh, the hardship.

A police car flew past in the other direction, siren blaring, and I paused until it faded before answering.

"Emmy's still there, apparently. We just wanted to stop by to say hello as it's been a while since she last saw Scarlet. I thought it'd be quieter outside of working hours."

And I was really, really hoping that Mack would have gone home by now. I glanced at my watch—almost nine and past Scarlet's bedtime. Emmy would most probably be furious at me for bringing her out at this hour, and rightly so, but I could hardly leave her home alone. The bag on the seat beside me contained her favourite books, Eric, snacks, and a blanket. Everything a reluctant spy needed to amuse a child while attempting to break into a high-security computer system.

The car pulled up outside the main gate at Blackwood, and the guard peered in through the back window.

"Isn't it kind of late to be out with a little one?"

Scarlet saved me once again. "I'm not tired at all! We're going to visit Emmy."

He sucked in a breath. "They're mighty busy in there."

I managed a smile. "She knows we're coming."

The guard shrugged. "All right, then."

The gates slowly opened, and I fumbled with the brooch to turn the camera on then did the same with the earpiece. A quick check in the mirror I carried in my purse showed my hair still covered everything up. Only my panicked breathing was likely to give the game away, and I forced myself to stay outwardly calm even as my heart raced.

"Do you want me to wait?" the driver asked as he stopped beside the main entrance.

"I'm not sure how long I'll be." But I *would* want to make a quick getaway. "I'll try to be quick. I'd be very grateful if you could wait."

He tipped his hat. "Yes, ma'am."

The only person in reception when I led Scarlet through the double doors was a cleaner, a girl my age moving the floor polisher back and forth as her head bobbed in time to the music playing through her headphones. A few weeks ago, that had been me, and just look at the shambles my life had disintegrated into since then. At least Scarlet was happier now. I had to look at the positives.

Even so, my feet dragged as we climbed up to the third floor, each step punctuated by Dean's voice in my ear.

"Why don't you take the elevator? Surely it's quicker?"

With Scarlet so close, I couldn't inform him that

nobody took the elevator around here, so I just kept climbing. The black doors of the Special Projects division loomed ahead, and I leaned forward into the retina scanner. The doors whooshed open, and we walked into... Oh, hell. What was going on?

I'd expected the usual skeleton staff, but there had to be fifteen people milling about in there. I spotted Emmy pacing in front of her office, and worse, the flame-haired figure of Mack seated behind her bank of screens. A dark-haired girl sat near Emmy, and when her gaze met mine, a chill ran through me and I quickly broke the eye contact. Logan glanced across from his desk and flicked one hand up in a wave before focusing on his screen again. Nobody else even noticed me except for Sloane, and Scarlet gripped my hand as she hurried over to us. I'd never met Sloane in person before, but I recognised her from my days of studying the staff directory.

"Taylor?"

I nodded.

"I'm so sorry, I should have called you. Now isn't a great time to meet with Emmy. There was an incident after we spoke, and things got a little busy."

"What's happening? Should I leave?"

In my ear, Dean piped up. "You're not leaving."

Sloane bit her lip and looked over her shoulder at her boss. "The problem's in Rybridge, so it's probably best if you stay here where we know it's safe. Maybe you could wait in the kitchen?"

"Sure, I can do that."

None of the tables were occupied, so I chose the one farthest from the door and settled Scarlet into a seat. Honestly, this was impossible.

"Do you want hot chocolate?" I asked her.

"Yes! And can you read to me?"

"As long as you help with the words."

"Okay. I've been practising at kindergarten."

We'd got through most of *Skipper the Cat*, much to Dean's annoyance, when Logan walked into the kitchen.

"You're still here?"

"Sloane thought it would be safer if I stayed."

He thought for a beat then nodded. "Yeah, she's probably right. One less thing to worry about."

"Did something bad happen?"

"Another one of those home invasions. You've seen them on the news?"

I'd started watching the headlines most days now, both to stay informed and to provide background noise in a quiet house while Scarlet was at kindergarten.

"Yes. The last one was a few weeks ago, right?"

He took a quick look at Scarlet, but she was engrossed in the book.

"Until tonight. They hit a house where Blackwood's got a monitoring contract. The wife hit the panic button, and we got there within five minutes, but there was a gunfight."

"Did anyone get hurt?"

Logan held up three fingers. "One of theirs, one of ours, and the husband..." He shook his head.

"Will our guy be okay?"

"The bullet only winged him, but Emmy's still pissed. She's got half of Blackwood out looking for the perps."

"Do you have any idea who did it?"

"Yeah, we do. They gave us the slip earlier. We're

checking their usual haunts, but we've got to tread carefully."

"Is there anything I can help with? A round of coffee?"

At least that way I'd be able to check on the situation out in the office. I got to my feet, ready.

"I'm sure everyone would appreciate that."

Except Emmy chose that moment to stick her head around the door. "Logan, we've got to go."

"Go where?"

"Cade just hit his emergency button, and I need all the manpower we've got."

My chest froze, while my hand grabbed for the nearest chair to stay upright. "Cade's hurt?"

"Daddy Cade?" Scarlet asked.

"He told her?" Emmy asked.

I nodded.

Emmy crouched down next to Scarlet. "Your daddy's gonna be fine. I just need to pick him up from where he's at."

"And then I can talk to him?"

"We'll see, okay?" Then to me, "You should take Scarlet home."

"Sloane said there could be criminals on the loose in Rybridge."

"Don't worry—I'm pretty sure we know where they are now."

A sob welled up in my throat, but with Dean listening in to the whole conversation, I hastily swallowed it. Cade was connected to the gang responsible for the home invasions, wasn't he? That was his undercover job.

"Why have your hands gone white?" Scarlet asked.

I looked down to see I'd gripped the back of the chair hard enough that my nails had left deep dents in the padding. Emmy reached out and squeezed my shoulder as I blinked back tears.

"Just look after Scarlet. Cade's a tough cookie, and we'll sort this out, okay?"

I managed to nod.

"Logan, we need to go *right now.*"

They hurried out, and when I risked a peek into the main office a minute later, it was in time to see Emmy disappearing out the door. Her parting words were to Sloane.

"Nate wants you in the basement. He needs a hand with something. Probably coffee."

Sloane followed her out, and I was left in silence with Scarlet.

Well, near silence.

"That was a stroke of luck," Dean said in my ear.

Luck? *Luck?* The man I'd fallen for was in danger, and my husband, who was far from the man I thought I'd married, brushed it off with a flippant remark. And now my world had been turned upside down yet again. I'd planned to explain everything to Cade, but what if he never came back?

I needed to buy myself time, and there was only one way to do that.

"Scarlet, can you wait here for a few minutes while I do something?"

"Are you sure Daddy will be okay?"

"That's what Emmy said."

"I'm tired."

I fetched the blanket and wrapped it around Scarlet's shoulders. "I won't be long, sweetie. Promise."

I almost bent to press a kiss to her forehead, but with Dean watching, I couldn't do that, not without him asking awkward questions. Instead, I fished out the memory stick I'd carefully placed in the side pocket of my purse and walked through to the main room, trying desperately to look as if I belonged there.

To my left, Mack's office lay empty, and when I hurried in there, her four screens showed floating pictures of her on a beach with a blond-haired man. Her husband? They looked a heck of a lot happier than I'd ever felt with Dean.

"Right, get down behind the tower on the left," Dean instructed. "Straighten up a bit so I can get a look at the ports. Yes, that's it."

Excitement tinged his voice, and I longed to rip out the earpiece and stamp on it. Soon after we got married, bored with doing nothing all day, I'd asked Dean if I could help with his business, and he'd brushed off my offer with, "It's all too complicated."

And now that he'd finally found something useful for me to do, I wanted to shove the damn memory stick down his throat and hope it hurt like hell when he shit it out.

But like the good wife he thought I was, I took the thing out of my pocket and prepared to insert it somewhere else.

"Which port?" I whispered.

"Bottom left."

"This one?"

"That's right. Leave it in place, and it'll wipe itself once the program's run."

I half expected alarms and fireworks when I pushed the thing home, but apart from a blinking green light, the machine remained quiet. Almost an anticlimax.

But even though no alarms went off, I couldn't afford to hang around. I checked nobody was watching then hurried through to the ladies' room, anticipating a difficult conversation with Dean. I very much suspected he'd have booked me a plane ticket to go back to California, and I wouldn't be getting on that flight. The last thing I needed tonight was another argument.

"That was terrifying," I whispered. "Do I need to do anything else?"

"No, that's it. But I think you should stick around in Virginia for a few more days in case we run into any more problems."

Oh, thank goodness. "If you think that's best."

"I do. I'll give you a call in a day or two, okay?"

"I'll be waiting."

Scarlet slept for the whole journey home, and she didn't even stir when the driver opened the door for us to get out.

"Do you need a hand carrying her, ma'am?"

"I can manage, but could you bring the bag?"

"Of course."

Safely inside, I made sure the doors were locked then carried Scarlet up to bed, hoping with every atom in me that I didn't have to break bad news about her father tomorrow. Emmy had said he was okay and she just needed to pick him up, but she wouldn't have had to empty the entire department to go with her if it were that straightforward.

"Sleep tight, sweetie," I whispered, giving Scarlet

the kiss I'd wanted to earlier.

She mumbled and turned over, and I backed out of the room, pulling the door closed behind me. At least one of us would get some rest tonight.

Down in the kitchen, I poured myself a large glass of wine. I was asking for a hangover, but I needed something to numb my anxiety, and without anyone to talk to, alcohol was the only answer.

"Don't leave us, Cade," I said softly, even though there was nobody to hear. "Please don't leave us."

# CHAPTER 34

CADE TRIED TO move, but his arms were stuck fast behind him. All that happened was an explosion of stars behind his eyeballs like someone had attacked his face with a cattle prod. Every tiny twitch sent a burst of agony through his nerve endings.

A painful attempt revealed he couldn't move his legs either, and breathing was difficult due to a tight band around his stomach. Fuck. This hurt more than shitting Legos. Eventually, he cracked open an eyelid and found Hawk seated in front of him in the same position as earlier—legs spread as he straddled a chair.

"The traitor awakes."

Oh, hell. The memories were coming back now. Deke, Ginger, the fight. Cade forced the other eye open as far as it would go—about halfway—and took in the view. Deke hadn't fared much better, although he'd been hog-tied and left in the corner rather than duct-taped to a chair. The faint smell of urine drifted through the room, and Cade spotted a yellow puddle spreading out from underneath the unconscious man. Smith and Sailor stood behind Hawk, and Ginger huddled on the bed, letting out the occasional whimper as she pressed herself against the wall. None of the other men seemed to notice her.

Hawk leaned forward on his elbows. "So, Pool Boy.

Talk."

In his army days, Cade had taken part in hostage drills, and the only information they'd been permitted to give was name, rank, and serial number. At Blackwood, he no longer had the latter two, and he didn't much feel like revealing his name either. He stayed silent.

Hawk nodded to Sailor, who stepped forwards and ran the edge of his boot down Cade's shin.

Well, at least that made the pain in his nose fade into perspective. Cade bit his lip to avoid crying out, and his mouth filled with the metallic tang of blood. How long had he been knocked out for? Did his emergency transmitter work? Was backup on its way? Or was he about to die in this hellhole?

He had no way of knowing.

And the stupid thing was, he half agreed with what Hawk was doing. Yes, his methods left a lot to be desired, but the ultimate goal was one they shared. And the chances were, Emmy might too. But Blackwood also had a paying client who wanted the gang behind the home invasions taken down. Cade hadn't known Emmy long enough to predict how she'd deal with that kind of conflict of interests.

"Who do you work for?" Hawk asked.

It didn't strike Cade as a great idea to admit that his employer was the reason Snake had needed to have a bullet dug out of his thigh earlier, so he clenched his teeth together as Sailor approached once more. The boot technique was crude yet effective, especially now Cade's grogginess had worn off.

Heavy footsteps sounded in the hallway outside, and Wolf appeared in the doorway, his pistol pointed at

Cade's head. There was no mistaking the anger in his eyes. It radiated out, cloying, constricting. Was that where The Darkness had got their name?

"Mouse tells me we've got a cop in our midst."

"Pop, I'm handling this."

"Bullshit. This is my club, and I'll deal with it." Wolf advanced on Cade, his hand steady. "The Darkness took you in, made you our brother, and this is how you repay us? By recording our conversations? What did you plan to do? Put my son in jail?"

Cade closed his eyes. Whatever he said to Wolf, it was sure to inflame the situation. Denial would clearly be a lie, and the truth? Well, Wolf wouldn't like that much either.

"Coward. Can't even watch your own death?" The *snick* of the hammer being cocked made Cade's guts twist. "Open your eyes, boy."

"Pop, don't do it."

"Stay back, son. Won't have no cancer spreading through my club."

"Not like this."

"I'm your father, Brendan, and as long as this double-crossing fuckhead is in my building, my decision rules."

Cade looked at Wolf, only to regret it as malice spread across the older man's face. His finger twitched on the trigger.

A vision of Scarlet popped into Cade's head, standing next to Taylor. He'd barely gotten to know his daughter, and he wouldn't even get the chance to say a proper goodbye. And Taylor? He should have done things differently on that flight home. Kissed her again rather than raking over his past, because now he'd never get the chance to tell her how he felt, and she'd be left with bad memories of him rather than good.

The corners of Wolf's mouth twitched, and Cade resisted the urge to close his eyes again. A coward was the last thing he wanted to be. He'd wanted to be a father, a boyfriend, and perhaps one day a husband. Now he'd be immortalised in an urn at Arlington, his life reduced to a simple marble plaque.

At least, that was what he thought until a blur of Ginger flew across the room.

"Don't!" she screamed.

The bullet whistled past Cade's ear and embedded itself in the wall beyond as Hawk snatched the gun away from Wolf.

"You may be my father, but your judgement's impaired, old man."

Sailor wrestled Wolf to the ground as Smith pulled Ginger out of the way. She began sobbing, and Smith looked perturbed by her tears. He raised an eyebrow at Hawk and shrugged.

"Get her out of here and find a box of tissues."

Hawk held up a roll of duct tape in front of Wolf. "Are you gonna let me handle this?"

"If anything happens to my club..."

"It won't. But I want answers first, and dead men can't speak." He turned back to Cade. "Just because I stopped my father from pulling the trigger doesn't mean I'm gonna let you live. Give me one good reason why *I* shouldn't shoot you right now."

Cade remained silent, desperately searching for the right answer, but before he could come up with something that wouldn't result in a painful death, an angel spoke from the back of the room. An angel with a crisp English accent and a confident tone.

"How about I give you thirty?"

# CHAPTER 35

WITH MOST OF the team at Blackwood out dealing with the aftermath of the home invasion, Emmy had rounded up whoever she could to pay a visit to The Darkness's clubhouse. Launching an attack on the place promised to be a logistical nightmare. The facility had once been a warehouse-slash-factory, and as their name suggested, the bikers didn't consider windows to be an important feature. There were three entrances—a front door that led into the residential area, another set into the rear which, according to Cade, accessed Wolf Hauser's private apartment, and a huge roller shutter at the far end where the auto shop was housed.

Half an hour after the first report of the shootings came in, the Blackwood surveillance unit two blocks away had spotted an Escalade with blacked-out windows speeding past, but a truck passing in the other direction meant they didn't catch the registration number. By the time they snuck up to The Darkness's warehouse, all was quiet. If the Escalade had gone there, it was safely tucked up behind the shutter.

So Emmy had been antsy about the place even before Cade's alarm went off, turning a bad day even worse.

But what was life without a few challenges?

The first part of the operation had gone surprisingly

well. Emmy and Ana took point with Dan and Mack tucked in behind. Mack had moaned like hell about leaving her computer screens, but she'd trained for every eventuality just like the rest of them.

"Look on the bright side," Emmy had told her. "At least you won't get eye strain."

"I might get shot at. How is that better than eye strain?"

"Stop being so negative and put your Kevlar on."

Another six of Blackwood's finest followed them through the front door, backed up by Logan's team of four at the rear. Carmen had climbed up the fire escape and onto the roof of the building opposite then hunkered down with her favourite sniper rifle, cheerfully announcing she was armed and ready. Secretly, Emmy sometimes thought she sounded a little too chipper at the prospect of having a moving target to fire at.

Agatha checked in over the radio, safely ensconced in the basement at Blackwood with Nate supervising. This would be the first live job she'd worked base on, and it'd be interesting to see how she performed. Emmy kept her fingers crossed. Mack needed a break before she burned out, and if Agatha could handle some of the smaller operations, it would take the pressure off.

Infrared analysis revealed a group of men sitting in a room to the right of the front door, a second cluster in a small room near the centre of the warehouse, and three men in Wolf's apartment at the rear. The plan was for Logan's four to start clearing from the back of the building, subduing the trio in their way while Emmy and Ana's ten took the front room. After that, they'd converge in the middle.

It seemed like a good plan until a shot rang out as Ana was picking the lock on the front door.

"Aw, fuck," Emmy whispered. Her grip tightened around her favourite Walther P88.

Ana didn't hesitate, just kept working until the door popped open a few seconds later. And in one way at least, it turned out that the gunshot was a good thing, because the six guys in the front room were all fidgeting around a doorway at the back, clearly trying to work out whether to intervene or not. Ten from Team Blackwood, six bikers, fifteen seconds, and it was over.

"Damn, I love Tasers," Dan muttered.

Slater and Isaiah stayed behind to sort out a longer-lasting solution while the other eight carried on down the corridor on the far side of the room.

"Our three are sleeping now," Logan said. "One of them had a bullet wound to the thigh."

"Then I guess that's who injured Shaun earlier."

"We've also got a laptop here, and the case next to it is monogrammed with the initials of this evening's victim."

"It's all slotting into place."

"Everything's still clear outside," Agatha put in.

Time to carry on. The building was a fucking nightmare. If anyone started shooting in there, body bags would be needed. The layout offered little cover, dead ends abounded, and the stakes were high on both sides.

And then came the words Emmy really didn't want to hear.

"Give me one good reason why *I* shouldn't shoot you right now."

Ana rolled her eyes but kept her gun steady as Emmy stepped forwards.

"How about I give you thirty?" Okay, so it was more like fifteen, but Emmy reckoned each of her people was worth two of anyone else's. Hawk started to bring his gun up, but Emmy stopped him with a sharp, "Stand still if you want to keep your head, and that goes for the rest of you assholes too."

"Go to hell," Hauser senior growled.

"I'd love to, but Satan's got a restraining order against me."

The old man lurched in her direction, but his son stopped him. "Stay where you are, Pop." Then to Emmy, "Who the fuck are you?"

"I'm the darkness to your sunny day."

Hawk just glared at her.

"Fine." Emmy jerked her head at Cade. At least, she assumed it was Cade under all the blood. "His boss."

"That doesn't answer my question."

"Emmy Black."

Hawk let out a long breath. "Motherfucker."

"Pretty sure I never did that. But I see you know who I am, which is good. It means you know I'm not lying when I tell you that you're surrounded by highly trained special-forces operatives with varying degrees of trigger-finger itchiness. Guys, say hi." A chorus of greetings came from the corridor outside. "See? If you try any shit, none of you'll get out alive. And we'll take this whole club apart. We've got you on the home invasions, and I'll work with the ATF and the DEA on your little faux pas relating to gun running and crystal meth."

"What did you do to the rest of our people?"

Emmy tutted. "They're sleeping on the job."

Hawk cursed again under his breath, and Emmy knew he was looking for a way out. Sailor too, although she suspected the big man was more brawn than brains. Smith was the unknown. Smart for sure, but did he present a threat in a situation like this? The older man in the room she recognised as Wolf, and although his eyes were filled with hatred, he didn't look to have a weapon. Then there was the unconscious dude and the woman in the too-short dress. Emmy would keep an eye on her. Women could present an unexpected threat, something she turned to her advantage all too often.

But in the meantime, Emmy decided to throw down another card. "I know who you are, Hauser. I know you were a good soldier once, and I also know that after the incident in Ukraine, you lost your nerve. Is that why you started targeting civilians instead of men who could fight back?"

"Emmy, no." Cade's voice came out as a croak. "That's not what's happening."

"What are you talking about?"

"It's not what you think." Cade coughed and seemed to be struggling for breath.

"Dan, get in here and help. We need water too."

It didn't take long for Dan to turn up with a full glass, and as she crouched at Cade's side and spoke softly to him, Emmy caught the words "broken ribs." It didn't take a genius to work out whose big feet had helped with that. She'd take that up with Sailor later.

Cade took a few sips of water and made another attempt to speak. "Those men getting killed are paedophiles. Hawk's trying to stop some network called

The Ring."

Emmy let her features fall into a blank mask as she mulled over that latest piece of information. Was Cade right? There'd been no indication of that kind of activity in any reports she'd seen, but he'd been right in the middle of things and she hadn't. To her surprise, it was Agatha who filled in more details.

"I know who they are. They may be called The Ring, but in reality, it's more like a necklace, and there are a whole bunch of them. One for each state, and a year or so ago, they began expanding overseas. I worked on a joint project led by the FBI to dig for more information, but they're so, so slippery. We barely got anywhere, and the project got shut down because of funding issues. But after I left, I sort of turned it into a hobby. Every so often, I pick up a thread and take a prod at their servers."

"I've heard of them too," Mack added from outside.

"Which ring are you after?" Emmy asked Hawk. "The Virginia one?"

The shock on his face was something he couldn't hide, mirrored by Sailor and Smith.

"There's more than one?"

"My sources indicate one for each state, plus a number overseas."

"Fuck." Hawk's bravado faltered, and he sat on the edge of the bed. "The Virginia ring's got over a hundred members, and if that's replicated in every state..."

"Not a palatable thought, is it?"

"The Texas ring is the largest," Agatha said. "Estimated at over three hundred members. California's lagging just behind, followed by Minnesota. Each ring has a leader, but we believe they're governed by a small board. It's scarily organised, much the same way as a large conglomerate. Not only that, they're fanatical about security, and they only ever use numbers, not names. Local leaders are designated by number one. The CEO, if you like, is called Zero. Dues are paid in virtual currency, and membership isn't cheap."

"Like Bitcoin?"

Hawk looked up sharply, and Emmy shook her head to indicate she wasn't speaking to him.

"Yes, Bitcoin. They were an early adopter. Before that, they used a convoluted system of offshore bank accounts, and I've got no doubt they'll switch again if something better comes along."

"And their activities?"

Agatha sucked in a breath. "Sick. On a day-to-day basis, it's photos and videos. They've been experimenting with a webcam service. Then there are the petting parties, and one-on-one sessions start at six figures."

Emmy's curse echoed Hawk's. "Look into it. If there's a connection between this Ring and any of our victims, I want to know about it."

"We've already got the evidence," Smith muttered. He'd turned from cocky to sullen.

Decisions, decisions. Blackwood had been hired by the widow Granger to find the people who shot her husband and ensure they got convicted. Or accidentally died while resisting arrest—Mrs. Granger hadn't seemed too concerned which. She was paying a generous hourly rate, plus a success bonus. The easy thing to do would be to drop Hawk and his buddies off at the police station and take Cade home to lick his wounds, but that would leave loose ends, and Emmy hated loose ends.

"Why did you turn vigilante? Why not take this evidence you claim to have and let the cops deal with it?"

Smith looked as though he wanted to speak, but Emmy pointed at Hawk. He was the leader, the biggest threat, and it was him she wanted to understand.

"Because the first member of The Ring we found was Steven Garland."

"As in Chief Garland?"

"The one and only."

"He shot himself."

"Because he realised I'd taken his laptop. He took out his service revolver, walked onto the back deck, stuck the barrel in his mouth, and pulled the trigger."

"You watched?"

"From his bedroom window."

"You didn't help?"

"If I'd known at the time why he did it, I'd have helped him to load the gun."

Emmy had never been keen on Chief Garland, and the rift between them had only grown when he accused her of killing her husband several years previously. When she'd heard the news of the dear Chief's death, she'd popped the cork on the bottle of Krug she kept chilling in the fridge for a special occasion.

Okay, bottles.

And there may have been a small party.

For about two hundred people. Nobody else had liked him either.

And of course, Emmy hadn't killed her husband, even though doing so would have made her a very rich woman. A billionaire, in fact, several times over. Emmy's husband was generous enough with his cash that the issue of money never came between them, and it also meant that her judgement was never clouded by the size of her bank account. Which was why she didn't really give a fuck about Mrs. Granger's success bonus. Blackwood's professional reputation was always an issue, but doing what was right trumped everything in Emmy's eyes.

Oh, and did anybody mention that her moral compass pointed in a different direction to most other people's?

She broke into a grin and beckoned Hawk to follow her. "Come on. Let's have a chat."

"A chat?" The unspoken words at the end of that sentence: *have you been smoking something?*

"Sure. A chat. A conversation I will absolutely deny ever took place should anyone ask me."

Hawk responded with a tentative smile.

"In that case, lead the way."

Emmy turned to the room. "We'll be back shortly. Just stay still, and nobody'll get hurt, yeah?"

Silence.

She turned to Hawk, eyebrow raised, and he nodded.

"Do as she says."

"Thank you. Dan, take Cade back to the office. Agatha, get Dr. Stanton ready and waiting. Ana, if anyone else moves, make sure they don't get that chance again."

Ana gave Emmy a salute as she motioned Hawk to walk down the corridor in front of her. The two women didn't need to speak to know each other's plans.

Ana's silence said, *We're all behind you.*

# CHAPTER 36

"WHERE ARE WE going?" Hawk asked.

Emmy smiled inside. Good. He already understood where the balance of power lay.

"Well, since you ruined my dinner plans, I thought we'd get something to eat."

"Food? You're thinking of food?"

"Got to keep my strength up. Besides, my nutritionist's got me on this raw food diet, and I really need a plate of fries."

Hawk tried to hide his eye roll, but Emmy caught it.

"If you want fried shit, there's a twenty-four-hour diner not too far down the road. Do you want to take my vehicle or yours?"

"Seeing as Snake had a hole in his leg, I'm assuming your Escalade could do with a valet?"

A couple of guesses there, but educated ones.

Hawk paused for a beat. "You'd better drive."

Emmy fished the keys to the Ford Explorer she was driving out of her pocket and radioed Agatha.

"We're gonna need another vehicle over here. Dan's using one to bring Cade back."

"On it."

Before she bleeped open the car, Emmy paused a few feet away. "What are you carrying?"

"Springfield Armory XD."

"How do you find the action on that?"

"Is that a serious question?"

"Why wouldn't it be?"

Hawk hesitated, then shrugged. "It's done the job so far."

"Do me a favour and drop the magazine out, yeah?"

With Emmy's Walther still in her hand, he had little choice but to comply. As a gesture of faith, she did the same and tucked the magazine into her pocket while the pistol went into the holster at her side. Hawk most likely had a backup gun somewhere, as did Emmy—a Beretta strapped to her ankle. Plus a second Walther in the door pocket, one switchblade at her wrist, and another under the sun visor.

They'd barely got half a mile when Hawk sucked in a breath and put his seat belt on. Emmy's driving wasn't that bad, surely? If she'd been a real bitch, she'd have brought Dan to act as chauffeur. Hmmm. Hopefully, Cade would get back to Blackwood in one piece. Wouldn't it be ironic if he survived a beating from a gang of bikers only to succumb to Dan's leaden foot?

A worrying thought, but there was no time to dwell on it.

"On the left," Hawk said.

Emmy put on the indicator and parked up next to a battered Honda on the far side of the lot. Apart from an ancient pickup with two flat tyres, the rest of the spaces were empty.

"Popular place."

"It gets busy early in the evening, but not so many folks go out late in Oakley."

*Living here must be a riot.* Emmy climbed out first,

but Hawk overtook her to hold the door as they went into the restaurant. Manners hadn't bypassed him completely, then. A brunette looked up from the counter as they entered, and she smiled broadly when she saw Hawk.

"What can I get for you guys?"

Hawk gestured for Emmy to go first.

"Cheeseburger and fries with a chocolate milkshake."

"Make that two cheeseburgers, and I'll have a root beer."

Someone had tried to modernise the place, as evidenced by the freshly painted walls and the menus adorned with cutesy clip art. But the counter still sagged, and Ol' Blue Eyes played quietly from the jukebox in the corner. On the plus side, there was a rear exit and plenty of windows should an escape be needed.

And through the plate glass at the front, it was easy to see the squad car that rolled up outside the front door.

"Oh, fuck," Hawk muttered.

"Relax. They don't know anything. If there was trouble, someone would have radioed through."

No, the cops working the home invasion case were all too busy bumbling around in Rybridge to take a trip out to Oakley tonight.

The overweight officer tipped his hat to Emmy and eyed up Hawk before settling back onto one of the stools in front of the counter. The metal legs creaked ominously. Hopefully, he didn't plan on hanging around for the night, because that would make the conversation Emmy wanted to have difficult. They couldn't just leave because firstly, that would look dodgy, and secondly, Emmy was bloody hungry.

"Coffee please, Sandy," he said, fishing through his pockets for change.

Emmy flashed the cop a smile. "Let me treat you. It's the least I can do to show my gratitude for keeping us all safe at night."

"Much obliged, ma'am."

Any possible suspicion: averted. She dropped a twenty on the counter and looped her arm through Hawk's, heading for a booth in the far corner. Just another couple out for a late meal as opposed to two warring factions about to negotiate their next move.

Fifteen awkward minutes of small talk passed while the cop blew steam off his coffee and finally drained the cup. Emmy learned that Hawk's first car was a Toyota, and he didn't like grits. She did her usual and made stuff up.

"I'm an avid fly fisher."

"Really?"

"Love it. There's nothing more relaxing than standing in a river in a giant pair of boots."

"I didn't think you'd have time for that."

"It's important to make time for these things. And I always have my chakras balanced once a week, otherwise I find I can't shoot straight."

After years of practice, she'd got the deadpan delivery down to a tee, and Hawk's brow twitched as she held his gaze. Would he call her out on the bullshit? Nope. This was fun.

But then the cop left, the food arrived, and they could get on with the conversation they were supposed to be having.

"So, I'm dying to find out. Why do you spend your

free time wasting perverts rather than, say, following in your daddy's footsteps and contributing to the country's drug problems?"

"I don't always agree with everything he does, but he's my father. You might not get that, but..." Hawk shrugged.

"I get it." And Emmy did, having a remarkably similar problem with father number two herself. "How about the first part?"

"Snake's daughter. She died."

"I read that in the file. I'm sorry."

"Your file tell you how she used to hug me whenever I came home on leave? How she made me smile no matter how shitty my day had been? Wait, maybe it told you how she drew me pictures and called me Uncle and sat down to read me stories that didn't involve war, blood, and death?"

"The data can only give us so much. That's why I'm talking to you now."

"Do you know what they did to her?"

"I've seen the autopsy report."

"The sanitised version? Or the one Chief Garland tried to hide, where the pathologist reckons she got raped repeatedly for several days?"

Suddenly, Emmy's plate of fries didn't seem so appealing. "The sanitised version."

"And how many more Garlands are out there? Men all too willing to abuse their positions of power as well as young children?" Hawk swallowed a mouthful of root beer. "How many more Barney fucking Sunshines?"

"Barney Sunshine? Are you serious?"

"As a coronary."

"Okay, point taken." Emmy leaned back against the cracked red vinyl. "But you're going about this all wrong. Using the home invasion thing as a cover was a good idea, but those crimes are linked, and people are gonna start digging harder just like we did. And whoever's running The Ring must already know."

"You think we don't understand how difficult this is getting? Why did Blackwood get involved, anyhow?"

"Widow number five hired us to, and I quote, 'find the animals responsible for my husband's death.'"

"You know who was responsible? The people running The Ring."

True. And that gave Emmy an idea. "Okay, so you've had a good innings. Six men shot, two knifed, and one whose head you bashed in with a hammer. Do you still have the weapons?"

"We left the hammer behind. It came from the house, anyway."

"The rest?"

"I know where they are."

"Good. Let's give the world the men responsible."

Hawk got halfway to his feet, face clouding over. "I'm not turning my team in. If anyone's going to prison, it's me. I'll take the rap for everything."

"For fuck's sake, catch up. I'm talking about framing the dudes who run The Ring. As long as all of this evidence you say you've got checks out, obviously."

He paused, one foot out of the booth. "It'll check out."

"In that case, we'll just make it look like they did the home invasions too, and everyone'll be happy. Well, not everyone, exactly. I'm sure the widow Granger won't be thrilled to find out her husband had a penchant for diddling kids, but I think this solution's as good a compromise as we're going to get."

"You'll help us?"

Emmy nodded. "But you've got to stop with the home invasions. I can't deny they've been good for business, but they're scaring the public."

"Then we'll have to find another way of working backwards through the ring."

"No, we'll have to find a way of skipping the links and going all the way to the top. You've still got the computers, right?"

"Mouse has been through them already."

"Fifty bucks says my people find something he's missed. He may be a good hacker, but he's not an investigator."

Hawk held out a hand. "That's a bet I'll gladly lose."

Emmy shook it, mulling over the new alliance. It promised to be an interesting one, as long as Hawk kept his people under control.

"We'd better sort out the logistics."

"First, I have a question. What put you onto us? Cade's been sniffing around for months."

"I'd like to claim credit for that, but he was actually there for a different matter."

Hawk sighed. "Shit. What?"

"Someone's selling grenades illegally, and the ATF thinks they're coming in through the biker community."

"They are, but not through The Darkness."

"You know who?"

"Yeah."

Emmy stared at him expectantly.

"I'm not a snitch."

"You know we'll find them eventually, and if you help us out here, we'll have more manpower available to track down The Ring."

Hawk closed his eyes as he fought an internal battle. Finally, he came to a decision. Thankfully the right one, otherwise Emmy would've been pissed.

"The Devil's Disciples out of Raleigh. And you didn't hear that from me."

"Hear what?" Emmy smiled, then popped a couple more fries into her mouth. "I need more ketchup." She added a liberal application from the slightly scummy bottle at the end of the table and chewed thoughtfully. "We'll need to sort out the blood evidence from tonight's crime scene too. Snake made quite a mess. Ever broken into a forensics lab before?"

"Nope. You?"

"I don't need to. I borrowed a pass a while back, and I haven't got around to returning it yet." Emmy used air quotes around the "borrowed." "Considering the line of work they're in, those guys are pretty lax with their security procedures."

Hawk shook his head, smiling now.

"And if we're gonna work together, Blackwood's taking the lead. I've seen your file, and you were good at what you did, but there's a hell of a difference between foreign espionage and a domestic investigation. Plus you've lost your edge."

Hawk's smile slipped. "How'd you see my file? That's supposed to be classified."

"Friends in low, low places."

"That job in Ukraine..."

He fell silent, and Emmy knew he was reliving the worst of it.

"Don't. It's the past. Learn from it, don't live in it. Do we have a deal? Blackwood takes point, and you assist where necessary?"

"Why are you doing this? It's not your battle."

Emmy briefly allowed memories of her own childhood to surface, of the small child men had twice forced themselves on before she learned how to fight back. Just enough to fuel her anger, then she locked them back up where they belonged.

"It's always my battle. It should be everybody's."

Hawk nodded. "Then yeah, we've got a deal."

## Chapter 37

EVEN THOUGH I'D set the ringtone on my phone as loud as it would go, I couldn't help checking the screen every other minute throughout the night. Eventually, when the sky began to lighten and I'd still had no sleep, I put the phone face down on the dresser by the bedroom door to force myself to get some rest. It didn't work. By the time Scarlet woke, I'd become a card-carrying member of the living dead with so little energy I couldn't even run a bath. I took the lazy alternative—dry shampoo and a spritz of deodorant.

"Can I have pancakes this morning?" Scarlet asked when I got downstairs.

Bless her, she'd tried to get dressed herself and ended up with mismatched socks and an inside-out T-shirt.

"We don't have time for pancakes this morning. You'll be late for kindergarten. How about you eat cereal today, and we'll do pancakes tomorrow?"

"With chocolate sauce?"

"Yes, with chocolate sauce."

I sorted out her shirt and fetched another pair of socks while she ate a bowl of cornflakes. With no word yet on Cade, I desperately tried to act normal so she didn't become alarmed.

"Is Daddy Cade coming back soon?" she asked in

the car.

"I hope so."

"Can we have macaroni and cheese for dinner?"

"As long as you help to set the table."

I managed to hold it together until she disappeared into the school building, but as soon as I got into the car, my throat grew tight.

"How were things at Blackwood this morning?" I asked the driver.

"Sorry, I only picked the car up and came straight here."

"Nobody mentioned any problems last night?"

"I only spoke to Eugene on the gate, and he didn't say a word about that."

That had to be good news, right? Eugene was grumpy, but he couldn't resist a good gossip. When I first started working at Blackwood, half of my information came from the chats I'd had with him on my way into the office.

Unless whatever had happened was so awful it was being kept closely under wraps. When one of my former colleagues at the hospital died in a car accident, management told everyone she was off sick until her next of kin had been tracked down. The possibility that Cade had gotten seriously hurt gave me chills.

When I got back to the house, I couldn't stand it any longer. My fingers shook as I dialled Emmy's number.

"Emerson Black's phone. Is this Taylor?"

"Yes."

"It's Sloane here. Emmy's busy, I'm afraid. Can I take a message? Or help with anything?"

"I was just wondering what happened last night."

Oh heck, now I sounded nosy. "I mean, I want to know whether Cade's okay. Because of Scarlet. I mean, if something happened to him, then I'd have to break the news, and she's already asking when he's coming home again."

"Things are still up in the air at the moment."

"Did they find Cade?"

"It's best if I get Emmy to call you when she's free."

Why wouldn't she answer the question? "Is he... Is he...dead?"

"He's in the infirmary. I'll leave a message for Emmy to phone, but try not to worry."

Try not to worry? Was she serious? The man I cared about had gotten hurt, and all I could do was sit at home and freak out. To take my mind off things, I pulled out three dishes and made a mega batch of macaroni and cheese, ready for Scarlet when she came home. I could freeze the extra. Eventually, I got distracted enough to grate off one of my fingernails and ended up throwing half a pound of cheddar away because I couldn't find the broken bit.

And still there was no news on Cade. I sent a message to him as well, trying to stay lighthearted, asking him to call when he got a second, but nothing. Either he'd been badly hurt, or I simply wasn't a priority, and the idea of that stung too.

By the time the driver came back to pick up Scarlet, I was a wreck. The nail I'd grated didn't look bad compared to the rest, which I'd chewed ragged in a return to the childhood habit I'd repressed for years.

"Have you heard anything more?"

He shook his head. "Sorry. But I reckon it's something big. The top dogs are all sequestered on the third floor, and they're not speaking to anyone."

That didn't sound good.

Scarlet ran out of kindergarten clutching a cardboard box decorated in crayon. Mostly animals, but I spotted the same three figures she'd drawn in the restaurant at Wonder World and prayed her dream wouldn't be shattered. Speaking got harder with each passing minute, so I just listened as she chattered the whole way home.

"Same time tomorrow?" the driver asked.

"I'll let you know if anything changes."

Scarlet ran up to her room as soon as we got in, eager to find Eric. She updated him on her escapades each day, and it made me sad that the one constant in her life was a cuddly toy. I headed for the kitchen to divide the macaroni and cheese into portions for the freezer, but I'd only gotten halfway when the doorbell rang.

My heart seized. I'd seen those TV shows where the police showed up to deliver bad news in person. We rarely got visitors, and this wasn't an area where door-to-door salesmen tended to travel. I longed to ignore the tinny sound and carry on with cooking like it'd never happened, but I couldn't.

Nervous, I pressed my eye up to the peephole, and my knees threatened to give way when I saw who'd come calling.

I yanked the door open and dropped my voice to a whisper. "Dean? What on earth are you doing here?"

He motioned me outside and reached past to pull the door closed. "We've got a problem."

No kidding.

"What kind of a problem?"

"Blackwood isn't just gunning for Draupnir, they're coming after us personally. We're all in danger, and our families too."

No. I couldn't believe it.

"Maybe it's somebody else? Everyone there's been nice to me."

"It's definitely Blackwood. Did you ever meet a woman called Agatha Lerner?"

"I don't think so." Her name didn't sound familiar from the staff directory, either.

"Well, that's who seems to be leading the charge."

"How do you know?"

Dean leaned down to kiss me on the cheek. "All thanks to you, when you helped me to break into their system last night."

He watched me closely, and I fought not to panic. What had I done? I really didn't think putting that memory stick into Mackenzie's computer would let Dean access the system. If it had, that meant I'd made a terrible mistake, and while I'd hoped Cade would be understanding of my situation when I explained it, now I'd blown it. A sob welled up in my throat, and I choked it back down. Dean mistook my devastation for embarrassment.

"Don't worry. It's understandable that you've been taken in by them. These people pretend to be what they're not for a living."

Could it be true? My world was flipping on its head faster than a slinky going down a flight of stairs, and I no longer trusted my own judgement.

"Are you sure? I mean, maybe this Agatha is acting on her own."

"It's possible there's a rogue element, but that

doesn't mean we're in any less danger. The attacks on Draupnir's servers quadrupled yesterday, and it's only a matter of time before the defences crumble. Lerner won't stop until she's wiped out anyone standing in the way of her plans."

I'd begun to doubt Dean over the last few months as he kept his distance, but when things got difficult, he'd dropped everything and flown all the way across the country to rescue me. Maybe I'd misjudged him as well.

"What should we do?"

"First, we need to get out of here. I've got a friend who's offered us a place to stay until we figure out our next step."

A slamming door caught my attention. "What about Scarlet?"

"Isn't there a babysitter she can go to?"

"I *am* the babysitter."

"Oh. Yeah. Of course." Dean sighed. "I guess we can take her with us, but it may hamper our chances."

"I can't just take her on the run. Her father'll be beside himself with worry."

"He'll understand. What else are you going to do? Drop her off at Blackwood with Agatha Lerner and her accomplices?"

"I don't know."

He looked at his watch then glanced back at the kerb. "Whatever you decide, we need to leave right now. I took a big risk coming here, but I couldn't bear to leave you behind."

And I couldn't bear to leave Scarlet behind to an uncertain future, especially with Cade stuck in the infirmary. Who knew what state he was in? I'd come to the realisation that I didn't want to stay with Dean, but short term, I had to go along with his plan and get us out of harm's way.

"I'll pack a case for both of us."

"Hurry. My car's around the corner. I didn't want to invite suspicion by parking it outside the house."

"Do you want to pull into the garage?"

"There's no time for that. Just throw the essentials into a bag and lock up."

"I should send a message to Scarlet's father and let him know what's happening."

Dean gave me a sharp look. "And who do you think monitors communications within Blackwood?"

"Uh, Agatha Lerner?"

"Precisely."

"Okay, I won't send anything."

"And turn the phone off. They can track your location."

I did as he said, then ran upstairs and found Scarlet sitting on her bed, playing with Eric and his friends.

"Sweetie, we need to take a little trip."

Her face lit up. "Wonder World?"

"Not this time, but how about you bring some of the toys Daddy Cade bought you?"

"Can we build a Noah's Ark?"

"We'll see."

Scarlet organised a collection of her favourite cuddly animals, and I shoved them into my suitcase along with toiletries and a few changes of clothes. Dean hadn't said much about where we were going, but he'd always insisted on staying in nice hotels whenever we took a trip, so I couldn't imagine we'd be slumming it.

And no matter what he said, I couldn't just leave without a word. I scribbled out a note and left it on the dresser where I hoped Cade would see it.

*Cade,*

*Have reason to believe Scarlet and I are in danger. I've taken her somewhere safe and will be in touch ASAP.*

*Taylor*

Then I hefted the case downstairs with Scarlet following. She eyed up Dean with suspicion.

"I don't know him."

"He's a friend of mine from California."

"Daddy told me not to go with strangers." She sat down on the sofa, arms folded.

Wonderful, trust Cade to have acted so responsibly. I crouched in front of her and squeezed her hand. "He's not a stranger, sweetie. I've known him for a lot of years."

"Are you sure it's okay?"

"Yes, I'm sure."

Scarlet's booster seat was still in the Blackwood car, so I did the next best thing and grabbed a cushion to go in Dean's rented Toyota while he grumbled about the amount of stuff I'd packed.

But then we were off, and I left a trail of burned bridges stretching all the way to Blackwood in my wake. I so nearly asked Dean to head over to the office so we could drop Scarlet off at the front gate, but memories of her arrival there stopped those words in their tracks. The poor girl had already been dumped there once, and I couldn't bring myself to do it a second time, and not only that, Agatha Lerner was an unknown quantity. I'd have given anything for Cade to have been home to ask for advice, but as he wasn't, I had to make a decision for his daughter and me.

I only hoped I'd done the right thing.

# Chapter 38

"COFFEE. I NEED coffee."

Mack's husband, Luke, rubbed his face as he stared at his computer screen. Lines of code that made Emmy's eyes hurt scrolled past, and he tapped away at the keyboard, frowning on occasion.

"Make it two," Mack said. "And that memory stick's still bugging me."

"Three," put in Agatha.

When they'd got back to the office in the early hours, Mack had found a thumb drive in one of her USB ports that she swore wasn't there before. A quick investigation revealed a database of recipes, including Mrs. Fairfax's famous chocolate fudge cake.

"I bet it was Bradley," Emmy said. "He probably brought it by to help you after that disaster of a dinner party."

"I keep telling him not to touch my computer."

"And I keep telling him not to touch my wardrobe, but he rifles through it every sodding day and throws out all the comfortable stuff. Have you tried calling him?"

"Yes, and he didn't answer."

"Toby gave him a box of valerian tea the other day. Bradley had one cup and snored all the way through a documentary on Versace. I bet he's tried drinking it again."

Luke cleared his throat. "Speaking of drinks..."

"Fine."

Emmy was only too glad to play glorified waitress while the geeks battled technology in their quest to find The Ring and its leaders. The initial information from Hawk's team checked out, just as he'd promised it would, and now Mack, Luke, Agatha, Nate, and Mouse were combing through the stolen laptops, the regular internet, and the Dark Web in the hunt for more clues. Servers, firewalls, VPNs, blah, blah, blah... Just give Emmy a damn gun. She'd grabbed a few hours' sleep on the fold-out couch in her office, door securely locked, and now she needed to prepare her team for a visit to the ringleader.

But first, caffeine. One of Emmy's pseudo fathers, Eduardo, had recently bought a second coffee plantation in his ongoing attempts to diversify from his core business of selling coke, which meant she and all of her friends had more Colombian roast than they could ever drink in one lifetime. The rich aroma drifted up as she dumped a scoopful into the espresso machine and pushed the button. What were the chances of convincing Eduardo to buy a chocolate factory too?

"Make one for me?"

An arm slipped around Emmy's waist and pulled her tight against a hard body. Her husband. A little of the tension she constantly carried inside herself eased.

"I thought you weren't getting back until tonight?"

"Job finished early. Surprise."

With their formidable reputations to uphold, Emmy and Black usually steered away from PDAs in the office, but with the kitchen empty, Black pushed his wife against the counter and kissed her breathless.

"Missed you."

"Missed you more."

A figure walked past the open kitchen door, and Black took a step back. "What's going on? When I spoke to you yesterday afternoon, you were planning a quiet evening in with Ana. Plotting your world domination," he added under his breath.

"Everything happened." Emmy updated him on the home invasions, The Ring, and Hawk's team.

"I wondered why we had a group of strangers camping out in the conference room. How's Cade?"

"Broken nose, concussion, blood in his urine, but the ultrasound's ruled out serious kidney damage. Kira gave him a sedative because he threatened to get up and help."

"And what about you? Have you slept?"

"I got a couple of hours."

Black traced the dark circles under Emmy's eyes with a fingertip. "Get a couple more. I'll look after things here."

"We need more information on The Ring, and I have to start putting a team together in case we have to visit people."

"Get some sleep, and I'll make the calls."

"Diamond, wake up."

Black's voice broke through the darkness in Emmy's mind, and her eyes flickered open.

"What is it?"

She'd known Black long enough that even groggy,

she could hear the urgency in his voice.

"We got a break."

"What kind of break?"

"Mack found a lead."

"Where? What kind of lead?"

"Victim number three's laptop. Apparently, one of The Ring's live events got cancelled at the last minute, and someone from the inner circle sent a message to let the attendees know. It got deleted, but Mack recovered part of it from the hard drive."

"And what does it tell us?"

"There are some sick fucks out there."

"Apart from that?"

"The person we're looking for lives in California. Mack and Luke are tracing the IP address back through various channels. Nick's in LA at the moment, and he and Micah are on standby with a team to pay a visit."

For a second, the control freak in Emmy had her mentally packing and heading for the airport, but she forced herself to park that idea. Nick was more than capable of handling the operation.

"I'll go and catch up with Mack. What time is it?"

"Almost two."

"Shit."

"Relax. You needed the rest. Mack does too, but you know what she's like when she gets her teeth into something."

"Yeah, I do. How are the new guys? Hawk's crew?"

"Not getting in the way as much as I feared. Mouse seems to know his way around a computer, Smith and Carmen have spent half the morning comparing guns, and Hawk's got some sensible things to say. I like the man."

"Me too."

Black gave her a sharp look.

"Put those green eyes away, you idiot. I'm talking purely in a professional sense." Emmy checked her face in the mirror and grimaced. "I'm gonna pay a visit to the bathroom. Meet you out there."

When Emmy got onto the main floor of her Special Projects division, the place was a hive of activity. Someone had thoughtfully provided donuts, and she snagged one before walking into Mack's office.

"Been sleeping on the job, boss?" Luke asked, but he was grinning.

"Yeah, and so should you. You look like shit."

"I keep telling myself I'll do one more thing, then another hour goes past."

"Seriously, get some sleep. Use my office if you want."

"I might just... Hang on... Mack, I've got something."

"What?" Mack pushed her chair back so she was sitting next to him. Even though he didn't technically work for Blackwood, Luke spent enough time there to have a small desk in the corner of Mack's office.

"A name to go with our address. Dean Montgomery. Has that come up anywhere?"

"No. How did you find it?"

Luke launched into a detailed explanation that sounded like a cross between torture and Swahili, but Mack nodded and smiled.

"Sounds right. We'll go with that."

"What's at this address?" Emmy asked.

Mack pressed a few buttons, and a satellite map filled the plasma screen on her wall. "A rather nice beachfront villa in Santa Barbara whose owner has a penchant for privacy. Nick's en route."

Emmy settled into the conference room, and over the next few hours, information on Dean Montgomery trickled in. Literally. Trickled. Usually when Mack and Luke began researching a person of interest, it flooded, and sifting through it required significant work. But by six in the evening, the file on Mr. Montgomery remained painfully thin.

"It's like he didn't even exist until six years ago," Mack said. "At least not under this name."

"We can't even find a picture of him," Luke put in.

"What do we want to do about visiting?" Nick asked from the speaker in the centre of the table. "We've taken a look from outside, and everything's quiet. I'm not sure he's even home."

"Go in when you're ready."

Nick held his team back until dusk, and in that time, apart from a lawn sprinkler coming on midway through the evening, nothing had stirred at the beach house. There didn't seem to be an alarm either.

"But that means nothing," Mack said. "If I didn't work for Blackwood, I wouldn't use an alarm, not an audible one. I'd build cameras into the house to alert me to any unwelcome visitors."

"So you could call the police, right?" Luke asked.

"Not exactly."

"I don't think I want to know."

Mack patted him on the hand. "That's probably for the best. Anyway, back to the beach house. Y'all need to take out the phone lines and the electricity. He'll most likely have battery units, but you can deal with them once you're inside. Keep your faces covered."

As the sun dropped, Micah donned a high-vis jacket and shinned up the nearest phone pole to cut the wires. Ten minutes later, the team entered the grounds of the beach house, pulling scarves and bandanas over their faces, and formed up outside the doors. Emmy watched via their body cameras from Richmond, fidgeting because she'd much rather be where the action was.

"Fuse box first," Mack muttered.

Nick didn't need to be told—he already knew his job. Once he'd flipped the main circuit breakers, his team turned on their flashlights and began searching the house. Fortunately, the high walls surrounding the property ensured they were out of sight of curious neighbours.

"Looks as if someone left in a hurry," Nick said when he reached the master bedroom.

The camera showed clothes strewn across the floor and bed. Nick opened the closets, but only one of them was messy. The other displayed neat rows of clothing, arranged by colour and type.

"This is all women's shit," Nick said.

"You reckon he had a girl with him?" Emmy asked. "We haven't seen one mentioned anywhere."

"I don't know. The stuff on the bed belongs to a man, and this doesn't look like it's been touched."

"So, what? He did a runner and left her behind?"

They both had the same thought at the same time, and said the same thing. "You don't think...?"

Micah walked into the bedroom. "You'll want to check this out. Along the hallway."

"It's not a body, is it?" Nick asked.

Micah shook his head. "What makes you think that?"

"A woman lived here, but it doesn't appear that she packed to leave."

"No, it's not a body. Haven't smelled anything bad either. No, this is...well..."

Computers. It was computers. A bank of servers with their insides ripped out, and what's more, it looked as if somebody had taken a hammer to the hard drives. A sharp intake of breath came from Mack, seated beside Emmy.

"Bastard," she muttered. To her, destroying technology was sacrilege. She'd even been known to name her servers. Blackwood's current rack-based system was called Henrietta.

"Bring back what you can," Luke instructed. "We'll see if we can salvage any of the discs."

Nick's team trawled through the rest of the house but found little of use.

"It's sterile," he said. "This isn't a home. I've stayed in hotel rooms more personal. Where are the photos? The vacation souvenirs? Takeaway menus? Junk mail? Books?"

"Maybe they took all those things with them when they left?" Agatha suggested.

"They took the junk mail and left most of the clothes? No way. I'd say Dean Montgomery and his woman lived a strange life, and I'd also hazard a guess that they're not coming back."

"Collect fingerprints and anything else useful you can find. We'll have to keep looking."

# CHAPTER 39

A TEAR ROLLED down my cheek, and I tried and failed to wipe it away before Scarlet saw.

"Why are you crying?"

"I have something in my eye. Grit. Dust, maybe."

I wrapped my arms tighter around her as we sat on the floor in the corner of the luxuriously appointed bedroom, or at least, that's what it looked like at first glance. The tripod at the end of the bed gave it away. The room wasn't a bedroom, it was a movie set, and I knew who the sick bastards wanted to star in their next video.

"I got grit in my eye once, and Mommy told me to blink until it came out. You should do that, Taylor."

"Good idea."

"When can we go home?"

"I'm not sure. Soon, I hope."

Although in truth, I no longer had a home. My entire life had fallen apart today, shattered into so many pieces I'd never put it back together.

Perhaps I should back up a bit, right? To the moment I realised things had gone badly, badly wrong...

When Dean picked us up, we'd driven through Rybridge, skirted a couple of small towns, and even gone past Blackwood's headquarters. If I'd known how awful things would turn out, I'd have grabbed the wheel and crashed us into the gatepost. Anything to avoid ending up where we were now.

But at the time, Dean had still been muttering about Agatha Lerner and what an evil person she was, and I'd believed him. I mean, he was my *husband*. I'd known him for six years, and he'd taken my once-broken life and fixed it as best he could. Why wouldn't I have trusted him?

Little did I know that he was about to destroy me.

"Where are we going?" I asked when he finally stopped bitching. Scarlet had fallen asleep in the back, thankfully, tired from kindergarten.

"Somewhere safe."

"But where? We've been driving for almost two hours."

Almost aimlessly, it seemed. I swore we'd been down one road twice. Dean drummed his fingertips against the steering wheel the whole way, which did nothing to settle my nerves.

"And we're nearly there."

Ten minutes later, he'd pulled off a narrow country road into a tree-lined drive. A guard hut stood inside the entrance, next to tall gates reminiscent of Blackwood's. A man strode out to greet us, greasy-looking with slicked-back hair and a gold tooth that glinted in the sunlight when he smiled in at a still-sleeping Scarlet.

"Dean Montgomery to see Mr. Hargrove."

"Yes, I have you on the list."

Their voices dropped, almost to a whisper, but I still heard what they said and the guard's words sent chills up my spine.

"I didn't realise you were bringing merchandise."

"Got a lucky break."

Merchandise? What merchandise?

"What's with the woman?"

Dean shrugged. "She's not important."

Not important? I was his *wife*. I almost protested, but another car pulled up behind us, and I didn't want to make a scene. Maybe Dean had downplayed our relationship as some sort of bizarre cover story?

The rented car rolled smoothly up the driveway, winding past an empty paddock and a rather phallic statue. I failed to see how that could be called art, although I was sure Bradley could explain it.

A mansion came into sight, three storeys high and painted in an odd shade of pink that reminded me of overcooked salmon. Proof that money couldn't buy taste. To one side, a small parking area held a handful of cars, all of them new, all of them expensive. A Mercedes, a Bentley, a Ferrari. Dean's Toyota stuck out in the same way I did on the rare occasions he dragged me along to a fancy party.

"What is this place?" I whispered as we got out of the car.

"Draupnir's headquarters."

"Offices? Where are we staying tonight?"

"Here. They also have rooms."

Scarlet woke up, groggy, as I lifted her out of the car. Dean had brought a small case of his own, but I didn't have any spare hands for my luggage.

"Leave it," Dean said, picking up my purse himself. "Someone'll fetch it later."

The butler, perhaps? He opened the front door as we approached, dressed in a dark-grey suit. I'd never been anywhere so classy before. Even Emmy didn't have a butler. We followed the man along opulent hallways, our feet making no sound on the plushly carpeted floor. A small girl came the other way, a couple of years older than Scarlet, only she was dressed in an evening gown. It seemed a little formal for the afternoon, but the lady holding her hand was well-dressed too.

"I didn't bring any party clothes," I whispered to Dean.

"Doesn't matter. You won't need any."

The butler paused in front of a set of double doors, then reached out with white-gloved hands to open them. He didn't step inside, just motioned us through.

A man stood at the far end of the room, gazing out the window, but he turned at our approach. I put him in his late forties, early fifties at a push, with tanned skin that stood out against his white dress shirt. Who wore a tie at home? The same kind of man who wore a made-to-measure suit, I figured.

He held out a hand for Dean to shake, but when it came to my turn, he took my hand in cool fingers and pressed his lips against the back of it. They curved into a smile, but his eyes stayed hard. Cold eyes, such a pale blue.

"Put the girl down."

"Sorry?"

"Put her down."

I didn't want to, but his tone left no room for argument.

"Sweetie, stand up."

Scarlet clutched at my jeans as the man bent to appraise her, her top lip quivering. *Please, don't cry.*

Finally, he straightened and faced Dean. "She'll do. We can use her tomorrow."

Use her? What were they talking about?

Dean smiled, and I knew he was nervous because of the way he rubbed the back of his neck.

"Let's call her a peace offering."

"Montgomery, it's going to take more than one girl to make up for the shitstorm you let rain down on this organisation."

"I'll fix it, I promise. I've already migrated everything to new servers, and I'll run things from here until it's going smoothly again."

"You'd better. I've already given you enough chances, and you know I don't tolerate dead weight."

Dean gulped. "I've got it, Mr. Hargrove. Uh, do you have a room for the girls?"

"Simms will find them one. This is your wife, I take it?"

"That's right."

"You can both join Sharon and me for dinner later, but first I want that webinar set up."

"Got it."

Mr. Hargrove turned away, and that was us dismissed. Dean led us towards the door, and the butler —Simms?—opened it as if by magic. Had he been listening in?

"I'll show the ladies to their room, sir."

Clearly, the answer to that was yes.

Dean trailed along behind as Simms led us down yet more hallways. Most of the doors leading off them were closed, but I glimpsed a library, a ballroom, and a lounge furnished with sofas that looked too uncomfortable to actually sit on. We went up two flights of stairs before Simms stopped next to a plain cream door with a brass handle and a big brass key in the lock.

"I believe this one will suit."

Dean fished the Toyota key out of his pocket. "Any chance you could get their case from the car?"

"Of course, sir."

Just like everything else in the mansion, the room was opulently furnished, the centrepiece a king-sized four-poster bed draped in deep-red velvet. A dark wood blanket box sat at the end, matched to a closet by the bathroom door. I glimpsed a shower stall inside. No bath. Great. Then I saw the tripod and turned back to Dean. Except it wasn't the Dean I knew. This man had eyes that rivalled Mr. Hargrove's, only darker blue.

"W-w-what's that for?"

"What do you think? Making movies."

"On the bed? Who?"

And then it clicked. The little girl downstairs, dressed to the nines. *Merchandise.* Using Scarlet tomorrow. Vomit rose in my throat, and I struggled to swallow it back down.

"Those sick freaks want to film Scarlet?"

"It's just business."

"*She's five years old.* What are they going to do to her?"

Even as the words left my lips, I realised I didn't want to know.

Fortunately, Dean just shrugged. "Younger kids tend to make a lot of money. Don't worry, they'll look after her."

I moved to slap him, but he caught my hand.

"Why? Why are you doing this? Why bring us here?

What did we ever do to hurt you?"

His eyes bored into mine. "You already know the answer to that, *wife*." He spat the last word.

"I don't!"

"Wonder World? Does that ring any bells?"

Oh, shit. "Y-y-you know about that?"

"Do you think I'm stupid?" He was shouting now. "I tracked your phone every damn day to make sure you stayed safe. You thought I wouldn't notice when you went to Florida?"

"You didn't tell me you were doing that."

"If I had, what would you have done? Left the damn thing behind? I sent an associate to the hotel to check you were okay, only for him to report you were playing happy families with the kid and some asshole. Did that ring on your finger mean nothing to you?"

"I was confused. I mean, you left me on my own in Richmond. The trip was a last-minute surprise from a friend."

"What friend?"

"Emmy Black."

Dean scrubbed his hands through his hair. "Fuck, you weren't supposed to be making friends with these people."

"They were nice to me."

"Nice? That man had his hands all over you. I've seen the damn photos."

"I'm s-s-sorry. Please, do whatever you want to me, but let Scarlet go. She doesn't deserve any of this."

"I need her now. Thanks to your lack of performance, Hargrove's beyond pissed."

"But I put the memory stick in Mackenzie's computer. You said you got the data you needed."

"Did you? Did you really? Bullshit. You did something to that thumb drive so it didn't work."

"Then how did you find out about Agatha Lerner?"

"From other sources. She was on a team investigating Draupnir when she worked at the FBI. It didn't take a genius to work out that she carried on her vendetta when she moved to Blackwood."

"You lied to me?"

"Don't act so surprised. You haven't been able to tell the truth lately either."

"Nothing happened between me and Cade."

Except for that kiss. The one I couldn't get out of my mind.

"Want to look me in the eye and tell me that?"

I tried, but my gaze wouldn't meet his.

"Thought not. Be ready for dinner at eight, and if you embarrass me, I'll make sure the girl suffers."

What had happened to the Dean I thought I knew? "How can you be so heartless? Did our marriage mean nothing to you?"

He shrugged. "Sex on tap, dinner on the table, a clean house? It was convenient."

That time, my palm did connect with his cheek, but not nearly hard enough. Dean forced it down to my side before I could have another try and motioned at Scarlet, sobbing silently at my side.

"Eight o'clock. Don't be late."

# CHAPTER 40

"THIS IS STRANGE..."

Mack sat back in her custom office chair, rubbing her eyes.

Emmy had eventually convinced her to catch a couple of hours' sleep, but she'd been back in front of her screen by five in the morning. Now, at eight thirty, she looked as if she needed her caffeine by IV. Was that even possible?

"What's strange?"

"The utilities at the beach house were in the name of Dean Montgomery, but the mortgage was taken out by a shell company. Trace that back far enough, and it's owned by a corporation registered in the British Virgin Islands. Guess who the sole shareholder is?"

"Dean Montgomery?"

"Dean Lake."

"Same man?"

"I'm guessing so, yes. Also, there was a jeep parked in the garage, but out of the three Dean Montgomerys in the area with licences, one's seventy-eight years old, which doesn't fit with the clothing Nick found, one lives with his mom and earns minimum wage at a fast-food joint, and the other's still in high school."

"What about Dean Lake?"

"Nothing registered to the home address. We've got

a list of five, and we're tracing through them at the moment. The LA and San Francisco offices are on standby to do the legwork."

Hawk walked in, carrying coffee for everyone. "You mind if I give Snake's wife an update? She's getting antsy."

"How much does she know so far?" Emmy asked.

"Pretty much everything. Don't worry, she'll keep her mouth shut."

"Bare minimum, okay? My husband's still negotiating with various agencies about how we're gonna cover all this shit up."

Hawk gave her a salute. "Understood."

"Anything more on The Ring?" Emmy asked Agatha.

With Mack and Luke concentrating on Dean Montgomery-slash-Lake, Agatha had continued digging for information on their primary target.

"I've been in contact with the members of the old task force, and the general consensus is that they're headquartered somewhere in Virginia. Several of the intercepts came from this state, and the Virginia ring was one of the first to be identified."

"I'd better go and get some target practice in, then."

Emmy wasn't kidding. She liked to shoot every day if possible to keep fresh. After an hour in the gym and thirty minutes on the range with Ana, Carmen, and Dan, she headed back upstairs to see how the hunt was progressing.

"Anything?"

In answer, Mack pointed at her plasma screen. A brown-haired, blue-eyed man stared back from a California driving licence.

"That's the right Dean Lake?"

"We believe so. He dropped out of sight six years ago after his brother got accused of raping a woman."

"And here's where it gets really interesting," Luke continued. "The woman Harlan Lake was accused of attacking was one Evelyn Sutton, and when Nick talked to the neighbours by the beach house, they said the woman who lived there was called Evelyn. Very quiet, apparently. Nervous."

"Do we have any more information on her?"

"We're looking, but we've been concentrating on Dean so far."

Sloane poked her head around the door. "Guys, I know you're busy right now, but the driver who picks Scarlet and Taylor up each day for the kindergarten run just called to say they're not at the house."

"Have you tried calling her?" Emmy asked.

"She's not answering."

"Did he get there on time? Maybe they took a cab? Or walked? It's sunny out today."

"I guess. I'll ask him to drive the route."

"Try calling the kindergarten too. And Lara. They're friends, right?"

"On it."

Emmy turned back to the screen. "What else have we found out about Dean Lake?"

Mack scrolled through the information. "His parents died when he was eighteen. Car crash. His only family seems to be Harlan, who's a junkie. He did a stint in rehab after raping Evelyn, which from the police report seems to have been a clear-cut case, but she refused to press charges."

"Why would she do that?"

"According to the officer in charge of the case, she forgave Harlan."

"Seriously? The guy raped her and she forgave him? I'd have chopped his fucking balls off."

"I wonder if that had anything to do with Dean?" Luke mused.

"What, like he convinced her to let him off?"

Mack shrugged. "If they were in a relationship, her sending his brother to prison would have been awkward."

"Who the hell has a relationship with their rapist's brother? I mean, even if they were already together, how did it last?" Ah, it suddenly dawned on Emmy. "The asshole didn't tell her. That's when he changed his name, right? He got cosy with her and convinced her to let his brother off."

"That's sick."

"We're talking about a man who's involved with a paedophile ring here. I'd say being fucked in the head pretty much goes with the territory, wouldn't you? What happened to the brother, anyway?"

"He's in prison now," Mack said. "For rape."

"Another one? Shit."

"Two, actually. Wait a second, I think I've found Evelyn's DMV record. I'll put it on the big screen. Hold on, is that...?"

Emmy stared up at the photo. She didn't shock easily, but her jaw dropped.

"Holy shit. That's Taylor." She thought back to Sloane's words a few minutes ago. "Fuck, and she's disappeared. Get rid of that picture, and don't tell Cade."

"Don't tell me what?"

The man himself appeared in the doorway, nose swollen, eyes black. Busted.

"Nothing. Not important. Where's my gun?"

He stepped forwards and Mack went to minimise the picture, but lack of sleep had obviously impaired her abilities because she ended up projecting the damn licence onto the wall instead.

"Taylor has a driver's licence?" Cade asked. "I always assumed she couldn't drive. Hold on, why is her photo with someone else's name?"

"Go sit down. Have some breakfast. Lunch. What time is it? Brunch?"

"I'm not interested in brunch. What's going on?"

"Should you even be out of bed?"

"Nobody's telling me anything, and I'm sick of being treated like an invalid."

"You *are* an invalid. You've got two cracked ribs and a broken nose."

Hawk wandered in, and Emmy stifled a groan. Could this morning get any more awkward?

"Cade, right?"

Cade folded his arms. "Yeah."

"Look, I'm sorry about the whole..." Hawk motioned at his nose. "I thought you were there to stop us."

"Yeah, I was until I found out why you were doing what you were doing. You've gotta learn the importance of dialogue."

"I kind of have. A bit late, I know."

"My ribs hurt like a bitch."

"I'm sorry about that too."

Emmy tried to herd them out of the room. "Excellent. Why don't you two chat over coffee?"

Cade stood his ground. "Not until you tell me what's happening."

Hawk leaned forwards. "Evelyn Montgomery? Is that the asshole's wife?"

"Wife? Taylor's married? She said she split from a guy... What was his name...? Dean, I think, but she never said they were married."

"Dean? She actually said she was with a guy called Dean?"

"I'm pretty sure. We'd both been drinking, but I think that's what she said."

Emmy looked at Mack, who shrugged. "Maybe if they split up, Evelyn working here was just a coincidence. A fresh start?"

No way. "I'm not buying that, even on sale. Besides... What Sloane said."

"What did Sloane say?" Cade asked.

This was not a conversation Emmy wanted to have. No, she needed to get to Cade's place and find out what was going on. Hmm, what to do? She opened Mack's desk drawers, one after the other, rooting through.

"What are you doing?" Mack asked.

"Uh, stuff."

Aha, that was what Emmy was looking for. Handcuffs. Three seconds later, Cade was securely attached to the door handle, and a minute after that, Emmy was running out of the building with Ana, Carmen, and Dan in tow, Cade's yells echoing behind them.

"Sorry," she shouted back.

"I don't think Cade's happy," Dan said as Emmy bleeped open the door to her husband's Porsche Cayenne.

"I'll explain later. He can be hot-headed, not to mention the fact that he's injured, and he'd only hinder things if he tagged along. Which he would insist on doing if he knew what was going on."

Carmen hefted a duffel bag into the trunk. She'd brought enough firepower to start a small war, and they all knew how to use it. Emmy hopped behind the wheel, fired up the engine, and sped down the driveway.

"Where are we going?" Ana asked.

Emmy loved those girls. She'd told them nothing, just mimed a gun, and they'd followed without hesitation.

"It seems Scarlet's nanny may be married to our suspect, and the driver who was supposed to drop them off at kindergarten this morning called to say they're both missing."

"You think she realised we're onto them and took the girl?"

"I don't know what to think at the moment." Emmy slammed a fist into the steering wheel. "Fuck it. I should have done a more comprehensive background check on her, but I went with my gut."

"Your gut's served you well in the past," Dan said.

"Yeah, but it seems to have let me down this time. Cade's gonna flip when he finds out."

"Maybe they just overslept?" Dan said, but her tone suggested it was a forlorn hope.

"Maybe. Load my Walther with the good stuff, would you?"

With Emmy driving, it didn't take long for them to

reach Cade's neighbourhood. Rather than parking in the driveway, she sped past the house and abandoned the Porsche at the kerb around the corner.

"No signs of life," Dan said. "No lights on, no vehicle in the driveway."

"I'm not sure whether that's a good thing or a bad thing. I'll knock on the front door while you guys go in the back, okay?"

Ana nodded. "Do you have a key?"

"Sorry."

"Doesn't matter."

It truly didn't. When nobody answered after Emmy had knocked twice, she picked the lock and opened the door in less than thirty seconds. Practice made perfect, and she'd had a lot of it over the years. The other three girls met her in the lounge, silent as Emmy pointed at the stairs. Two by two, they crept up them, only to clear every room with no signs of life. In the master bedroom, Emmy picked up a note from the dresser.

"What's this?" She read it out loud. "*Cade, have reason to believe Scarlet and I are in danger. I've taken her somewhere safe and will be in touch ASAP. Taylor.* Is she for real?"

"Why would she think they were in danger?" Dan asked.

"Maybe she didn't," Ana suggested. "What if she left the note to lull us into a false sense of security when she's the danger all along?"

"I don't know." Dan shrugged. "I was talking to Lara the other day, and she said Taylor loved that kid. Acted more like a mom than a nanny, and it isn't easy to fake that."

Emmy paced the lounge, frustrated. Nothing about

this case made sense. The bad guys were the good guys, and now it seemed one of the good guys may, in fact, be rotten.

"Where could she have gone? She didn't have a car, and the driver didn't pick her up. We need to check cab companies, her bank account, and her company credit card."

Dan put out an arm to hold Emmy still. "Bet you the husband picked her up. They're both missing, remember? She'd only have thought Scarlet was in danger if someone told her that, and it wasn't us. Who else did she trust? It all comes back to the husband."

"I don't get why she was even working at Blackwood. Until two days ago, we weren't investigating The Ring."

"*We* weren't, but Agatha was. And she slipped up once, remember?"

"You reckon she infiltrated us because of that?"

"Can you think of a better reason?"

"Not right now. Dammit, we need to find that kid."

# CHAPTER 41

DINNER LAST NIGHT was awful. I'd worn jeans as a protest, pleased to look out of place beside Sharon, Mr. Hargrove's wife. It turned out she was the woman I'd seen leading the young girl when we first arrived, meaning she didn't merely turn a blind eye to her husband's activities, she actively participated in them.

My attire had earned a scowl from Dean, and a harsh whisper to, "Behave yourself, or else."

I'd bitten my tongue through the pretentious appetiser and main course, and the old Evie would have stayed silent for the entire meal. But spending time with folks who had genuinely cared about me and encouraged me to speak meant I'd grown in confidence. And the wine helped too.

"Why do you do this?" I asked as Simms brought dessert.

"Do what?" Hargrove asked.

"Abuse children."

Dean kicked me under the table, but Hargrove only laughed.

"That's a very subjective view. How do you know they don't enjoy it?"

For a moment, I was speechless. "How can you even ask that?"

"While our talent is with us, they're very well looked

after."

"But you're videoing children doing... Well, I expect the things are very much illegal."

"The age of consent is such an arbitrary figure. In Angola, it's twelve."

"We're not in Angola."

He waved a hand at me. "But why should it be any different here?"

"Because a twelve-year-old is a child. They can't even understand what they're consenting to."

"That's just your opinion. Everybody's entitled to one."

I didn't even have an answer to that. "You're also using children under twelve. Scarlet's five, for goodness' sake."

"Evie..." Dean warned.

Hargrove smiled, an evil grin that chilled my blood. "Don't worry. We'll break her in gently."

"You're sick."

"Another opinion. I say I'm merely part of a group with different sexual tastes to you. Think about it—sodomy was illegal in the United States until recently. In many countries, homosexuality is still a crime, yet here in America, gay people can get married now. I hope in my lifetime, love between an adult and a younger person will also be legalised."

The man was certifiable. "Gay marriage is legal between two *adults*. And in the meantime, you're just going to carry on exploiting children. How can you do that?"

"Supply and demand, Evelyn. There are many people out there who share the same passions we do, sadly driven underground by a society resistant to change."

I turned to Dean. "How can you support this? Don't tell me you're into paedophilia too?"

He shook his head. "No, I just do the computers. Business is business. You enjoyed spending the money I earned for long enough."

"If I'd known where it came from, I'd have chosen to live on the streets instead."

"And you'd be there now if I hadn't taken you in."

"You bastard..."

"Evie, remember what I said earlier."

I bit my tongue for Scarlet's sake when what I really wanted to do was stab Dean in the eye with a fork. The smug bastard finished his strawberry roulade and licked the spoon.

"Delicious."

Simms walked over and took his plate, then raised an eyebrow at me.

"I'm not hungry."

"Suit yourself," Dean said.

Sharon Hargrove finished her bowlful in dainty mouthfuls, avoiding eye contact with anybody at the table. She hadn't said a word throughout dinner. I couldn't even begin to understand her.

Simms served coffee and petits fours, and I resisted the urge to throw my cup at somebody. Both Dean and Hargrove made tempting targets, but I was too worried for Scarlet's safety. Eventually, the most painful meal of my life ended, and Dean escorted me back upstairs.

"You were incredibly rude tonight, Evie. If you act like that again, there'll be consequences."

"You're insane, all of you."

"Rich people aren't insane, merely eccentric."

"And you basically kidnapped me."

"We're married."

"I want a divorce."

Dean chuckled. "If you'd been this feisty over the last few years, I might have enjoyed fucking you more."

"I hate you."

His mouth hardened into a thin line. "Suit yourself. You're here to look after the girl. Make sure she stays in line. If she doesn't behave, we won't need either of you anymore."

I knew what he was implying, and that made me tremble inside. Either we behaved, or we were dead. But I couldn't let him see my terror. Instead, I turned and shoved the bedroom door open, then slammed it behind me. The key clicked in the lock.

As soon as I got inside, Scarlet leapt off the chair by the window and ran towards me. "Taylor, where did you go? I was scared."

"Sweetie, I'm so sorry."

"A man brought me food, but it wasn't as nice as what you make."

"Did you eat it?"

"Some."

At least she'd keep her strength up if she ate. "Good girl."

"Is it time for bed yet?"

Yes, but I couldn't bring myself to sleep in the four-poster monstrosity. Who knew what despicable acts had taken place there? Instead, I rummaged in the blanket box and found a spare quilt.

"How about we camp out by the window tonight? That way we can watch the sun come up."

"On the floor?"

"It'll be fun."

She looked dubious, but she came and snuggled next to me on the floor anyway. Above us, the metal bars spanning the window glinted in the moonlight. We were in a prison. A five-star prison, but a prison nonetheless.

And as I was the one who'd got us there, I was the one who needed to figure out a way to escape.

Escape... Escape...

Most of a day passed, and I tried to stay calm for Scarlet's sake even though my insides felt as if they were being mauled by sharks. Our suitcase had arrived overnight, and I dug through it looking for something—anything—that might help our predicament, but all I'd thrown in were clothes and toiletries. Unless I could squirt shampoo in somebody's eyes or hit them with a shoe, the contents were useless. Needless to say, Dean had taken my phone.

The room offered a couple of options—the tripod and a pair of brass candlesticks, one on each nightstand. I hefted the nearest and tried a few practice swings. They were heavy enough to do damage, but if I tried and messed up, what consequences would that lead to for Scarlet?

Simms brought breakfast, leaving a tray by the door before locking it behind him again. Scarlet grinned with delight at the waffles with chocolate sauce, but I couldn't eat a thing. The same with lunch. Now, as the afternoon drew to a close, every sound from the hallway outside made me feel sicker.

And then the lock clicked.

"Ah, Mrs. Montgomery. Lovely to see you again. I do hope Simms has been looking after you."

Hargrove walked in, followed by another man, younger and lighter in build, dressed in a pair of fitted slacks and a button-down shirt.

"Stop calling me Mrs. Montgomery. I want nothing to do with that man anymore."

"As you wish. I've brought Guillaume up to meet our newest star. They'll be doing a scene together later this evening."

"Over my dead body."

Hargrove's eyes hardened, and the veneer of congeniality he'd shown at dinner last night disappeared.

"That can be arranged."

I clutched Scarlet tighter against me as Guillaume trailed a finger across her cheek. *Tres jolie.*

"How can you do this?"

"It is simple." His French accent was smooth, easy to listen to. A complete contrast with the words coming out of his mouth. "I enjoy it. She will enjoy it too."

"Can't you..." I closed my eyes and swallowed down bile. "Can't you do something with me instead?"

Hargrove chuckled. "You're far too old for our audience, I'm afraid. Tonight's viewers have been promised a girl from age category one, and that's what they're paying good money to watch."

I turned away, blinking back tears.

"Of course, my tastes are eclectic, so I'll be happy to oblige you later. We can't have you getting frustrated now you've fallen out with your husband."

"It wasn't an open offer."

"I know. But I actually prefer it when my women struggle. The challenge, you know? And secretly, they like it too."

The man was delusional. For the first time in my life, I wanted a person dead. No, the second. Because I'd gladly have put a gun to Dean's head at that moment too.

"Well, I'll leave you in Guillaume's capable hands. He'll arrange things the way he likes them. And Lorraine will be with you shortly to assist with clothing, hair, and make-up. She's been one of our girls for many years, although now she's passed that golden age, we've had to move her to the other side of the camera."

Hargrove left, pulling the door closed behind him, while Guillaume fussed with the drapes. Lorraine duly turned up a few minutes later. She couldn't have been more than eighteen, and while she gave us a flickering smile, her glassy eyes spoke of a crushed soul.

"Mr. Hargrove said he wanted something classic for tonight. Dark eyes, red lips. It'll match the dress we've got picked out." She motioned to a garment bag she'd draped on the bed when she came in.

Scarlet clapped her hands. "Will I look like a princess?"

Lorraine's head bobbed up and down. "Yes, just like a princess."

"A princess..." Guillaume nodded behind them. "I like this idea. I'm sure we 'ave a crown somewhere. Let me look."

He walked out, and I got ready to make a run for it, but then the lock tumbled, keeping us all in. Lorraine didn't seem in the least perturbed by that, but I guessed she'd been there many times before.

"How can you participate in this?" I asked her.

"They take care of me. It's not so bad once you get used to it."

"How long have you been here?"

She counted on her fingers. "Eleven years."

Freaking hell. She couldn't have been much older than Scarlet when she arrived.

"But what about your parents?"

"I don't really remember them. Mr. Hargrove says they didn't want me."

"And you believed him?"

"He wouldn't lie."

"You think?" The poor girl must have been brainwashed. Mind you, I'd spent six years trusting Dean, so what did that say about me?

Lorraine pinched her lips together, concentrating as she outlined Scarlet's eyes. Smokey black, so far from the sparkles she loved.

"Don't worry about Guillaume," Lorraine said. "He's one of the good ones. Gentle."

"That doesn't make it right."

She just shrugged.

The door swung open as Lorraine finished zipping Scarlet into a red evening gown that matched her name. Tight on the top, slashed to mid-thigh, absolutely unsuitable for a child. Even I wouldn't have worn it out in public.

Guillaume looked her up and down, nodding his approval, then produced a small golden tiara. "Look what I found. Perfect."

Scarlet's eyes lit up, and I wanted to cry for her. She had no idea what was in store, and I didn't know what to say. Should I try to prepare her? Or wait to console her afterwards?

What a decision to have to make.

Lorraine packed up her make-up box and disappeared, leaving us alone with a child molester and rapist. The terrifying thing was, if any woman saw Guillaume on the street, she'd most likely be enamoured with his accent and boyish good looks, never suspecting the river of filth that ran under the surface.

Now he fiddled with the pillows and stood back to appraise the scene. I eyed up the door.

"We need to fix this lighting. It is too bright." He stepped over to the light switch, cutting off our exit, and dimmed the overhead chandelier. "This is better."

The candles flickered into life, and he knelt in front of Scarlet, cupping her face in his hands as he bent forwards to press his lips to hers. She looked to me for help, confused.

And I saw red.

What I was doing barely registered as I swung the candlestick at Guillaume's head, not quite striking dead centre, but it knocked him to the side and away from Scarlet. He grabbed my ankle as she stumbled backwards.

"You bitch!"

I tried to pry his fingers off me, but he wrapped his other arm around my waist, holding me tight against him. Dammit, he was stronger than he looked.

"Run, sweetie!"

"What?"

"Hide-and-seek. We're playing hide-and-seek. You run and you hide, okay?"

"Okay."

Good girl. She sprinted from the room as Guillaume backhanded me, and stars flickered in my peripheral vision. I scrambled backwards, trying to get a grip on the bed.

Guillaume's eyes widened, and I felt rather than saw the flames at my back. Shit! The candles must have set fire to the bedcovers. Bitter smoke filled the room as Guillaume pinned me to the floor, using his body weight to keep me still. My arms flailed, and he shifted his grip to my throat, squeezing.

"You crazy *salope*. You've ruined everything."

I couldn't get a breath to reply. Instead, I beat my fists on his back, but it was pointless. I'd failed Scarlet, and I'd failed Cade. My strength ebbed, and my arms flopped uselessly at my sides. Only for my left hand to connect with the candlestick. I used the last of my energy to strike Guillaume's head, and someone must have been smiling down on me because rather than his hands wringing out my last drop of life, he collapsed, a dead weight on top of me.

The darkness receded, enough for me to push him off to the side, and I stumbled away from the fire. Holy crap, the whole bed was alight! I took one last look at the sick bastard's motionless body then ran from the room, pulling the door closed and locking it behind me. Guillaume could go to hell.

Now I needed to find Scarlet so we didn't join him.

# CHAPTER 42

WHEN THE GIRLS got back to Blackwood, Cade was waiting in reception with murder in his eyes.

"We should have gone in the back way," Dan muttered.

"Can we have this argument in private?" Emmy asked, then headed for the stairs without waiting for an answer.

Cade hurried to catch up, wincing as he caught the door. "Where's Scarlet?"

"We're not entirely sure. Somewhere safe, apparently."

"Who the hell is Evelyn Montgomery? Mack wouldn't tell me anything until you got back."

"Let's go into the conference room, shall we?"

Maybe get a coffee, some snacks. Anything to put off telling Cade his daughter had disappeared.

Alas, once they'd got inside, he blocked the door.

"Now."

"Okay, okay. Uh, it seems Taylor, or Evelyn, may be peripherally involved with this Ring."

Cade's face, now clean-shaven, cycled through blush, then off-white, then rose, then cherry, then garnet. Good grief, Emmy had been looking at too many of Bradley's paint swatches.

"You mean you hired a paedophile to look after my

daughter?"

"I don't think she's actually a paedophile herself."

"You don't *think*? What happened to background checks?"

"We did one when she joined Blackwood, obviously, but only a basic one since she was just cleaning. Then... I kind of went with my instincts."

"Your instincts?" He turned away, fists balled. "Well, your instincts are fucked, aren't they?"

Mack held up a hand. "Hold on a second. Don't blame Emmy for all of this. Chances are, the advanced background checks would have come back clean anyway. Dean Montgomery's a good hacker from what I've seen, and it wouldn't have been difficult for him to concoct a cover story. Heck, I can do it in my sleep, just like I did for you with The Darkness until you lost your damn voice recorder."

"I only lost it because I was preventing a woman from being raped. Would you rather I'd ignored that?"

"Of course not. I'm just saying—"

"Enough!" Ana said. She didn't raise her voice. She didn't need to. "Stop arguing. Cade, I know what it's like to lose a daughter, but apportioning blame won't solve anything. We need to work out how we're going to find her."

"That shouldn't be too difficult." Black's voice came from the doorway, and everyone turned to stare at him. "Nate has a small confession to make."

Nate Wood, one of Blackwood's co-founders and Black's best friend since their days in the Navy SEALs, looked a little sheepish as he walked into the room.

"What have you done?" Emmy asked.

He blew out a breath. "You recall the problems we

had locating Tabitha after she went missing?"

Ana's daughter. Yes, it would be difficult to forget. "We all do."

"I didn't want to encounter those difficulties again, so I've been experimenting with a new generation of kinetic-energy-powered tracking devices." Nate was Blackwood's Mr. Gadget. He spent half of his working life playing commando and the other half sequestered in his basement lab. "They're really quite powerful now, and since we co-invested in that satellite company, we've been able to link up to the whole network via—"

"Nate, we don't need to know the techno-details. Are you saying you fitted one of these to Scarlet?"

"During the medical she had when she first came here."

"Why the hell didn't you tell us this earlier?"

"I didn't realise she'd gone missing until now."

Ana narrowed her eyes. "Who else has one? Tabby?"

He nodded. "And Josh, and Libi, and Caleb. Call it an insurance policy."

Dan got to her feet. "I can't believe you put electronic shit in my son without telling me."

"He was cool with it. I told him you'd get mad if you found out."

This time, it was Black's turn. "Enough! Scarlet's an hour away, and we need to retrieve her." Everyone shot up and jostled for the door. Black pointed at Cade. "Not you. You're injured."

"But—"

"Do you want to get handcuffed to something again? We're not having this operation compromised by making allowances for broken bones. We've got enough people who are in good shape."

Cade dropped back into a leather chair. It was clear he didn't like the situation, but nobody argued with Black. Well, except Emmy. She kind of liked taunting him, especially in the privacy of their own bedroom. It guaranteed fireworks.

But right now, the only thing she wanted to explode was Dean Montgomery's head.

Emmy's Special Projects team was used to working with tight deadlines, and it only took two hours for them to come up with the outline of a plan once Nate tracked Scarlet to a country estate forty miles outside of Richmond.

"Registered to the Draupnir Foundation," Luke said. "A not-for-profit organisation committed to rehabilitating children from troubled backgrounds."

"Where did you find that out?" Emmy asked.

"From their website."

"You're serious? Pornographers masquerading as a charity?"

"Sure looks that way. And since it's a private residential treatment centre, there's no requirement for the place to be licensed."

Emmy pulled a chair up beside Luke and studied the information available. Assuming Draupnir had used genuine photos, the inside of the property looked to have been modelled on the palace of Versailles except with extra gold. Had a leprechaun thrown up in there? Even Bradley would have cringed.

It was difficult to get an idea of the interior layout,

which made planning trickier, but from the photos of the grounds and the satellite images Mack had obtained, the surrounding woods stopped a hundred yards or so from the mansion. At least there were plenty of ornamental hedges, trees, and fountains to cover their approach. Emmy paused on a view of the front facade, thinking.

"Someone's got money, huh?" Luke said.

"We can climb up those stone columns to get to the third floor." She leaned in, squinting. "But the windows have got bars on. Why do they need bars? Actually, I don't want to know." A sigh escaped her lips as she pushed the seat back. "Ana, we need to pack explosives. The small charges."

The sun was low in the sky as Team Blackwood crept through the woods surrounding the Draupnir estate. They were running with open radio channels, and Mack, Agatha, and Luke kept them updated with new information as they received it.

A couple of Agatha's former colleagues from the FBI had arrived too, ostensibly to ensure the hastily contrived public-private operation ran within the rules, but Emmy had heard the pair of them taking bets on the body count as she strode out of the office with a pistol strapped to each thigh and a pair of knives clipped on her belt. A further FBI team was on standby to assist with the aftermath, but as usual, they'd let Blackwood do the tricky part first.

"Main man's called Kelvin Hargrove. Forty-nine years old," Mack said. "Fifty bucks says he's got a hidden past too, because I can't find anything on him going back further than fifteen years. Pictures are on their way through. He's married to Sharon, twenty-five years his junior, former child beauty queen. Anybody want to bet on how healthy that relationship is?"

"I'm sure he'll trade her in for a younger model soon," Dan said.

Black's voice came through, loud and clear. He'd joined the team along with Nate, who declared he'd been cooped up in the basement for too long and needed some fresh air. "Objective one: find Scarlet. Objective two: find Evelyn Montgomery. Objective three: Kelvin Hargrove. Objective four: Dean Montgomery. Objective five: 'find' the computers that went missing from the nine home invasions we've been investigating. Someone did bring those, right?"

"In the trunk of vehicle four," Hawk said.

"Good. Agents Betts and Hamblin, you didn't hear that last part. Objective six: have fun, people."

A series of confirmations echoed over the channel as the team settled in to wait for dusk. With the grounds to cross, they'd decided to make their move with a little darkness to help.

Except things didn't quite work out that way.

"Is that smoke?" Carmen asked from her position to the west, situated on a small rise with a sniper rifle and scope.

"Where?" half a dozen people asked at the same time.

"Top floor, one, two...five windows from the back."

"I do believe it is," Nate said. "Flames too, and someone yelling from the window. Sounds like French."

"Let's go," Black decided. "Take advantage of the confusion."

Fourteen shadows ran across the lawn to their chosen entry points. For Emmy and Ana, that was up the fancy stonework and onto a second-floor balcony, through a set of double doors and into...

"Fuck me, we've landed in Hawaii."

One end of the room held cameras, lights, and a rack of skimpy beach outfits, while at the other, a pair of sun loungers sat beside a mock pool cabana backed by a painted tropical paradise. They'd even brought real sand in. Emmy bet that got into all the wrong cracks.

Out in the corridor, shouts came from other parts of the house, but no gunfire yet. So far, so good. Emmy and Ana ducked into an alcove as a woman ran past followed by three young girls. None of them appeared to be a threat.

Nate's voice came through Emmy's earpiece. "Someone's let the French guy out of that room, and the fire's spreading on the west side of the third floor. Black and I'll check for prisoners. Avoid it if you can."

Emmy hated the idea of her husband being near the flames, but trusted that he knew what he was doing. She needed to concentrate on her own job, which was to clear the east side of the second floor with Ana.

Their area seemed to consist mainly of movie sets—a jungle, an office, ancient Egypt complete with a disturbingly stiff asp, and a school classroom. At least somebody had already set the place alight, which saved Blackwood from having to do it themselves. Because this building was going to the ground.

Beyond the pervert's playground, they found a series of locked rooms, keys on the outside. Emmy stood on one side of the first doorframe, Ana on the other, using the walls as cover as they swung the door open. A girl cowered on a plush bed, her eyes fixed on the barrel of Emmy's gun. Emmy guessed her age at thirteen or fourteen.

"Do you know how to get out?"

She nodded quickly.

"How many others along this corridor?"

The girl held up six fingers.

Emmy swore under her breath. "Go. The place is on fire. Run, and keep running until you get outside. Do you understand?"

Another nod.

Emmy jerked her gun, and the girl took off.

"Six to go. Three and three?" The threat from these girls was minimal.

"Works for me," Ana said.

Three minutes, six rooms cleared, and six more girls running for the exit. The youngest couldn't have been older than seven, and Emmy was mentally toasting Kelvin Hargrove's balls on little bamboo skewers when they heard voices coming from farther along the hallway.

"Put her down!"

Emmy caught Ana's eye and mouthed, "Evelyn?"

Ana didn't need to confirm. They may have been working together for less than a year, but each *knew* how the other would react. Mirroring each other's movements, they crept along the corridor and burst into the next room.

Well, there were objectives one and two. And three, by the looks of things, although the man's face was half-hidden behind Scarlet while he used her as a shield. Hargrove had a gun pointed at her head, and he was trying to walk to the door, but Scarlet clung onto one of the velvet curtains with such a determined look on her face that Emmy snorted a laugh despite the dire straits they were in. The asshole had about as much of a clue how to deal with a child as she did, which was to say no idea at all. Evelyn stood to one side, pale as a ghost, screaming at him.

"Take me instead. She hasn't done anything to hurt you."

Great. A hostage situation. Emmy hated those.

"Or better still, be smart and drop the gun, then put the girl down, and you might have a chance of walking out of here."

But Hargrove wasn't smart. He swung his gun towards Emmy as she ducked next to a hideous statue of... Was it really a giant vagina? It certainly seemed so, because Ana was standing behind the matching cock on the other side of the doorway. Someone needed to talk to this guy about his decor.

Evelyn wasn't smart either. She launched herself at Hargrove, and the loud *pop* as his gun went off in the small room made Emmy's ears ring. He lost his grip on Scarlet as Evelyn collapsed at his feet.

Two more shots fired, louder this time—one from Emmy's Walther, the second from Ana's Glock—and Hargrove fell to the floor as well. He wouldn't be getting up again.

"Rear of the second floor. We need medical help. Objective one's safe, two's down, and three's down permanently."

Black answered, and Emmy breathed a sigh of relief. "Clear up here, and objective four's dealt with too. On our way."

Ana tucked her gun into her waistband and picked up Scarlet, trying to comfort her. It didn't work. The little girl's tears overshadowed Evelyn's groans as Emmy rolled her over. Blood was already seeping through her pale-pink top, and when Emmy pushed it up, she could see the neat entry wound caused by Hargrove's 9mm Beretta just below Evelyn's navel. Judging by the blood spreading across the carpet, the bullet had gone all the way through.

And the smoke was getting thicker.

Like all of Blackwood's team, Emmy and Ana carried individual first aid kits on their belts during operations, and Emmy tore hers open.

"Evelyn, can you hear me?"

"Mmm."

"Can you move your feet?"

Her toes twitched. Thank goodness. At least that meant spinal cord damage was less likely. Where had the bullet come out? Emmy felt underneath Evelyn until her fingers hit the exit wound to the left of the entry. More blood oozed out.

"What do you need?"

Thank goodness. Black was there. "Can you keep an eye on her airway? Nate, we need fluids. Mack, get an ambulance on its way."

"We've got to get her outside," Nate said. "The fire's spreading. Everyone else is on the lawn."

Emmy looked around the room. "Get that chaise longue. We'll use it as a stretcher."

While Nate dragged it over, Emmy packed gauze against Evelyn's abdomen, but when she applied pressure, blood flowed out between the woman's legs.

Oh, hell. That meant the bullet had angled down and gone through her uterus, which was a heavily vascular area. Blood loss could be a big problem.

As gently as they could, they lifted Evelyn onto the makeshift stretcher. Nate took one end, Black lifted the other, and Emmy held the dressing in place as they half jogged for the front door, coughing from the rolling smoke. Ana ran in front with Scarlet, taking the stairs two at a time, the little girl beyond tears as she stared wordlessly over Ana's shoulder at Evelyn.

In the full-height atrium, Emmy almost tripped over a man's body dressed in a pair of dark sweats. His head looked sort of...dented, but familiar.

"Is that...?"

"Objective four?" Black answered. "Yes."

"What happened?"

"Would you believe he tripped and fell over the third-floor balcony?"

"I'd absolutely believe that."

Ana shoved the front door open, and the others burst out behind her, gulping in air. Dan ran up with an IV line and a bag of fluids and fitted a cannula while Carmen held a flashlight. Evelyn had fallen silent now, and that worried Emmy more than her groans.

"Mack, how long for the ambulance?"

"Two minutes. The FBI had one waiting nearby."

"Hang in there," Emmy muttered to Evelyn.

Emmy had always trusted her gut, and despite the evidence to the contrary, she struggled to believe Evelyn was a bad person. After all, when they found her, she'd been trying to save Scarlet even though Hargrove had a gun. And then she'd sacrificed herself to help Emmy.

They let the house burn as FBI agents swarmed over the property, sorting out the group of young girls huddled under an old oak tree fifty yards away and hunting down the various assholes who'd fled from the fire. Carmen used her infrared scope to assist with locating them, and by the time a crew of medics lifted Evelyn into the ambulance, there was a row of eleven men handcuffed face down in the gravel.

"Will Taylor be okay?" a small voice asked from behind Emmy.

Ana was still holding onto Scarlet. "I hope so, little one. I really hope so."

# CHAPTER 43

MEMORIES OF DRAUPNIR came back in flashes—Guillaume, the fire, Scarlet in that bastard's arms. Then the pain, radiating out through my stomach. Emmy was in the picture too, at least for a while, and then everything went dark.

Now the light was so bright it hurt my eyes, but most of the pain came from my abdomen. Every time I breathed, it burned, and eventually I wondered if it might be easier to simply stop. Really, what did I have left to live for?

"How are you feeling?" A nurse leaned over me, blocking the light for a few blessed seconds.

"I don't want to be here." My voice came out croaky, and my throat stung too.

"Not many people do, hun. Do you want some more painkillers?"

"Yes, please."

The pain eased a little, and the darkness returned. I wished it would last forever.

The next time I opened my eyes, it wasn't the nurse standing over me. Emmy's blonde hair brushed my cheek as she straightened my pillows.

"You're awake?"

What were the chances of passing out again? I had no idea what to say to her.

"Sort of."

"How are you holding up? Evelyn? Your name *is* Evelyn?"

"Evie." I couldn't meet her gaze. "Everything hurts."

"Do you want me to call the nurse?"

"Not really." I just wanted to die quietly with the minimum of fuss. It wasn't as if anyone would miss me. But I needed to ask one question first. "How's Scarlet? Is she okay?"

"She's back home with barely a scratch on her. Do you feel up to talking about what happened?"

I didn't ever want to talk about it, but I supposed I owed Emmy an explanation for the mess I'd caused, especially when that mess had nearly gotten her shot.

"I guess so."

She sat on the edge of the bed and stared expectantly.

"Uh, it all started when somebody attacked Draupnir's servers and Dean traced it back to Blackwood. He told me Draupnir was a rival security company, and if I didn't help him to break into Blackwood's systems, he'd lose his job. I should have refused. I know that now."

"But there was no guarantee you'd even get a job with us."

"Dean said he did a deal with the agency who find you cleaning staff."

Emmy huffed out a breath. "Looks like we're finding a new agency, then."

"Sorry."

"Don't be. We need to tighten up our procedures."

"I hadn't worked there for long when I decided I couldn't do what Dean wanted. Except when I tried to tell him, he wouldn't listen or let me come home, and every time I spoke to him, he put more pressure on. He changed. And then...in that horrible place..." I choked back a sob as Dean's words came back to me. "He said he only married me because I cooked him dinner and cleaned the house, and s-s-slept with him."

"That wasn't the only reason. At least, we don't think so."

"Really?"

Emmy reached out and squeezed my hand. "I'm sure you remember the name Harlan Lake."

This time, I couldn't hold back the tears. "Y-y-yes."

"Dean was his brother."

Every drop of blood in me turned ice cold. "That can't be true. Dean told me he didn't have any siblings."

"He lied, honey."

The full enormity of what she was telling me hit like a truck. No, screw the truck. It was as though a jumbo jet had ploughed into me.

"But Dean was the one who convinced me not to press charges against Harlan. Do you think that was because they were related?"

"It seems likely."

"You referred to Dean in the past tense?"

"I'm sorry. He died in the fire."

By rights, I should have been upset, but I just wasn't feeling it. Instead, a weight had been lifted off my chest.

"I'm not sorry. Not one bit."

"Really?"

"He stole six years of my life. I've had time to think about it since I've been in Richmond. Every time I got scared to go out, he never encouraged me, not once. Just said it was fine, and that I should stay at home if that made me happy. Cooking and freaking cleaning." How would my life have turned out if I'd never met him? Sure, it would have been more difficult at first, but I probably wouldn't have ended up so damned naïve. "It was only when I came here that I started to live again, and now I've lost everything. I don't even have medical insurance, so I've got no idea how I'm supposed to pay all the bills."

"Blackwood's covering that."

"But why? When I...did what I did?"

"You weren't the driving force behind that. And you cared for Scarlet, didn't you? Genuinely?"

"I love that little girl."

Emmy squeezed my hand again. "She adores you too. She keeps asking how you are. Oh, and also why you hit some bloke who sucked her face. We told her he was a fucking pervert. Not in those exact words, obviously."

"Guillaume." I shuddered at the mere mention of his name. "They had him lined up to make an adult movie with her that evening, so I hit him with a candlestick and accidentally set fire to the whole building."

Emmy burst out laughing. "Nice one. Couldn't have done it better myself."

"Do you think I'll ever be able to see her again?"

"Cade's angry right now. He needs space. Maybe one day..."

"Don't worry, I understand. I blew it. I planned to

tell him everything, but he was away, and then Dean threatened to come and get into Blackwood somehow himself, and I panicked. He made me wear a camera and earpiece while he watched me put his stupid virus into Mackenzie's computer, but I couldn't bring myself do it."

"The thumb drive with the recipes? That was you?"

"Bradley gave it to me, and they looked the same from the outside. I just wanted to buy some time until Cade got back, but then Dean came and took us away. He told me Agatha Lerner was a renegade agent."

"She's not."

"I was so stupid."

"Dean did a real number on you, didn't he?"

"How can I ever trust anybody again? He's left me with nothing. Well, I've got a few thousand dollars from cleaning, but I don't suppose I'll be able to work for months, so that won't last. Do you know how long it'll be before I get out of here? Nobody's even told me how badly I'm injured."

Which was never a positive sign, and when Emmy closed her eyes and let out a long breath, I knew the news wasn't good. But I could still move my limbs, at least. What did the bullet hit?

"You took one round to your abdomen, but it went through your uterus as well as your bowel. The surgeons had to remove part of your small intestine. They repaired the damage to the rest as best they could, but it's doubtful you'll ever have children. I'm so sorry, Evie."

Emmy stroked my hair and passed me a tissue as I cried, devastated for the loss of the child I'd always wanted but would never have. Between that and failing

Scarlet and Cade, I felt hollow inside.

"I-I-I expect you think I'm silly. I mean, g-g-getting so upset over something I never had. Dean didn't want children, but I guess I just always hoped..."

The stupid thing was, it had been a lucky escape. If I'd had a baby with Dean, a girl, would she have ended up as one of Draupnir's slaves?

"I kind of do understand why you're so upset." Emmy stared off into the distance, out of the window where a bird soared on an air current. "I lost a baby once. But only three other people know about that, so I'd appreciate it not going beyond this room."

She gave me a sad smile, and the enormity of what she'd just told me swelled inside my chest. Not only because it was incredibly sad, but because of the trust she'd shown.

"I'll never tell a soul."

"I know. And it does get easier with time."

"I'm so sorry." I echoed her earlier words.

"Sometimes, I think it was fate. If that baby had been born... There would have been difficulties. And the idea of being responsible for a small child terrifies me."

She stood up, and I understood she didn't want to talk about her loss any longer. I still needed to process the news about mine too. Secretly, I'd hoped that my game of happy families with Cade and Scarlet would become permanent, but like Emmy said, fate had conspired against us. And my husband. Or was he...?

"If I married Dean Montgomery, and that wasn't even his name, what does that mean? Was it legal?"

"Honestly? I have no idea, but I'll get my lawyer to look into it."

"I can't afford any legal fees."

"Forget the cost. Just concentrate on getting better, okay?"

The nurse came in and Emmy slipped out of the room, leaving me alone with thoughts I didn't want about people I couldn't have.

"Would you like something for the pain?" the nurse asked.

"Trust me, pills aren't going to help."

# CHAPTER 44

SINCE YESTERDAY EVENING, Cade had been sequestered in the basement infirmary at Blackwood's headquarters, and just in case he got any ideas about escaping, Dr. Stanton had switched his clothes for a paper gown then stuck him with a needle full of something that left his mind feeling weirdly disconnected from his body. Yes, it meant he could breathe without fire ripping through his lungs, but pain was the least of his worries when his daughter was missing.

Even spaced out and semi-naked, he'd considered making a break for it to find out what the hell was going on, but then he saw the guard hovering in the hallway outside the door and had a rethink. The watchdog was Emmy's idea, no doubt. The cunning bitch. Every so often, a colleague would venture downstairs and talk to the man in a hushed whisper, but each time Cade asked what the news was, he got the same answer.

"The operation's ongoing. Nothing's confirmed yet."

Cade had been contemplating making a toga out of the sheet, setting off the fire alarm, and making a run for the elevator when Dan arrived to give him an update. The clock said eleven thirty p.m., but as he'd waited for news of Scarlet, every second had felt like a decade.

"What's going on?" he demanded the instant she walked in. The time for asking nicely had long since passed.

"Scarlet's safe. A little shaken, but she's not hurt."

"Where is she?"

"At Riverley with Ana and Carmen."

"You left my daughter with Ana?"

"Look on the bright side—if anyone tries to get near her, they'll wind up wearing their intestines as a necklace."

"Don't you think she's been through enough? I should be the one taking care of her."

"Have you seen yourself in the mirror? You look like an extra in a horror movie, and as you said, Scarlet's been through enough." Dan's voice softened. "Ana's weirdly okay with kids. She was braiding Scarlet's hair when I left."

Cade wasn't going to win the argument—he understood that. Attempting to negotiate with Dan was pointless because she could be almost as stubborn as Emmy when she wanted, so he decided to dig for more information instead.

"What happened? Where did you find her?"

"Everybody's busy unravelling things. The cops, the FBI, an army of attorneys... Someone'll fill you in on the details tomorrow."

"Why can't you fill me in now?"

"Stuff's still going on."

"What stuff?"

"Paperwork, clear-up, that kind of thing."

Paperwork? Yeah, right. "Is that a bloodstain on

your pants? And why do you smell of smoke?"

"Ethan thought we'd barbecue for dinner."

"Bullshit. There was a fire?"

"Get some sleep." Dan backed towards the door, leaving Cade with a thousand unanswered questions as frustration replaced his fear. "See you in the morning."

"I'm sorry."

Cade hadn't expected Emmy to be quite so forthright, but she came straight out and apologised. Nine o'clock in the morning, and the doctor must have slipped him a sleeping pill in the early hours because even eight hours later, his eyes kept closing all by themselves and his brain lagged two paces behind Emmy's words.

"I fucked up. When I asked Evie to look after Scarlet, I should have checked into her credentials more thoroughly."

Who? Oh, right. Taylor.

"Evie? That's what she's calling herself now?"

Emmy nodded.

"Then she's still alive?"

"In the hospital."

Cade's heart shouldn't have lurched, but it did. Until yesterday, he'd been falling for... He struggled to think of her as Evie, even if the name did suit her better. Anyhow, he'd been falling in love with her—too quickly, he knew that now—and her betrayal hurt like a motherfucker. The loss had been fast and painful, like tearing off a Band-Aid, except it had ripped away chunks of his soul instead of just a layer of skin.

"Badly hurt? Is that why Dan was so evasive yesterday?"

Emmy nodded. "Evie was still in surgery. She'll live, but barring a miracle, she'll never have kids. She took a bullet for Scarlet."

Fuck.

"What the hell happened?"

Emmy gave Cade a précis of yesterday's events, starting with the moment they realised Scarlet was missing and ending with Evelyn Montgomery's emergency operation. By the time she'd finished, Cade wanted to strangle Dean Montgomery with a barbed wire garrotte. Bare hands were too kind for him.

"And I'm not saying this to mitigate what I didn't do," Emmy said, finishing up, "but I genuinely don't think Evie's a bad person. She just met the wrong men at the wrong time, and both of the shitheads turned out to be from the same gene pool."

Gene pool? Cesspool, more like.

But while Taylor-slash-Evie might have taken on Kelvin Hargrove at the end, she'd still been the one to get Scarlet into the situation in the first place, not forgetting the fact that she'd come to Blackwood as a spy. A fucking spy.

"If Scarlet hadn't arrived on the scene, do you think Evie would've carried on with her original plan? To break into the computer network?"

"Who knows? Dean did a number on her head—brainwashed her—but the longer she was apart from him, the more she learned to be herself again." Emmy shrugged. "Without the access to the third floor Scarlet provided, Evie would've got caught sooner rather than later, and the chances are, Dean Montgomery would have abandoned her to her fate. He seemed like that sort of person."

"I don't know if I can forgive her." And damn her for making him feel this way. "Right now, I just need to be there for my daughter."

"Take as much time off as you need. Bradley can help until your ribs heal up. Stay at Riverley if you want."

No way. The place was only one step up from an asylum most of the time.

"I'd rather be in my own home. Scarlet's had enough upheaval in her life already."

"Understandable. Want a ride to pick her up?"

"Dan thought my face might scare her."

Cade had taken Dan's advice and looked in the mirror, and she'd been right in her assessment. He'd have slayed in a zombie movie. A shower might have washed the remains of the dried blood off, but there wasn't much he could do about the row of stitches above his eyebrow, his split lip, or his swollen nose. At least he'd lost the damn beard now.

"She only said that because we didn't want you wading into the middle of things last night. Too much stress. But like you said, Scarlet needs stability, and she's been asking for her daddy."

Cade hated to raise the question, but... "Which one?"

"You, you idiot. Otherwise I wouldn't have mentioned it."

His heart did another stupid flip. Perhaps he should get the doctor to check that out? Run an ECG or something. But that could come later, after he'd seen his daughter and started on the long journey to rectify the damage done by Montgomery and Hargrove.

He hadn't entirely forgiven Emmy either, or Nate for putting a fucking tracking device in his daughter without asking permission first. But they'd gone some way to redeeming themselves with yesterday's rescue operation. Nobody but Emmy's team could have pulled that off, and that had meant the difference between a few awkward questions from Scarlet and a lifetime of pain.

Yes, he'd take some time off. Time to heal, time to think, time to be a father. Then he'd decide where his future lay, and Scarlet's too.

"Then thanks," he said to Emmy. "A ride sounds good."

# CHAPTER 45

EMMY DIDN'T COME back to the hospital the next day, but Lara peeped around the door mid-morning and caught me wiping away the tears I couldn't seem to stop crying.

"I'd ask if you were okay, but I know that's a really stupid question."

"Well, I'm alive." I tried to make a joke out of it, but the smile wouldn't come, and I felt my face crumple. "I'm not sure whether that's a good thing or a bad thing right now."

"It's definitely a good thing."

"You're about the only person who thinks that. Have you heard the whole story?"

"Nick and Emmy told me most of it."

"I can't believe she doesn't hate me for what I did."

"Emmy doesn't look at the world through the same eyes as everybody else."

"I'm beginning to understand that."

My mouth felt all dry, but when I tried to sit up, a pain shot through my stomach and I winced.

"You want the water?"

"Yes, please."

If I couldn't even reach for a drink, how long would it be before I could take care of myself again? One of the reasons my fourth-floor apartment cost so little was the lack of an elevator, and I'd need to find work soon to pay the rent. It wasn't as if I could just run back to California. What was left there? A foreclosed house and reminders of the man I'd grown to hate?

Lara passed me the glass, and I sipped gratefully through the straw. Having her there with a friendly smile gave me some hope for the future, at least. Hope that I'd be able to meet new people and resurrect something from the ruins of my life. A big part of me still wished I'd died at Draupnir, but that wasn't what kismet had in store for me, so now I needed to deal with it.

Although I couldn't help poking at old wounds.

"Have you heard anything about Scarlet?"

"I looked after her yesterday while Cade went into the office."

"Emmy said she was doing all right?"

"She seems to have come through this better than anyone. We spent an hour swimming, and now she wants a mermaid tail."

"Has she mentioned anything about the fire? Is she having nightmares?"

Because I sure was.

"From what I understand, Ana sat down with her when they got back to Blackwood, and they talked things through. That was kind of surprising because..." She lowered her voice to a whisper. "Between you and me, Ana's really scary."

"Who's Ana?" I didn't remember her name from the staff directory.

"Emmy's height, short black hair, moves like a panther."

"I think I saw her once in the office. And again at

Draupnir. She was one of the people who came to rescue me."

She'd had a gun in her hand and eyes like the devil himself, so yes, I understood Lara's assessment. But if Ana had helped Scarlet, she couldn't be that bad.

"Seeing her once is enough."

"And how's Cade?"

Lara wrinkled her nose. "Still a little upset about everything."

"That's what Emmy said too. Do you think he'll ever speak to me again?"

She shrugged. "He's kind of tetchy, what with his broken ribs and nose."

"His *what*?"

"Oh, shoot. Nobody told you?"

"I knew he was hurt, but nobody said he had broken bones."

"His undercover job went wrong. It turned out the people he was investigating were also after Draupnir, just coming at it from a different direction. There was a bit of a fight before everything got sorted out, but you didn't hear that from me. I'm not supposed to know those details, but I overheard Nick talking on the phone."

I leaned back into the pillow and closed my eyes. More pain caused by Dean and Hargrove. They'd hurt everybody I cared about.

"I'd do anything to turn back the clock."

"But what happened to Cade was nothing to do with you."

"I guess."

"Enough with blaming yourself." She reached into a bag at her feet. "I've brought you an eReader, a phone, a portable DVD player, chocolates, a few puzzle books... oh, and grapes."

"You didn't need to do that. I don't even have anyone to phone."

"Of course you do. Me, Nick, Emmy, Bradley. Bradley wanted to come and visit too, but I thought you might want an extra day to recover first."

"He does have a lot of energy."

"He's been using it for shopping. Nick brought your clothes back from California, but Bradley still insisted on buying you a whole new wardrobe."

This was crazy. All of these people helping me? I didn't deserve it. "Can you thank Nick for bringing my things? I still need to sort out the house, but hopefully I can do that from here. I'm not sure I can bring myself to go back to the West Coast again, even if I manage to scrape together the money for a plane ticket."

"We kind of figured you wouldn't want to go back there. Do you want to sell the house?"

"I just want to give the keys back to the mortgage company and never think of it again. I don't even know if I *can* sell the place. Everything was in Dean's name, and he used a false surname, so I'm not sure where that leaves me. Emmy said she'd look into the legalities."

"Then leave it to her. She'll fix it. Do you want any of the contents? The furniture? Nick said the house was mostly empty."

I shook my head. "Dean liked it that way."

"Nick was the other extreme when I first met him. You literally couldn't move in our house for all the trash he'd accumulated over the years. But it's all good now. You've got a choice of five spare bedrooms."

"What?"

"Well, you can't go back to your apartment sore like this. We, uh, cancelled the lease and moved your stuff from Cade's."

"You did what?"

"We were worried about you being on your own. Please don't be mad. Bradley's already offered to help you find a new place when you're better, and I'm sure he'll even decorate."

"I don't deserve any of this."

"Your ex did some really nasty things to you, and I understand how that feels. Mine nearly killed me. So, Nick and I are going to help you get back on your feet because it's the right thing to do."

"I don't know what to say. I'm so sorry somebody hurt you."

"Don't say anything. It's all in the past now for both of us, and one day, you'll be stronger because of it. I know I am."

"Thank you."

Lara just smiled. "I think we should watch a movie now."

The doctors let me out of the hospital a week later, when I could walk and dress myself again. The twinges of pain in my gut were a constant reminder of what I'd lost, but Lara was right. I needed to look to the future. That meant trying to smile as I unpacked in my temporary bedroom, even if I could barely move from the mountain of flowers Bradley had brought. At least it was cheery.

At first, I felt like a waste of space, but Lara got me

to help with table plans for her latest charity dinner, then the menus and invitations. After living with Dean for so many years, one of the few things I'd learned was how a computer worked, so I set up an event website too.

"You're good at this," she said. "Ever thought of going into the events planning business?"

"The idea of talking to all those strangers the way you do terrifies me."

"It used to scare me too. I always felt like the ugly duckling, really self-conscious, but Nick spent so long telling me I was a swan that eventually I started to believe it. And do you know what? I don't care what those people think of me anymore. And the less I care, the more respect I get. Weird, huh?"

"Really weird. But I'm still not sure I'm cut out for events planning. In fact, I'm considering going back to nursing. I really enjoyed it before I met Dean."

"Well, I think you'd make a great nurse too."

Back in San Francisco, before we moved to Santa Barbara, I'd taken a one-year vocational course to become a Licensed Practical Nurse, but I'd been out of the field so long I'd be more or less starting from scratch. Still, Lara supported me all the way, finding details of the courses and helping me with the forms. A month after the fire, I began to feel as if I was worth something again.

Despite the fact that I'd moved into their home at short notice, Nick and Lara never once made me feel like a burden. And when Lara announced that the Blackwood girls were coming over for dinner one evening, rather than lock myself in the bathroom and cry like I would have just one short month ago, I followed one of Mrs. Fairfax's recipes and made an appetiser of baked Camembert.

They started arriving at seven—Dan, Mack, Carmen, Tia, Georgia, Chess, Sofia, Ana, even the mysterious Agatha. Emmy brought up the rear with Bradley, who I'd learned was an honorary member of their little club. Being the new girl felt awkward at first, but the conversation soon flowed along with the wine.

"So, Hawk's starting work at Blackwood on Monday?" Sofia asked.

Emmy nodded. "Yeah. Just as an entry-level investigator until we see how he gets on, but somebody's happy."

She pointed at Agatha, who'd gone quite pink.

"What?" Agatha asked.

"Every time I looked at you today, you were staring at him," Mack said.

"I was just, uh, thinking."

"About licking him, I bet."

"We need to run a pool," Emmy announced. "Hawk and Agatha. How long until they can't keep their hands off each other?"

"I doubt he even likes me."

Carmen reached out for the bottle of wine. "But he's definitely single. Smith told me."

"Why are you spending so much time with Smith, anyway? You're married."

"Because apart from Slater, nobody else appreciates the beauty of a gun like I do. Smith's a close third. How's Mouse getting on?"

"He's a little odd," Mack said. "Blunt to the point of rudeness sometimes, but also sensitive. I keep having to reassure him about everything. And he only drinks out of blue cups."

"But does he know what he's doing?"

"He writes code like a demon."

"Then who cares about blue cups?"

"Not me. He's taken some of the non-sensitive stuff off my plate, and the extra pair of hands means I can finally catch up on some sleep. Oh, and Sailor said he'll stop by tomorrow before he heads off to Thailand."

Tia leaned back with a sigh. "I wish I could spend six months on the beach."

"Just ask your hot boyfriend to take you," Dan said.

She rolled her eyes. "I would, if he wasn't spending all of his time locked in the studio with *your* hot boyfriend."

I didn't know most of the people they were talking about, but it didn't matter. The sense of camaraderie was the important thing. For the first time in my life, I felt as if I belonged somewhere, even if I was only on the periphery, and I didn't want to leave. There were just two things missing: Scarlet and her father.

# CHAPTER 46

"THE CENTREPIECES ARE arriving at four. I've seated Carolina di Matteo as far away from her ex-husband and his new wife as possible, and the kitchen knows that Bruno Carmichael on table six can't eat anything with red meat, dairy, gluten, refined sugar, chilli, or onions."

Or flavour, it seemed.

Lara paused in her attempts to shoehorn the long list of donated gifts into the charity auction schedule, her scribble-covered papers spread over the dining table at Adler House. "You're a star. Honestly, I couldn't have done this without you. Are you sure you don't want to come tonight?"

Go solo to a ridiculously fancy charity dinner? Not likely. Emmy had jokingly offered to set me up with a suitable man—at least, I thought she was joking—but all I wanted to do was kick back on the sofa with a glass of wine and another box of the chocolates Bradley kept buying me. He'd encouraged me to go tonight too by bringing me not one but three evening gowns, complete with more accessories than some New York fashion shows.

"I'm sure."

"Scott Lowes is going to be there."

Trust Lara to tempt me with the Hollywood A-List.

She'd been thrilled when he accepted the invitation. But even though the delectable Mr. Lowes may have commanded thirty million dollars per movie, there was only one man I wanted, and he hailed from the East Coast, not the West.

"I'd rather stay here."

"Slater offered to go with you. I know I'm with Nick, but I've got eyes, and Slater's..." She blew out a breath and grinned.

"It's very kind of him, but..."

The doorbell rang, and Lara leapt to her feet, scattering papers across the massive dining table. "Darn it! That'll be the make-up lady. I keep telling Bradley I don't need all this fuss, but he insists."

Saved by the bell.

Oh, heck. I almost forgot to update the seating plan to say that Duncan Paulson's new date was a vegetarian. A last-minute replacement, according to his personal assistant.

"Taylor!"

I looked up in time to see Scarlet fly across the room and launch herself at me.

"Oof." I'd been feeling better, but hit by a speeding five-year-old, I doubled up in pain.

"Scarlet, be careful."

I recognised that voice, and shivers ran through me when I saw Cade watching from the doorway. A different Cade. He'd lost weight, and I'd never seen him without a beard before.

"Hi." I didn't know what else to say.

"Hi."

"Taylor, I want pancakes. Daddy Cade doesn't do them right."

He shrugged. "Apparently, mine have lumps."

"Uh..."

Should I offer to make them for her? Because I would, but I didn't want to do the wrong thing.

"Can I have chocolate ice cream with them?"

I glanced at Cade, helpless until Lara stepped in.

"Why don't you come through to the kitchen and try my pancakes? I'm sure I can find some chocolate ice cream."

"Don't you have to get ready?" I whispered.

She waved a hand. "It's fine. You talk to Cade."

Nice idea, but what on earth was I supposed to say? We'd reverted to the same awkwardness that had filled the space between us when we first met.

Thankfully, he spoke first. "Did she hurt you?"

"Not really. My stomach's just a bit tender still."

"I should have told her not to hug you."

How could I tell him I'd take a hug from Scarlet even if it left me in agony? Because her sweetness outweighed everything.

"It's fine, really. How are your ribs? I heard you broke them."

"Yeah, they're okay."

The gulf widened again, and Cade shifted from foot to foot.

"Do you want something to drink? Or eat?"

"She's missed you. Every single day, she's been asking for you. I don't know what to tell her."

"I've missed her too." So, so much.

Cade came closer, and now I saw the tension in his shoulders. It matched my own. He took his hands out of his pockets before he sank into a chair opposite me and picked up the pen Lara had been writing with.

*Click. Click. Click.*

"Emmy said I should talk to you. I... She... Taylor... Evelyn... Shit, I don't even know what to call you."

"My name's Evie."

Hopefully Evie Sutton soon. Apparently, even though Dean had used a false surname, our marriage was legal, but at least I didn't have to deal with the hassle of a divorce. I couldn't wait to have my maiden name back. Emmy had promised her lawyer was on the case with the paperwork.

"Evie." He smiled for a second. "It suits you, better than Taylor." But then his expression grew serious once more. "You lied to me. To us. To everyone."

"I know. And I mostly wish I could undo it. But if I did, then I'd never have come to Virginia, and I'd never have met you and Scarlet. And while I'll apologise forever for all the hurt and pain I caused, I'll never be sorry for that part." I'd had enough time to think things through now, and the time I'd spent with Scarlet and Cade was something I'd always treasure.

"Emmy said your husband pushed you into everything."

I nodded.

"How could you let him do that?"

"Because I was nothing. He spent six years making sure I had no confidence and no self-esteem, and just for once, I wanted him to be proud of me." A tear rolled down my cheek. "And look how that worked out."

"I'm sorry for your, uh, loss."

"It was no loss. I only wish I'd never met him in the first place."

"If I'd known you were married, I'd never have made a move on you in Florida. That's not the type of man I am."

"I know. But I can't be sorry for that part either."

The pause continued on and on until Cade finally cleared his throat.

"So, what are your plans now? Are you staying in Richmond?"

I nodded. "I don't have any family, and I'm not going back to California. Lara's offered me a place to stay until I can get a job and find a new apartment."

"Do you have anything lined up?"

"I'm hoping to become a nurse again."

"Nothing definite yet?"

"I'm doing all the applications at the moment. I won't be able to lift anything for a few more weeks, anyway."

"Because... I was wondering..." Cade scrubbed a hand through his hair. "I'll be starting work again soon and... Look, do you want your old job back?"

A tiny bud of hope blossomed in my chest. "Are you serious? After everything that's happened?"

"You were ready to give up your own life to save my daughter. That's the kind of person I want looking after her, because I'd do exactly the same. And when we were talking about your past, you said forgiveness was important, that holding a grudge was like poisoning yourself. I've felt that bitterness over the past month, and it's time to let it go."

"I've been thinking about that too, and I'm not sure I'll ever be able to forgive Dean."

"I guess I can understand that. What he did was in a whole different class of asshole."

I stifled a giggle.

"Just don't let it eat away at you. And Evie? No

more lies."

"I'm never lying to anybody again."

"Then what do you say? About the job?"

My smile grew so wide I worried my face might split. "I'd love to look after Scarlet again."

Cade smiled too, not so big, but it was there. "She'll be happy with that too. But it'll have to be different this time. Live out."

"That's fine. I can get a little apartment and a car."

"Then we're sorted?"

"We're sorted."

That was the best offer I could ever have hoped for, and I was still beaming when Scarlet scurried in holding a plate out in front of her.

"Taylor! We made you pancakes. I put extra ice cream on for you."

Lara followed her in, carrying three more plates on a tray. "We figured everyone could use pancakes."

"What about your dinner tonight?"

"Between you and me, I'm not so keen on nouvelle cuisine. Pancakes are much tastier."

"Is Taylor coming back home?" Scarlet asked Cade.

"Taylor's got a new name now. She's called Evie. Isn't that pretty?"

Pretty? He thought my name was pretty? Or was he just saying that?

"Why?"

"Because special girls are allowed to change their names occasionally."

"Oh." She mulled that over, licking chocolate ice cream off her spoon. "Am I special?"

A bubble of laughter escaped because I saw where this was going, but Cade, busy scooping pancakes into his mouth, clearly didn't.

"Of course you're special."

"So I can have a new name?"

Ah, now he realised. He looked up at her, hesitant. "What new name do you want?"

"Pocahontas."

Lara got the giggles and covered her mouth with her hand while we waited to see how Cade would react.

"Pocahontas? That's, uh, difficult to spell."

Scarlet folded her arms and stared at him. "P-o-c-a-h-o-n-t-a-s. Evie taught me reading."

"People might get confused."

"Are you confused?"

I took pity on him. "Scarlet's a lovely name. And I thought we could make cakes tomorrow and write our names on them, but Pocahontas might not fit."

"You think I should keep being called Scarlet?"

"I do."

She shovelled up her last mouthful, dripping melted ice cream across the table. "Okay, I'll keep being Scarlet. Now I need a piss."

She hopped off her seat as I choked on a piece of pancake. Lara stared open-mouthed while Cade rolled his eyes to the ceiling.

"Sweetie, where did you hear that word?" I asked.

"Emmy said it yesterday."

"I was stuck for a babysitter," Cade whispered.

"That's a grown-up word, and it's not polite. You want to be polite, don't you?"

She nodded solemnly.

"So, you say 'I need to go to the bathroom.'"

"I need to go to the bathroom."

"Good girl. You remember where it is?"

"Yes."

She ran off down the hallway, and I heard the door to the half bath slam.

"I'm glad you're coming back," Cade said.

That made two of us.

# CHAPTER 47

OTHER WOMEN MAY have lusted after a jet-setting lifestyle or a high-powered career, because that was what society geared us to aspire to, right? All the glossy magazines, the TV shows, the ads on the internet... But I found my happiness in a simpler way: in a small house with Scarlet and her father, when he was home.

My gourmet dinners consisted of macaroni and cheese, a visit to the art gallery meant sticking another of Scarlet's drawings on the fridge, and my manicurist was a soon-to-be six-year-old child. Mackenzie had tracked down a copy of Scarlet's birth certificate, and everyone was desperately trying to keep the date a secret from Bradley. After a discussion, Cade and I decided a quiet dinner with a few gifts and a cake would be more appropriate than whatever circus he might come up with.

And according to Carmen, he took the "circus" part literally. Her son's fifth birthday party had featured a big top and forty-three acrobats, and to this day, Joshua couldn't stand clowns.

Things with Cade had been strained at first, but by the end of the third week, we'd settled into a routine, and I even dared to hope we'd become friends again. Until his ribs healed fully, he was restricted to office duty, which meant he came home every night and ate dinner with us most evenings.

And tonight had been no different, except he'd arrived home earlier than usual to finish off some work on his laptop. And when I said "work," I meant I'd been listening to him playing around with Scarlet the whole time I cooked dinner.

"Need a hand?" he asked from the doorway.

I turned around and started giggling.

"What? You think the glitter's too much?"

"I want to be a hairdresser when I grow up," Scarlet announced.

I stepped forward for a closer look. She'd added a lifetime's supply of gel to Cade's hair, spiked it up, coloured it blue, and sprinkled it with silver glitter.

"Where did the blue come from?"

"What blue?" Cade asked.

"A Sharpie," Scarlet informed him.

His eyes widened. "I think I need to take a shower before dinner."

"I'll keep yours in the oven. Good luck."

An hour later, Scarlet kept yawning while a blue-tinted Cade swirled the dregs of a bottle of Pinot Noir around the bottom of his wine glass. I didn't touch alcohol in the evenings because I had to drive back to Adler House afterwards. Emmy's lawyer had come through, and the sale of the beach house had been completed five days ago, but even though I had forty thousand dollars sitting in my bank account from the equity, I was still living with Lara. Nick was away quite often at the moment, and she said there was no hurry for me to move out.

"Normally, I'd go with him to LA," she told me. "But I accidentally got volunteered to run another fundraiser seeing as the last one was so successful."

"That's good, though."

"I know. I just miss Nick, that's all, and the house is so quiet when I'm on my own."

"I like the company too."

And I really did. Having proper friends was a whole different experience to the superficial acquaintances I'd hung out with in the past, and I finally began to feel good in my own skin.

Up until last week, money had been tight, so I still didn't have my own car. But Cade had bought an SUV so we could take Scarlet places, and I borrowed that each night to make the short trip back to my temporary home. He said he didn't mind, and he preferred to ride his bike to the office anyway.

But tonight, rather than walk with me to the front door, he settled onto the sofa. "Want to watch a movie?"

"Together?"

"No, I figured I could watch on the TV upstairs while you stayed down here. Of course together."

"I'd like that."

"Any preferences?"

I shook my head. I'd have quite happily watched a blank screen as long as I was doing it with Cade. Because no matter how much I tried to persuade myself otherwise, I was still crazy about the man. How many times had I relived that kiss with him in my sleep? I'd lost count. Sitting down to watch a movie might not have been a big deal to most people, but for me it meant a step back towards the way things were before, even with him at one end of the sofa and me at the other.

He ejected *The Enchanted Library* out of the DVD player. "Let's give anything Wonder a miss. I know all the words by heart now."

"Have you still got that little shell bra Scarlet made you?"

"Yeah, somewhere. Reckon I should get the mermaid's tits properly covered up, shouldn't I? Actually, I know just the man to do it now."

"It probably wouldn't hurt, especially when she starts having friends to visit. Kids always ask such awkward questions."

"Remind me tomorrow. I'll get it organised."

Cade picked out an action movie, and I struggled to follow the plot as I kept sneaking glances towards him. Eventually, I began to drift off and caught myself just as I keeled over into his lap.

"Sorry! I really should go before I get too tired to drive."

Rather than help me up, he rested one hand on my side and twirled my hair around the fingers of the other.

"But you'll miss the end of the movie."

As well as Cade's gentle touch.

"Okay, I'll stay." It wasn't a difficult decision. "I can make a coffee after."

Except the coffee never happened. I woke in a comfortable bed, both familiar and unfamiliar, with the faint smell of Cade's aftershave drifting around me.

Holy hell! He'd put me to sleep in his bed. Where was he? A quick check either side revealed I'd slept alone, which meant he must have taken the sofa. Dammit, this was the sweet side of him I found hard to deal with. Hard because I wanted to throw myself at his feet and beg him to do bad things to me.

But not at this very moment. Because my hair was stuck to one side of my face, I'd drooled in my sleep, and my eyes were all gummy. Oh, and I really, really needed to pee. What was the time? Eight thirty. Dammit, I'd overslept too. At least it was Saturday, so I didn't need to take Scarlet to kindergarten. I could freshen up, make breakfast for everyone, then sneak back to Lara's for fresh clothes.

The house was still silent, so I made a dash to the bathroom and hastily stripped off yesterday's dress. The oversized woollen sweater thing wasn't my usual choice, but Bradley had bought it for me, so I figured I should wear it at least once. Now, what was there in the way of toiletries? My things were no longer by the sink since Lara had picked them up ages ago, but after a quick rummage, I found a spare stick of deodorant at the back of the cupboard under the sink. Thank goodness. And a comb and cleanser too.

I untangled my hair, but as I stared at myself in the mirror, a tear rolled down my cheek. Last time I stood there, I was a whole person, but the woman looking back at me now was damaged goods. The scars on my otherwise flat stomach were testament to that. I'd never have stretch marks, just the puckered round hole where Hargrove's bullet had ripped apart my insides and next to that, the angry scar from the emergency laparotomy. A constant reminder of my stupidity.

I gave in and let myself cry freely, and when the door clicked open, it took a few seconds to register that Cade was standing there. In a freaking towel. I didn't know which bit of myself to cover first. Hadn't he heard of knocking?

"Why are you upset?"

"Hello, I'm half-naked here."

He ran his eyes up and down my body, and one corner of his lips quirked up. "I'd have to be a saint not to notice that, and I'm no saint. Why are you crying?"

"It doesn't matter."

"Yeah, it matters." He followed my gaze downwards in the mirror. "Your scars? You could get a plastic surgeon to lessen the impact."

"Emmy said that too."

"You don't like the idea?"

"No, I need to keep them as a reminder not to get mixed up with the wrong man again."

He took another step closer. "Define the wrong man."

"One who lies. One who takes advantage of me. But it's not just the scars outside, is it? D-d-do you know what happened inside?"

He nodded.

"I'll never be a mom."

"You already are."

His words made me glow and ache at the same time. "But what if I lose her again? It would break me."

"You won't. I promise you won't. You won't lose either of us, okay?"

Cade wrapped his arms around me, and the awkwardness of having this conversation skin-on-skin was eclipsed by his strength as it flowed into me.

And his lips on mine.

Our first kiss paled into insignificance when his hands roamed over me, and as his tongue teased the seam of my lips, I opened up and invited him in. Oh hell, I hadn't even brushed my teeth. Not that he seemed to care. He pinned me against the counter with his hips, and what pressed into me suggested other parts of his anatomy were happy with the situation too.

Then he pulled back, leaving me breathless.

"I promise I'll never lie to you, but I want to take advantage of you every damn day, peach. What do you say?"

"You mean... You and me?"

"Unless there's some other asshole I don't know about?"

"There's no one." Words failed me, so I stood on tiptoe and kissed him back. My bra disappeared somewhere, and Cade's towel fell to the floor, leaving my panties as the only barrier between us. Then he ripped those off too.

"Are you okay with this?"

No, I was terrified, but I was more scared of missing out. So I bit my lip and nodded.

Another searing kiss, then, "Shit. I don't have a condom. They're in my bedroom."

With a five-year-old girl on the loose.

"I'm not going to get pregnant."

"I'm clean, I swear."

He picked me up, cursed as he tripped over his towel, and then we landed up against the wall in the new, smaller shower. But that barely had time to register before he pushed inside me.

"Fuck, you're tight."

I screwed my eyes shut, consumed by a pain as delicious as it was burning. "I think that's something to do with your size."

Dean had barely touched the sides.

Nor, it appeared, had Dean known what to do with

it, but Cade certainly did. I wrapped one leg around his waist to get closer as he thrust, and a warm haze spread inside me, an ecstasy I'd never felt before, and his lips... his hands... They were everywhere.

And then it happened.

"Daddy! I need to go to the bathroom."

Cade paused, smothering a laugh. "Can you use the toilet downstairs?"

"Okay. And can you pick up Evie? I want her to come and make pancakes."

He lifted me clean off the floor. "Evie'll be coming really soon."

"You're so bad," I whispered.

"Shhh."

But I couldn't stay quiet, not now he was even deeper inside me. Only one thing for it. I reached out and turned on the shower to cover up the sound of my moans as a supernova burst inside me. I couldn't stop shaking as Cade gave one final thrust and filled me with his heat, and for a few minutes, we just stood there, letting the water cascade over us.

"Are you okay?" he asked, lips brushing against mine.

"I don't even know what planet I'm on at the moment. What just happened?"

"We had shower sex, peach."

"I mean at the end."

His eyes widened. "You've honestly never had an orgasm before?"

I shook my head. No more lies—that was what I'd promised.

"I thought you were kidding about that. Six years and the man never made you come? He was an even bigger asshole than I thought."

"Did you mean what you said about taking advantage of me?"

"Peach, I want to take you to bed and bury myself in you for a week. No, a month. A year." He smiled against me. "But apparently, you're making pancakes."

With Scarlet still downstairs, I gathered up what was left of my clothes and ran through to Cade's bedroom with him following.

"You wrecked my panties," I hissed.

He only smirked. "I'll buy you a new pair so I can do it again."

"I'm serious. What am I supposed to wear? And what do we do? The car's still downstairs. Should I leave and come back again? Pretend I arrived while she was on the toilet?"

Cade shrugged. "If you want."

"You're no help."

I pulled my dress on, only for him to lift it up again, running his hands up my sides as he kissed me senseless.

"Cade! I'm being serious."

"So am I. Very serious. About you."

I got lost in another kiss, then came to my senses and pushed him away. "I'm going to fetch underwear. Do me a favour and get the frying pan out. And the mixing bowl."

He pulled on a pair of jeans, laughing, and gave me a salute. "Whatever you say, boss."

Playful Cade. A side I hadn't seen much of, but I

liked it. I gave him one last peck on the cheek and yanked the door open.

"Evie! I didn't know you were here already."

Oops.

Cade appeared behind me, tugging on a shirt. "Evie stayed here last night so she could make you pancakes."

"Yay! Is she moving back in now?"

He raised an eyebrow at me.

"Uh..."

"Up to you, peach."

Of all the decisions I'd ever had to make, that one was the easiest.

"Yes, sweetie. I'm moving back in."

Cade grinned while Scarlet jumped up and down, clapping. "And is she gonna be my new mommy?"

"Do you want her to be your new mommy?"

She put her hands on her hips and gave him an "are you stupid?" look.

An arm snaked around my waist, and he pulled me back against him. "Seems like you got yourself a promotion, Evie Sutton."

Scarlet did a strange dance that involved wiggling her butt a lot, then scampered off along the hallway.

"I need to tell Eric!"

"What was that?" I asked Cade.

"The dance? She's also been spending time with Dan lately."

"I meant the whole moving-in bit."

"I guess it comes with the 'I want to bury myself in you for a week' part." He nuzzled my neck. "Looks like we're having our pancakes *sans* underwear this morning."

"I hate you."

But I was lying, and we both knew it. I loved him.

# EPILOGUE

OVER THE NEXT few weeks, my life turned into everything I'd ever wished for. I had new friends, a cosy home, a beautiful daughter, and a gorgeous man to sleep next to at night. Okay, not so much of the sleeping part. I'd resorted to afternoon naps.

Each day, I caught up on the news while I cooked dinner. The home invasion case had been officially closed, and according to Cade, not only had the FBI found all the stolen computers in the trunk of Kelvin Hargrove's car, their investigators had unearthed a backup tape containing a list of Draupnir's clients in a fireproof safe in the mansion. Over the past few weeks, they'd slowly been rounding the sick freaks up, and lawyers from coast to coast were rubbing their hands together in glee. Nine of the girls found at the house turned out to be kidnap victims, and one of them had been missing for five years. Five years of hell, but at least it was over now. The others were runaways Hargrove had brainwashed into performing for his clients, or in several cases, acquired from their disgusting parents. Fourteen bodies had been found in the grounds—that was the worst part—but only two of them had been identified so far.

I still burned with anger about what he'd gotten away with for so many years. Once or twice, I found myself wishing that he and Dean had survived the fire, but only so I could have the pleasure of killing them myself.

But enough of the negativity. I had a new part-time job, which meant that two days a week while Scarlet went to kindergarten, I helped Dr. Stanton out in the infirmary at Blackwood. Just with routine vaccinations and medicals at first, but it gave me a change of scene and fulfilled my wish to return to nursing, if only in a small way.

And being with Cade brought out an adventurous side I never knew I had. Last weekend, he'd convinced me to get on the back of his motorcycle, and we rode out to visit a friend of his in a little town called Oakley. In a tattoo shop. At least I looked the part, because Cade had bought me a leather jacket.

The man who ran the place made me nervous at first, partly because he was enormous, but mostly because the snake tattoo winding its way up his neck looked so damn realistic.

"Good to see you again, Pool Boy. Your nose is looking straighter."

"Pool boy?"

Cade tightened his arm around my shoulders. "Long story."

"And who's the lovely lady?"

"This is Evie, my girlfriend."

His girlfriend. It was the first time he'd called me that, and damned if it didn't make me smile.

The man held out a hand to me. "Snake."

Of course.

"This a social visit, Pool?"

"Actually, I need a favour."

Cade told Snake about the mermaid shells, and the big man's shoulders shook with laughter. "So you want her to look demure, is that it?"

"It's for the best."

"And how about you, lady?"

"Oh, no. I'm not really that sort of girl."

"Datin' Pool here? I'd say you were exactly that sort of girl. I'll do your art free of charge."

I was about to decline again, politely, when Cade whispered in my ear.

"Do you trust me?"

"Yes."

"Then you're getting a tattoo."

While I'd have felt sick at the thought of giving up that sort of control to Dean, with Cade things were different. He really did act in my best interests and showed it every day with actions rather than words. And so I did as he said and lay back on the padded table, gripping his hand while Snake worked, and when the not-so-scary-after-all man finished, I almost cried for the first time in weeks.

"It's beautiful."

"They're peach blossoms."

Pretty pink flowers covered up the scars on my stomach, pale petals with a darker centre. Snake had worked the lumpy texture into the design and turned the ugly mess into a work of art.

Cade leaned over to kiss the corner of my mouth. "Figured you didn't need reminding not to get mixed up with the wrong man anymore. Because I'll spend the rest of my life proving I'm the right man, and I'm never letting you go."

Dammit. "I need a tissue."

But this time, I cried happy tears.

Two days until Scarlet's birthday, and Bradley still hadn't found out. So far, so good. I was waiting with her in reception at Blackwood for Cade, and then we were going to the party store to pick out balloons. Tomorrow, we planned to bake a cake, which if the last attempt was anything to go by, would involve Cade watching TV and licking out the icing bowl while his daughter and I did all the hard work.

But I didn't care. He talked to me while I cooked, and he always helped to clear up the mess afterwards. That house was filled with love and laughter, and each day, the memories of Dean grew dimmer. Three weeks had passed since my last nightmare about Harlan Lake, and even when he did pay an unwelcome visit, Cade woke me from the pain and held me tight until good dreams eclipsed the bad.

"Do either of you want a drink?" asked Lottie, the receptionist. I'd gotten to know her a little too, and she made amazing oatmeal-and-raisin cookies.

"No, thanks. Cade won't be long."

Scarlet got out her colouring book while I watched the news on the big screen opposite. Another FBI bust. Another high-profile paedophile being led off in handcuffs. Although we tried not to mention the past, Cade had told me the ongoing series of arrests was tied to Draupnir, and just thinking about it made me sick.

So I tried not to.

Instead, I focused on happy things. Like this morning, when Scarlet called me Mommy Evie for the first time. Because I knew now that life was a series of key moments, some good, some bad, and I had to embrace the joy it could bring and deal with the woes as best I could. And I also knew that Cade would be by my side, helping me through it all.

Unless it involved cooking.

Agatha walked past and gave me a friendly wave. "Cade's on his way down. He just stopped to talk to Emmy."

I waved back. "Have a good weekend."

"You too."

The doors whooshed open, but instead of silence when they closed again, I heard the sound of footsteps. A woman dressed in tight jeans and a scoop-neck top with her boobs spilling over strode towards me with the guard from the gate hurrying along behind.

"Ma'am, if you'll just take a seat, I'll try to locate him."

"No need, Scarlet's right over there." She opened her arms wide. "Come to Mommy."

My heart stuttered, then stopped.

No. *No, no, no.* This couldn't be happening. The little world I'd built for myself crumbled apart brick by brick.

Scarlet dropped her crayon and gripped my arm, nails digging in as the woman kept coming. Cindy. That was what Cade had called her.

"Time to go, darlin'. Didn't I promise I'd be back for you?"

"I don't want to go."

"Don't be silly. You got any stuff to bring?"

I finally found my tongue. "You're not taking her."

Cindy put her hands on her hips in a stance that

mirrored Scarlet's on occasion. "And who do you think you are?"

"Her—"

I was going to be diplomatic and say nanny, but Scarlet cut me off.

"This is my mommy Evie."

Cindy narrowed her eyes, and a clump of mascara flaked away and dropped to the floor.

"Been getting your claws into my kid, huh?"

"You abandoned her at the gate."

"Naw, I left her temporarily with her father. Where is he, anyway?"

"I'm here." Cade appeared at my elbow. "And Evie's right. You're not taking Scarlet."

"Well, didn't you clean up well. You were always kinda rough in high school, not that I minded that. And I *am* taking Scarlet. Her being here was never a permanent thing."

"Split up with your new boyfriend, did you?"

"That's none of your damn business."

"It's every bit of my business if it impacts my daughter. The daughter you neglected to tell me I even had."

Scarlet's head was going back and forth, and I recognised that lip quiver. The first tear fell as I crouched beside her.

"Sweetie, it's okay. Don't cry."

"I wanna stay with you and Daddy Cade."

"You can."

"Over my dead body," Cindy snapped.

Heels clicked on the floor behind us. "Do you want to be buried or cremated?"

I looked up, past the five-inch stilettos and the

fitted pencil skirt, the tailored jacket and the diamond necklace, and took in the fierce expression on Emmy's face. Boy, I was glad that wasn't aimed at me.

"Evie, take Scarlet up to my office."

I hesitated a second too long.

"Now."

She spoke quietly, but the effect was still deadly.

I scooped Scarlet up and headed for the stairs, but I still caught the first part of the conversation.

"You abandoned a five-year-old child with strangers, wearing shoes that didn't even fit, lied to her first father, sprang the news on her second father, and didn't even leave a phone number. And now you think you can come into *my* building and create a scene? Lady, you're fucked in the head."

The door closed behind us. Scarlet was sobbing, I was close to it, and I don't know how I made it to the third floor, but when I stumbled through the door, the only reason I didn't sprawl on the floor was because Ana caught us.

"Is there a problem?"

"Scarlet's mom came back. Emmy t-t-told me to come upstairs."

Ana shrugged. "Then it's okay. Emmy will fix it."

She wandered off, leaving Logan to shepherd me into Emmy's office.

"Scarlet's mom turned up, huh?"

"She wants her back."

"Doesn't matter what she wants. Cade loves his daughter, and Emmy fights for her own. Just sit tight."

"But what if Cindy wins?"

"Against Emmy? Bitch doesn't stand a chance. Do you want a drink? Coffee? Water?"

I shook my head, but Scarlet spoke up. "Can I have a cookie?"

Logan ruffled her hair. "I'll see what I can find."

He headed for the kitchen, and Scarlet asked, "What's a bitch?"

I smothered a laugh. "That's another grown-up word, sweetie."

Almost an hour passed, and a stranger in a suit appeared. Steel-grey hair, but he couldn't have been older than thirty-five. He got out a laptop and typed away for a few minutes before fetching a pile of documents from the printer and disappearing again.

I shuffled over to Logan. "Who was that guy?"

"Emmy's lawyer."

"Is that a good thing or a bad thing?"

"I'm gonna go with good."

I'd unpicked half of one of my sweater cuffs out of sheer nervousness by the time Cade appeared with Emmy. Her expression gave nothing away, but then Cade looked at me and smiled. I left Scarlet on the sofa and ran over.

"Is it okay? Please say it's okay."

"She's ours for good."

"What? How?"

"Money," Emmy said. "Ten grand direct deposit and Cindy signed away all parental responsibility. Some people aren't cut out for motherhood."

"You paid her off?"

"Consider it part of Scarlet's birthday present. The other part's waiting on the runway at Silver Springs. You three need a break. Now, sod off. I don't want to see any of you near work for at least a week."

She headed towards Logan, and I stared after her,

open-mouthed. "Was that her way of telling us to take a vacation?"

Cade already had Scarlet in his arms. "She doesn't need to tell me twice."

Three hours later, an overjoyed little girl ran up the steps of Emmy's jet.

"I can't believe she's sending us back to Wonder World," I said to Cade.

"Under the dragon-like exterior, she's not a bad boss. But we'll have to enjoy it while we can, because I'll be going out on assignment again when we get back."

My heart sank. "Like an away-for-months-at-a-time assignment?"

"That was a one-off. But I'll be away some nights."

"I can deal with that. I'll miss you like crazy, but I'll deal with it."

He leaned into me as we settled into our seats. "Love you, Evie."

The three words I'd wanted to hear for so long, and they sounded every bit as sweet as I'd imagined.

"I love you too."

I curled into his arms as the plane took off, taking us back to happy memories. Scarlet got out her pencils and started drawing. She was turning into a proper little artist, and I loved her creativity. Her writing was coming along nicely too.

As the plane descended over Florida, she held up her picture for us to see. "I drew us. Look!"

Three figures, holding hands, and she'd already

gotten the message about her new name: Scarlet Duchamp. She'd printed it underneath the smallest person.

"Did I get all the letters right?"

I looked at the rest. Cade Duchamp. Oh, heck. Evie Duchamp.

"Sweetie, you got my second name wrong."

"I did?" She reached for the eraser, but Cade took it out of her hand.

"Leave it."

She shrugged. "Okay."

But I started shaking. "Cade..."

He leaned closer, so close his lips brushed against my ear. "Marry me, Evie. Marry us."

I gripped his hand, and my eyes stung as I turned to press my lips against his. "*Nothing* would make me happier."

# WHAT'S NEXT?

**The Blackwood Security series continues in Quicksilver, releasing in 2019.**

*Help me.*

English teacher Corazon da Silva attends the funeral of Isabella Morales, but soon afterwards, two desperate words whispered over the phone shake her to the core. Is her best friend really dead?

With little interest from the Colombian police, Cora goes undercover to hunt for Izzy in America. The journey promises to be dangerous, but she's not worried because her big brother, Rafael, is watching her every move.

The only problem? Rafael's an assassin, and he's just shot somebody he shouldn't have. Now they're in a race against time to find Izzy before dangerous enemies catch up with him, and Cora isn't the only person with a hidden agenda.

For more details: www.elise-noble.com/silver

**My next book will be Cursed, the first tale in the Electi series, releasing in September 2018.**

Rania Algafari never asked to be different, and when she escaped the war in Syria and moved to the UK, her only goal was to live her life in peace. Get up, go to work, avoid talking to the dead, that sort of thing.

But not everyone dies quietly, and Rania's soon being pestered by one ghost, blackmailed by another, and distracted by a handsome private investigator who's got his own reasons for wanting to solve a particularly gruesome murder.

While Will Lawson doesn't mind using unorthodox methods to crack a case, he's never had to contact his witnesses via a seance before. But the clock is ticking, and Will and his unlikely sidekicks need to hunt down a killer before he's dispatched to join the spirit world himself.

For more details: www.elise-noble.com/cursed

**If you enjoyed The Scarlet Affair, please consider leaving a review.**

For an author, every review is incredibly important. Not only do they make us feel warm and fuzzy inside, readers consider them when making their decision whether or not to buy a book. Even a line saying you enjoyed the book or what your favourite part was helps a lot.

# WANT TO STALK ME?

For updates on my new releases, giveaways, and other random stuff, you can sign up for my newsletter on my website:
www.elise-noble.com

**Facebook:**
www.facebook.com/EliseNobleAuthor

**Twitter:** @EliseANoble

**Instagram:** @elise_noble

I also have a group on Facebook for my fans to hang out. They love the characters from my Blackwood and Trouble books almost as much as I do, and they're the first to find out about my new stories as well as throwing in their own ideas that sometimes make it into print!

And if you'd like to read my books for FREE, you can also find details of how to join my review team.

Would you like to join Team Blackwood?

www.elise-noble.com/team-blackwood

## END OF BOOK STUFF

I'm writing this as I watch *Wonder Woman*, so forgive me if there are typos. (I may also be drinking wine). How have I managed to miss out on the DC expanded universe films for so long? I've already binge-watched *Dawn of Justice* and *Suicide Squad* today, and now I'm just trying to work out whether I'll have time to fit in *Justice League* before I fall asleep.

Or die of heat exhaustion, whichever comes first. It's been thirty degrees (Celsius, not Fahrenheit for all you Americans who insist on using the wrong temperature scale) for weeks now, and Britain DOES NOT HAVE AC. We spend our days eating ice cream and complaining about the heat (we get plenty of practice from complaining about the rain), and our evenings battling mosquitos and watching football, at least until England lose in the World Cup.

Anyhow, back to Blackwood. Originally, Cade started off as a minor character in Red Alert, and he was never supposed to be a potential suitor for Tia. That love triangle plot kind of wrote itself, which is always a nice thing to happen because it saves me a lot of thinking.

Even though Cade lost out originally, I liked him and decided to bring him back in his own book. This time, I wanted to write a story with motorcycles in, and because I can't possibly write a normal freaking plot, I thought it would be fun to make Cade and Evie less than enamoured with his biker lifestyle. For the record, there's no bike sexier than a Ducati, except perhaps for a Ducati being ridden by David Gandy or Chris Hemsworth.

And I got to bring Lara back too, which was fun because I've hardly seen her for ages. When Evie needed a friend, Lara seemed the perfect choice because she's so damn sweet, plus they've both had to deal with dating assholes.

So, what's next?

At the moment, I'm writing the third book in a new series. The Electi is best described as supernatural romantic suspense—a group of girls put on earth for one reason and one reason only, which is to get justice for murder victims and free their trapped souls. The only problem is, squaring things involves killing people, and who wants to do that? The first book, Cursed, should be out in September if all goes according to plan.

The next Blackwood book will be Platinum in the Elements series. Everyone knows Roxy and Gideon are meant to be together—except Gideon, it seems, who's busy denying the obvious while fighting with a group of evil assassins plus Emmy and Sofia. And after that will be Quicksilver, which sees Emmy and Black head back to Colombia under less than ideal circumstances.

Enjoy the summer! (Or winter if you're in the southern hemisphere)

Elise

Bronze (2019)
Nickel (TBA)

## The Blackwood UK Series
Joker in the Pack
Cherry on Top (novella)
Roses are Dead
Shallow Graves
Indigo Rain (2019)

## Blackwood Casefiles
Stolen Hearts (2019)

## The Electi Series
Cursed
Spooked
Possessed
Demented (TBA)

## The Blackstone House Series
Hard Lines (TBA)

## The Trouble Series
Trouble in Paradise
Nothing but Trouble
24 Hours of Trouble

## Standalone
Life
Twisted (short stories)
A Very Happy Christmas (novella)

Printed in Great Britain
by Amazon